STEALING *his* THUNDER

BETH BOLDEN

CHAPTER I

THE WIND WAS STEADY, the tape attached to the top of the goal posts fluttering in it. Dawson lifted his head, letting it wash over him. Cataloging every minute brush of the air against his skin.

Wind, despite popular opinion, wasn't the end of the world when it came to a field goal.

Spending the entirety of his career before this playing in Baltimore in December and January meant he'd had to figure out how to kick even if there was a wind. Especially if there was wind. Because if there was inclement weather, there was going to be wind. And in Maryland and Pennsylvania and Buffalo—all places he'd kicked over his ten-year career—there was one fucking guarantee from September to January and that was inclement weather.

"Hey, Daws."

There was only one person who would attempt to talk to him right now.

Dawson sighed, resigned, and turned towards his holder, who also happened to be the punter.

The rookie.

Cameron was not the only rookie on the team, but he was the rookie on the team who routinely broke the unspoken bubble of space that Dawson kept for himself during games.

He looked up at the rookie.

Marty, the special teams coordinator, had said he'd talk to him, but apparently he hadn't done it yet or he hadn't done it clearly enough that the rookie got it.

This Sunday, they were in Miami, which wasn't usually the windiest, except when there was the dreaded *inclement weather* and yep, it was coming. During halftime, Marty had come up with the latest weather report, and it looked like they were going to just get this game in before a storm rolled in.

But right now, there was only that steady wind. Enough that it needed to be compensated for, mental calculations that Dawson needed space and time and focus for.

Space and time and focus that the rookie was currently dividing up.

"What's up?" he asked flatly.

He was going to have to talk to Marty again, and Dawson didn't love that.

In Baltimore, this never would've happened. In Baltimore, he'd moved on the sideline like he had a physical barrier between him and the rest of the team. But this wasn't Baltimore.

Baltimore had dropped him like a hot potato when he'd had the season from hell last year, all those years of loyalty and blood, sweat, and tears erased with one simple fact: professional football was a business, and he'd become a liability.

Cameron rocked back on his heels. He was tall for a punter, and Dawson had to crane his head a bit, just to look into his light brown eyes. "Just wanted to check in. The wind—"

"Yep," Dawson interrupted. "I felt it."

"Figured you did. Gonna have to compensate some."

Back in Baltimore, Dawson would've given any guy who approached him right now the kind of stink eye that would have them avoiding him for the rest of the season. But now, today, he couldn't stop thinking about how everything had changed. He wasn't in purple and black anymore. He was in bright blue with silver accents, his dark blue helmet sitting behind him on the bench. Toronto colors, now, and he wasn't exactly in a position to be an asshole to the rookie. Who also happened to be his holder.

"Agreed." It was harder than it should've been for Dawson to grit out the word and he wondered when it had become so tough for him to *not* be a dick.

Oh right.

The divorce. The criminal proceedings against his ex-father-in-law. The money he *should've* had in his accounts.

Dawson took a deep breath, felt the wind again for a second, and added, "What do you think?"

"Couple of degrees, but keep it steady, 'cause it's not gusting," Cameron said.

Dawson nodded his agreement, telling himself firmly that the fact he and the rookie agreed was a good thing. It meant he knew what the fuck he was talking about. But then that hadn't really ever been under debate. Cameron had won the punting competition in camp and had barely seemed to break a sweat doing it.

He *should* be damn good.

"It kinda sucks we're in Miami in September. Would've preferred the sunshine in December," Cameron said.

Dawson gave up and shot him a glare. A *tempered* glare, sure, but still a glare.

"Oh yeah." Cameron winced. "Sorry. You probably want to uh . . .focus up."

And on cue, on the field, the Thunder offense came to a stop at fourth and two, right on the twenty-three-yard line.

Marty glanced over at him, inclining his head towards the field, and yeah, they were going to kick the field goal.

Aidan jogged over to the sideline and made a brief but impassioned argument to go for it, but Dawson already knew how that was going to go.

He took one last practice kick into his net, and then he and Cam and Joey, the long snapper, jogged out onto the field.

On his way past, Aidan was still grumbling under his breath about how they could've gone for it and gotten the first down, but he patted Dawson on the helmet anyway, giving him a love tap of support and encouragement.

The wind stayed steady as the Thunder's field goal unit took their positions.

Dawson did what he did every single time he kicked a field goal. Hundreds, *thousands,* of field goals, he'd kicked this exact same way.

Deep breath, facing the goal posts, checking the wind one last time.

He met his holder's eyes—in Baltimore it had been Nicky, but now it was Cameron—and nodded. Stepped backwards, stepped to the side.

Took another deep breath.

Heard the whistle, and like a well-oiled machine, the ball was snapped to Cameron, who caught it.

He didn't *fumble* the ball, not exactly. He got it turned and positioned properly but only half a second before Dawson's foot met it.

Dawson didn't need to hear the intake of the crowd as the ball sailed through the air, just narrowly missing the right upright.

He'd already known it wasn't going to be good.

Dismay bubbled inside him but Dawson wiped his expression clean before it could make it to the surface. There'd been enough pictures and videos of him staring at missed field goals, of balls barely missing the target, last year.

There didn't need to be any more.

He felt a tap on his shoulder as he headed back towards the sideline, but Dawson didn't have to look up to see who it was.

Cameron.

"Sorry, man," he said, all the dismay Dawson had carefully kept away from his face painfully obvious in Cam's voice and in his expression.

It wasn't fine, so Dawson wasn't going to say it was fine, so instead he just gave the rookie a nod.

It might not have even been his fault. He'd technically pulled the ball down and rotated it properly, getting it set before Dawson had kicked it.

But it was still a slight wrinkle in a system that should be perfectly smooth, that should work flawlessly and effortlessly every single fucking time.

It didn't matter whose fault it was, who had made the wrinkle—if it was Dawson, again, or if it had been Joey, fucking up the snap, or if it had been Cameron, not getting the hold just right.

Dawson hit the sideline. Aidan tapped him on the back again, a brief touch, similar to what he'd done before the kick, and exactly how he'd have done it if Dawson made it.

Dawson knew it because when they'd both played for Michigan, he'd tapped him exactly the same way, too many times to count.

At least, Dawson thought as he tugged his helmet off and set it on the bench, they were still ahead, and that field goal hadn't been for the lead—only to pad it further.

He'd had one too many experiences last season where his fuckups had cost the Ravens the lead—or even the game.

He wouldn't wish that feeling on his worst enemy.

In Baltimore, everyone had known to give him space before a kick—but definitely after a missed kick. Apparently nobody had the memo here, because he heard footsteps behind him, deliberately stopping.

Dawson sighed, pressed a finger between his eyebrows. He almost wished he had a headache, because maybe that might explain why that field goal hadn't been good. Turning around, he was surprised that it wasn't Cameron there again, wanting to apologize again, maybe to go over every moment of that play.

It was Marty.

"I'm not gonna say I told you so," Marty said.

Dawson made a face before he could pull it back. Hopefully there wasn't a camera watching him still—though who was he kidding? There was *always* a camera watching.

"Except that it sounds like you're gonna say exactly that," Dawson complained.

Marty said nothing, just shrugged. The knowing look on his face before he turned to check in with another staff member said it all.

When Dawson had gone to Marty last week to bitch about Cameron not giving him space on the sideline, Marty *had* said he'd talk to him. But he'd also argued that the biggest issue wasn't that the rookie didn't know to keep his distance; it was that they were on two different wavelengths, and until they got their shit together and jived, their kicking unit wouldn't be as good as it needed to be.

Dawson hadn't ignored him, but he hadn't agreed either. He'd made an effort. Okay, a *minimum* of effort, but still some kind of an effort.

He was thirty-two years old, newly divorced, his ex-wife was now with the guy she'd fallen in love with while Dawson had been killing it at his job, and his bank accounts weren't as comfortable as they should've been. He was tired and disgruntled and a little bitter, and the last thing he wanted to do was to take a rookie under his arm and teach him everything he should already know.

Especially not a rookie who reminded him, uncomfortably, of how he'd felt coming into the league ten years ago. Wide-eyed, naive, hanging on every word from the vets, shocked but pleased at any sliver of opportunity he'd gotten, even though he'd fought like hell for every single one.

But Cameron was even more of all that than Dawson had even been.

He was raw and unproven and untested and so fucking talented he made Dawson's teeth ache.

Cameron did at least know enough to keep his distance until the end of the third quarter.

Aidan had driven the offense down the field and scored a touchdown to extend the lead to fourteen, so the missed field goal had disappeared out of everyone's mind—except his own.

They'd gone out and kicked the extra point and it had gone in, ball straight down the center of the uprights, their kicking team working like clockwork. Like they'd never missed at all.

But Dawson remembered.

It was a hard kernel of unpleasantness, a rock in his shoe. Impossible to forget, even though Dawson knew he had to forget it.

Maybe he wasn't the only one, if the way Cameron came up to him after he'd kicked off to the Miami receiving team was proof.

"Hey," Cameron said.

Dawson wanted to tell him that he was attempting casual and it wasn't working, the anxiousness was written all over his young, open face.

"You haven't gotten much work in today," Dawson said.

Because he knew what Cameron wanted to talk about, but he really, really, *really* didn't want to discuss what had gone wrong.

He'd already be thinking about it, and there was no way Marty wouldn't force them to go over every second of the play on Tuesday, over and over again until Dawson wanted to scream about it.

"Best work in the world, when your team moves the ball well enough they don't need you to punt much," Cameron joked. But there was still that tightness around his eyes. Dawson couldn't miss it.

"Yeah," Dawson agreed.

"I just wanted to say—again—that I don't know what happened, but it won't happen again."

He sounded very confident. Sure of himself.

It was a common trick special teams guys liked to use. *Fake it til you make it. Fake it til you believe it. Fake it til it's true.*

"Sure," Dawson said, even though there was a loud, insistent part of him that wanted to yell that the stupid trick didn't always work. It hadn't worked for him last year, anyway.

At first his head hadn't been quite on straight.

Then it had rolled right off his body. Dawson had become a train wreck of a person, no matter how he tried to visualize differently.

Cameron huffed out a frustrated noise. "Don't brush me off like that, Daws."

Dawson hadn't ever suggested Cameron start calling him that. He'd just done it. Like it was expected. Like it was okay.

It was bitter and stupid and sulky that it wasn't, so Dawson hadn't corrected him.

"I'm not brushing you off," Dawson claimed, but he was.

They both knew he was.

Even worse, Marty knew it, and Marty was going to have his ass for it.

"You are, and it's not cool. I don't know why we missed that kick—"

Dawson gave up holding it in and rolled his eyes. "*I* missed that kick, rook."

"I know, but—"

"No," Dawson said, making it clear he wasn't going to argue about it. "I missed it. You got the ball down and positioned right."

Cameron really looked like he wanted to keep arguing.

There was even a part of Dawson that wanted him to. But while Cameron and Joey were both integral members of the team, the only one who really mattered—the guy taking the actual kick—was Dawson.

The physical side of their job wasn't all that challenging—at least compared to the skill level required of Aidan or Nate or Mo—but the mental focus required was unique and challenging.

So many people thought if they were only athletic enough, they could kick field goals or punt decently, and sure they could. But could they do it when it mattered most? Could they do it a hundred times, flawlessly, the exact same way? Could they do it when the pressure was at its most demanding, when winning the game was on the line?

The game ended. The Thunder won by fourteen, and Dawson kicked another extra point, but wasn't called onto the field for another field goal attempt.

He told himself he was happy about that as he climbed the steps onto the jet that was taking them back to Toronto, but there was a part of him inside that burned with the injustice of not getting another try. A part that had wanted to redeem himself.

He flopped down in the same seat he'd grabbed on the first flight to a preseason game, towards the back, but away from the guys who played cards, because that wasn't usually his scene, but he didn't want the absolute tomb-like atmosphere of the front of the plane either.

A second later, Marty dropped down next to him, big wad of his omnipresent bubble gum tucked into his cheek like a squirrel with a nut.

Dawson shot him a look.

"Hey, man," Marty said casually.

He had a feeling he was in for another lecture, and he wasn't particularly looking forward to it.

"What is it?" Dawson asked. Asking without saying, *I thought I'd get another thirty-six hours to lick my wounds before you started dissecting them?*

"We need to talk about Cam," Marty said, not bothering with any friendly preamble.

The plane was filling in. He could see Cameron up front, in the quiet section, because from what Dawson had noticed, he liked to watch something on his tablet during flights, earbuds firmly in place.

At least Marty hadn't dragged him back here—or dragged Dawson to the front.

"Here I thought you wanted to talk about that kick," Dawson said.

Marty, twice his age and with a lifetime of NFL experience in special teams, looked unamused. "Daws, you remember your first Pro Bowl?"

"Kind of hard to forget it," Dawson grumbled. He was old, but not *that* old.

"First time we met," Marty said. "You know what my first impression was?"

Dawson tipped his head back against his seat. "I know you're going to tell me."

"Young kid. Raw. But fucking talented. If he could only get out of his own way. And then you did, and kept doing it."

"I've heard this story before and I know how it ends."

"Yeah, you think you do. You think it ends with your last season, with you going off the rails. But it doesn't have to end that way."

"This sounds suspiciously like the pep talk you gave me when you convinced me to sign with the Thunder," Dawson retorted without much heat. Marty was kind of a pain—but he *liked* him. Had always liked him, from the first time they'd met, at that Pro Bowl.

When Baltimore had released him, Marty was the only special teams coordinator who'd come to *him*. His agent had spent the weeks post-release—post-*firing*, Dawson had thought of it—making agonized noises about how they were going to have to make the rounds, make Dawson look confident and good again, that he was probably going to have to win a kicking competition in camp. Something he hadn't done in ten years.

But then Marty had shown up with his inspirational speech, like he actually believed, despite all evidence to the contrary, that there was still something special in Dawson. Like he still deserved to be pitched *to*, instead of being forced to pitch *himself*.

"It's not the same thing at all," Marty dismissed. "We're not really talking about you. Though you're in a dramatic enough snit you probably think everything *is* about you."

Dawson squeezed his eyes shut. Willed himself to be anywhere else.

"God, take it easy on me, old man," Dawson ground out.

"No," Marty said unrepentantly.

Dawson ground his teeth together. "Fine. *Fine.* Who *are* we talking about?"

"Cam, of course. You need to work with him."

"We *are*. We're on the field together every practice. You're there. You see it." Marty directed it, more like, though Dawson had been in the NFL long enough that he probably could've orchestrated their practices himself.

"Yeah, sure, on the field, yeah. Could get your timing down a bit better. Get more familiar with each other. That comes with time. You know what else helps with that?"

Dawson knew what was coming. He just didn't have to like it. "No."

"Yeah, you do—"

"Yeah, I do. What I mean is, *no*, I don't wanna become his best bud or his rookie comfort blankie."

Marty elbowed him hard as the plane started to taxi. "You've become kind of an asshole. That kid I met at the Pro Bowl ten years ago would be disappointed in you, Daws."

"Can we go back and tell that rookie not to get married, either?" Dawson didn't bother to hide his bitterness. Didn't think he should, at this point. He was bitter, and frankly, he *deserved* to be. He'd gotten fucked over. Literally. Figuratively. Every single freaking way you could get fucked over, he'd endured.

"You and Brynn were happy, once."

"Were we though? Or was she just happy that I was good and getting better? She liked the prestige and the money. Liked being a WAG."

"Daws," Marty warned.

"Easier to pretend that it was always shit," Dawson muttered by way of explanation. "Easier than thinking of how it got fucked."

Marty patted him awkwardly on the arm. "It's gonna be okay. I know it doesn't seem that way now, but it will be."

"Thanks," Dawson said dryly.

"But I mean it," Marty said, his voice going serious, "you're gonna have to do something about this. I've talked to Cam, and he says you're nice enough—which I'm sure is a fucking lie—"

"Ouch," Dawson interrupted.

"Real talk, you've been a grumpy asshole since you showed up in Toronto," Marty said.

"If I am, it's 'cause I deserve to fucking be."

"Maybe, yeah. You've been through it, Daws. Here's the thing. I know Cam's been trying, but you're being difficult. I don't know why."

"You don't know why?" Dawson huffed out a breath.

Marty winced. "Okay, I know why."

The captain announced over the PA system that they'd reached their cruising altitude and they'd be in Toronto in a little under three hours. Three hours for Marty to badger him to death about the rookie.

Dawson didn't say anything, with the hope that maybe Marty, not the biggest talker in the world, would give up.

But he seemed intent on making his point because he kept going. "Sure, you're a little pissed off. A lot pissed off, maybe. At Brynn, sure. At her daddy, no question. At Baltimore, for not having more faith in you as a player. But I'm telling you, none of that's Cam's fault. He's just trying to do his job, best as he can, and you're making it hard on him. Hard on yourself, too, to be honest."

"Did you practice that?" Dawson asked flatly.

Marty grinned at him. "How was it?"

"Eh," Dawson said. "Middling. Could use some work on the delivery."

"Come on, man. You know what you need to do. You just need to do it."

It wasn't that easy, and Marty probably knew it, but this was as much of a pep talk as Marty was apt to make. Frankly it was more than Dawson had even expected.

"I'll think about it," he said.

Marty's expression was full of frustrated resignation. "Do more than think about it."

Dawson could've offered more excuses, but they all sounded painfully transparent even to him, and it was more than a little embarrassing how much he'd already exposed all his wounds—some of them still bleeding sluggishly, refusing to close.

"Alright," Dawson said and hoped that he wouldn't make himself a liar.

CHAPTER 2

Cameron could see a tiny sliver of Lake Ontario out of the corner of the biggest window in his living room if he craned his head just right while he was on the far end of his couch.

It wasn't the nicest apartment tower in downtown Toronto, but Cam had still nearly choked when he'd heard the monthly rent. His dad had needed to remind him again how much money he was making now—and how much money he'd probably end up making if he stayed the Thunder's new punter through an entire season and they signed him to an extended contract.

Still, Cam was pretty sure he was paying a shit ton of unnecessary money for that sliver of a view. Even though it was barely visible, Cam had found himself not bothering to occupy the middle of his couch, but instead sitting in that one spot on the very end, figuring that if he was paying for it, he might as well get as much enjoyment out of it that he could.

It was a one-bedroom place, tiny honestly, but even though it felt like it was barely bigger than the closet he'd had at his dad's house in Montana, the walls didn't feel confining. Instead, they felt cozy, like they were keeping him in, keeping him safe and whole and *together*.

"When's the last time you left your apartment?" His dad's voice echoed against the bare-ish walls. Cam shifted uncomfortably, jostling the phone balancing on his knee.

"I leave every day. I have practice," Cam reminded him. "Remember, Dad? I'm a football player. Kind of hard to do that in a five-hundred-square-foot apartment."

His dad made a disgruntled noise. "Not today you weren't. It's your day off. Did you go do something fun? See any more of the city? Hang out with anyone? Even go to the grocery store?"

"Dad," Cam chided. "This is civilization. We get our shit delivered."

Maybe the only thing he really *liked* about Toronto, besides the team: the ability to get just about anything he could think of delivered right to his door.

It meant he never really had to leave his apartment if he didn't want to, and the truth was, he *didn't* want to.

A fact he had scrupulously tried to keep from his dad and from his teammates, but obviously he hadn't done a very good job, because his dad was pressing now, like he *knew*. Or had, at the very least, guessed.

"Cameron," Shane Greene warned.

"Just saying," Cam retorted, but without much heat.

"I'm worried about you. It seems like you never go out," his dad said. "Every time I call, you're at home."

"You're just calling at a good time. And um, we went out twice, the last couple weeks, as a team. Remember that bar I told you about?" Cam wasn't going to mention that the first time his teammates had dragged him to Vault, he'd nearly had a heart attack.

"You go out by yourself?"

"Uh," Cam hesitated. He didn't want to lie, but he also didn't want to make his dad worry, the way he was worrying now.

"Kid, you can't hide away in that little box."

"It's not *that* little," Cam argued. But it was. It was a tiny-ass apartment, and he probably *shouldn't* be so happy here. When he'd first walked in, before he'd signed on the dotted line, he'd actually worried that living here would feel confining. He remembered asking the sales manager showing him the place where the nearest green spaces and parks were, because he'd been sure that he'd not just *want* to see a tree, but *need* to see a tree.

But then he'd moved here for camp, and the thing had *almost* happened, and suddenly the four walls of this apartment had started to look really good. Not right away, but more and more each day, then each week.

"It's fucking tiny," Shane griped. "I hate the thought of you cramped in there."

"Dad, it's really not that bad. I like it." That wasn't a lie at all. He did like it, but what he wasn't going to share was that he probably liked it more because of what it wasn't.

"I'm just worried about you. And then yesterday—Hall looked pretty pissed on the sideline."

Cam winced, glad that Dawson hadn't overheard that comment. He'd have believed no matter what that Dawson wouldn't have liked everyone to know how much he hated missing the kick. But with how well Cam knew Dawson now, he was becoming so much more familiar with how deep that frustration would go.

He'd tried so hard to hide it on the sideline during the game. Cam had watched him school his expression like somehow not showing the wound of the missed field goal might change the ball's final trajectory.

"Yeah, it just . . .it was just one of those things. He's solid." Cam hesitated. Unsure of how much he should say. He'd never worried about sharing with his dad before, but ever since coming to Toronto and starting his professional football career for real, it was tougher. "I think I probably fucked up the hold."

"You got the ball down in time."

"Barely," Cam said heavily. He'd been thinking about that two seconds for the last twenty-four hours and now even if he looked at the tape and it proved it wasn't his fault, it still wouldn't matter.

"Kid, you need to take it easy on yourself. You've only been holding for him for what . . .a few weeks?"

Cam didn't need to tell his dad that it wouldn't matter if he'd never held for Dawson before last week's game, that it didn't matter if he was unpracticed and unprepared, that mistakes—even slight, barely even mistakes like yesterday's—weren't something he could get away with. Especially now that he was in the NFL.

If he couldn't do it, there'd be a hundred guys behind him, aching for the chance.

But he didn't say any of that. There wasn't any point in rehashing it. Maybe his dad had lived in the middle of nowhere, Montana, for practically his whole life, but he still was a lifelong football fan. He understood.

"We're going to get it figured out," Cam said optimistically. More optimistically than he currently felt, anyway.

"If this whole thing doesn't work out—" his dad started to say, but Cam cut him off.

"Dad," Cam said in a hard voice. "*No.*"

Shane gave an embarrassed laugh. "God, I sound like one of *those* fathers now, don't I?"

Cam rolled his eyes. "You wouldn't be any good as an over-involved sports dad, anyway. You're too emotionally healthy for that shit."

"Yeah, probably. Doesn't mean I'm not tempted into it, once in a while. Having you so far away sucks. I trust you can take care of yourself—you've got a good head on your shoulders, kid—but doesn't mean I don't worry sometimes. On days like yesterday. Days like today, when I think you're just gonna hide in that apartment forever."

Ugh. *Ugh.* Cam hated the guilt that swamped him.

"Sorry, Dad. I wish—" Cam cut off. Unsure what else he could say. Unsure what else he *should* say.

He'd felt okay leaving his dad to his busy, fulfilled life in Montana. But every once in a while it hit him how much he just plain missed having him around.

Other dads cared more if their sons succeeded in making it to the NFL or the NHL or to MLB or whatever overachieving goal they'd set for them than they did their actual *sons*. But Shane had never been like that. He'd wanted Cam to have goals and aspirations, sure, but Cam had never felt like achieving those was a requirement for his dad's love. He'd have it, regardless.

He'd have it even if he didn't make it with the Thunder, or with any other team that tried him. Even if he went back to Montana and picked up the threads of a life he'd put together as a backup plan: managing his dad's veterinary business with the business degree he'd gotten in college.

"You're fine, kid," his dad said softly.

It would be a small life, but probably a satisfying one. There was a part of him—stronger than he'd expected—that wondered if he should just call it now. Tell his dad that maybe this whole NFL experiment had been crazy. Pushing too hard, pushing way past his comfort zone.

But he didn't need Shane to tell him that if he was out of his comfort zone, maybe that wasn't a bad thing.

"Actually," Cam admitted, "I'm not sure you're wrong."

"About?"

It was hard to be honest, especially now. Hard to admit what he'd refused to even really acknowledge to *himself* back then, and to do it now, to his dad, knowing how he was going to react.

Cam swallowed hard. "I haven't really wanted to leave the apartment."

There was an understandable silence from his dad. Then he cleared his throat. "Kid, it's not that surprising. Toronto's a big city."

"Yeah it's that. It's . . .it's scarier than I thought it would be." And scarier, too, to admit it to his dad. "And well . . ."

"Well?" Shane prompted.

God, this was so hard to say. "I know people say big cities are different, but they really are."

"Kid, what happened?"

"Nothing really. When I say it, it's so stupid. But I got lost late one night. Ducked into the PATH—you know, one of those tunnels under the buildings? Ran into a bad group of guys. I think they were a bad group of guys, anyway. I wasn't sure—didn't want to risk it though. Got out of there, fast. But they followed me. I was sure I was gonna get jumped." And for *what*, Cam had thought then. He didn't even *own* anything that was worth money. Just his contract, and that was a piece of paper and cash in the bank, not in his pocket.

There was another tense silence, like his dad was having trouble not losing his shit. This was exactly why Cam hadn't told him. "And?"

"And it was fine, in the end. I ran into another group, different guys. I think they were drunk, but cool, you know? Asked them for directions, made it back to my place in one piece. But . . ." It had been hard to admit any of this, but it was harder to admit *this*.

"You've got to just spit it out, Cameron," his dad said, a little sternly, but mostly all Cam felt was the love echoing across the line.

"It was fine. It was totally fine. But it might not have been. And I've never felt like that before. Not once. Not ever. And it freaked me out. Reminded me that I was . . .you know, really far from home. Away from everything I've ever known."

"Yeah." Shane's voice was heavy. "That would be a lot to deal with."

"I shouldn't let it get to me, but I keep thinking, every time I go out, what *could've* happened, you know? And I don't like it. I don't want to worry."

"I don't want you to either." His dad's voice was so gentle. "That sucks. But every big city's gonna have dicey moments like that, you know? You grew up in a small community. Knew every person. Even when you went to school, I bet you never even worried about it. Never even thought about it."

"I didn't," Cam admitted. "Not until it was almost too late."

"Hey, listen to what you're saying, okay? *Almost* too late. *Almost*. It didn't happen. And now you're aware."

Cam swallowed hard, still trying to tamp down the embarrassment wiggling through his stomach like worms. He'd never been ashamed to tell his dad something before, but he'd hidden this for months now.

"Yeah," Cam said.

Not just from Shane—but from his teammates too, because the thought of telling them was even worse than confiding in his dad. They already thought he was too young and too naive. Imagine if they knew just how stupid he really was.

It made him seem so weak and useless. He was strong, sure, a professional athlete, but what good would that have done against a whole pack of guys?

"Let me guess," his dad said, "you haven't told anyone about this."

"No shit," Cam said dryly.

Shane hummed under his breath.

"They already think I'm some kind of gullible country idiot," Cam grumbled.

"What do they think about you not ever leaving your place?"

"I *leave my place*," Cam argued. "I told you. I have to."

"So they haven't noticed?" His dad's tone had gone arch, *knowing*.

"A few comments, but not like . . ." Cam didn't say, *I'm good at hiding it*, but he was.

His dad hummed again, like he didn't quite believe him—but it was the truth.

And didn't that suck even more than the fact Cameron's breath went short and fast whenever he had to leave his bitty apartment.

If a group was going out, he'd go out with them. It was easy to hide in a group. But he didn't go out alone anymore, and since Dawson was pretty occupied with his own shit, and Joey, the other guy who made the third leg of their special teams triumvirate, had a family—a wife and three kids—Cam had been sort of on his own. A lot.

The rest of the team was wrapped up in their own problems on and off the field.

Aidan was trying to get the offense to gel—working harder than he should've behind an offensive line that was still struggling to protect him. Trevor was a rookie, too, but he was constantly revolving around his older stepbrother, Lane. Their running back, Jaden, had been a rookie last year, but from the first time Cam had met him, he'd seemed ages and ages removed from where Cam was.

Nate was kind, but he had his hands full with the defense.

There were a few rookies there, too, but Nate had taken them under his wing, and it hadn't really seemed like there was room for Cam there.

Everyone believed that someone else was looking out for Cameron, and he hated to correct their misassumption, because that would mean *admitting* to shit he barely even felt comfortable admitting to himself.

"You need to get out," Shane said bluntly.

Cam considered arguing, even though he knew his dad was right.

"Okay," he finally said.

"I mean it," his dad reiterated. "Go to the grocery store."

"Alright," Cam said. He could do that. Well, next week, anyway. He'd already gotten his meal plan service delivery this morning, and like absolute fucking magic, his groceries at his door, this afternoon.

"Cam, I mean it," his dad said warningly.

"I mean, I *will*, just not today. I've got everything I need for the week."

"Cam," Shane repeated, same tone of voice.

"What? I don't *need* anything," Cam argued.

"What you need is to get out of that goddamn apartment." He could hear his dad pacing in their living room, boots clicking against the worn hardwood. "You could go get dinner somewhere."

"Alone?" The word escaped from Cam's mouth before he could snatch it back.

His dad sighed. "Okay, how about this—there's that exercise center in the basement, right?"

"Yes," Cam said hesitantly. He didn't want to go work out.

"And it has a swimming pool, right?"

He had a feeling he knew where his dad was going.

And as expected, Shane said, "You should go down there for a bit. Swim around. Try to relax. It's safe there, even if you're on your own. You need a keycard to get into your building. It'll be good for you to get out of your apartment and it'll be a good first step."

Cam thought it made him sound a little pathetic—that he needed the reminder that his building was safe—but it wasn't a terrible idea.

"It's not a bad idea," he said.

"Cameron Alexander Greene," his dad said, exasperated. He didn't need to say, *stop fucking around and just say you'll do it,* because he heard it, anyway. Message received.

"Fine, fine, I'll go," Cam said, pulling himself off the couch.

"One more thing," Shane asked casually. "You meet anyone yet?"

Cam wasn't sure if this was more or less embarrassing than admitting to his dad that he'd gotten freaked out by how big of a city Toronto was. "You know the answer to that."

"Even someone . . .uh . . .temporary?"

"God, Dad," Cam said, his cheeks flaming bright red. "*No.* And even if I did, I wouldn't want to talk about it with you."

"You said it was one of the reasons you wanted a bigger city," his dad reminded him. "It would be easier to uh . . .um . . .what is it you said? Hook up?"

"God," Cam repeated. "Please never say that again, okay?"

He reminded himself how lucky he was that his dad had always been unflinchingly supportive of his sexuality, even if being gay in small town, Montana, wasn't full of its own challenges.

"Well, I want to know how you're doing! How else am I supposed to know if I don't ask?" Shane didn't have to say, *because you're not going to volunteer anything, not like you used to.*

"The answer is *no*. But I'm sure I'll get there. Like comfortable enough to download an app and actually follow through or even go to a gay bar."

"Uh. Yeah. Good."

"Can we not talk about this anymore?" Cam begged as he headed towards his bedroom to change into his swim trunks.

"I'm good with that," his dad said, chuckling self-consciously. "Not because I don't approve! Or because I think it's wrong or disgusting or—"

"Please," Cam pleaded. "I don't think that. I promise."

"Okay, good."

"Yes, you're the most supportive. Nobody's ever taking your ally crown away."

"Thank goodness," Shane said dryly. "You have fun, okay? Text me when you're back."

"Dad," Cam warned.

"Not because I think you'll be unsafe! Or because I'm worried. Just because . . .just because, alright?"

Cameron smiled. It was hard not to. He loved his dad, and his dad loved him. "Alright."

A second later, he hung up, and after putting his phone on the charger by his bed, pulled out his swim trunks and an old T-shirt. He changed, shoved his feet into a pair of sneakers, and grabbed a towel from the narrow linen closet on the way out the door.

The elevator ride down to the basement level with its fitness center and pool was quiet. It was late afternoon on a Monday—too early for anyone to be coming home from their corporate jobs.

There were a handful of people in the fitness center, on the treadmills and ellipticals, a smaller group spread out among the weight machines. Cam headed right to the sign that identified the entrance to the swimming pool, bypassing the locker room.

When he pushed it open, he wasn't surprised to see it empty.

Well, *almost* empty.

There was a single figure on the far end, sitting on the edge of the pool, head down and feet dangling in the water.

After pulling off his T-shirt and shucking his shoes, Cam stole another look at the guy, taking in the messy dark hair—all that was visible—and then realized a second later that he *recognized* that messy dark hair.

And the shoulders.

And the thighs.

It was Dawson.

Cam swallowed hard.

He'd known, in a very abstract way, that Dawson was living in his building. He'd made a hesitant comment about it, early on just after winning the punter job right out of training camp, and Dawson had brushed him off.

That had kind of sucked, for sure. But he'd begun to understand more, the more time he'd spent around Dawson—almost exclusively on the field, but that was okay, because it had given him a perspective on how much shit was currently balancing on those broad shoulders.

Proving that he was still the future Hall of Fame kicker. Dealing with his divorce. Fighting to get his money back from his snake of a father-in-law.

Cam hesitated, wondering if he should go over there.

Then Dawson lifted his head, and those bright hazel eyes met Cam's.

Shit. There was no pretending he hadn't seen him now. No grabbing his stuff and retreating.

Dawson tilted his head, saying without a single word that Cam should come over.

This was definitely not what he'd thought would happen. Cam thought he'd come down here, maybe have to avoid a knot of kids, or an older retiree swimming laps. Or he'd have the pool all to himself.

"Hey," he said hesitantly as he approached Dawson.

He had the same thought he always did when faced with the guy—*God, he's hot*—and then he pushed it right down, because Dawson's hotness was not important.

Not because Dawson wouldn't be interested in a guy. Before he'd gotten married, he'd had his pick of women *and* men in the Baltimore dating scene. Cam might or might not have watched from afar, from his small-ass town in Montana, and thought, *that might be me, someday.* Depending on the day, he'd imagined himself *as* Dawson and as the guys Dawson had taken home.

Cam had never imagined they'd end up on the same team.

But now they were, and Dawson barely seemed to tolerate his presence. Certainly never went out of his way to seek Cam's company.

If he'd ever had any insanely fantastical expectations, reality had punctured those succinctly.

"Hey," Dawson said. "I forgot you lived in this building."

Cam internally winced. If he wanted more evidence that he never crossed Dawson's mind, then here it was.

"Yeah," Cam said.

But then Dawson actually surprised him by gesturing next to him. "You wanna pop a squat?" he asked.

"Uh," Cam hesitated.

"Or are you here to be all productive on our day off, and swim some laps?"

"No. No laps," Cam said. He settled down next to Dawson, making sure to leave at least a foot between them as he dipped his feet into the pool. The water was warm and felt refreshing against his skin.

For a long moment, neither of them said anything.

Cam couldn't speak for Dawson but he knew *he* couldn't think of anything to say. Didn't want to bring up the Thunder, because it was their day off, and on top of that, that missed field goal from Sunday was lingering between them like a bad smell.

He wanted to talk about it—talk it out, at least—but he knew this wasn't the right place to do it. Besides, there was no way Marty wouldn't end up going over the footage with them tomorrow with a fine-tooth comb.

Cam was surprised when Dawson turned to him, the corner of his mouth quirking up. "So you gonna tell me why you came down here, then?"

"You actually want to know?" He shouldn't have said it with so much surprise. Cam knew it. But he didn't realize just how ugly that was until Dawson's expression crumpled.

"Shit, I've been an asshole, haven't I?" Dawson tipped his head back.

Cam knew he shouldn't feel guilty—that was really on Dawson, who'd been the one to do it in the first place. He'd just, in the mildest way possible, called his stupid ass on it.

"Uh, yeah, well, for a good reason," Cam said, surprising himself again, by not being as tough on Dawson as he really should've been.

Dawson reached over and smacked him on the side.

"Ow," Cam said reflexively, even though it didn't really hurt. Burned a little, but more from the fact that it was Dawson's hand touching him on bare skin.

Despite how many times he told himself to not think it, Dawson *was* a hot guy.

"You don't need to be so nice to me," Dawson said.

"Why not?" But Cam knew exactly why not. *Because you don't deserve it.*

"Because I don't deserve it." Dawson's tone was morose. Which was exactly why Cam had held back.

"You've been going through a lot of shit," Cam argued.

"Rook, I appreciate the defense. Trust me, I do. But I really don't deserve it. I've been . . ." Dawson swallowed hard, and even though Cam was trying to ignore it, his eyes followed his Adam's apple as it bobbed—tan and smooth. "I've been sort of shit to you."

"Not that shit," Cam said loyally.

Dawson shot him a look.

"Okay, kind of shit," Cam corrected gently. "But you had good reason. And everyone's been sort of distracted, so that makes sense. I get why. It just . . ." *It just sucks that everyone forgot about me.*

Dawson straight up put his hand right on Cam's bare thigh. He'd never thought his swim trunks were short or long, or really had *any* thoughts about their length, but now he was praising every deity out there that he'd made sure there was a good amount of bare thigh showing.

A good amount of bare thigh that Dawson could touch any dang time he wanted.

Even if he didn't mean it *that* way.

"Wait," Dawson said, "what are you talking about?"

"Um, what *you* were talking about?"

Dawson let go of his thigh. Cam didn't let himself cry about it—he *didn't*. He was just being a good bro, a good teammate. That was all. "Are you telling me that nobody's been making sure you're good?"

"I wouldn't say *nobody*," Cameron said, so he didn't have to say who exactly *had* been watching out for him.

"Then who? 'Cause it sure as fuck hasn't been me. I've been . . .well, you know. Distracted. Messed up."

"Exactly." Cam nodded enthusiastically, hoping that would be the end of it.

"Rook, don't fucking change the subject." Dawson's tone had gone stern, and a thrill shouldn't have shot down his spine when Cam heard it, but well . . .he was only human, right? And his dick had already established, unequivocally, that Dawson was a hot guy.

"Sorry."

"Marty told me I was being a self-centered ass, but I didn't want to believe him." Dawson said it like he wasn't even saying it to Cam—more like he was lecturing himself.

"I wouldn't call you entirely a self-centered ass," Cam offered.

"Well, I'm sorry, anyway." Dawson let out a hard breath. "Forgive me?"

Like Cam was ever going to get that tilted smirk-smile of Dawson's and not fall for it. "Sure. Of course."

"I'll do better," Dawson said.

Cam wondered what that would look like, but before he could ask, Dawson opened his mouth again. "What *have* you been up to?"

"What do you mean?"

"Like, what have you been doing? Where have you been? I haven't spent much time up here, but I know it's a great city. Vibrant."

Cam pressed his lips together. *I'm afraid to leave my apartment. That's how great it is.*

"I know we've been to Vault," Dawson continued, like he hadn't realized yet that Cameron hadn't actually answered him. "But I bet you've found all the other good spots." He nudged him in the thigh. "Cute guy like you, I bet the boys are all about it."

"Uh," Cameron hesitated. He wasn't sure when his brain had shorted out. The fear that Dawson might find out the truth that had gripped him suddenly? Or that Dawson had called him cute?

"I'm almost a little jealous," Dawson said. He threw his arms up and stretched, then set them behind him, propping himself up. Cam watched this performance, trying to ignore the pull of his muscles, the ripple of his shoulders.

Sure, he saw naked bodies all the time in the locker room. But that didn't mean he was immune when it came to Dawson, or that he could be immune when all that mouthwatering shit was right there.

Right there for the taking.

Maybe if Dawson thought he was cute, he wouldn't even push him away.

"Jealous of *what*?" Cam questioned. He was hooking up *less* than he had in Montana, which was actually pretty fucking sad when he thought about it.

"Jeez, dude, how much ass you're probably getting. A young hot player? Fresh from the middle of nowhere? I bet they're just eating you up."

Cam didn't know whether this was a worst or a best-case scenario.

"They're not," Cam said flatly.

A confused frown appeared on Dawson's face. "Huh? I thought you were gay—"

"I am," Cam interrupted, before Dawson could go on.

"You with someone?"

"No, I just . . ." Cam huffed out, embarrassed. Telling his dad had been hard enough. Telling Dawson felt impossible. "It's weird to go out by myself. I'm not used to such a . . .big place, you know? It's *so* big. Big and strange."

Comprehension dawned horribly on Dawson's face. "Shit. Nothing bad happened to you, right?"

"No, no," Cameron said. He didn't *have* to tell Dawson what happened. Or what *almost* happened. "It's just a lot to handle, that's all."

"Well, I can't say I'm cool or hip necessarily, but maybe—"

"No, it's really okay. It's okay." Cam could feel the red flush creeping up his cheeks. "I'm okay."

Could he use a hand that wasn't attached to his own arm once in a while? Sure. But he was managing. And maybe with some time and adjustment, he'd be okay, again. He'd learn to keep his fear controlled—without Dawson finding out his issues or even more embarrassingly, trying to be his wingman.

"Jeez, okay, I guess I really *am* old and uncool," Dawson said wryly, rubbing his jaw. "Don't hold back, rook."

Cameron wondered, for a single wild second, how Dawson would react if he told him exactly how little the ten years between them mattered.

But of course he didn't say that, because he wasn't insane, and he wasn't about to screw it up, now that Dawson was finally acknowledging his existence outside a football field.

"Not *that* old or uncool," Cam said instead. He risked a quick nudge of his own, right back at Dawson.

Dawson chuckled under his breath. "Keep telling yourself that."

"I'm gonna," Cam said. Hesitated. Took another risk—this time bringing up a subject that felt . . .loaded. But if they didn't talk about it now, Cam knew they'd have to face it tomorrow regardless, and tomorrow it would feel worse. Everything magnified by the seriousness of the building they were in. Today, it felt lighter. More casual. "Are we gonna get our asses kicked tomorrow?"

"Don't know why *you're* worried," Dawson said, making a face.

"I'm worried 'cause it's on all of us, not just you," Cam argued. "I didn't—"

"You didn't," Dawson interrupted, not letting him get the rest out. Patted his knee absently, hazel eyes distant and lost in the past. In the near past, on Sunday when he'd missed the field goal? Or farther back? Last year, when he'd had the worst season of his career? Or farther back even than that, when he'd reigned as the best kicker in the NFL?

"You're still money. You know?"

Dawson's gaze swiveled to him again. "Alright. If you think so." He sounded almost amused. Like Cam was saying it to be funny. Or to placate him, which was even worse.

"I mean it," Cam argued. He was beginning to think it wouldn't matter what he said, it wouldn't make a damn bit of difference to how Dawson saw himself. It was humbling and more than a little humiliating.

"I know you do," Dawson said, smile wry. "But yeah. Probably gonna regret waking up in the morning. And I'll—*we'll*—deserve it."

Cameron nodded. He'd been through his share of shitty practices. Probably not as many as Dawson, but enough to know what it was probably going to be like.

He gestured at the pool. "I think I'm going to . . .uh . . .get in?"

"Sure," Dawson said absently, and as Cameron slipped into the pool, he told himself that even as bad as tomorrow was probably going to be, they'd have each other.

But when he emerged on the other end of the pool and glanced back, Dawson was gone. Disappeared like he'd never been there at all.

CHAPTER 3

"I CALLED YOU YESTERDAY," Aidan said, jogging over and catching up with Dawson as he headed towards the field.

"Yeah," Dawson said. He hadn't been much in the mood to talk. Not since he'd gone to bed, replaying that stupid field goal on his eyelids, and then woken up to a text from Brynn. **Wanted to tell you before you heard it anywhere else, but Carlos and I are expecting. Due in the spring.**

"So?" Aidan questioned, giving him that same look he'd done back in Michigan. A little disgruntled, a little offended, like there was anyone on earth who'd get a call from Aidan Flynn and then *not* call him right back.

But Dawson hadn't been in the mood. The fucking understatement of the century.

He'd told himself that his ex-wife wasn't trying to rub her happiness into his unhappiness, but it felt like she kept pressing on every bruise, never letting them quite heal.

He didn't even know if he wanted kids, but of course, now he couldn't stop thinking about that other life, the one he'd lost. The one where they'd stayed together, in Baltimore. Where her dad hadn't stolen his money. Where she'd become pregnant with *his* kid.

It didn't matter that he hadn't been particularly happy. It didn't matter that they'd both barely been going through the motions of a marriage.

That sliding-doors moment still beckoned tantalizingly, a wolf in sheep's clothing. Tempting and nearly attractive enough to lure him in, before it swiped hard at his tender midsection with its sharp claws.

"So I was busy," Dawson said to Aidan.

Aidan made a face. "That's *my* excuse, now," Aidan said, annoyingly self-righteous. Annoyingly happy, too. Like he'd finally gotten a boyfriend at the ripe age of thirty-three and was going to be insufferable about it for the rest of eternity.

Dawson was happy for his friend. While also wishing Aidan would fall right into the nearest black hole and stop harassing him.

"Yeah, yeah, you're happy as fuck. We know," Dawson grumbled.

"Still doesn't tell me why you didn't call me back."

"Maybe 'cause you *called* me like a freaking old man," Dawson said.

Aidan's face did something hilarious. Worth every bit of the shit he was about to get dished right back. "You're literally only a year and a half younger than me," he said blankly.

"It's enough." Dawson paused. "I went out, actually."

Aidan looked skeptical. "Did you really or are you just saying that?"

"I go out!" Admittedly, not often, and usually only when someone else made him, but he *did* do it. He wasn't sure if he'd call heading down to the swimming pool so he wouldn't have to look at the blank walls of his apartment any longer *going out*, but nobody was going to stop him from calling it that.

And if pressed, he *could* say he'd run into Cam, too. Almost like it had been planned.

"Could stand to do it a bit more," Aidan said. "I wanted to know if you wanted to come along to the linemen's dinner this week. Trying to get a count."

"I'm not a lineman," Dawson pointed out.

Aidan grunted in frustration. "I know that. I'm just trying to make sure everyone's feeling good. You know, *welcomed*."

"You mean you're trying to make sure I'm not throwing myself off a cliff after missing that field goal on Sunday, and you're too busy fucking—or getting fucked by? I'm not sure which and please don't tell me—your hot new boyfriend to pencil me on for a separate date, so you're just going to group me in with something already on your schedule."

Aidan stared at him incredulously. He didn't seem to know where to begin with what Dawson had just said. And Dawson had to admit that when he word vomited these days, that was often the reaction. "Do you even listen to the shit that comes out of your mouth?"

"Rarely," Dawson said wryly.

"I am *not* making sure you didn't throw yourself off a cliff," Aidan said slowly. "But yeah, I know you're going through it—"

"And this is exactly why I didn't call you back. I don't need to be coddled," Dawson said. "You should get that I don't want to talk about my feelings. When have you ever wanted to talk about *your* feelings?"

That got him an actual Aidan Flynn smile. Never an easy feat to accomplish, though easier than it had been, before Levi had shown up and Aidan had fallen in love with him.

"Fair," Aidan said. "But you're good?"

"Solid. Never been better," Dawson lied breezily. "About to have a fucking great practice. How are you?"

Aidan just rolled his eyes. Patted him on the shoulder as he walked past. "You're so full of shit, Hall," he said.

And yes, that was true. Dawson was totally full of shit.

He was a shit teammate.

Had been a shit husband.

Was possibly now a shit kicker.

Dawson made a face at his own bad mood.

And then, of course, that was when a voice piped up behind him. "Hey, Daws," Cameron said sunnily.

He wasn't *always* this upbeat, but he was usually unflinchingly and unfailingly positive in a way that Dawson only resented because it made him feel even grumpier.

"Hey," Dawson said, trying to fake it til he made it, because he remembered a little too well how guilty he'd felt last night when he'd realized that nobody had been looking out for the rookie.

It should've been his job. He'd known it and he'd still let it slip through his hands, telling himself a bunch of lies that someone else was taking care of Cam.

But of course, nobody else was. Why would they?

"You ready for this?" Cam asked, but he was still smiling, like he might actually enjoy Marty kicking his ass into next year.

"Sure," Dawson said, lying again.

He couldn't say he'd slept any better last night than he'd slept the night before, but at least he'd slept *some*.

When the alarm had gone off, he'd shaken out of sleep, the remnants of some kind of dream he didn't want to remember lingering in the corners of his mind.

He and Cameron at a club, flashing lights and pulsing bass, and he'd been watching from the edges as Cam danced with one guy and then another and then kissed a third.

There was an unsettled heat at the base of his stomach as the images flashed through his mind again.

"Come on, you two. Time to get to work." Marty approached, dispelling any discomfort Dawson felt.

He'd just dreamed about Cam because he'd seen him at the pool, and they'd talked about going out and hooking up. It was just his brain dredging up recent events and re-forming them into a new pattern. That was all. It didn't mean anything.

He definitely hadn't felt a flare of what might be jealousy if he looked closely enough at it. So he didn't.

Marty put them through their paces.

Warmups. Stretches. He had them jogging five times around the field. Joey, whining the whole way, complaining that he hadn't taken the cushiest job on the special teams unit if he was going to have to actually *work*.

Cameron said nothing. Just bent his head and got to work, like he believed they'd earned every drop of sweat falling to the turf.

Dawson made a couple of comments under his breath to Joey, but only when they were out of Marty's earshot.

He was already on Marty's shit list. Deservedly. He didn't need to bring more crap down on his head.

When they finished running, Marty leveled him a look. "You ready?"

Wiping his face with a towel, Dawson laughed without amusement. "Am I gonna kick til my leg falls off?"

"Ha," Marty said. "Why would I do that? You know how to kick a goddamn field goal."

"Sure," Dawson said.

"I'm confused," Cameron inserted.

"What he's saying is it's not about the kick," Dawson said flatly.

"Yep, we're only going to work on mechanics today." Marty gestured to Joey. "Let's get set up."

"Told you it was my fault," Cam told Dawson as Joey pulled a big bin of footballs over to the five-yard line.

"God," Dawson whined, "it's not *always* about you, rook. It was all of our fault, okay?"

Cameron only grinned at him with delight. "Told you it wasn't just your fault."

"Oh, get over there," Dawson grumbled, gesturing towards where he'd be holding the snapped ball but the truth was he was having to actively tamp down his own answering smile, and that was something. More than he'd expected, for sure.

The rookie wasn't just cute, he was unexpectedly sly in a way that shouldn't be attractive but *was*.

Dawson still didn't let himself think about it.

Cam wasn't the smoothest, most reliable holder he'd ever had but he was better than the other punter that Cam had beaten out for the starting job. Though he'd not wanted to admit it to Cam's face, he'd gone to Marty to advocate for him, way back in training camp.

The other guy had been experienced, sure, with several NFL seasons under his belt, but Cam had way more upside. He was so easy to fold in. To be there and be present, but never make a big deal out of it. Dawson had known how straightforward it would be to form an easygoing-but-hard-working triangle between him, Joey, and Cam.

But Dawson was beginning to wonder if he'd taken Cam's ease for granted.

It made it so painless for his gaze to just slide right past him and lock back in on his own problems.

Marty worked them hard, the sheer repetition wearing Dawson down, forcing him to focus only on how his muscles moved, imprinting the exact motions into his brain and body.

They were only kicking extra-point distance—but Dawson could feel the rhythm echoing in the bones of his leg and his foot, his abs clenching with tension as he drilled ball after ball between the uprights.

By the time it was over, over an hour later, Dawson was dripping sweat. Even Cam had beads of sweat on his forehead. He shook his hands out, tense and sore from the number of times he'd caught the ball.

Joey had gone totally taciturn, lips clamped together into a grim line.

"Well, that sucked," Cam said, but even that sounded fucking happy.

"Please don't tell me you enjoyed that," Dawson said as they dragged their tired asses up towards the locker room.

"Yeah, if you did, I'd be worried about your masochistic ass," Joey muttered.

"Amazed you actually know what that means," Cam said, laughing under his breath.

Joey exchanged a knowing glance with Dawson. He knew he should keep his fucking mouth shut, but when had Dawson ever been good at that? Never, that was when.

"Like you'd know *anything* about it," Dawson snarked back.

Cam's eyes went wide. Surprised. "Why, you wanna show me, Daws?" he teased.

Shit.

Joey started to laugh, even though they were all exhausted.

"Yeah, he called your ass there, bud," Joey said.

Dawson rolled his eyes. But he felt it, the press of Cam's suggestion against his skin, even if it was a joke, as he stripped down in the locker room and staggered into the showers.

Clearly, he needed to get laid. Especially if he was thinking about showing the rook the pleasure of a well-placed bruise. Of a grip that was a shade too tight.

He was still feeling it after grabbing his burrito bowl at the cafeteria. Knew he should go sit with Aidan, who was pressed thigh to thigh, laughing at something Levi was showing him on his phone. That was definitely the safer choice. Maybe a slightly aggravating one, if only because the pair of them were so smug. Trevor and Lane were sitting at the same table, exchanging glances like they were currently eating shards of glass. So they were being like *that*.

But then he looked over, at one of the far end tables, and Cameron was sitting there—not alone, that would have made the decision easy—along with a few of the backup defensive guys.

Brynn had never believed him when he'd told her about the semi-rigid hierarchy of the NFL cafeteria situation. "It sounds like we're back in high school and I'm worried about the popular girls," she'd said, rolling her eyes.

But it could be exactly like that, and *worse*.

It was up to leaders like Dawson to make sure that it never got that bad.

He sighed heavily and took his tray over to where Cam was sitting.

"Hey," he said to Cam, who looked up in surprise. Like he'd written off Dawson ever sitting with him. Like he'd just expected Dawson to take his stupid ass right over to where Aidan was sitting.

"Hey," Cam said, through a bite of chicken caesar wrap.

The two defensive guys eyed him like they thought he was lost.

And wow, that was a problem. How had things gotten this bad without Dawson even realizing it?

He gave them both a nod and then told himself he could do better than that. "Hey, I'm Dawson," he said, and took in their surprise that a vet and a starter, probably a guy that would end up in the Hall of Fame with a gold jacket one day, was acknowledging their existence.

Double shit.

"Hey," the one with the broader shoulders said. "I'm Duke."

"Jack," the other one said.

"Nice to meet you guys," Dawson said. There were only fifty-two other guys on the fucking roster. There was no excuse for him to not know everyone's name.

"I was on the Ravens' practice squad two years ago," Duke said. "Good team."

Dawson barely held back the face he wanted to make.

Real nice fucking team. Letting him go like he was washed up and old, just because he'd missed a few kicks.

But he was trying not to be bitter about it. Not succeeding, maybe, but *trying*.

"Oh yeah," Dawson said, trying for casual agreement.

"Come on, dude," Cam argued, "you can't think that, not after they treated Dawson here like a piece of trash."

Dawson's eyebrows skidded up, but Duke didn't look surprised.

"Yeah, we know you're obsessed with Hall," Duke teased.

And Dawson realized they'd discussed this before. How often had Cam sat with these two at lunch?

"Ride or die," Jack agreed and then fist-bumped with Duke.

Dawson tried not to blush. "You're exaggerating."

"Dude, we're really not."

It was Cam's turn to flush bright red. "Guys," he warned.

"He'll go to bat for you, no matter what," Duke said, sounding amused. "He practically wrote a presentation about it. Showed us a whole YouTube of all your career highlights."

Cam cleared his throat. "We don't need to talk about that."

It was very stupid. Dawson shouldn't feel any kind of way about this. But he was touched. Thrilled. In a place he had *zero business* feeling a thrill when it came to the rookie.

"I think we do," Dawson joked.

Cam looked so fucking earnest. "You've just made so many money kicks, in important spots. You've won championship games and even a Super Bowl. Like you are lights-out, Daws, and nothing's changed."

It felt good, being glazed like this, the rookie gazing at him with those sweet brown eyes and that even sweeter face.

He wanted to bask in it for a moment longer.

"Thanks," he said.

A month ago, he might've argued, but it was true. He *had* won championships and there was a Super Bowl ring in the drawer next to his bed, at home. A Super Bowl he'd brought home with a fifty-four-yard field goal.

"I—*we*—got your back," Cam said, patting him on it.

For a split second Dawson wanted to ask if he'd meant what he'd started to say: that *he* had his back. Not the team. Not the collective table. But *him*.

But that would be insane and Dawson was trying to not be insane today.

Still, after he finished his food, he caught Aidan by the trash can.

"Hey," he said, "is that dinner invite still open?"

Aidan looked at him bluntly. "Yes."

"Count me in." Dawson hesitated. "For two spots, actually."

Raising an eyebrow, Aidan asked, "Who else is coming?"

"I'm gonna bring the rookie," Dawson said.

Aidan's eyebrow notched even higher. "Oh, yeah?"

"Don't," Dawson said. His face was burning brighter now than it had when Cam had been praising him. "It's just . . .it's not like that."

"Like what?" Aidan asked innocently.

"Like whatever your suddenly dirty mind is thinking."

Aidan lifted his hands in mock surrender. "I wasn't thinking a damn thing, Daws, but if you want to bring him, the more the merrier."

"Someone has to look out for the rookie." Dawson hated how self-conscious he sounded. How defensive.

It *wasn't* like that.

"That's what I keep telling you," Aidan said, slinging an arm around Dawson's shoulders. Chill and relaxed in a way that Dawson was still getting used to. "You're just finally listening."

"Yeah, yeah," Dawson grumped. Hating the guilt that swirled in the base of his stomach. "Mark us down for all of them, going forward."

"Seriously?"

"You can afford to buy two more of us steak on a weekly basis," Dawson argued.

"It's not about that. It's just been pulling teeth getting you to do *anything* with the team, and now, suddenly, you're there and you're there with the rookie. You *sure* it's not like that?" Aidan was not usually the kind of guy who teased. Especially not over *this*.

But Levi's dick apparently had magical properties.

"Jeez, way to make a guy feel bad," Dawson said. Hesitated. "Well, *worse*. Way to make a guy actually feel worse."

"Daws," Aidan said sympathetically. "I'm here if you want to talk about it."

"Honest to God, if I did, you'd be my first call," Dawson promised. That made him feel itchy, too. Everyone expecting him to talk about his fucking feelings, and that was the last thing he wanted. He just wanted to focus on anything else.

Of course, he hadn't been doing a very good job of that, either.

"Good," Aidan said. Giving him one last squeeze. "I'll put you and Cam down for the dinner. And it's good you're hanging out with him."

"Yeah, yeah," Dawson said, brushing the praise off.

It was the least he could do, and he could definitely stand to do a little bit more.

CHAPTER 4

It had been a long day. Cameron was tired, in a way he wasn't always on Tuesdays.

The repetitive field goal practice had taken it out of him, and he hadn't even been the guy making kick after kick, like a machine that didn't even know how to miss.

He was nearly to his car, the sun setting behind the players' parking lot, when a voice stopped him.

"Hey, wait up."

Cam turned, surprised at the voice and the guy it belonged to.

He couldn't remember the last time Dawson had gone out of his way to spend so much time together during a workday.

Even after yesterday, running into each other at the pool, he hadn't expected this.

He figured you out. He saw right through you. Knows exactly what fears are going through your head.

But even if that was true, Cam hadn't gotten even the tiniest hint that Dawson judged him for it.

"What's up?" Cam asked, slowing to a stop a dozen yards from his truck.

"Shit." Dawson exhaled hard, putting his hands on his knees as he tried to catch his breath. "I'm gonna regret that tomorrow."

"Probably." Cam shouldn't be endeared but he was. For a split second, he wondered if Daws was going to ask him to do something else he'd regret in the morning.

"Come on," Dawson said, gesturing towards his SUV. "Get in."

Oh God, was *he?*

"What? Uh. How?" He wasn't proud of how his voice stuttered, but how was he supposed to keep it level?

Dawson rolled his eyes. "We're going to dinner, rook. You good with that?"

"Like uh . . ." He could *not* make his mouth form the word *date,* but he was thinking it.

Dawson just laughed. "Rook, you're getting ahead of yourself, aren't you?"

"Uh." Apparently that was all the vocabulary he had left.

"So neither of us sit in our empty apartments, alright? Isn't that a good enough reason?" Dawson's voice was teasing. "You okay with that?"

Cam swallowed hard. "Yeah. For sure. Sounds good. But my truck—"

"Oh jeez, rook. I'll give you a lift in the morning. We're coming from the same place. Why are we both driving through this ass Toronto traffic, anyway?"

"Not sure," Cam said, feeling like his throat was strangling him.

"Well, are you gonna come or not?"

Cam barely stopped his jaw from dropping. "To dinner?" he questioned.

"Yes, *to dinner,*" Dawson said with exasperation.

Cam nodded. "Yeah. Yeah, we can go to dinner."

He followed Dawson to where he'd parked. New car smell spilled out as he opened the door.

"I don't suppose you have any ideas on where to go," Dawson said as he pulled out of the parking lot.

"Me? Uh, no. Not really." Cam was afraid that exposed his ugly habit of hiding in his apartment. But it was also the truth, and it seemed like

Dawson might've guessed anyway. Hadn't he just said, *so we don't sit in our empty apartments?*

That was as good as calling Cam out for what he'd been doing.

"Me either," Dawson confessed. "But Aidan sent me a list of suggestions, and I thought we'd start at the top of the list."

They stopped at a red light and Dawson pulled his phone out of his pocket, and clicked something, hooking it up to the car's Bluetooth.

"How do you feel about Thai?"

"Thai food?"

Dawson shot him a look as they hit the freeway. "Yes?"

"Um, yeah. I like Thai." He wasn't really that familiar with it. Had enjoyed Thai a few times, sure, but someone else had ordered for him. Since coming to Toronto, he'd gotten Chinese food a few times, because that was familiar enough, since there was a small authentic Chinese restaurant in his hometown.

But Thai felt like a step farther, and he never knew what he'd like—or what he should order.

Maybe it would be okay to admit that to Dawson though.

"Rook, if you want something else, we go someplace else," he said simply. Like it really was no big deal.

"No, no, we can go to Thai. I just . . ." God, to admit how uncultured he was *was* embarrassing. "I just don't have a lot of experience with Thai food."

There. He'd gotten it out.

Dawson hummed under his breath. Glanced over, zero judgment in his expression. "Not a lot of call for Thai food in Montana?"

"I mean, I'm sure they have it in Missoula or Billings. Bozeman, for sure. But I'm from Phillipsburg, which definitely doesn't. There was probably one in Helena, where I went to school, but by then . . ." Cam trailed off. He'd said it, sure, but he didn't really want to *expound* on his naivety or his fear surrounding it.

"You didn't want to expose yourself as some hick?" Dawson asked kindly.

"Uh, yeah. Exactly."

"Don't sound so surprised. I was a good ol' farm boy from Iowa," Dawson said wryly. "A long time ago, but that kid definitely existed, and he was at least as embarrassing as you. Probably more, because he acted like he *did* know everything, even though he knew fuck all."

"I didn't know that," Cam said. "But you went to Michigan, yeah?"

Dawson chuckled. "Yeah, my old man is still bent about that."

"Still?"

"There's not much to get pissed about in Iowa." Dawson paused. "Though he's plenty pissed off these days, and that has nothing to do with Iowa."

Cam never knew whether it was acceptable—or allowed—to mention Dawson's divorce or the case against his father-in-law.

"About the um . . .thing?"

Dawson laughed louder this time. "Jeez, rook, you can at least say it. Yeah. He's pissed as hell about what happened. Don't know who he's angrier at. Brynn or her dad or the Ravens. Take your pick, honestly. I keep having to talk him down from flying out here and start throwing punches."

"That's sweet, actually," Cam said. His dad would do the same thing. Maybe not the punches part, but the flying-out part. If he thought Cam was struggling, he'd be here in Toronto in a minute.

"Yeah, he's a good guy. I should spend more time with him, but you know, the season . . ."

"Yeah." Cam nodded. "It's hard. I miss my dad."

"Just your dad?" Dawson slid him a sideways glance.

"Yeah. Mom died young—I was only eight."

"Shit, that sucks," Dawson said.

It had. But his dad had been so great, always, he'd missed her, of course, but he hadn't really felt the lack of love in his life.

"It's alright, honestly. We're just close. I worry about him out there, all alone."

"Phillipsburg is small, huh?" Dawson turned down a side street and pulled the SUV into an empty spot on the curb.

"Oh yeah. Fucking tiny." Cam shut the door behind him. It wasn't a bad neighborhood at all, but his pulse still thumped unevenly as he took in the very metropolitan trappings around them.

"Toronto must be a real wake-up call," Dawson said casually, but he was watching Cam intently—Cam could feel his gaze on him—as they walked down the sidewalk.

"Sure," Cam said.

"Cam," Dawson said, nudging him. "Don't front with me. It's okay to be a little—or a lot—freaked out."

"I'm not." But he was. But telling his dad the truth was so much different from telling the hot guy he was trying to impress at his brand-new job.

"Uh-huh." Dawson didn't look convinced as he stopped in front of an unassuming storefront. "I think this is it."

"You're gonna order for me, right?" Cam asked apprehensively as they walked inside.

They grabbed a table and Dawson pulled one of the plastic laminated menus from behind the napkin holder. "What?" he questioned.

"I don't know what I'd like . . ." Cam trailed off.

"So, figure it out," Dawson said. He put his elbows down on the table and leaned in. "You're never gonna do that if I do all your hard work for you."

"Ugh, I don't like you," Cameron complained.

"False accusations," Dawson said, laughing. "All lies."

Cam harrumphed, and even though he was apprehensive, pulled out a menu of his own. The foreign words made him slightly apprehensive, but for idiots like him, there *were* pictures of some of the dishes, and he was in the middle of analyzing them when he felt a touch on his hand.

Glancing up, he realized Dawson was touching him, concern written across his expression.

"If you're really . . ." Dawson trailed off. "I'm happy to give you some pointers, if you want."

"What did you *just* say about doing all my work for me?" Cam asked archly, realizing suddenly that he wasn't sure he wanted or *needed* Dawson to order for him. Maybe he wasn't experienced but that didn't mean he was incapable of figuring it out.

And if he ordered something he hated? Well, he'd order something else and send the leftovers home with Dawson. That guy was a human dumpster. He'd eat just about anything; watching him eat over the last few months had proven that.

"True. Well, the offer stands."

"What are you gonna get?"

"Probably the green curry—that's spicy, so be careful if you don't like heat—and probably an order of the fried rice. And um, maybe also these beef satay skewers with the peanut sauce. Aidan's text said specifically not to sleep on those."

"Hungry?" Cam asked, raising an eyebrow.

"And it's good leftovers. When I get home after practice, sometimes the last thing I wanna do is figure out what to eat. I've got the meal service shit, sure, but *ugh*, that's just so . . .well, you have it too, so you know how it is."

"Cardboard masquerading as food?"

Dawson gave him a commiserating look. "Exactly."

"Didn't you—your—" Cam stopped abruptly, realizing he didn't know what Dawson's ex-wife's name was. Didn't know if he should really be bringing her up at all, even though he had earlier and it had been okay. But this was different. More personal.

"Didn't Brynn feed me?" Dawson laughed, a little bitterly. "Sure. But she was shit in the kitchen, too, so it wasn't really a big difference when she moved out."

Cameron stared at the menu. "I'm sorry," he said, even though that seemed like a sentiment that wasn't nearly heartfelt enough. But what else could he even say?

"Yeah, I wanna say *me too*," Dawson confessed, leaning in again, "but then I think about how unhappy I was—how unhappy we both were—and I think, am I really sorry? I'm sorry it got ugly, for sure, and even sorrier that her dad is an asshole and stole from me. I'm sure fucking sorry the whole mess distracted me from what I'm good at. From my job. But other than that . . ." Dawson took a deep breath, and he looked like he was really realizing this for the first time, expression tinged with surprise. "I guess I'm not *that* sorry."

Cam wasn't sure how he was supposed to react. "Uh."

"Shit. Sorry," Dawson said, and then winced. "I didn't mean to unload like that. Maybe Aidan's right and I *should* be talking about it."

"He's Aidan Flynn, I can't imagine he's ever wrong," Cam said. Had he been starstruck the first time he'd met the Thunder's QB1? Maybe a little. It was hard, when Aidan looked like *that* and not only had that natural air of confidence to him, but two Super Bowl rings.

"Oh boy," Dawson said, groaning. "He's wrong all the fucking time. Don't tell me you think he's hot, too."

Dawson didn't sound very happy about that possibility—actually pissed off about it, in fact—that Cam was tempted to tell him that while *yes*, Aidan was hot, he found Dawson hot too. Hotter, in fact.

But Dawson was finally including him. Sitting with him at lunch. Asking him to dinner. Chatting with him like he wasn't just the stupid rookie, afraid to leave his apartment, but like he was a friend. He couldn't fuck it up by making things uncomfortable. Not now.

"Uh yeah, don't *you*?"

Dawson made a face. "When you've seen him puking in a bush outside a shitty frat house in Lansing, it sort of sucks the hotness out," Dawson said frankly.

The waitress appeared then, and they ordered. Cam hesitantly pointing to a handful of pictures, and Dawson confidently rattling off dish after dish like he'd been ordering Thai food for years. Then he added two orders of the beef satay skewers—because, he said, "You didn't, and if Aidan finds out I didn't take his rec, he'll be insufferable."

"Aidan doesn't strike me as the puking-in-a-bush type," Cam wondered, because they were apparently still talking about Aidan. He was way too put together for that, even when he'd been younger. Controlled, even.

"Oh, he's not. Not normally. Not even back then, but once in a while? Like I mean *really*, once in a while. Like maybe once. But once is all it takes, you know? Once I saw him crouched over that bush, it was all over."

Cam had had a few friends like that back in college. Friends he'd thought, *maybe*, when he'd first met them, and then even if he'd found them attractive, they'd ended up firmly in friends territory.

"Anyway," Dawson continued, "do *not* assume that Aidan Flynn's some kind of perfect football god, because he's not. He's an idiot like the rest of us."

"Even if he sends you restaurant recommendations?" Cam asked.

"*Even* if he's stupidly self-sacrificing and goes out of his way to invite us to the o-line dinner. Which we're going to, by the way."

"We are?" Cam wasn't sure why they would, but he wasn't about to turn down an invite, especially not if it was Aidan Flynn issuing it.

"Yeah. He's woken up from his cock-drunk state and realized that he's left us alone, which . . .I'm not mad about that, to be honest, because he's an annoying busybody, but we'll let him have this one."

"We will?"

Dawson shot him a look. "Rook. Keep up."

Cameron couldn't help the smile that bloomed across his face, even though he'd tried to keep it under wraps. "Alright," he said. "If we're invited, I suppose we'd better go."

"Damn straight," Dawson said, grinning. "Plus, it's on Aidan's dime and he's a snob, so it'll be good."

Their food arrived then, looking delicious and smelling even better, and Dawson added as he picked up a beef skewer, "Don't tell him that though. His ego is big enough."

"Oh. Okay." Cam was still having trouble actually saying anything to Aidan's face, so he didn't think that was going to be too much of a problem.

"Dig in," Dawson said, between bites of beef satay, "and don't let me eat all of these. Trust me, you're gonna want to try one."

They *were* delicious. Tender and bursting with flavor, and the peanut sauce on the side? Cam was tempted, for one single moment, to pick it up and just slurp the entire bowl down.

His noodles were really good, too, and it lifted his confidence just a little that he'd done a good job picking for himself, even though all he'd had to go on was the description and the picture.

"Yeah," Dawson said, smirking, as Cam barely came up for air. "I knew you'd do okay." He reached over, patting Cam on the hand. "You're too hard on yourself, rook."

Cam stared at his plate, already half-gone. "You were right," he said. "Toronto has been a real eye-opener."

"Yeah?" Dawson glanced up. There was still no judgment in his face. "I bet it is. And I should've realized it sooner that nobody else was watching out for you."

Humiliation flashed in his stomach, hot and fast. "I'm twenty-two. A grown man. I don't need to be watched out for," Cam retorted.

"Yeah, you do," Dawson argued mildly. "The fact that you don't think you do means you *really* do. The NFL is a big adjustment, even for guys coming from the major colleges. And you definitely didn't come from one of the big schools."

"No," Cam agreed. Western State had been tiny, and he'd only gotten national attention for his skill because they'd ended up playing two top twenty-five teams for a much-needed payday his senior year. Otherwise, probably very few pro GMs would've even known he existed. But he'd had some really great punts exactly when his team had needed them, and people had sat up and taken notice.

"This is the way," Dawson said, between bites of fried rice. "The way things are done. The vets watch out for the rookies. But I didn't the way I should've. Guess that's another thing I'm sorry about."

"You don't need to be," Cam argued. That embarrassment was still curdling in his stomach, no matter how good the food was. He didn't want Dawson's apology or to be treated like some hick who didn't know anything—even if that might be partially true.

"Yeah, I do." Dawson's hazel eyes were soft and serious. "I was stuck in my own shit. And Joey might've done it instead, but he's busy with that whole pack of kids, and there's a hierarchy to these things. You should know about that. Even at a small school, things can't be that different."

"Yeah, I get that because it wasn't. Not really," Cam said. It was why he'd been demurring to both Dawson and Joey, because they both had lots of NFL experience, and because Dawson was one of the team captains.

He wasn't about to force his company—or even worse, his fucking issues—onto Dawson.

"That why you were sitting with Duke and Jack at lunch today?"

"Maybe I just like them," Cam said, aware of how defensive he sounded.

"You can like them, but they're still practically practice squad guys. You should be hanging out with the starters. *You're* a starter, rook."

"Joey spends all his time with the linemen, and then you . . ." Cam swallowed hard. "You've known Aidan a long time, so it tracks that you'd hang out with him."

"Shit," Dawson said, and Cam knew he'd said too much because realization was dawning, clear and obvious on Dawson's face.

"Don't—" Cam warned, fork clattering to his plate.

Dawson shoved another beef skewer at his face. Cam didn't want to take it, but it was hard to resist when they were *that* good. After dipping it in the heaven-sent peanut sauce, he groaned a little around the first tender bite of meat.

"Yeah, for sure we're never telling Aidan how right he was about those," Dawson muttered under his breath. "But back to *you*, I get it. I was with Aidan, and you weren't gonna encroach on Aidan Flynn at work."

It was true, but Cam didn't like admitting to being intimidated. "Yeah, sort of, I guess. But I *do* like Duke and Jack. They're cool guys."

"Cool enough to show a whole presentation about me?" Dawson asked, his eyebrow lifting up.

"Ugh, don't listen to them. It wasn't a *presentation*, it was just me pointing out a few things when Duke kept defending the Ravens, when they shouldn't ever have treated you like that—"

"Yeah, they probably should've," Dawson said flatly and then looked surprised again, like he'd never expected to admit that out loud, or to admit it to Cam.

"No," Cam argued. "Sure, there was a tiny rough patch, but it wasn't that long or that rough."

"It was long *and* it was super rough," Dawson said honestly. "I was there for it. It still sucks that they didn't feel the same kind of loyalty to me that I felt for them. I'm allowed to be pissed about that, and I *am*. But this is a business, and the sooner you realize that, the less this stuff will fuck you up."

Cam nodded, though he secretly wasn't sure he'd ever be realistic enough about his situation for it *not* to fuck him up. He'd stayed focused and told himself a hundred times—maybe even a thousand—during training camp, that if he didn't win the position from the old punter, that was okay. He'd end up somewhere, even if that somewhere wasn't Toronto.

"It was a lot to expect you to deliver under those circumstances," Cam argued. He wasn't going to let Dawson beat himself up when he'd been through a war in his personal life, frankly was *still* going through it, to some extent, and that was the reason why he'd had so much trouble making kicks when they mattered.

"Yes but no." Dawson sighed. "Anyway, I've been way too focused on my own shit. I'm sorry for that. And I'm gonna try to do better. Try to do *different*, anyway."

"Okay," Cam said, swallowing hard. It felt good to hear it. Maybe Dawson hadn't known he was struggling—not necessarily drowning, but no question churning up the current as he trod water—and maybe Dawson wouldn't ever have the full picture. But that he was stepping up now felt good. Reassuring, honestly.

"So expect a lot more of these dinners," Dawson said. "We're both new to Toronto, so it only feels right we should work our way through Aidan's list."

"How long *is* the list?" Cam wondered, picking his fork back up and shoving another forkful of delicious noodles into his mouth. If all the recs were as good as this one, he was going to get spoiled.

"Decent enough. We can add some more places, too, if you've got your eye on anything you want to try," Dawson said. "I know Aidan doesn't strike you as the guy you'd go to for a *best of Toronto* list but that guy is so disciplined, if he's going to eat something off the meal plan, he's going to make sure it's damn good when he's doing it."

"Makes sense," Cam said. He paused. Wondered if he'd earned enough of Dawson's attention and trust to ask what he wanted to. Belly full of good food, he decided even if he hadn't, he was going to ask anyway. "So you really *never* with Aidan Flynn?"

Dawson laughed. "God, rook, you are adorable. Really fucking cute. Sorry to burst all your fantasies but no, we never did. We were just friends. I didn't even know Aidan was queer, to be honest. Kind of disappointed I was like the *last* to fucking know."

"Sucks." Cam exchanged a commiserating glance with him.

"Probably better for everyone I didn't." Dawson grinned. "We'd have been a hot mess."

"One of those, for sure," Cam retorted.

"Aw, you *are* cute."

As they finished up dinner and Dawson argued about grabbing the check—promising he'd let Cam pay for the next dinner they shared—Cam kept thinking about that. It was *nice* Daws thought he was cute, but the more he turned it over in his head, the more he didn't love the way he said it. Like Cam was some kind of small purse dog that you'd pet the head of and then barely spare a second thought for.

"What time are we leaving tomorrow?" Cam asked as they walked into the elevator. He pressed his floor and then realized, belatedly, that he didn't actually know which floor Dawson lived on.

Dawson shot him a look, complicated and layered. Some guilt, some apology, a wry kind of humor like he'd just realized that they'd lived in the same building for months now, and Cam had never even been to his place. He pressed Nine.

"Eight? Traffic blows no matter what time we leave, which I'm sure you've discovered," Dawson said.

"Yeah," Cam said. "Food's good here, sure, but the traffic is ass."

"Just wait til the winter," Dawson said knowingly.

Cam chuckled as the elevator came to a stop at his floor. "From Montana, dude."

"Oh. Right." Dawson shot him a lopsided smile. "Well, see you to-morrow morning, rook?"

"Sounds good," Cam said, nodding.

Dawson patted him on the shoulder briefly, and there it was.

Like he was a purse dog.

Cam told himself it was better to be a purse dog than to be forgotten. But he found it hard to quite believe it, even after he'd let himself into his place and put the leftovers into the fridge.

Still, it was an improvement to pull up the text convo with his dad and be able to send, **hung out with a teammate tonight. grabbed some food, it was really good.**

Because, Cam thought later as he relaxed into bed, it *had* been.

CHAPTER 5

Dawson hadn't even realized he was feeling alone—not *lonely*, per se, because it was basically impossible to feel lonely in a place like Toronto, and around a football team like the Thunder, who all clung a shade too close, but on an island of sorts—until he and Cam started carpooling.

"I don't know why you weren't doing that before," Nate said to him in the weight room when Dawson expressed how nice it was to have company on the long and often infuriating drive to the practice facility every day. "You guys live in the same damn building."

"I didn't even think about it," Dawson admitted. God, he'd been so preoccupied with his own shit.

"Pretty self-absorbed of you," Lane joked.

Dawson rolled his eyes. "Don't need to tell *me* that."

"I kinda think we do," Aidan added, and next to him, Mo nodded.

"I don't need a lecture," Dawson retorted without much heat. Maybe he *had* needed one, but he'd figured it out, hadn't he? He'd fixed it. Well, not entirely, but he was on his way to fixing it.

He looked over at where Cam was stretching on one of the big mats.

"I kind of thought I was gonna have to give you one," Aidan said in a low voice, flicking his hand towards Cam's figure on the mat. He was moving into some yoga poses now, shorts pulling across his ass.

Dawson glanced away. It was a really nice ass. He was divorced. Not dead. And while he might be long since inoculated to Aidan's hotness, it wasn't the same with Cam.

Maybe he could get him to puke in a bush.

"What are you talking about?" Dawson asked suspiciously, afraid he *did* know what Aidan was referring to.

"Please, you think he's adorable," Aidan said. "And he's well . . ."

"Pretty fucking green?" Lane answered for him.

Dawson rolled his eyes. "This convo is not good for anyone. Not for me, not for you, and definitely not for *you*, Lane."

Lane's eyes gleamed with mischief. "Afraid I'm gonna move in on your rookie, Hall?"

"He's not *my* rookie, and no, because the guy's got good taste. Better taste than you."

"Ouch," Lane said, lifting his hand for a high five with Mo.

Aidan gave them both a brief but hard look.

"The rookie has a name, and he's—" But Aidan didn't get any more of his speech out before Lane interrupted him.

"Naive? Innocent? Way too sweet for any of us?"

Dawson ground his teeth together. "All of those things, sure." If Aidan couldn't finish his lecture, then Dawson would do it. "But he's a good kid. Deserves better than to be harassed by you guys."

Lane rolled his eyes, but Dawson wasn't really worried about him. There was only one rookie Lane had been looking at, and he might talk a big game about hooking up and might talk an even *bigger* game about disliking the guy, but the rookie wasn't Cam.

He finished up his reps and glanced over at the mat. Cam was there still, laughing with Duke.

Maybe Lane wasn't who Dawson should be worried about.

"Your face is gonna freeze like that and good luck ever getting anyone else to marry you."

Dawson looked over and of course it was Aidan, looking smug and annoying.

"God, I hate you," he said, punching Aidan in the arm. "Go be superior someplace else."

Aidan only shot him a knowing glance.

"Maybe where your hot boyfriend is," Dawson muttered under his breath. He polished off his water bottle and headed over to the dispenser to fill it. Not surprisingly, Aidan followed him.

"You know I wasn't giving that warning for Lane," Aidan said, leaning against the wall, knowing look gleaming in his blue eyes.

"He's the best person for you to give it to. The guy's living out his Grindr-hookup fantasies."

"Don't think so. Not anymore, anyway. But don't change the subject."

Dawson was afraid he knew what Aidan was trying to get at, and he really didn't want him to say it out loud.

"Don't," Dawson warned.

"So you admit you need the warning?"

"No. *No.* The guy's like a baby. A rookie. Why would I be interested in him?" Dawson's mind was not cooperating and was currently ticking off reasons why he might be: 1) most definitely cute, with an even cuter ass, 2) talented, 3) funny when you got him out of his own head, 4) and saw a version of Dawson that wasn't a total fucking failure.

"I want to remind you that you kicked my ass about Levi, and you were right to do it."

"That's different. You were like a robot with a failing battery, and when he showed up, it was as if you'd finally gotten plugged in again."

"I'm going to ignore that sort of fucked-up metaphor and focus on the point. *My* point. You look at him. I know you do. And he sure looks back, Daws. And that's not a bad thing. I know you've had a hard go of it recently—"

"And that's it, the extent of this conversation," Dawson interrupted casually.

"Why do you never want to talk about it?" Aidan complained. "You make me feel like a bad friend."

Dawson took a long drink of water and shot Aidan a look. "'Cause you're a fucking terrible friend, Aidan."

Aidan had the nerve to look wounded, and now, it was even worse because Dawson felt guilty about it.

"Not that you actually *are* terrible. You're ride or die for your guys, you've always been. I knew when I signed here that you'd watch out for me. Be a good teammate. But you're always fucking pushing."

Aidan frowned, confusion creasing his forehead. "Daws, that's what good friends *do.*"

Was the worst part that Aidan was probably right? Or that after all of Aidan's insistent patience and pleas to talk about his goddamn feelings, he'd ended up confiding in Cameron instead the other night?

Aidan would surely pick the latter, but Dawson would always, *always* pick the former.

"Okay, I'm only gonna say this once." Dawson fixed his gaze on a point just over Aidan's shoulder so he didn't have to see his eyes as he said it. "I've been feeling pretty fucking sorry for myself. Some of it justified, some of it not. And it sucks to realize that. That while I've been pouting about how things shook out, it's like the world moved on without me. I'm still trying to catch up. I don't need to talk about it. I don't *want* to talk about it. It sucked. It *sucks*. End of story."

"Daws—" Aidan started to say, hand coming up to cup Dawson's shoulder.

"No," Dawson said flatly. "Don't say you're sorry."

Aidan looked almost relieved. And that was better than anything else. Maybe Levi had actually, finally turned him into a real boy.

"Okay," Aidan said. "But my original point stands. Cam gazes at you like you're a god, and that's gonna feel good."

"He does not," Dawson scoffed. He nearly told Aidan that Cam actually thought *he* was the hot one, but Aidan didn't need any more boosts to his ego. It was already healthy enough, especially with Levi in his bed now.

"He does," Aidan argued mildly. "And you might pretend that you don't, but you're looking back."

Dawson wanted to argue. But then he'd checked out Cam's ass earlier, hadn't he? He'd have to be a lot stronger man than he was to be faced with that slender, muscled curve and *not* look at it. It was just aesthetic appreciation, that was all.

"I'm not saying *don't*, because you're not Lane, thank God. We have our hands full enough with the demon twins. But like . . .step carefully, alright?"

"He's not a child," Dawson argued and then regretted saying anything at all.

"Right. Of course he's not. But like . . .everything's new to him. Remember how that was?"

Dawson did. How underwater he'd felt his whole first season in the NFL. "I'm watching out for him, that's all."

"Well, I'm glad you're doing at least that now," Aidan said.

Dawson smacked him on the arm. "You're the fucking worst."

Aidan grinned. "Yeah, yeah. But you love me, secretly."

"Enough people love you, secretly," Dawson said.

A complicated look passed over Aidan's face. "Yeah," he agreed.

Dawson raised an eyebrow. "You wanna talk about *that*?" he asked, gesturing across the room to where Mo had joined Cam and Duke.

"I really, really don't," Aidan said, glancing briefly at Mo and then looking away.

"Remember that the next time you whine at me about sharing *my* feelings," Dawson told him.

Laughing, Aidan chucked a fist under his chin. "I missed you, you know? When you were in Baltimore."

"I'm not surprised," Dawson said.

"Okay, how about this: if you're gonna fuck the rookie, at least don't fuck *up* the rookie?"

Dawson rolled his eyes. "I'm not gonna fuck the rookie."

Aidan didn't look like he believed him, which was fine. Aidan wasn't the end-all, be-all of everyone's sexual desires. Frankly Dawson hadn't been convinced that Aidan even *had* sexual desires, not until Levi had shown up in Toronto and Aidan couldn't stop looking at him.

But as much as he didn't like it, Aidan's words followed Dawson through the day. Through practice, watching from his spot on the field as Joey and Cam practiced hitting punts that landed within the five-yard line.

He could kick pretty damn far for a punter, no question, with a leg strength that belied his slender stature. But he had the accuracy too, which not every punter had. Most of them were just damn good at booming kicks, but not pulling back when the occasion demanded it. Dawson hadn't met a punter yet with such a fine-tuned ability to judge exactly how much force was needed on a kick to pin an opposing team on the other side of the field.

It was just admiration of skill, that was all.

His high school English teacher would have insisted he was protesting way too much.

Brynn would probably tell him competence porn was a thing. After all, it had won *her* over. Carlos had been her personal trainer, and there was a part of Dawson still very much pissed that his normally intelligent ex-wife had fallen into *that* trap.

His words hung around at lunch, with Cam on one side of him and Duke and Jack across from him as he ate his chicken salad.

Did Cam look at him like Aidan said? Or was Aidan just seeing desire everywhere, now that he'd finally experienced it for himself?

No question, there was a thread of hero worship going on there. Dawson's ego, bruised and battered, *did* enjoy that. A good reminder that at some point, not that long ago, he'd been aspirational. The kind of player other special teams guys talked about in hushed whispers.

He'd been proud of that. Probably *too* proud, which was what his dad was always saying came before a fall.

But Dawson didn't think that was all of it, either. It felt good, sure, and soothed a hurt. No question about it. But other guys had reached out, after Baltimore had released him, and he hadn't been tempted to cash any of the checks their gazes promised.

They drove back to downtown together, as they had for the last few days, now. It felt good to even have Cam next to him in the seat, even if he was quiet. So it couldn't just be the sweetness of Cam's hero worship.

"Offensive-line dinner tonight," Dawson reminded him as they were in the elevator heading up to their apartments.

"Right," Cam said, nodding. "Should be a good time. I heard Lane and Trev were crashing, too."

"Ugh, the demon twins," Dawson muttered.

"Hey, they're pretty nice," Cam argued.

"Don't let them be *too* nice to you," Dawson warned.

"What?" Confusion crossed Cam's face.

"Just . . .don't let Lane charm you."

Cam was straight-up frowning now. "Lane's not interested in me."

Dawson considered saying that he shouldn't be, but that would probably come across shitty, like nobody, ever, should be interested in Cameron, when actually the opposite was true.

There were *plenty* of reasons why anyone would be interested in Cam. It felt like Dawson had spent all day turning them over and over again in his head.

"See you in a bit," Cam said, when the elevator hit his floor.

"I'll order an Uber for us," Dawson said, and Cam gave him one last look before the doors shut behind him.

Dawson dumped his stuff by the door and, after showering again, headed to his bedroom and its walk-in closet. He had clothes in it, of course, because he had to wear clothes every day, but it had been so long since he'd actually cared about looking good.

He still wasn't sure he cared, but when he grabbed the first shirt off the hanger, he did at least glance at the mirror and make sure he didn't look embarrassing.

Positively, Aidan could give a shit about what he was wearing, so he wouldn't catch any strays for wearing a variation of what he'd worn the last few times they'd gone out to Vault.

Maybe if he was actually trying to hook up, he'd make an effort.

But the idea of going through all the small talk and posturing and then maybe if everything went okay, figuring out how two lives meshed together all over again? Dawson's skin crawled. He didn't think he could do it. Maybe he should download an app. Or he could stick to what was easy and what was already working, which was his right hand.

After checking his email, responding to a message from his agent, and spending thirty minutes flopped on the couch watching ESPN and sucking down a Gatorade in anticipation of the booze he'd probably be drinking, he headed downstairs.

There were a handful of figures scattered around the front of their building, but only one caught Dawson's eye.

He was wearing jeans that fit his ass like a second skin, and a dark button-up that hugged him in all the best ways. Emphasized the curve of his hips, and the slenderness of his waist. Dark hair curling over the smooth tan skin of his neck.

Dawson did a double take and angled himself a little closer as he waited for Cam. He *was* fine with his right hand, if he could think of guys like this when he touched himself. And this guy was worth thinking about; Dawson's gaze kept getting caught on shoulders and thighs and the tiny bit of visible skin he could see between hair and collar. Imagined, for a single second, what it would feel like under his tongue.

And then the guy turned around and Dawson nearly choked.

It was Cameron.

Here was the thing: Dawson *knew* the rookie was attractive. Had known it but was steadfastly ignoring it, for a hundred very good reasons.

But it was going to be even harder to ignore it now.

Dawson debated running away, despite that he'd never been a coward, even through the worst of the shit he'd been through. Gave himself a firm pep talk-slash-warning and then headed over to where Cam stood.

"Hey," Dawson said. Suddenly wishing that he'd not just grabbed the first Thunder-branded polo shirt he'd found in the closet.

"Oh, hey." Cam grinned, giving Dawson's shoulder a pat. "Looking good."

Dawson wasn't sure he'd go that far. But Cam *was* looking good. Good enough to eat.

Down, boy.

"Uh yeah. Thanks. Ditto." Dawson forced his gaze to slide past Cam's front, then down to his phone. "Car should be here in a minute."

Cam nodded, like everything was normal.

And everything *was* normal, except Dawson.

He'd seen the rookie dressed up before, right? They'd gone out to Vault at least twice, but he couldn't remember what the guy had been wearing before. Clothes?

Certainly not *these* clothes.

"You've been quiet today," Cam observed as Dawson tried to fall into his phone screen, tracking the car that was supposedly just around the corner but that had yet to appear.

"Uh, just . . .preoccupied, I guess." It was early October in Toronto; he should not be sweating under his collar.

"You're not still worried about that kick on Sunday, are you?" Cam frowned, his eyebrows narrowing together. "'Cause we've worked hard this week. It's not gonna happen again."

"It wasn't *your* fault," Dawson said automatically. Realized his mistake in activating Defender Cam only when he curled a hand around his bare forearm and squeezed supportively.

Dawson made the mistake of looking up into his eyes. Regretting that yes, Cam was at least two inches taller. His eyes were brown, yes, but a rich and dark brown, with tiny flecks of green and gold. Beautiful fucking eyes.

Was this because they'd ended up at the swimming pool the other night? No, because he'd been too distracted that night, both by his own fucking distress and his realization that Cam was struggling, too. Then there'd been the dream.

But those had just been stray thoughts, coalescing into nonsense scenarios.

It didn't feel like nonsense, now.

"Daws," Cam said, "it wasn't *your* fault, either."

"I know," Dawson said quickly. Too quickly. Another mistake. They were piling up now and at some point they'd stack up too high, wobbling uncertainly, and Dawson was afraid of what might happen if they all came falling down.

A honk forcibly yanked him out of his spiral, and Dawson realized a second later that the car was here, and the driver had been probably been sitting there for at least a minute, watching them stand too close together. Watching Dawson gazing into the rookie's eyes like he might find not just the secrets of the universe in them, but the magic answer to all the bullshit cluttering up his brain.

They climbed into the back seat, Cam sliding over on the bench, Dawson offering an apologetic glance to the driver as he pulled the door closed behind him.

"It's not far," Dawson said to Cam.

Cam glanced over, and Dawson was relieved to see that his smile was as bright as it had been before. This was okay, then. He didn't want to jar Cam too forcefully out of his comfort zone.

"You always crash Aidan's offensive-line dinners?" Cam asked.

"Actually, never," Dawson admitted. "At least not at Michigan and not here, either, but he's being his normal nosy self. He'd have invited me earlier, I think, but Levi had him pretty well distracted."

"He doesn't seem that different to me?" Cam observed.

Dawson laughed. "You didn't know him before. In his pre-Levi heyday, he made a triple espresso look chill."

"Only by reputation, yeah," Cam admitted.

"Oh that's right." Dawson shot Cam a knowing look, then deliberately ignored how the fire flicked to light in the base of his stomach as they shared it. "You thought Aidan was hot."

Kept the inevitable question to himself. *Do you* still *think Aidan's hot?*

Cam groaned. "Don't remind me. And for God's sake, don't tell *him*, okay?"

"Don't worry. I'm not about to boost his ego like that," Dawson said. *Not about to fuck my own, either, even though that would probably be better for everyone.*

A minute later, they pulled up in front of the restaurant and slid out of the car. The hostess clocked them when they walked in and immediately led them back to a private room situated at the back of the restaurant.

"Hey, glad you two made it," Aidan said, greeting them. He tugged Dawson into a bro hug and then did the same with Cam.

"You mean, you're happy we crashed?" Dawson joked.

Aidan shot him a look. "Please. If it gets you out of that sad, pathetic apartment, you can crash every single goddamn week."

"Shit, if you're telling *me* I'm pathetic, then I must be pretty bad off," Dawson said, scrubbing a hand over the scruff covering his jaw. Maybe he should've shaved. Cam had, and he looked fresh, clean, jawline so sharp it could cut glass.

"You're not," Cam retorted loyally. "Not even close. You're Dawson Hall. Like a fucking legend."

Aidan tilted his head, staring right at Dawson.

He didn't need to hear Aidan say it to know what Aidan was thinking.

Watch it with the rookie.

But Aidan's warnings were unnecessary. Dawson had invented them first.

"Dude, you came." Dawson thought he recognized the voice, and his first guess was confirmed when Dawson saw that Duke was behind Aidan, white teeth flashing bright against his light brown skin, as he greeted Cam.

Like he'd been *hoping* Cam would show up.

Damn, what had happened to Cam being *his* rookie?

Cam hugged him too, Duke balancing his drink in one big hand, pulling Cam into the group he'd been with—Nate and another defense player, whose name Dawson couldn't remember.

"Oh yeah, apparently you're not the only one crashing," Aidan pointed out under his breath, but he looked pleased. Like this was actually what he'd been gunning for this whole damn time.

So much for keeping Aidan on his toes.

"Come on, you totally planned this," Dawson said, eyeing the long table with its number of place settings. "It's not a surprise that we're all here."

"Not all me," Aidan said smugly. Levi appeared then, like magic, wrapping an arm around Aidan's waist and tugging him in proprietarily.

Aidan glanced up into his boyfriend's face, way too pleased with himself.

Dawson had forgotten about this—or purposefully pretended that he wouldn't have to witness it.

At practice and in the team facility, they were fairly chill about the PDA. Pretty much the whole team and the entirety of the coaching staff had either been told or figured out that the QB1 of the Toronto Thunder and his left tackle were dating, but they weren't as obvious about it when they were at work.

But even though this was technically a team event, it wasn't open to everyone, and Levi's fingers were stroking Aidan's waist and Aidan was gazing at him like he owned the best dick on the eastern seaboard.

"I'm gonna go uh . . .see Duke and Nate," Dawson offered.

Aidan raised an eyebrow. "You actually know who Duke is?"

If he hadn't been watching Aidan robot his way through life, thinking that all he'd ever need was a football and a playbook, Dawson might have thrown back that he was surprised that *Aidan* knew who Duke was, considering how wrapped up he seemed to be in Levi these days.

But the truth was, Aidan, as insufferable as his happiness was, deserved this, and Dawson was genuinely thrilled for his friend.

"He's a cool guy," Dawson said, tilting his chin up, like it hadn't been *Cameron* who'd introduced them.

Aidan smiled knowingly. He'd probably guessed, but Dawson wasn't going to call him on *that*, either.

"Sounds good," Aidan said.

Aidan had been the poorest little rich kid forever. It was wonderful seeing him find someone who cared about who *he* was, not just about the trappings he'd always carried around, heavy but inevitable.

If Levi lifted those burdens, for an hour or an evening or even a fucking moment, Dawson would tolerate Aidan's obvious coupling up.

There was nothing to do *but* head over to where Cam had ended up, like Dawson was following him around like a puppy.

It didn't help that Cam's grin widened when he saw Dawson coming in his direction.

"Hey," Nate said, nodding. "Good to see you at one of these, Hall."

"You gonna call me pathetic, too?" Dawson wondered.

"Nah," Nate said, punching him lightly on the arm. "You're solid, man."

"Hey, if we're calling anyone pathetic . . ." Duke trailed off and shot Nate a sharp look. "It's Nate Dogg here."

"What?" Cam asked, a frown creasing his forehead.

"Who's that hockey player friend of Wes'?" Duke asked.

"He's nobody," Nate muttered.

"Now, that's not true. I looked him up. He set all kinds of records in college. Was supposed to be like the next coming of Sidney Crosby or something."

Nate made a disgruntled noise. "Dude, the guy isn't even a *forward*, he's a defenseman." He looked put out—because he was having to explain this, or because he was having to talk about the guy at all? It was unclear. "Crosby's a forward. You know, the guys that score points? You ever even watched a hockey game?"

"More than you," Duke teased. "At least before you met a hockey player and realized how hot they are."

"Oh, that hot friend of Wes'?" Cam asked.

The hockey player *was* hot. There was no question of it. Hotter than Aidan, even if Dawson removed the vomiting-into-a-bush handicap. But *God*, it was like Cameron thought every guy on the planet was attractive, except for him.

That should be good. It should not rankle Dawson. Shouldn't get his back up.

But he didn't like it.

Duke nodded enthusiastically. "The last time we went to Vault, guy tried to talk to Nate, and he just iced him out."

"He's such a dick," Nate muttered under his breath. "Swans around like he's real hot shit."

It was at least nice to see someone else suffering, so Dawson said, "He kinda *is* real hot shit."

Nate rolled his eyes, looking unimpressed. Like Ramsey was actually right here and he was hoping to take him down a peg or two. Or ten.

"We're gonna have to agree to disagree on that," Nate said. "He's fucking annoying is what he is. I wish Wes would stop bringing him around."

"Maybe they're together," Cam said, and the hopefulness in his voice, the sheer fucking optimism made Dawson feel so old. God, other than Aidan and Levi, it was like he'd become permanently allergic to happily-ever-afters.

When he saw one, all he could think of was all the ways it could catastrophically implode. *That's fucked up*, a whole host of voices in his head chimed in.

Dawson didn't know whether it was better or worse that one of them even belonged to his ex-wife.

"No way," Nate said, tone edgy. "Wes's still in love with his ex."

"Well, the hot hockey player turned Lane down flat," Duke said. "He told me. Was all pissed off about it."

"Maybe he just didn't want to fuck Lane." Nate's voice had gotten steelier.

"More like he didn't want Lane to fuck *him*," Duke muttered.

Nate smacked him on the arm. "We don't do that kind of sexist, homophobic bullshit here, Adams."

"What?" Duke whined.

"Getting fucked isn't just for the smaller guy," Cam said knowingly.

Dawson really hoped that nobody was looking at how he went hot all over, his face no doubt flushing red.

"Not that you'd know *anything* about it," Nate added.

Duke shrugged, clearly unbothered. "I can't say I'm into guys, but it *is* interesting. Plus the gossip is top-notch, especially on this team. Who else is fucking who? I want in on the ground floor."

"Nobody but Aidan and Levi," Nate said.

"*Yet*," Duke retorted.

Dawson willed his flush away, but before anyone could comment on how poor of a job he was doing—or before, even worse, Cam noticed—Aidan announced that the waitstaff was about to come around and take orders, so they should all take their fucking seats sometime this year.

He ended up seated towards one end of the table, Wes—a late arrival, which after the whole convo Dawson had been having with Nate, Duke, and Cam, was probably a relief—on one side and Cam next to him. Within easy view of Dawson, which was both a good and a bad thing.

Wes was only a few years older than Cam, but Dawson, observing over the edge of the menu he was supposed to be reviewing, wondered if they'd end up friends.

He *wanted* Cam to have friends. Wanted him to be included. Wanted him to be a significant part of this team because he *was*, and it mattered to Dawson that his teammates saw him the same way Dawson was beginning to.

But despite that, there was a thread of jealousy, of *envy*, that wound its way through him.

He wanted to be the guy making Cam laugh.

He wanted Cam to be the sunshine brightening all his shadows, dismissing his heartbreak.

What if Cam did that for Wes, instead?

It would be fine. It *would* be fine. Because Dawson was not interested, and even if he was stupid enough to be, the reality was he was currently a wreck of a human. Hardly good for anyone in this state.

Dawson glanced pointedly back at his menu.

"You alright?" Nate asked.

It was embarrassing that he'd been spotted. "Sure, yeah," Dawson said, as easy as he could.

"Sure thing. That tenseness in your shoulders has nothing to do with the rookie over there," Nate said under his breath.

Dawson forced himself to relax. "I'm good," he repeated. Nate didn't look convinced, but it didn't matter because that was the moment the waiter appeared next to him, ready to take his order.

He ordered a steak and a salad, side of mushrooms, and a glass of red wine, telling himself that they just had the walkthrough tomorrow.

It was a good event, full of laughter and some pointed teasing, but then Aidan had been hosting these dinners for years. Still, he appeared to be really relaxing into the job in a way he hadn't ever before, and Dawson was sure that was entirely because of the guy on his left.

Levi was in great form tonight, arm casually slung around Aidan's shoulders. He'd nudge him every minute or so, and whatever observations he was murmuring into Aidan's ear were making him laugh in a way that Dawson didn't think he'd ever seen before.

The dinner wound to a close, guys beginning to depart in pairs. A few of them were making plans to go out for another drink, after, but Dawson knew he had too much resting on this game—*every* game, if he was being honest—to spend too much time drinking two days before he had to be in top shape, physically *and* mentally.

He collected Cam and detoured on the way out of the restaurant to say goodbye to Aidan. Aidan, whose head was tipped in close to Levi. They weren't kissing currently, but it wasn't too much of a stretch to imagine they might've been a minute ago, or Levi might say fuck it and plant one the moment Dawson and Cam left.

"Hey, we're off," Dawson said, and Aidan rose, giving him a quick hug. "Thanks for thinking of us."

Cam was silent next to him. Thinking of how he wished he might be the guy in Levi's position?

Dawson needed to get his head examined, that much was clear. He'd mentally imagined Cameron with practically every guy here during this stupid dinner. Every guy except *him*.

"'Course," Aidan said. "Feel free to show up every week." He shot Cam a separate smile, bright and genuinely welcoming. "You too, rook."

"Uh yeah, sure. Thanks," Cam stammered.

A minute later they were on the sidewalk again, Dawson pulling up the Uber app on his phone.

"Should I warn Levi you're going to try to steal his man?" Dawson half-joked, trying to ignore the burn of jealousy in the base of his stomach.

"No. *No.* God." Cam rolled his eyes. "You're embarrassing."

That much was true. It was genuinely embarrassing how much he was beginning to crave the rookie's attention on *him* and nowhere else.

Dawson slipped his phone into his pocket and tried to ignore the brisk wind that had not been nearly so brisk a few hours ago. "Oh, Aidan," he said in a mock-seductive voice, "you're so hot. So good at football. Let me punt all your balls."

Cam choked out a laugh, and Dawson wanted to pat himself on the back for the flags of color rising hot on his cheeks.

"That's not . . .trust me. That's not what I want to say. Or who I want to say it to."

Is it Wes? Lane? That hockey player everyone's talking about?

But Dawson didn't ask because he didn't want to hear the answer.

It wasn't going to be him. Cam worshipped his leg. The kicking prowess that he'd once possessed as easy as breathing that now felt distant and slippery. Impossible to grasp.

"Okay, sure," Dawson said and heard the disbelief in his voice.

But Cam just laughed again, nudging Dawson's side with his elbow. Sharp but gentle. His eyes were wide and guileless, full of stars.

Dawson looked away.

The car pulled up to the curb a second later, saving Dawson from whatever very stupid thing he'd been tempted to say or do next.

But after they'd slid into the back seat, Cam let his arm fall into the middle, brushing against Dawson's.

"Thanks for inviting me," he murmured, his words barely audible over the Leafs game the driver had on, the play-by-play droning endlessly.

"It was no big deal."

"A big deal to me. Making sure it was . . .making sure I was getting out, seeing people. Seeing new places. Means a lot to me." Cam's tongue flicked out, licked his bottom lip.

Dawson knew he should look away. Knew Cam wasn't flirting with him, but he still wanted it. Wanted to bask in that sunshine, even when it wasn't meant for him.

"Anytime." Dawson tried for breezy casual but didn't quite get there.

He finally tore his eyes away from Cam's face, watching as Toronto at night flashed by the car window.

Less than a minute later, the driver pulled up at the entrance to their building and they climbed out.

Cameron was at least quiet as they walked towards the elevator. No more earnest thank-yous and no more big puppy eyes.

That should've made it easier for Dawson to bid him goodbye when the elevator opened at his floor, but it didn't quite.

Because after he was gone, Dawson felt the empty space next to him as acutely as he ever had.

CHAPTER 6

THE THUNDER WERE ONE of the few teams in the NFL that didn't require players to stay in a hotel the night before a game. They offered the option—for players who craved that feeling of routine every single week, whether they were home or away—but Dawson liked his own bed. His own pillows.

The mattress on his king-size bed was the one thing he'd really given a shit about after he and Brynn had divorced. He'd ended up buying a new one, but the same brand. The one that felt like he was sleeping on a cloud.

Money was tight, but not *that* tight.

He could still have a great bed where he could, *theoretically,* get a fabulous night's sleep.

It was not the bed's fault that sleep was elusive these days.

Normally, he'd sleep like a baby. But Dawson was tired this afternoon, so tired he actually considered attempting to take a nap.

But before he could get closer than rising from the couch, his phone rang.

His phone only rang these days for a very select handful: his parents, his agent, and his lawyer. He'd considered adding Aidan to that list, but Dawson was beginning to suspect he'd abuse that privilege, with the number of times he'd called, "just to check in."

Dawson sighed and answered. It was, as he suspected, not his parents or his agent, who all knew better than to call him the afternoon before a game.

"Hey," Simon Burns, his lawyer, said. "Glad I managed to catch you."

"Yeah," Dawson said. Whenever Simon called, it was not usually good news. For a victim, he'd imagined that hearing from his lawyer would make him feel better every once in a while, but that never seemed to happen.

"There's a new plea on the table from Ackerman and the defense," Simon said. "The prosecutor wanted me to discuss it with you."

"Is it going to piss me off?" Dawson asked archly.

Simon chuckled under his breath, which probably meant, *yes*.

"We've talked about this, Dawson," Simon said. "He's going to probably plea out. It's a white-collar crime."

"Does it matter what kind of crime it is? It's still a fucking crime. Richard Ackerman stole from me. From a whole bunch of people."

"I know." Simon at least sounded understanding. He'd been invaluable during this whole process. Been the one to call up an old friend in the district attorney's office and get more eyes on the case. Get it bumped up in the case load.

Dawson didn't need to be reminded that there were far worse crimes out there. Criminals who'd killed and raped and stolen.

Stolen shit that couldn't be given back.

"So what's the plea this time?" This was not the first time Ackerman and his defense team had come up with a way for him to wiggle out of this.

Sometimes Dawson felt guilty for using all his football player privilege to make sure Ackerman got adequately punished, but then he remembered that it wasn't *only* his money that his father-in-law had stolen.

He'd siphoned funds out of lots of people's accounts, including a bunch of middle-class households that couldn't necessarily ever replace what had been lost.

"Still trying to avoid jail time," Simon said. "His defense team is pushing hard for house arrest, because of how high profile this case has gotten."

"And? What does the prosecutor think?" Dawson demanded. He wanted Ackerman to go to fucking jail. He wanted him to sit in a tiny little box and think about how Dawson had been his son-in-law, with a front seat to how goddamn hard Dawson worked to earn every cent, but he'd stolen everything from him anyway.

But Simon just sighed.

Yep, Dawson had fucking called it. Nobody had any balls. They wanted Ackerman to get by on a technicality. To only be restricted to his cushy-ass house.

As far as Dawson was concerned, that wasn't even a punishment. Not enough of one. Not even remotely.

"Shit," Dawson muttered.

"And I talked to Alex," Simon said, referring to Dawson's agent, "and he thinks it would be better for everyone if Ackerman settled with a plea bargain. Less distracting press, less media focus on how that affected you last year."

Dawson took a deep breath and let it out slowly. "He doesn't want me to testify." He couldn't blame Alex for being wary. When he'd been in the middle of all this shit, last season, there was no question it had negatively impacted his game.

And like all bad cyclical shit, the worse it had gotten, the more impossible it had been to pull himself out of it.

"You doing the deposition was tough enough."

It hadn't been easy, that was for sure. But the truth was while Dawson was a victim, he wasn't the centerpiece of the prosecution's case. That was the forensic accountant he'd hired when Brynn had filed for divorce and suddenly nothing was what it seemed with his accounts.

"You said they wouldn't even ask me to testify if it went to trial," Dawson reminded his lawyer.

"If the prosecution keeps rejecting the pleas? If I was Ackerman's defense team, I'd make it a media circus, and you'd be the key to that, Dawson."

"Fuck," Dawson muttered.

"Think about it. I'll send the particulars over by email. Review it. I know you have a game tomorrow."

"Yeah."

"We have some time to offer an opinion. And I'll remind you again, it's just an opinion. Ultimately it's the prosecutor's decision on whether they want to take it or not."

"Right." Dawson tried not to sound pissed off about it, but he could tell he hadn't quite pulled it off.

"It's going to end and be over, and you'll be able to get back to your normally scheduled life soon," Simon soothed.

But even as he thanked Simon for the call and promised to review the plea that came through in his email, he knew that was untrue.

He couldn't turn back the clock.

When Brynn had declared she wanted a divorce, everything had changed. He'd been forced to pull the blackout curtain back on his unhappy marriage and take a hard look on how long he'd been skating by with just "fine." Then, the shit about the money had come out, and everything had gotten worse, capped off by suddenly sucking at his job.

He'd never be able to put all those genies back in their bottles. Dawson knew he was forever changed by what had gone down last year.

He knew who he'd been; he just didn't know who he was going to become.

It was difficult not to imagine his dad giving him a blunt look and saying, "and who you are has got nothing to do with you? You make your own self, Daws. You always have."

He could sit here and mull over all the shit, marinate in every way he'd gotten fucked, or he could *do* something else.

Dawson stood and grabbed his keys, not even letting himself think.

A minute later he was riding the elevator down to Cam's floor.

He didn't text, because he was afraid if he did, he'd chicken out.

But right now, all he was thinking about was how he felt *better* when Cam's sunshine was soaking into him. At the dinner, he'd been jealous because he'd wanted it on *him*, and the only one keeping him from having those rays was himself.

Dawson knocked on the door once, then again.

He was just about to do it a third time when suddenly there was no more wood under his fist, the door swinging open.

Dawson nearly swallowed his tongue.

Cam was wearing only a pair of low-slung sweatpants.

It wasn't like they didn't all strip down in the locker room on a frequent basis. They did. There was no real room for privacy in professional sports. But Dawson had tried not to look—not at Cam, not at *anyone*. And before that, what felt like an eternity ago, but was actually only like a few weeks, he'd not even been *interested* in looking at anyone. He'd been too busy feeling sorry for himself.

Well, he wasn't feeling sorry for himself now.

He was fucking *looking* and didn't know how to stop.

Cameron wasn't the hottest guy in the world or the most ripped, but there was something about the graceful slide of one muscle into the next—traps to pecs to abs—that made Dawson's throat dry and his tongue too big for his mouth.

"Hey," Cam said happily, eyes lighting up at Dawson's presence in his doorway. "What's up?"

"I…uh…" At some point, and at a point that couldn't have been that long ago, Dawson had considered himself fairly charming. He'd gotten around Baltimore's single scene, guys and girls alike, before he'd met and married Brynn.

But Cam short-circuited his brain.

He wanted to touch him, and not just with his hands, either.

Cam raised an eyebrow. "You okay?"

"I'm not gonna be if Aidan figures out I'm looking at you like this," Dawson confessed. And okay, he hadn't meant to say that out loud, but apparently the brain molecules that hadn't just been fried within an inch of their lives had lost their connectivity to his mouth.

Cam had the nerve to actually look shocked. "What are you talking about?"

They didn't need to have this conversation right here—frankly, they shouldn't be having it at all, but having it in the hallway of their building was *worse*—and Dawson pushed into his space, until they were nearly pressed together in the tiny entryway of Cam's even smaller apartment.

Dawson opened his mouth and snapped it shut. "Nothing."

Cameron was still smiling, but the corners of his lips turned up farther, into a sly little look that shouldn't have turned Dawson on, but did. "You can't do that. Come on. What does Aidan have to do with this? And how are you looking at me?"

He had two options: tell the truth or run away.

Dawson told the truth. "You're . . .well, you're attractive, okay? And Aidan would probably be pissed if he knew about it."

"What, and *what*?" Cam demanded. He pressed a palm into Dawson's chest.

"Aidan—"

Cam laughed like it had been startled out of him, and it sounded like bottled sunshine. Dawson wanted to roll over like a dog and just bask in it. "I don't want to hear about Aidan," he interrupted. "I want to hear about *you*."

Dawson was sure Cam was hardly annoyed about it—he hadn't seemed that way, anyway—but it still felt embarrassing to admit to the attraction. Especially like this. God, at one point, he'd had moves.

That day felt so far removed it was like it hadn't ever existed at all.

"I'm divorced, not dead," Dawson muttered. He waved his hand. "And you're . . .well, you know."

"No, I don't, which is why I keep asking," Cam said. He hadn't moved his hand, and now his fingertips curled into the fabric of Dawson's sweatshirt.

Like if Dawson tried to get away, Cam wasn't going to let him.

"You're hot, okay?" Dawson swallowed hard. He wasn't going to add, *and I'm attracted to you*, because he thought that must be obvious enough and also because he wasn't stupid enough to take this even further.

"Thanks." It turned out Cam had an adorable divot of a dimple when he smiled that wide.

"You're welcome."

Neither of them moved, but Dawson knew he needed to, before he did something even dumber than admit to Cam's face that he was hot.

"So you gonna tell me about this Aidan thing?" Cam asked.

Dawson made a face. "No?"

Cam had the nerve to laugh delightedly. "Yeah, I think you are, Daws. Come on. What does *this* have to do with Aidan?" His fingers dug more insistently into the thick fabric covering Dawson's chest.

"Nothing, really—he'd just tell me it was a bad idea. And he would be right."

"What would be a bad idea?" Cam gazed at him guilelessly. "You're attractive, too."

Dawson groaned under his breath.

"It would be better—*easier*—if you thought that about just about anyone else on the team."

"Maybe not Aidan or Levi," Cam said thoughtfully. "Or Wes."

It was the worst thing Cam could've told him. Or maybe the best. Dawson was unclear. "Actually, Wes—"

Dawson wasn't sure if he was relieved or disappointed that Cam interrupted him before he got the whole thing out.

"Wes's still hung up on his ex," Cam said, and for the first time since he'd opened the door, there was a whisper of a frown on his face.

Dawson glanced away. "Yeah, he is." *And I'm still fucked up, a real hot garbage fire.*

"This isn't a big deal," Cam said and patted Dawson's pec reassuringly before he finally pulled his touch away.

It was actually the biggest deal. Dawson wanted to tell him that since his divorce over a year ago, he'd not looked at anyone and wanted them, not until Cam.

But they were playing with fire enough as it was.

Maybe Cam even knew it, because he turned and walked into the living room then, grabbing a sweatshirt on the couch and tugging it on.

Dawson watched the last of his bare skin disappearing and told himself that he wasn't disappointed. That he didn't enjoy every second of the still-tanned muscles of Cam's back rippling as he covered up.

"So," Cam said, that dimple returning, "what's up?"

"Oh. Yeah." He'd come down here for a reason. Not *just* to ogle the rookie in all his shirtless glory. "Um, I wanted to know if you wanted to go for a walk with me. I gotta get out of the house, and figured you might need that, too."

"Got me all figured out?" Cam teased, but he was still grinning, like he'd just won the lottery.

"Not entirely, but—" It was all Dawson got out before Cam wrapped an arm around his waist and tugged him in close.

That two inches Cam had on him had never seemed like a thing, but it felt like a thing now.

Dawson froze.

"I know you said it was a bad idea," Cam said. His mouth was hovering only an inch above Dawson's. The arm around his waist wasn't holding him tight enough that Dawson couldn't get away if he wanted to.

The problem was that he didn't want to, even if he *needed* to.

He pulled himself away. "Uh," Dawson mumbled.

"I know, bad idea and all that, but could be fun," Cam said, shrugging. Like it was no big deal that he'd almost kissed Dawson.

"Fun?" Dawson parroted back.

"Oh come on, you're not too old that you've forgotten what fun is."

Maybe he had. Because ten years ago, he'd have been enthusiastic about the prospect of kissing Cam, even if it was only fun.

But then ten years ago, he hadn't seen the dissolution of a marriage and nearly the mirrored dissolution of a career he'd fought so hard for.

"Not that old, no," Dawson agreed. He could tell Cam how tempted he'd been, but if he told him just *how* attracted he was, how much his hands were itching to bury themselves under Cam's sweatshirt and find the bare skin underneath, he had a feeling pulling away wouldn't be quite so easy the second time.

"Didn't think so," Cam said, the corner of his mouth quirking up. "But yeah, let's go for a walk. I could get out, too."

He grabbed one of those puffer vests and shrugged it over his sweatshirt and slid his keycard into a pocket of his sweatpants, along with his wallet.

They were in the elevator, when Cam turned to him again. "Sorry," he said, that dimpled smile back in full effect, "but you sort of distracted me. Are you okay though?"

"Why wouldn't I be?" Dawson shoved his hands into his pockets. They were cold, sure, but also maybe then he wouldn't be thinking about touching Cam again.

They'd fit together, better even than the late-night images his uncooperative imagination had supplied.

"I don't know, you looked upset when I opened the door. And not just 'cause I was shirtless. And you said you *had* to get out. So I wondered."

Dawson sighed. He supposed that he'd already been too honest today. Why not push it a little further? "My lawyer called. It's funny. I was thinking how, even once in a while, when he does, it should be a good thing, right? And it never fucking is."

Cam looked surprised. "Never?"

"Sometimes it feels like the only one who wants my father-in-law to pay for this shit is me."

"That can't be true," Cam soothed. "He's on trial, right?"

He pushed the door open to the late afternoon. It was blustery today, only a bit of weak sunshine showing through the clouds. Dawson didn't have a destination in mind, but picked one direction and Cam just followed along, like where they were going didn't really matter.

"Well, sort of." Dawson barked out a bitter laugh. "They did arrest him. But then they released him, until the trial. And now it looks like that's not even going to happen."

"What?" Cameron's incredulity felt good. *Right.* Like finally, someone's mirrored Dawson's own.

"I know, right? It freaking sucks." The tall buildings were shadowing the sidewalks and Dawson shivered, wishing that he'd grabbed something more than just a sweatshirt.

"I can't believe they wouldn't even go to trial."

"They keep telling me it's just a white-collar crime. Like because nobody got hurt, it doesn't really matter. They're going to let him plea out, keep him on house arrest, which isn't really even a punishment. Not when my money bought that house he's going to be living in, all cushy and easy."

"Shit." Cam paused. "Someone *did* get hurt. You got hurt, Daws."

Maybe that was the biggest evidence of the ten years between them. Because Dawson felt the discomfort of that accusation crawling up his spine, but Cam said it like it was nothing, like it was perfectly okay for Dawson to admit to it.

The world hadn't told him yet, over and over again, that it wasn't okay to be vulnerable. Had never punished him for admitting to it.

"And it's even worse than that. I think my lawyer and my agent *want* this plea deal to go through. They're both so afraid I'm going to fuck up again I feel like no matter how I fight it, it's inevitable that I will."

Suck on that, world.

Cam stopped abruptly, jaw dropping open in shock. People on the sidewalk wove around them like they weren't even there. And maybe, Dawson thought, they weren't. Maybe this was a hallucination or a dream. Maybe he'd wake up any moment now.

"Daws, no," Cam said fiercely. "*No.*"

He shrugged uncomfortably. "It's just how it feels. Like they're so sure it'll happen. Maybe it will. No matter how much I don't want it to. No matter what I do to prevent it."

"See, I know that's bullshit. And you should know it, too." Cam took a deep breath and finally started walking again, knocking his shoulder against Dawson's. "You're lights-out. You've always been lights-out."

"Not always," Dawson muttered.

"I know Duke was joking about this, but like, do you *know* the stats? I do. Do *you* know how many kicks you missed last season versus your norm?"

Dawson was sure at one point his agent had given him a rundown of the numbers, but he'd blocked it out. It hadn't mattered to the team, so why should it matter to him?

He shrugged.

"Four field goals. You missed four more field goals than your normal, and they fired you. That's . . .that's fucked up." Cam actually sounded really pissed in a way Dawson had never heard before.

"Huh." Dawson hadn't realized it was *that* few. He'd seen the percentages, of course, though he'd tried not to think about what they represented. Now that he did, it was hard not to be even more pissed.

"It's fucked up," Cam repeated firmly.

"You're good for my ego, that's for sure," Dawson joked weakly. "Got any more of this presentation you want to share with me?"

Cam stopped on a corner, waiting for the light to change. "Couple of YouTube montages I could send over," he said thoughtfully.

"Uh, no, no. I'm good." When Dawson looked over at him, Cam's eyes were twinkling mischievously, and he had a feeling he'd be seeing those videos at some point.

"You sure?"

"Pretty sure." Dawson rolled his eyes, but he felt warm inside in a way he hadn't in a while.

"I could also tell you how hot you are," Cam said.

Dawson's heart raced in triple time, but before he could remind himself—or Cameron—how bad of an idea it was, even if it was just "fun," he only laughed and added, "Don't worry, I won't. But it's true, anyway."

"Alright." Dawson's mouth was dry. "Guess you won't."

Cam shot him a look. Warm and questioning. "Nope. It's a bad idea, right?"

Even though Dawson knew it, sure as anything, deep down in his bones, he still felt a pulse of disappointment. Too much reality intruding into a moment that could've lived forever in his fantasies.

"Want to grab something hot to drink?" he asked, gesturing towards a cafe, lights shining out of the window.

Cam nodded and they went inside, Dawson holding the door for him.

CHAPTER 7

Cam was acutely aware of the fact that while on the outside, he was acting normal.

All while screaming the roof down internally.

He sipped his hot chocolate opposite Dawson and kept trying to be normal. Even if he didn't know what normal was anymore.

Dawson Hall thought *he* was hot.

Dawson Hall was attracted to him.

He'd had a bad day, and instead of sulking alone in his apartment, Dawson Hall had sought *him* out.

Had just showed up, like it was nothing, like it was no big deal.

But it was a huge fucking deal.

"God, why is it already so cold?" Dawson complained, cradling his cup of hot chocolate close to his chest.

"It's October still, Daws," Cam teased. "It's gonna get a whole lot colder."

"Ugh, don't remind me." How was Dawson so cute even when he was bristling with grumpy annoyance? Cam was beginning to think he'd be cute, no matter what. His stomach went all gooey, just thinking of how it was mutual, now.

Maybe it *was* a bad idea. He'd said it, and they'd both agreed it was, but he had a feeling that it wasn't going to end there.

If anyone could use some fun to loosen him up, it was Dawson Hall.

"It was cold in Baltimore, right?" Cam asked.

"Not as cold as Montana," Dawson retorted.

That was probably true. "I can always warm you up," Cam offered mildly, knowing exactly the face Dawson would make at his suggestion.

Hopefulness sliding into reluctant resignation, finally ending in denial.

"I'm good," Dawson said, even though it was obvious he hadn't gotten any warmer in the last ten seconds.

Cam felt like he was existing in an alternate universe, and it didn't even matter if Dawson shook his head decisively, because Cam had seen the way he'd wanted it, before he'd buried the desire.

The last bits of the sun were reflecting off the skyscrapers as they headed back towards their apartment building.

"You feeling any better?" Cam asked.

"I'm fucking freezing," Dawson complained and Cam laughed.

"Don't argue," Cam said and wrapped an arm around Dawson. Despite his slender stature, his dad had always called Cameron his little space heater.

"I'm not arguing," Dawson muttered, and to Cam's surprise, he leaned into Cam's body. "Remind me to get a warmer coat."

"Or you could just always take me with you," Cam joked.

"Like a personal blanket?" Dawson glanced up at him. There was that look again, flashing across Dawson's face. Cam caught it before it was gone. A split second of desire, quickly hidden.

"Sure," Cam said easily, hoping that if he was chill about it, then maybe Dawson would let himself have it. Have *him*.

But Dawson just laughed. Didn't shrug him off, though, and stayed tucked tight against him, all the way to their building. Only when they approached the front door did Dawson finally pull away.

He tossed his empty hot chocolate cup into the trash.

"Actually," he said, "I *do* feel better."

"Warmer or—"

Dawson shot him a look. "We both know what you were asking, earlier. And yeah. I do. I didn't think I would. I didn't think there was any hope. Best-case scenario was a distraction."

"Happy to be that, too," Cam said. He wouldn't be this way with just anyone, ready and willing to give them whatever they wanted, whatever they needed, but Dawson made it easy.

"You're too nice, rook," Dawson said, swiping his card and pulling the door open. They slipped through, to the warmer lobby.

"I like to think I'm just nice enough," Cam insisted. What he didn't tell Dawson was that he might *not* be this nice to just anyone.

Dawson made him crave things. Stupid, silly things. Like him smiling. Like for that thundercloud he carried around with him constantly to lift once in a while. For every field goal he attempted to sail right through the uprights. For him to take what he wanted, even if it was a bad idea.

He'd admired the guy from afar—Cam supposed some people might call it hero worship—but that had made sense. He'd had the life Cam wanted. That he'd worked so hard for. Validation and approval for all his life choices. A career and a team and a family. It hadn't mattered that Dawson was *just* a special teams guy. Or that he was queer. He'd gotten everything anyway.

Or at least it had looked that way to Cameron.

"You ever think about trying to play a position?" Cam asked as they got into the elevator because that was simpler than asking Dawson, *do you ever wonder if you made all the right decisions?*

Dawson just chuckled under his breath. "You mean, do I ever wish that I got a fraction of the respect and money and validation that the skill players get? Sometimes, yeah. But I was shit at throwing. And catching. And not very good at running either."

Cam couldn't help but laugh. "Still shit at running," he teased, nudging Dawson as he pressed the buttons for both their floors.

"Better than you," Dawson retorted, but Cam had done his job, because Dawson was smiling now. "And yeah, joke was on every coach, because they figured out real quick after that how good I was at kick-ing. Never missed, not back then."

"Still barely miss now," Cam inserted.

Dawson rolled his eyes, but he shot Cam a fondly exasperated look, heavy on the former, light on the latter.

"Anyway, hard to be too mad about it, when there *is* something I'm good at."

Cam was happy he'd said he *was* good at kicking, no qualifications, no addendums, no *well, not like I used to be.*

"I played some wide receiver in high school," Cam said.

"Seriously?" Dawson was even laughing now.

"I was awful," Cam said. "But one game the punter got hurt and at halftime they asked, is there anyone who can kick the ball? And I said, sure, I can try it."

"Sure, you can try it," Dawson muttered under his breath. "Like it's easy."

"It wasn't easy," Cam said. "But I did it. And when the guy was healthy again, they ended up benching him. He took my spot as a WR."

"How was he?"

"Total stone hands. Dropped every pass they ever threw him," Cam said, grinning.

"That why you didn't end up at a big school? Because you started so late?" Dawson asked.

The elevator dinged to a stop on Cam's floor. He hesitated. They were still talking. He was enjoying himself, and it sure seemed like Dawson was. But he didn't want to overstep and invite himself to Dawson's floor.

But he didn't even have to ask, because Dawson pressed the Doors Closed button and turned to Cam, expectant look on his face, like he was thinking, *I asked you a question you still haven't answered.*

"Uh, mostly because I went to a small school. Really small high school, actually. Not a lot of scouts showed up there. I only decided to keep playing initially to help my dad with the costs. And then I got better in college."

"Yeah, you sure did," Dawson said.

It was impossible not to feel some type of way about Dawson watching *his* footage on YouTube, even though Cam had watched plenty of his.

"Good enough when I finally got a decently sized stage, I got some attention," Cam added.

"I watched that game live," Dawson said. "Wisconsin versus Western State. They paid you guys a shit ton of money to fly to Madison and play them. And you nearly beat them in their own home stadium. A big part of why was you."

"We had good special teams at Western. Coaches always preaching the basics. Maybe we couldn't compete with flash or with size of guys. But we could do all the simple things right."

The elevator opened onto Dawson's floor and it felt so right to trail behind Dawson to his apartment. He swiped them in and Cam mirrored him. Slipping his shoes off by the door. Hanging up his coat on the hook.

It was the first time he'd been in Dawson's apartment. Unsurprisingly, it was not that much bigger than Cam's. Laid out about the same. Same bare white walls, but despite the fact that he probably should've known better, Cam was still taken aback that they were so white and *so* bare.

That there were only a few pieces of rudimentary furniture and no personal mementoes at all.

Sure, Dawson had gotten divorced, and maybe a lot of his stuff was still stored, but surely he had *something* more than this?

"Special teams is all about the basics," Dawson said, nodding. "You want something else to drink or . . .?"

Even though it had been entirely Dawson's idea for Cam to come to his place instead of returning to his own apartment, Dawson looked suddenly uncomfortable.

Like the reality of it was only now entering his mind, seeing Cam standing in his living room, with its one IKEA couch and coffee table.

"No, I'm good," Cam said and decided that he'd have to do something to break the ice. He glanced around, like he hadn't noticed the lack of decor right away and was just realizing it now. "Kinda bare in here."

A flush crept up Dawson's cheeks. "Uh. Yeah. Sort of, I guess."

"You guess? I don't have any stuff because I've never had stuff," Cam said. "But you . . ." He didn't need to say that Dawson had been married. Established. He'd owned a big house in Baltimore with his ex-wife, probably full of stuff. A decorator's showpiece, no doubt, where she could host all the other team wives.

"But I had stuff? Yeah, I had stuff." Dawson leaned against the counter. "Kind of like how you played wideout, probably."

"But you didn't—"

"Didn't want any of it? Didn't take any of it? Wouldn't have cared if it all burned in a fire? All of the above?"

It was easy for Cam to see the difference now, when it was so stark. Only a minute ago, Dawson had been amused. Laughing. And now he looked like he was trying to swallow a bitter pill that was too big for his throat.

"Sorry," Cam mumbled. "I shouldn't have . . .I'm sure it was hard."

"Yeah, it was. But it was all hers, you know?" Dawson's voice softened. He flopped down on the couch next to Cam and propped his feet up on the coffee table. "You're too young to know what this is like, but I woke up one day and realized I didn't like anything about my life. It belonged to someone else. Someone I'm not sure ever existed. So I let her keep it all. Meant I had to pay her less alimony if she kept the house too. So win-win, there."

"If it was stuff she wanted, yeah," Cam said. He had a feeling, even though Dawson wasn't saying it, the person he'd become—the person he didn't know if he recognized—had been someone he'd been to please his ex-wife. Cam knew people did that. Molded themselves to fit into a relationship. But he'd never been in a relationship before, so he wasn't sure he understood the desire.

"Though her dad stealing a bunch of money from me helped that, too."

Cam didn't know what to say. "How's the new life so far?"

Dawson chuckled. A little bitterly, still, but not entirely. Not caustic, like before. "So far, not too bad. It's all my own, I'll give it that. Nothing here but what I want."

Hard not to wonder, when Dawson glanced pointedly over at him, sitting on Dawson's couch. Cam wanted to scoot in closer. Feel his leg pressed to Dawson's. Maybe indulge in a few bad ideas. But he didn't.

"What about what you need?" he asked instead.

"Huh. A novel concept," Dawson said, deadpan, and they both laughed. "Fuck if I know."

"Fuck if I know either," Cam said, reaching out and bumping his knuckles against Dawson's.

In some ways, they were both still figuring their shit out. Cam because he was starting out. Dawson because he was starting *over*.

"You're a good kid," Dawson said.

Cam made a face. "I'm—"

"Yeah, yeah. Twenty-two. A full-grown adult. Not a kid. I should know better. Aidan got so much flack for continuing to call Riley a kid long past when he actually was."

"Wait," Cam said, no longer stuck on the fact that Dawson kept trying to push him into a *do not touch* box. "He called Riley—as in *Riley Flynn,* who won a Super Bowl—a kid?"

"Literally called him 'the kid,'" Dawson confirmed, nodding gravely. "Like I said, not a smart guy. Not crush-worthy. Puking in bushes and calling his Super Bowl–winning brother a kid."

"Don't tell me you're jealous," he teased. If Dawson was, wouldn't that be something? Real jealously, *ugly* jealousy was different, but a little dose of healthy envy? When it might motivate Dawson to maybe make a bad idea a reality? Cam wouldn't be against that.

"Hell no," Dawson said. "Why would I be jealous of Aidan? He has to put up with Levi's ugly-ass shorts, and besides, you're here, right now, on *my* couch." He even had the nerve to look smug about it.

So smug that Cam really had to wonder if maybe the bad idea was beginning to look a little less bad, even to Dawson. It sure was to him.

"Levi's shorts, they're . . .uh . . .bright for sure," Cam said.

"Practically fucking eye-searing," Dawson agreed. "Besides, you're my rookie. Not his." He glanced over at Cam then, expectantly, like he wanted Cam to confirm that was true.

Dawson must be freaking blind, because Cam had been *his* rookie from the first time they'd met, at training camp. Dawson sauntering in like he owned the place, dark curly hair mussed, his intent hazel eyes taking in every single inch of Cam. Like they were taking him apart. Seeing exactly how he ticked.

Cam might've gotten off about it that night. Just that look in Dawson's eyes—*Dawson Hall*, looking at *him*—had been enough. Even the memory was enough now, coupled with the easy companionship of this afternoon, for Cam's cock to twitch about it.

Not now. Not when we're still convincing him it's a good idea, Cam told it. *Or a not-bad idea.*

"Not gonna complain about that," Cam said lightly. He had a feeling if he made it too serious—made it into something that wasn't just "fun" or a "distraction"—then Daws might freak out about it.

"Good." Dawson nodded, sounding satisfied with that.

They sat there for a minute in silence. Dawson had more of a view than Cam's sliver. Not much, but a few more inches, and it was nice to see the dusk falling down on Lake Ontario. They hadn't had bodies of water in Montana, not where Cam lived anyway, and it was easy not to take it for granted.

Dawson turned to him. "You didn't decide to stay in the hotel the night before?"

"Nah," Cam said. "Picked my bed out 'cause I liked it so much, so why would I want to sleep anywhere else, if I can help it? Besides, it's not like I have a lot of distractions at my place."

"Same," Dawson said. Then he glanced over at Cam again. Cam wasn't counting, but it definitely wasn't the first time. Or the first time his eyes flicked to Cam's lips, before rising upwards, to a safer zone. He *was* thinking about it, enough that Cam hoped he might change his mind.

"Thought you wanted a distraction?" Cam teased, elbowing him gently. "Why else am I around?"

"You're more than that." Dawson looked surprised by his own admission. "I mean, dude, I like you. You're a chill person. Always pumping my ego."

"And you think I'm attractive," Cam said, waggling his eyebrows. "You said so yourself."

Dawson laughed. "Shit, I created a monster, didn't I?"

He had, but Dawson had yet to comprehend what kind, and if that was true, Cameron wasn't about to enlighten him.

"I'm an angel."

"Fuck, that's not even remotely true," Dawson said, not sounding upset by this possibility at all.

"Aw," Cam said, pouting. "I'm hurt."

Dawson smacked him on the thigh. The pain smarted for a second, but Cam only wished it would've hurt more. For longer. Not because he was a masochist or liked pain with sex, but because he might've felt Dawson's touch linger longer.

"No, you're not. Not even close. You love it."

"Yeah," Cam admitted. He knew he had an innocent, sweet-ish face. Could even be convinced to use it to maximum effect, on occasion.

It was impossible not to wonder if Dawson would ever like that.

Dawson gave a half-groan. "You're killing me here. You'd better go, before I decide the bad idea is starting to look good."

"I think that means I *should* stay," Cam insisted, but he rose to his feet anyway. If—no, *when*—he got into Dawson's bed, he wanted Dawson fully on board, not overthinking and wondering the whole time if it was a mistake.

"You would think that. Incorrigible," Dawson complained, but despite that, the way he was gazing at Cam, fondly exasperated, told more of the story.

"My middle name," Cam joked as he walked to the door, Dawson trailing behind him. He slipped his shoes on and grabbed his coat from the hook. "I'll see you tomorrow?"

"Yeah," Dawson said, nodding. "We're gonna have a good game."

Cam liked that he said *we*. That they were a *we*, now. That it wasn't just Dawson versus all his ghosts and bad memories and the internalized pressure he put on himself, but *we*, tackling all those together.

It was the *we* that propelled him forward, pulling Dawson against him into a tight hug. "I never doubt it, not for a second," Cam murmured into Daws' ear.

Dawson was shorter, slightly, but more solid. More filled out. Still, they fit together. Better than even Cam had fantasized about. So good, in fact, that it *was* hard to let him go.

Finally, Dawson wiggled away, and Cam was pleased to see how pink his cheeks were. "You *are* incorrigible," he said, but it didn't sound at all like a bad thing.

Not one bad idea in sight.

CHAPTER 8

DAWSON SHOULD'VE KNOWN WHAT Marty was going to say when he wandered over in his direction during pregame warmups.

The special teams coordinator crossed his arms over his scrawny chest and flicked his gaze up and down as Dawson finished his stretches.

"What?" Dawson asked.

"Saw you laughing with the rook, a few minutes ago," Marty said.

At least Cam wasn't present for this conversation, since he was halfway across the field now, at the fifty-yard line, chatting with the Texans' punter. They'd attended one of the big senior bowls the year before.

Pro football was a pretty small community, but special teams guys formed an even tinier one. They all knew each other, at least by reputation, and usually even better than that.

It hadn't surprised Dawson that Cam would know the other team's punter, especially since he was also just starting out.

"Yeah," Dawson said, nodding. "You gonna give me your version of the lecture or Aidan's?"

"What does Flynn have to do with this?" Marty demanded.

Dawson regretted bringing him up. "Nothing," he claimed.

The look Marty shot him loosened his tongue. "Okay, he keeps worrying I'm gonna take advantage of Cam's 'hero worship' or whatever he keeps wanting to call it. That I'm gonna fuck him up or something."

Marty barked out a laugh. "Might be good for both of you if you actually managed to pull that off."

"Ouch." Dawson winced.

"Guess it's my own lecture, then," Marty continued like Dawson had never said anything. "It's good you two are getting closer."

"It was just a few laughs," Dawson argued, even though it was most definitely not only that. They'd spent hours together over the last week. They'd gone to Thai, and then the offensive-line dinner, and then their walk yesterday afternoon.

Why didn't he want to admit the truth to Marty? Maybe because the truth felt more dangerously close to what Aidan was worried about than what Marty kept pushing him for. His behavior wasn't entirely altruistic. Or platonic, for that matter. It was those things, too, but Dawson knew he wasn't *only* being a selfless, good team-mate.

"Then why did a little bird tell me you brought him to Flynn's dinner this week?"

Dawson rolled his eyes. "You're the biggest gossip on this team, and I want you to know, that's really saying something, considering who else wears a Thunder uniform."

"Thanks," Marty said.

"That wasn't a compliment—"

"Kinda was, whether you meant it or not."

"Was there anything you actually needed besides harassing me about how much me and Cam are hanging out?"

"Not really," Marty said, shooting Dawson a big dumb smile, when the opposite was much more accurate.

"You scare me," Dawson joked. It was *mostly* a joke, anyway.

"Good," Marty said, grinning. He tilted his head up, feeling the breeze coming in. "Watch out for the breeze swirling at the west end of the stadium, if you end up kicking that way. Wind comes right off the lake and it can be unpredictable."

"Got it," Dawson said. He was tempted to remind Marty that he'd said the same thing before every home game they'd played so far, but he had a feeling Marty actually meant something else entirely.

"'Course you do," Marty said gruffly, patting Dawson on the back before heading over to the bench to where Shane, the defensive coordinator, was leaning against the metal slats.

A second later Cam appeared in his sight line, jogging back from his little meeting with the Texans' punter. "Everything good?" he asked.

"Just Marty reminding me about things I already know."

"Like how freaking amazing you are?" Cam teased.

"Kinda, yeah. I think."

Cam grinned. "Good. Means I don't have to do it, too." He nudged Dawson's arm with his elbow. "It's time to admit it, Hall. You're pretty fucking amazing." He dropped his voice to something softer and quieter. "And on top of that, you're pretty fucking hot, too."

Dawson couldn't help the laugh that startled out of him.

"Too much?" Cam sounded delighted that it might have been.

"Too much. Way too much." But he was smiling too, now, and when the game started, Dawson had to admit that he felt more relaxed, none of that crawling anxiety between his shoulder blades that he'd felt during every single kickoff this season.

He was still on his game—focus came too naturally to him by now for him to *not* be—but he wasn't in his own head about it.

From his spot on the sideline, Dawson watched as Aidan and the offense drove down the field. It wasn't as seamless as some of the earlier Thunder teams Aidan had played on, but this particular team felt grittier. Acker, the right tackle, got a holding penalty, but then they pushed through, getting two big passes to the tight ends, Lane catching one for thirteen yards and Trevor getting the first down on the next play.

Every time it seemed like they were going to stall out—a sack happened, despite Levi and the offensive line's best effort to keep the defense out of the backfield, or an incomplete pass, or a rush attempt that went nowhere—they fought back.

This team was beginning to look tough. Took a hit to the chin, but they still kept coming.

They'd made it to the red zone when Cam wandered over. Dawson had noticed him glancing over every so often and had been expecting it. He'd actually waited longer than Dawson had anticipated.

"You ever think it's weird that when things are going well, they don't really need us?" Cam asked.

Dawson laughed. "Yeah, a lot of hurry up and wait."

"Guess we can kick the extra point if they get in," Cam said and held up his hands in mock surrender as Dawson shot him a half-hearted glare. "Yeah, I know all about jinxing, you don't need to lecture me about it."

"You don't believe in it?" Dawson had never met another football player—especially another *special teams* football player—that wasn't superstitious to a painful extent.

"Hell no," Cam declared. "If I can touch it and feel it and make it happen, then it's real. If it's not, then it's not important. Just something in my head that I can tell to fuck off."

"You're crazy. Totally fucking crazy," Dawson said, shaking his head.

"For *not* believing in superstition? Kind of the opposite, isn't it?" Cam was smiling, still, though Dawson was kind of beginning to believe that he couldn't really do anything else.

When Aidan finally took the ball in himself, rushing in the touchdown from four yards out with a gorgeous pump fake, crossing the line untouched—the defense didn't even seem to realize he'd kept it himself until the refs were calling a touchdown—Dawson turned to Cam.

"Guess you were right," he said.

"Guess so." Cam's dimple popped again, and Dawson had to mentally force himself not to think about how it might feel like the perfect groove for his tongue.

"Come on," Dawson said and picked up his helmet. "Let's get this shit done."

The refs confirmed the touchdown call—even though it had been an absolute no-brainer—and then Dawson got set up, watching carefully as Cam knelt to receive the snap.

Dawson took a breath and then another, then signaled for the ball.

It hit Cam's hands perfectly, then after he held it, Dawson's foot sent it hurtling right between the goal posts.

Just like they'd practiced dozens of times during the week.

"Textbook," Marty said, when they got back to the sideline.

Dawson nodded. He didn't want to build a castle in the sky about making an extra point. He'd made them last week too. Even made one after he'd missed that field goal.

It wasn't quite the same and Marty knew that, but Dawson knew what he was trying to do.

Dawson didn't know if he should feel warm and supported that his coach was going out of his way to reassure him or if he should feel embarrassed that he needed the reassurance at all.

"Yeah, felt good," Dawson said, setting his helmet down on the far end of the bench.

"It's coming together," Marty agreed. "But that doesn't mean cut it out and ice the poor rookie out now."

Dawson rolled his eyes. "Would I do that?" he asked. Then wished he hadn't, because he wasn't sure he wanted Marty to answer that question. It might not be *no*, and it should absolutely, unequivocally be *no*.

"You? Nah." Marty patted him on the shoulder.

And no, he wouldn't. Not now. He didn't think he'd be able to leave Cam alone now, not on purpose, not even if it was probably a better, smarter idea.

The Texans settled for a field goal after a long drive that sucked up the rest of the first quarter, but the next time the Thunder's offense took the field, they sputtered out near the fifty-yard line, and Cam jogged out to punt the ball.

He made punting look easy and totally effortless, even though Dawson knew exactly how much work and repetition and brainpower went into the minutest calculations.

Obviously, Cam's most important job was to get it as far away from the opposing team as possible, but also without kicking it into the end zone, because that would mean the ball would be set on the twenty-yard line.

The one-yard line was always the goal, but that wasn't always possible.

Now? It was definitely a possibility, and when Marty leaned in, giving last-minute instructions to Cam before he went out there, Dawson had a feeling that was what he was saying.

Pin them to the very far end of their side of the field.

Dawson watched as Cam took a deep breath and Joey snapped the ball to him. He wound back and kicked, a graceful perfect arc.

The rest of the special teams unit ran the ball down, but it was too late.

A second later, it bounced right into the end zone.

Cam shot him a wry look as he jogged back to the sideline.

It was hardly the end of the world—the Thunder defense, led by Nate—was pretty good. They could hopefully hold the Texans, even if they were starting at the twenty-yard line.

But Dawson could see from the way he brushed off Marty's supportive back pat and the expression on Cam's face after he yanked his helmet off he wasn't happy with himself.

Normally, Dawson liked his space on the sideline. How many times had he bitched at Marty for Cam not preserving it? But now he was the one breaking containment and heading out of his nice little bubble to where Cam was hovering next to the hydration station, twisting a paper Gatorade cup between his hands.

"Hey," Dawson said.

Cam shot him a look. "Are you going to say it was a fine punt? 'Cause it wasn't—"

"It was a fine punt."

Cam shot him another look, maybe the most annoyed he'd ever looked with Dawson. Dawson didn't like it, but only because he preferred Cam's sunny optimism better. Counted on it, he realized, and he didn't want Cam to lose it over one punt that mattered very little in the scheme of things.

"Hey," Dawson said when Cam didn't reply, "you said I was going to say it, so I figured since it *was* a fine punt, I might as well put it out there."

"You a comedian now?" Cam wondered darkly.

Dawson shrugged. "It was really fine. You pinned them to the twenty."

"Could've pinned them to the one. *Should've* pinned them to the one."

"Jeez, dude, lighten up." Dawson slung an arm around Cam's shoulder pads. Even with the breadth and the thickness of them, he still felt slight under Dawson's touch.

Fits perfectly against you.

Dawson ignored that voice. This was about more than that. He didn't want a single drop of sourness to grow into a stream and then poison all of Cam's optimism.

Not like what had happened to him.

"I can't believe it's *you* saying that to *me*," Cam grumbled.

"As president of the *Needs to Lighten Up* Club, I'm the most qualified to tell you that it's a requirement."

Cam shook him off. "I'll get it next time."

"Yeah, you will." Dawson had no qualms saying it. In the preseason and in the first three regular season games, Cam had been on the money.

"Don't patronize me," Cam said.

"I'm not. I'm really not." Dawson playfully chucked his fist under Cam's chin. "I mean it. Lighten up. Do I need to bring Marty over here to show you something on the tablet? Maybe a YouTube compilation of your greatest hits?"

Cam laughed then, like he couldn't believe Dawson had said that. "No. No. I'm good."

"Finally," Dawson teased. "That's the smile I like to see."

"Do you?"

There was the political answer. The *this is a bad idea* answer. Then there was the truth.

"Well, yeah, rook. Of course I do."

Cam's smile only grew, and maybe even if it hadn't been smart, Dawson couldn't say he regretted it.

On top of that, it was harder than it should've been to return to his empty bubble at the other end of the bench.

Dawson didn't know what that said about him or his current level of focus.

"You gotta lock in," Dawson muttered to himself and looked out onto the field, where Nate had just sacked the Texans' quarterback for the first time in the game.

Aidan and the offense would be getting the ball back with plenty of time to get another score before the end of the half—which they did, extending the Thunder's lead.

Dawson kicked another textbook extra point and kicked off, giving the Texans the ball back for the last two and a half minutes of the second quarter.

He'd picked up his helmet and was getting ready to head back into the locker room, feeling good about what they'd done, but then Duke, filling in for an injured safety, jumped in front of the Texans' quarterback's throw and picked it off.

Duke made it almost to mid-field before he got tackled.

Marty shot Dawson a look across the sideline as Aidan and the offense went back on the field. There might be enough time for a touchdown, but it was more likely Dawson would get called out for a last-second field goal, if Aidan could get them in Dawson's range.

Dawson had the stray thought of, *what even is my range, anymore?* before he shut it down. His range was what it had always been. In Baltimore he'd kicked dozens of fifty-plus-yard field goals.

He could do it again. There was no question in his mind that he could.

Did Marty and the coaching staff agree with him?

Dawson set up the ball on the tee in front of his net and, instead of watching Aidan's progress down the field, kicked it half a dozen times, focusing on making sure he was in a peak warmed-up state.

The roar of the crowd told him the offense was making progress. He heard the announcer call out a first-down play, a pass caught by Lane. Then a nice screen pass to Jaden, their running back.

When he looked up next, Marty was standing there, just outside the circle of space Dawson preferred.

"You good?" he asked.

Dawson nodded.

"They could keep going but I think they're gonna run out of time. You're gonna have to be ready. No time to really get set up properly."

He nodded again. Had expected that, and a glance up at the enormous play clock confirmed it.

"I'm ready," Dawson said. "Whatever it is. Send me out."

Marty tilted his head and then gave him a sharp nod. "Okay."

Dawson wasn't going to fuck up Marty's faith in him. But even more than that, he wasn't about to fuck up—anymore, anyway—his faith in himself.

By the time the offense finally ran out of time and Aidan spiked the ball, stopping the clock with just enough time for Dawson, Cam and the rest of the kicking team to run out onto the field, it was a fifty-one-yard field goal.

Not the longest he'd ever kicked, but still a significant distance.

Cam's smile had disappeared and in its place was an expression full of intense focus. Dawson had a feeling it mirrored his own.

This field goal wouldn't make or break the game, probably, but it would be great to go into the locker room leading seventeen to three.

It was impossible not to feel some pressure, but at least it felt manageable.

Nothing like when he'd kicked the Super Bowl–winning field goal.

Dawson took his position, the ref blew the whistle, and then there was nothing else to do but his job.

Joey snapped the ball, Cam caught it out of the air and positioned it, and then Dawson's foot connected.

It was less than a second, and he let out a harsh breath as the ball sailed right through the uprights. For a moment, he was worried it might veer left with the wind, but he'd taken that into account with the angle, and it still easily made it through.

Cam jumped into him like an excited puppy. "What a fucking great kick!" he exclaimed.

Joey rolled his eyes, but he was smiling too. "Sick shit, man," he told Dawson, patting him on the helmet.

Aidan met him on the sideline. "Good show, bro," he told Dawson, hand on his back. "Knew you could do it."

And Dawson felt the corner of his heart that *had* been bruised and blackened begin to beat to life again.

CHAPTER 9

IT HAD BEEN SUCH a good game Cam decided that doing this just made sense.

There was nothing to be afraid of. They were just streets. It was bustling right now, people milling around the stadium complex after the game, wanting to celebrate the win, with the Thunder beating the Texans thirty-four to ten.

He would be perfectly safe heading home to his apartment building before changing and heading out later to the victory party at Vault that Aidan and Levi had quickly put together in the locker room after the game.

Pulling out his phone, Cam sent a quick text to his dad, responding to his series of encouraging and excited messages he'd gotten during the course of the game. **Thanks,** he typed back. **Feels good. You'll be proud—I'm headed home, on my own. Will be safe.**

His dad's response came in almost immediately. **Proud of you, kid. For more than one reason :)**

Cam tucked his phone into the pocket of his pants and headed out towards the causeway that led from the stadium to the grid of streets.

He'd put a hat on over his wet hair and he kept the hood of his jacket up, and not surprisingly, there seemed to be no recognition from anyone he passed on the street.

That was the kind of under-the-radar situation Cameron was used to. The kind of under-the-radar situation he counted on.

Players like Aidan and Nate and Lane—even Levi and Griff and, to some extent, Dawson—always drew attention.

People recognized their faces, and a lot of the time they got stopped for autographs and selfies, and even the occasional drunken, belligerent comment if they hadn't won the game.

Maybe Cam got paid less and got less attention, but he also got *less* attention, and that could be kind of a blessing. Nobody was ever going to send the punter death threats.

And if they did, Cam would understand the fans' frustration, because he probably would've fucked up pretty damn bad.

It was only a short ten-minute walk from the stadium to the apartment building. On the way to the game, he'd driven with Dawson, but Dawson had said something about heading over directly to Vault with Aidan and leaving his car in player parking until tomorrow. He'd looked over at Cam and Cam had just given him a shooing motion, making it clear that Dawson didn't need to worry about him.

And if Dawson didn't need to worry about Cam, then *Cam* wasn't going to worry about Cam.

The streets were still pretty full when he made his first turn.

His breath came a little faster when he made the second, but it seemed like everyone was just trying to get wherever they were going, on this Sunday evening. He passed several groups of people, one of all guys and several others that were mixed, men and women both, and was proud his footsteps barely faltered.

Before, he hadn't kept a wary eye out. He'd taken his safety for granted. But he'd learned that lesson *almost* the hard way, and he wouldn't fall into that trap again.

Cam had thought it would be harder to take this step, but he realized as soon as he used his keycard to get into the side door of his building, that it had been actually *really* easy. Nobody had looked twice at him. Nobody had even remotely threatened him. Nobody gave a shit that they'd passed him by.

He was going to be okay. *Better* than okay, in fact.

It was just a ten-minute walk home, but as Cam rode the elevator up to his floor, he felt like he'd slayed a dragon.

Climbed right through the thorns and walked right up to the castle where it lurked. Drew his sword like it was easy, and just struck him down.

In his apartment, he grabbed a beer from the fridge, popped it open, and went to his closet to figure out what he could wear that might convince Dawson that a bad idea might actually be a good one.

An hour later, he was dressed, hair done, and he shrugged on his coat after slipping his wallet and phone into his pocket. He could call an Uber, but he was going to be doing that on the way home, probably, with Dawson in tow, and so wouldn't it be smarter—and additionally brave?—to walk to Vault on his own?

It wasn't that much farther than the walk from the stadium had been.

On the elevator ride down to the ground floor, he pulled the directions up on his phone, and decided, *yes*, he could do this. It was no big deal. Acting like it had been such a big deal had been the whole problem.

He was an adult. He could walk somewhere, by himself, after dark, without panicking.

And Cam believed that, at least up until he turned down one of the side streets about halfway to Vault, and realized it was basically empty.

Dark, too.

A few streetlights were shining, but it was more of an alley than an actual street and Cam hesitated in the opening. He couldn't call an Uber now. Not to go less than a quarter mile. He just needed to get through this alley. It was *just* an alley.

So what if there was a group of guys at the other end? They were just guys. They weren't going to jump him. Not everyone was out to get him.

But Cam's breath came in shorter and shorter pants as he walked deeper into the alley.

The farther he went, the more he knew he shouldn't be doing this. Maybe it was still safe—relatively, anyway—but his brain was screaming that it wasn't. That he'd fucked it all up again by being overconfident.

By thinking he'd slayed the dragon, when it was only sleeping, dormant in the long nights of winter.

Shit.

Cameron tried not to look at the guys as he passed them.

He shouldn't have worried, but it didn't help his mounting anxiety that they barely gave him a second look as he walked out of the other side.

A minute later and he was in the alley with the Vault entry, and if he ran almost the whole way there, who could blame him?

By the time security let him in, he was out of breath and sweating along his hairline, despite the fact that it was *not* warm outside.

Painfully aware of his panic, Cam tried to head to the bathroom, but there was a big group of Thunder players milling around the central bar, and of course they all saw him.

Even worse, Dawson was with them.

And total catastrophe, Dawson picked up his drink and sauntered over, ready to intercept him.

"Hey," Dawson said as he approached, like nothing was wrong. Like Cam wasn't red and blotchy and sweaty and feeling like he might pass the fuck out.

Cam opened his mouth and nothing came out.

Dawson's expression morphed from friendly and open to concern in a second.

"Shit, you okay?" he asked, putting a hand on Cameron's arm.

Humiliation surged through him. It was bad enough that he was having what must be an anxiety attack right here, in this cool-as-fuck bar, about something as ridiculous as walking through a dark alley, but even worse, he was doing it in front of *Dawson*.

"Come here," Dawson said, taking him by the arm and leading him out of the main room, away from all the people, ducking into one of the rooms. An *empty* room.

In another mood, on another night, under different circumstances, Cameron would be thrilled at the pleased look on Dawson's face and how fast he got them alone, but this was nothing like he imagined.

"Breathe, okay?" Dawson said, his empty hand reaching up and gently pressing against Cam's diaphragm. "You're good. I promise. You're totally good."

"I'm good," Cam croaked.

"That's right. You're good. More than good." The corner of Dawson's mouth curled up in a wry smile. "You're fucking great, rook."

Cameron took a deep shuddery breath. And then another. His chest was loosening, one moment at a time, with every second that passed. And the hysterical part of his brain that hadn't been sure if he *would* be okay was beginning to truly believe that Dawson was right. He *was* good.

He wasn't sure he was *great*, but Dawson sounded earnest enough when he said it, hazel eyes full of concern and conviction, it was hard not to agree with him.

"Yeah." Cam let out one last unsteady wheeze, and then before he'd thought it was possible, he was breathing normally again.

"There we go." Dawson curled his fingertips into Cam's shirt. "You wanna tell me what happened now?"

He sure fucking didn't, but he was calm enough by this point to know that he really should.

"Just . . . still struggling with the big-city shit," Cam said.

Maybe he shouldn't like the sympathy and understanding blooming in Dawson's gaze. But it was hard not to feel it like a balm. Cam hardly ascribed to any of that toxic masculinity bullshit about always staying strong and never letting anyone, especially another man, see you at your worst, but there was something comforting in realizing that he trusted Dawson enough to show him even his vulnerable underbelly.

"Big-city shit?" Dawson asked softly.

The whole story spilled out of Cameron before he could stop it. What had almost happened when he'd first moved to Toronto. How he'd struggled after that with the fear. How it had felt better. How *Dawson* had helped him feel better. The walk home from the stadium, and thinking, stupidly, that he was all fixed.

"It's not stupid that you thought that," Dawson said, expression gentle. His hand trailed down Cam's chest and took his hand, squeezing it. "You always believe in the best of any situation and I find that kind of fucking miraculous."

It was insane that Dawson saw him as miraculous, when, instead, it was actually Dawson. When he'd listened to that whole word-vomit situation and there'd not been a single moment where it seemed or looked like Dawson was judging him for any of it.

"It was kind of stupid, though," Cam argued.

Dawson just shrugged. "Or optimistic, maybe. But you're okay now? I'll make sure—I know I didn't before, and I wish I'd known this because I *would* have—"

"I know," Cam interrupted before Dawson could torch any of Cam's hopes and dreams with the declaration that he was going to *take care of him now.* Like a helpless puppy who had to be carted around.

Dawson shot him a chiding look. "Let me say this, okay? I know I said something like it before, but I shouldn't have just left you alone like I did. That was shitty of me, but especially shitty when you were going through this. It's not a bad idea to be cautious. You should *still* be cautious."

"You didn't know."

"No, but I could tell something was up. Just . . ." Dawson took a deep breath. "It was easier to think about my own baggage than to worry about someone else's. But that's changed. I promise."

"I'm not a kid. I don't need to be like . . .*monitored.*"

Dawson's gaze trailed up and down him. Cam's skin tightened, like it was a size too tight for his body. It should've been impossible to feel aroused, not when he'd been so panicked and then now that he was worried Dawson would shove him irrevocably back into the *teammates only* box, but it was hard not to intercept that look and not be moved by it.

"Trust me, I know you're not a kid. You're a rookie, sure, but you're a friend and a teammate, and . . ." Dawson's quiet voice trailed off.

"And?" Cam prompted, because he thought Dawson's reluctance meant what he was hoping it meant.

Dawson shook his head, like he was trying to clear it. Ran a hand through his unruly dark hair. "It's *still* a bad idea."

"But it's an idea, anyway," Cam said, grinning. Pleased that it *had* been what he'd been imagining.

Dawson rolled his eyes. "Doesn't mean you should be getting any ideas."

"Sure," Cam said. But the truth was, he'd long moved past the *getting*-ideas stage. He *had* ideas. Bad and good, comingled together in a tangled web he wasn't sure he wanted to separate.

"Why do I think you don't really mean that?" Dawson asked, but he was smiling.

It was so easy to lean in, let his eyelashes flutter, to flirt a little. "Do you *want* me to mean that?"

He fully expected Dawson to put more space between them, to gently but inexorably push him away, the way he had been. But Dawson didn't. Dawson shifted a half inch closer, until they were nearly pressed together, thigh to thigh, chest to chest.

"I should," Dawson murmured. "I *could*."

But his meaning was clear enough; he didn't want to. He wanted to get even closer. Take that bad idea and turn it inside out, until all it felt was good.

Desire spiked inside Cam as he finally took in their surroundings. Before, he'd only registered that they were alone. Now he realized that Dawson had pulled him in the library-themed room with its long blue velvet curtains framing the cushioned seats along the one far wall, the gold twisted ropes pulling back the fabric dripping with fringe.

He nearly suggested they go sit down. Maybe get a little more comfortable.

But before he could, Dawson pulled back.

"We should find the other guys. You want a drink?" he asked.

A drink wasn't even in the top three of things that Cam wanted, but he had a feeling everything else was still off-limits.

This wasn't the moment Dawson's resolve was going to crumble; that was still coming. It wasn't going to be easy to wait out all of Dawson's concerns—his insistence that this was a bad idea—but the reward was more than worth it.

It would be good between them. That much Cam knew for sure. It was only a matter of time before they got there.

"Sure," Cam said easily and followed Dawson out of the library and back into the main bar.

More players were gathered around its shiny mahogany oval now. Wes was there, that blond hockey-player guy with him. Nate and Duke and Jack, standing next to them.

That was where Dawson steered them. "Hey, look who I found," he said casually, like Cam hadn't arrived ten minutes ago, totally losing his shit.

He'd never imagined that Dawson would spill his secrets, but it felt good to be protected, anyway. And he was additionally relieved that nobody else seemed to have noticed his meltdown, because they all gave him a welcoming nod and went back to their conversation.

"I'm just saying," Wes' hockey friend said, "I could play football, sure. I could catch a ball. No problem."

"No problem," Nate muttered under his breath, looking put out. But Cam noticed that he was still here. A dozen or more other guys were milling around, but he was here, like he was glued to the hockey guy's every word.

"But," the hockey player continued, "are you gonna be able to get out there on skates and put in twenty minutes of ice time, chasing around Connor McDavid or Mitch Marner?"

Nate made a face. "Why the fuck not?"

The hockey guy—Cam was pretty sure his name was Ramsey—just laughed. And looked damn good doing it. So good Cam had to wonder if he practiced that shit in a mirror.

"You ever skate before, even?" Wes asked.

"It can't be that hard," Nate claimed.

"Oh, honey," Ramsey said pityingly.

"You better hope he never calls you on that, Bishop," Duke said.

Nate looked like he was just about ready to demand to be taken to Scotia Bank Arena right the fuck now, to test their claim that he couldn't pull it off.

"Football isn't easier than hockey," Nate argued.

"Kind of seems like it is," Dawson pointed out dryly.

The bartender approached, and Cam ordered a gin and tonic and, glancing over at Dawson, ordered him another glass of red wine. The same brand that he'd drunk the last time they'd been here that he'd said he'd liked. That seemed like a safe enough bet.

By the time he pressed it into Dawson's hand, it seemed like the football-versus-hockey argument was getting heated.

Well. *More* heated.

Cam was like Dawson; perfectly willing to concede to Ramsey's argument. Sure, there was a lot of specialized skill in football. A lot of people thought punting was just kicking a ball, and he knew that was absolute bullshit. But he wasn't doing that on a thin piece of metal balanced on a slippery surface.

"You ever go out on the ice, I bet you'd go over like one of those giant trees in the forest. Like a redwood, yeah?" Ramsey chuckled to himself, like he found his own joke so funny it didn't even matter if anyone else laughed.

Nate ground his teeth together. He looked about five seconds from throwing Ramsey against the bar.

Cam kind of hoped he might; that would be extremely entertaining while simultaneously being hot as fuck. He wasn't attracted to Nate or Ramsey, particularly—his dick was way too focused on Dawson these days—but they were both ridiculously good-looking.

"I've got better balance than that. Best balance in the league," Nate argued.

"Sure," Ramsey said and ducked his head. "Something I gotta check. Good to see you guys again."

A second later he was gone, and Nate still looked murderous.

Wes shot him a sympathetic glance. "You shouldn't let him rile you up like that," he said, nudging Nate with his shoulder. "He enjoys it too much."

"Seems like he could enjoy it a little more," Cam pointed out.

Everyone's face swiveled in his direction. Nate looked shocked and not in a good kind of way. "Are you fucking joking?" he barked.

Wes just laughed, though. "Oh my God, of course the rook says it. Yes, Nate, you two enjoy pulling each other's pigtails."

"He's just an . . .an . . .an *asshole*. Smug and hot and annoying."

"Hot, huh?" Wes teased.

Nate shook his head, cheeks unexpectedly flushed. "That's just, like, an *objective* opinion. I bet you if you polled this entire bar, even the straight guys would be like, oh yeah, that dickhead Ramsey's hot."

"Probably," Wes conceded.

Nate turned towards the bar, hunching over its shiny surface, flagging down the bartender. Ordering a shot. "Fucking hockey players," he muttered under his breath.

"Should I not have—" Cam murmured, leaning in so only Dawson could hear him. His curls brushed against his cheek, smelling like citrus and spice. Cam swallowed the longing that swept through him.

As annoying as it was, they were apparently on *Dawson's* schedule, here.

At least Dawson wasn't protesting that he was even interested, like Nate was.

"No, that was hilarious. And true to boot. They should totally hate-fuck about it."

Cam nodded. "Nate is looking awfully pent up these days."

The tension in the defensive captain's shoulders was undeniable as he threw back one shot and then barked out a request for another.

"Yeah, but if they did, imagine the fallout," Dawson said. He was apparently viewing everything, including the Nate-Ramsey situation, through the same *bad idea* lens these days.

"What do you mean?" Cam asked, sipping his drink. Even though he had a pretty decent idea of what Dawson had intended to say. He just wanted to hear Dawson say it out loud; maybe then he'd realize how much of a non-issue it actually was.

"I mean, if they do hate-fuck about it, what's going to happen the next time they're both here? And it's going to happen. Ramsey's practically Wes' shadow these days. They're gonna be awkward and it's not going to get better."

"Or they could have fun and keep having fun?" Cam suggested, maybe a trifle optimistically.

Dawson chuckled. Reached up and patted Cam's cheek. "You're adorable."

"I'm not naive," Cam complained.

"Never said you were. You're just . . .*always* just so glass-half-full," Dawson said.

"And that's adorable?" It was hard not to ask, out loud, why that wasn't sexy or hot or irresistible, but Cam swallowed the question back, along with a good-sized swig of gin and tonic.

"It sure is. I also think . . ." Dawson trailed off.

"You think?" Cam prompted.

"I never spent any time long on injured reserve, not like Ramsey. But it must suck. Kind of like how it sucked when my life fell apart. He saunters around like nothing can touch him, but I've done that too, so I know what it looks like. If things get weird between him and Nate, then he can't be friends with us. And he should be friends with us."

That was not what Cam had expected Dawson to say.

"Oh," he said softly.

"Yeah. *Oh*." Dawson's gaze was knowing.

"That makes . . .yeah. I can see it. You think that's why Wes brings him around all the time, even though he doesn't like football?"

Dawson nodded. "I do. Wish some of my teammates back in Baltimore had been nearly that observant or that dedicated."

"They weren't?" Cam was mad, just thinking about it. Dawson had played for the same team forever. Had been with the same guys for many of those seasons. Why *hadn't* they realized he was hurting?

"Not really. Kind of wish I'd been like him." Dawson gestured over to where Ramsey was holding court with Aidan and Levi and Griff now. "Really fucking good at hiding it."

"I could tell," Cam said. He didn't add that he hadn't known Dawson nearly as long as some of his ex-teammates. But it had been obvious to him that Dawson was hurting. That his self-confidence was shot. That he could use a friendly shoulder. He'd tried, initially, but Dawson had seemed oblivious to it.

"Yeah, well, you're not like those guys, rook. You're special." Dawson ruffled his hair, and it didn't feel like a patronizing gesture you'd do to a kid; it felt like more, like Dawson just wanted to touch him, any way he could. Especially with the intimate way his fingers lingered against his scalp.

"Thanks," Cam said, gazing down at Dawson's face. "Ditto, obviously."

"Obviously," Dawson echoed, but he looked pleased, anyway.

"We got each other's backs." Cam thought it was obvious that was true, but it was still something else to see the impact of his words hit Dawson.

Like maybe he hadn't realized it. Or that he had, but he just hadn't known the extent of it.

"Can you just stop being . . ." Dawson waved around him. "Like for a freaking minute?"

"Stop being what?"

Dawson stared at him, the look in his hazel eyes naked with want. But before there was any bad-idea indulgences, he looked away. "Like *you*," Dawson said, moistening his lips and then tipping his glass back, draining at least half of it. "I suppose it was too much to hope I'd have to outlast a Cameron Greene seduction onslaught."

"Oh, you thought *that* was seducing you?" Cam fluttered his eyelashes in an exaggerated movement.

Dawson laughed. "You weren't."

Cam nudged his hip with his own. "When I do, you'll know."

"Jesus," Dawson muttered and finished his wine with another large gulp.

CHAPTER 10

Dawson wasn't going to make the same mistake twice—or more like a dozen times, at this rate, but who was really counting? *Not him.* He kept an eye on the rookie all night long. Stuck close, even though that was both an exercise in patience *and* in torture.

Watched as Cam laughed and chatted with what felt like half the team. For a while, Lane and Trevor tugged them into their orbit, Lane insisting they take shots while Trevor made a disgruntled, disapproving face. But Trevor ultimately took the shot when Lane held the tequila up to his lips, giving in with a self-conscious chuckle.

They'd rotated through the various knots of different players. It was one of the reasons Dawson had liked being special teams—the offense *and* the defense both liked to claim them. Maybe before he hadn't done his due diligence, but celebrating a four-game win streak to kick off the season, everyone was acting like the next guy over was their new best friend.

Dawson didn't want the bitterness to invade this night, but it was impossible not to wonder absently how it would feel when they were more games in. When they inevitably lost. If they ever lost *badly*.

He'd been around long enough that he knew some teams weathered those storms better than others. It was still too new to know how *this* team might ride out a rough sea.

It was almost one in the morning when Cam leaned into him, soft, slightly sleepy eyes blinking up at him, and said, "I think we should probably head out."

He looked tipsy, but not drunk. Something he'd probably be grateful for in the morning.

"Yeah, you done partying, rook?" Dawson asked, tucking him into his side. Cam might be slightly taller, but it was a revelation how well he still fit against him like this. "I'll call a cab."

"No," Cam argued. "Let's walk. I want some fresh air."

"Fresh air, huh?" Dawson pulled him towards the exit, concern rumbling at the base of his stomach. Concern he didn't want to voice out loud, but he couldn't *not* ask. "It's pretty late. You sure you'd be okay with that?"

Cam blinked down at him, his eyes softening even more. "Well, *yeah*," he said. "You're with me."

Gooey warmth spread through Dawson's chest, even as he told himself—insisted, really—that it didn't mean anything.

"Alright, walking it is," Dawson said. Not only because he wanted to prolong this soft, sweet bubble between him and a tipsy, pliant, affectionate Cam, but because it might help remind Cam next time that there was nothing to be afraid of. A little bit of exposure therapy.

But when they got outside, it was drizzling. A cold unpleasant kind of rain, where the moisture sank its claws in and didn't let go.

"Just give me a sec," Dawson said, fumbling for the phone in his pocket. He was maybe a fraction more sober than Cam, but he wasn't *sober*, either.

"Nooo," Cam whined. "Come on. Let's walk. It's not so bad. Barely even raining."

"You gonna say it's barely even cold, either?" Dawson asked dryly, shivering even as he pulled up the collar of his jacket.

He checked the directions on his phone and they set off. Even though it was late and the weather sucked, there were still a few people out on the streets.

"Weeeellll," Cam said, drawing out the word, shooting a sheepish glance in Dawson's direction.

"Yeah, yeah, this was all your idea. I'm gonna remind you of that," Dawson pointed out as they turned a corner.

"We should go to the PATH, instead," Cam said. "I know there's an entrance in the basement of our building."

"What happened to fresh air?" Dawson wondered.

Cam shrugged. "It's cold!"

Maybe if Cam was fractionally less adorable, he could resist doing whatever he said. But so far, his track record of doing that recently was not very good. He *wanted* to make Cam happy because every time he did, Dawson felt a little warmer from the brightness of his smile.

Dawson knew just enough about the PATH—the underground network of pedestrian tunnels that crisscrossed the city—to be dangerous. He knew how to take the entrance in their building to the building that housed his favorite Chinese restaurant. He and Aidan had walked through the underground corridors a few times when he'd first gotten to town.

But he certainly hadn't been doing it recently, and his memory was more than a little foggy. Or maybe that was the glasses of wine he'd drunk.

Still, he was pretty sure this big skyscraper here had an entrance that if he went the right way *would* take them to their building.

He tugged Cam's arm and they hurried in, the security guy at the desk giving them a sleepy half-look as they walked towards the escalator that would take them to the bottom floor.

Cam leaned against the edge of the escalator. Water droplets dusted the top of his hair. And somehow—Dawson couldn't figure out how—he was still smiling.

"That was a great night," Cam mused. "We didn't have places like that in Montana."

"I'm not sure there's many bars like Vault," Dawson agreed.

"But it wasn't just the bar, though it is pretty freaking cool," Cam said. "Everyone's so . . . I don't know . . . loose and happy. And *together*."

"Four-game win streak," Dawson pointed out.

Cam shot him a look as they hit the basement floor. During the day, this was a food court, with various restaurants and a coffee shop as well as a bookstore, but at night, there were gates over all the storefronts, and it was quiet.

They were alone.

"I don't think it's just that," Cam argued staunchly.

"Easy to be happy when you're winning."

He didn't want to burst Cam's happy bubble. Dawson never wanted to do that. But he didn't want him to be caught off guard when the vibes inevitably changed. Because they always changed. Dawson being here in Toronto at all was proof of that.

"The guys have something to prove and I think they're excited that they have the chance to do that."

Dawson rolled his eyes. He didn't *want* to be a Debbie Downer but this was naive, even for the rookie.

"You don't really believe that. I promise—we're gonna lose a game, probably in some kind of extra shitty way. Either get blown out when we shouldn't be, or on like the last fucking play. And nobody will be teasing you about taking a tequila shot and Aidan won't be buying drinks and slinging his arm around everyone like they're his new best friend."

For a second, Dawson hadn't realized that Cam had stopped. But when there was nothing to his very blunt declaration but silence, he glanced over. Realized he'd left the guy behind.

No, Cam had *stopped*, right in his tracks, and was staring at Dawson with an incredulous expression all over his face.

"What?" Dawson wasn't sure if what he felt was guilt or self-consciousness. "Let me guess—you think that's bullshit too."

"It is bullshit. It's absolute bullshit. And even if it *does* happen, it doesn't mean that none of this stuff tonight was real, or true—"

"I didn't say that," Dawson said quickly.

Yep, no question about it at all. That was definitely a stomach-churning sweep of guilt gnawing at his innards.

"Yeah, you kinda did," Cam said, frowning. "And it's *bullshit*."

There was nothing Dawson wanted more than to agree with Cam. But he'd been there last year, when it hadn't been bullshit, it had been his *reality*.

When everything had soured, and instead of boosting him up, the team had turned their backs on him.

As beautiful as Cam's sunshine was, there was something Dawson recognized in it—maybe even how *he'd* been once—and when those beliefs had been stripped away, it had hurt like hell.

Maybe he could help the rookie avoid that painful realization.

"You believe that everything is just going to work out? Easy? Just like that?"

Cam's eyebrows screwed together. "I never said it would be *easy*."

"But you do. You believe it." Dawson hadn't realized he'd gotten so close. Not until Cam stumbled backwards half a step, one of those big cement pillars at his back.

"I . . .well, yeah. I do. I *do*." Cam said the last with defiance.

"That's—"

But Cam didn't even let him get the rest of the thought out before he was continuing, pressing a palm right against where his heart was hammering away in his chest. "So things *don't* work out sometimes. You got divorced. Your money got stolen. Your team dropped you. Those were all shit deals, okay? Nobody's gonna argue with that. But here's the thing, I can't go around believing the sky is always gonna fall. I don't think *you* even want to go around believing that either."

Dawson opened his mouth to argue, and then snapped it shut again, because damnit, the rookie was right. He didn't want to. Part of why he'd been so angry—why he was *still* so fucking angry—was that he didn't know *how* to go back to that guy. The one who'd been sure that with time and effort and maybe even a sprinkling of luck, he'd get exactly where he'd always dreamed and *stay* there.

He was just different now. The whole experience had soured him, and maybe even ruined him, and Dawson fucking hated it.

"See? I told you," Cam said smugly. His fingers curled into Dawson's coat. Around the placket. He tugged him closer.

Dawson knew he should be putting some space between them. If either of them moved another inch or two, he was going to be doing something he couldn't take back. A certified Bad Idea.

"Sometimes," Cam continued, "we just have to stay the course. Have hope that things will turn around. Even if it seems like they won't. Maybe the end result sucks, but the journey doesn't have to."

"Thanks, Mr. Self Help." Dawson had meant to say it in a snarky, kind of snide sort of way. But it came out all soft and tender instead. Like he wasn't being sarcastic at all, but meant every single word.

Cam smiled. "You think I got a future?"

If Cam did, it would mean sharing him, and without doing any Bad Ideas at all, Dawson already kind of hated that thought. *Should* Cam's optimism be shared? Probably. But Dawson was greedy, and he wanted to hoard all of it for himself.

"Maybe," Dawson hedged. "But if you go share it with the world, who's gonna sit here and keep me from drowning in my own pessimism?"

"Good point." The corner of Cam's mouth quirked up. "We can't have that."

"I'm already pathetic enough." Dawson wasn't entirely stupid. He wasn't a rookie, still. Not on the field, and not off it either, though it had been a *long* time since he'd done this: flirted and then held his hands up to the fire, like he wanted to get burned.

Like he couldn't *wait* to get burned.

His brain was screaming *Bad Idea, Bad Idea, Bad Idea,* but his body was doing the exact opposite, because somehow he was now pressed against Cam, still backed up against the pillar.

It was hot. So hot. Even hotter when Cam tilted his head down. Looked Dawson straight in the eye and said, "You gonna let me save you?"

It was stupid and more than a little crazy to assume that he could.

But Dawson nodded anyway, hypnotized by the way Cam was gazing at him. Like he really could perform miracles. Like he *would.*

Then Cam leaned in and closed the last inch between them, lips soft against Dawson's. The feel of their mouths moving together, even in a sweet, nearly innocent kiss, felt like getting yanked up, right out of the water he'd been flailing in.

It was a good kiss. Despite being young, Cam wasn't overly eager. He held back, tongue flicking out and then retreating, like he was worried Dawson might pull away.

Dawson thought he probably *should,* but he wasn't going to.

It felt so good. Too fucking good.

Cam's arms curled around Dawson's waist and he tugged him in a little closer, and *oh,* Dawson could do better than that.

He tensed and used a sudden burst of strength to turn them, pushing Cam back against the pillar. Cam whimpered into his mouth, and Dawson's pulse accelerated with the knowledge that this was what they both wanted.

Cam, even though he was taller, caged in with Dawson's body, their kisses growing hotter and wetter.

Dawson's lips found Cam's jawline. His whole body tensed as he found an especially good spot and Cam made a glorious noise in the back of his throat.

It would be so easy to get carried away, because this was the best thing Dawson had felt in forever. Even his foot connecting with a ball, nailing a fifty-plus-yard field goal in a clutch moment hadn't felt like this.

Dawson had told himself he wouldn't do this, but maybe it had been inevitable. How could he be expected to resist something so utterly irresistible?

Cam's fingers dug into Dawson's waist and then slid around, digging into his ass.

A throat cleared itself behind them and it was a bucketful of cold water dumped right on Dawson's arousal.

He pulled back. Separated them, even though it was the last thing he wanted to do. Especially when Cam was leaning against the pillar, long and lean and so gorgeous. Lips red and wet from Dawson's mouth.

There was a security guard behind them, looking sheepish. "Sorry, just doing my rounds," he said.

There was recognition in his eyes. At least they were both out and the fact they were both kissing people of the male sex couldn't have been *too* much of a shock. That they were kissing each other? That was probably pretty freaking surprising.

"Sorry," Dawson said. "Uh. We'll move along."

The guy nodded, a smile tilting the corner of his mouth up. "Good game," he said, and turned to go back upstairs.

Pleasure was banked, warm and smug, in Cam's brown eyes when Dawson met them.

"Guess we probably surprised him," Cam observed as Dawson glanced around, trying to remember where the PATH entry was here.

"Probably," Dawson agreed. It was easier to say that than to talk about it.

He finally spotted the sign, way over in the corner. If he hadn't been looking for it, he wouldn't have found it.

It was just expedient to grab Cam's hand, tangling their fingers together as he tugged him in the right direction. It was definitely less intimate than what they'd been doing less than five minutes ago.

"You're not freaking out," Cam observed as Dawson pushed the entry door open and Cam walked into the narrow passageway.

"Should I be?"

Cam shot him a look. "You were the one who said it was a bad idea."

"It's still *not* not a bad idea."

"When you figure out what that means, let me know, alright?"

Dawson sighed. "I mean, maybe it was inevitable. And it feels good. Right? You liked it?"

"Daws," Cam said with an edge of suffering to his tone, "*I* kissed *you.*"

"Well, you might've not liked it." He hadn't been with anyone since Brynn, and he couldn't even remember the last time he'd kissed her. Which really . . .that said it all, didn't it? But to say he was out of practice was putting it mildly.

Cam barked out a laugh. "Yeah, okay."

"I mean it," Dawson said.

"You were there." They took a turn and then another and Cam glanced back at him. "It was hot."

He'd thought so, but then it had been so long since he'd touched someone in a non-platonic way—or been touched in return—that he wasn't sure his standards were way out of whack.

Cameron had blown them way out of the water, anyway, but that didn't mean the feeling was reciprocal.

"Wait," Cam said suddenly, "you liked it too, right?"

Dawson reached out, his fingers ghosting up and down Cam's spine. "You were there, weren't you?" he teased.

"Okay, yeah. It was hot," Cam repeated, chuckling under his breath. "We could uh . . .do it some more?"

Dawson sure wanted to. Wanted to do more than kiss, too. His cock was still half-hard in his jeans, and every pulse of his heartbeat reminded him that it *had* been too long.

But he didn't know what Cam's expectations were. He was still a pretty shit bet. Ten years older and kinda washed up. Out of practice. Grumpy and self-absorbed.

Cam could do a whole lot better.

If Dawson had wanted another indication of how he wasn't really worthy of Cam's attention, the spike of jealousy he felt when he thought of someone else more deserving touching him was pretty convincing.

He could list out all those reasons. But then, he probably didn't have to. Cam had spent time around him. He knew what Dawson was like. And he'd kissed him anyway.

"It's not a difficult question," Cam pointed out when Dawson had been quiet, trying to decide between what he *wanted* to say and what he *should* say.

"I was gonna say, I'm a shitty choice, but then you know all the reasons why that is," Dawson said.

"You're not *shitty*," Cam argued, sounding like he was gearing up for a passionate defense on Dawson's behalf. A defense he definitely hadn't earned.

"But then," Dawson said, before he could get started, "it doesn't have to be anything serious, right? Just having some fun. Letting loose. Getting off."

Cam stopped again. Tilted his head, like he was analyzing what Dawson had said. "That what you want?"

Dawson didn't know what he wanted. It was Cameron, in some kind of way, but this way felt easiest. Safest. Maybe it was still a bad idea, but this probably protected both of them from the worst of the fallout.

If there's fallout, the remnants of the optimistic part of Dawson's brain pointed out softly.

"Yeah. I just . . .I . . ." Dawson shoved his hands in his pockets so he didn't grab Cam and kiss him again to avoid this conversation. To avoid saying something like, *you're going to figure out sooner rather than later that I'm a bad bet, and this'll make it hurt less when you do.*

"I suppose," Cam said, full of thoughtful consideration, "that would probably make it a *less* bad idea."

"Exactly."

"If anyone deserves to have some fun, it's probably you," Cam agreed.

"Shit," Dawson said, laughing. "Little harsh, don't you think?"

Cam nudged him with his shoulder, indicating their doorway, out of the last corridor, "You said it, not me. You wanna have some fun? Okay, let's have some fun."

Cam had never had a boyfriend. He'd had a handful of hookups in high school, and then some more regular friends-with-benefit arrangements in college. He'd always been happy enough with those.

Deciding that after all those casual situations now he wanted to get serious, and that the person he wanted to get serious with was Dawson Hall would be ridiculous.

Which is why you're not doing it, Cam told himself firmly. Dawson had said it himself. They were just having fun. The chemistry was good. The kiss had been spectacular. It was the perfect opportunity to blow off some steam. Easy. Simple. Straightforward.

Dawson hadn't had to say he hadn't hooked up with anyone since his marriage had ended; it had been written all over his face and in between his uncertainty after the kiss had ended.

Which was why Cam wasn't particularly surprised when they got to Dawson's apartment that he got weird and nervous. He'd already assumed he was going to have to drive this, at least the first time.

It wasn't *easy* for Cam either, but he did it anyway: as soon as Dawson pulled his coat off, Cam following suit, he pushed him right against the wall by the door, kissing him again.

Any protest Dawson made was swallowed up by Cam's mouth, and he melted under his touch.

Cam pulled back for a moment. "Been a while?" he asked casually.

Dawson looked deliciously flustered, a flush riding high on his cheekbones, his hair mussed. "Is it that obvious?"

It was, but Cam wasn't about to tell him that. He'd get all up in his head again, worrying about whether it was going to be good for Cam. Newsflash: Dawson turned Cam on so much it wouldn't have mattered if he'd been celibate for *years*.

"No," Cam murmured, "just wondering how long it's been since anybody did this."

Dawson's shocked and swift intake of breath as Cam dropped to his knees was so fucking satisfying. The way he groaned deep in his throat and the back of his head hit the wall behind him made Cam's dick throb.

"Too long," Dawson agreed roughly, one of his hands drifting down to Cam's hair, tangling gently in it as Cam undid his belt, his zipper on his jeans. Carefully pulled out his cock.

It wasn't long but it was thick, twitching against Cam's palm as he gave it an experimental stroke.

Cam wrapped a hand around Dawson's thigh, enjoying the way it tensed under his touch. It was even more satisfying when the cock in his hand flexed, too.

"You like this?"

Dawson laughed, rough and needy. "I don't hate it."

"What do you like? I want to make it good for you."

There was that desperate laugh again. It lit up Cam inside, thinking that he'd driven Dawson to this—that he could drive him even further.

He flattened his tongue and, sliding Dawson's cock along it, got his first taste.

"God," Dawson panted. "Not sure you're gonna have to do anything special to make me—" He cut off with a muttered *fuck* as Cam took him a little deeper.

He was just sort of feeling his way, figuring out what made Dawson tick, but Dawson was already making these insanely needy noises above him, like he could come from just a little exploration. Cam had wanted to make it last, but it was becoming rapidly clear that Dawson just wasn't going to.

So he switched gears. Taking his cock deeper, sucking it hard, tongue flicking in and out of his slit, humming as Dawson's precome coated his taste buds.

Dawson's hand tightened in his hair, not pushing him, but winding in, the bite of pain ratcheted up both Cam's arousal and his determination to make Dawson lose it.

His thigh was flexing, the muscles contracting under his palm, and Cam wished he wasn't leaning against the wall, because he wanted to feel his ass as he sucked him down. All that plush muscle clenching and releasing, like he was already imagining thrusting into Cam's mouth—or Cam's ass.

Cam groaned around Dawson's dick, mouth filling with spit.

He wanted to make it last. This was so hot—way hotter than it had any right to be—but they were both riding the edge now. Cam pressed a palm to his own dick, throbbing in his jeans. Giving pleasure always turned him on, but tonight, because it was Dawson or because it was how earnestly Dawson gave himself over to it, it was undoing him right alongside.

Then he pulled back. Glanced up. Swore he saw God in Dawson's face. "You wanna come in my mouth or on my face?"

"Fuck," Dawson muttered.

"Come on," Cam teased. "Tell me, Daws." He twisted his hand more insistently, more precome blurting onto his tongue. He was close. Cam could tell.

And he wanted it to be good. So fucking good that Dawson wanted more. That Dawson wanted this all the time, because Cam already knew *he* did. Once was definitely not going to be enough.

"Mouth," Dawson said, panting. "God, your fucking mouth."

Cam took him deep again, sucking hard, and there was one single glorious flex of what felt like Dawson's entire body and then he was shaking apart. Coming down Cam's throat until he pulled back a little, at the very end, savoring it on his tongue.

His knees were shaking when he rose to his feet, arousal a live, pulsing thing in his blood. He could barely get his jeans undone as Dawson pulled him in, palms cupping his cheeks and kissed him long and hard, tasting his own come.

For a second, Cam thought that was all it was going to take. Dawson's plush lips working against his, his tongue in his mouth, his palm barely grazing over his aching erection.

But then a hand closed insistently around Cam's wrist, holding him firm. Keeping him from doing anything that *might* actually set him off finally.

Dawson pulled back. "No," he said.

Fire burned through Cam at the word. He wasn't usually into being given orders. That had never done anything particularly for him before. But Dawson saying it sternly like that, in a voice already fucked out from his own orgasm?

That was a whole different story.

"But—" Cam whimpered pathetically. He was so horny. Couldn't ever remember wanting anyone the way he wanted Dawson.

"If we're doing this, we're doing this my way," Dawson said and took him by the wrist, pulling him along the hallway, tugging Cam into what had to be his bedroom.

"What's your way?" Cam asked, as he fell onto the edge of the bed. If his knees had been wobbly before, they were jellified now. And he hadn't even come yet.

Dawson didn't answer. Just leaned over Cam and began to strip him out of his clothes.

Shoes first. Then socks. His jacket. His shirt. His pants. His briefs.

Then he was totally naked, staring up at Dawson, who was the opposite.

"Oh yeah," Dawson said, a tongue flicking out to lick his reddened bottom lip. "Shit, you're fucking gorgeous."

Cam leaned back on the bed and believed him.

"See," Dawson continued, even though it sort of felt like he was talking to himself now, "if we're gonna do this, I wanna enjoy it. Take my time with you."

"I—" He didn't need it. He wanted to tell Dawson that. But that thought—really, all the thoughts left in his brain—got swallowed up in Dawson's mouth as he leaned over the bed and kissed him.

Hot and lush and leisurely, like they had all the time in the world.

For a long minute, it felt like all Dawson was going to do was kiss him. Cam might have been really alright with that situation. He was a great kisser, and the electricity that sparked between them made it one of the hottest makeout sessions he'd ever had.

But the thrum of arousal was insistent in his veins, and when Dawson's mouth finally slid lower, to his neck, then lower still, teeth nibbling at his collarbone, he groaned out his approval.

"God," Dawson murmured into his skin, humming as he went. "Wanna mark you up. Make sure everyone knows."

He didn't say what he wanted everyone to know. That he was fucking Cam? That Cam was fucking him? That maybe, incredibly, Cam was *his*?

But no, if that was true, then Dawson wouldn't have gone out of his way to clarify ahead of time that this was just a fun hookup, an exceptional way to release some steam.

If Cam really wanted to be his, he wouldn't have gone along with it so readily.

But he had, and so far it was both: fun *and* exceptional. There hadn't been any releasing yet, but Cam was already panting for it, because he knew it wasn't going to be a disappointment.

"Can I?" Dawson asked, lifting his head.

"Can you make me come? *Please*," Cam half-begged.

Dawson just chuckled. "I mean, can I mark you up?"

The guys in the locker room might notice and give him shit for it, but who cared? Cam wasn't worried about that. He nodded.

"Good."

Cam saw a flash of a smug smile before Dawson ducked his head back down and began to suck a mark into his collarbone. Then around his nipple, tongue flicking out, just barely grazing its surface, making Cam cry out at the unexpected pleasure shooting through him.

"So good," Dawson muttered, like that was the worst realization he could have come to. And that filled Cam with a buoyant happiness; they weren't going to do this only once.

His tongue was wet against his abs, then, like he was tracing the lines of them, the muscles contracting under its exploration.

Then finally, Dawson sank to his knees, and the first brush of his palm against the head of Cam's cock made him yelp embarrassingly loud.

He bit his bottom lip and tried to stifle his noises.

"No," Dawson ordered. "I wanna hear you. Let me hear you, rook."

Then he tucked Cam's cock into the wet heat of his mouth, one hand an insistent pressure against his thigh and the other reaching up, cupping his balls.

Cam could barely hold it together, now. He wanted to drag the joy of this out, spinning it endlessly until it swallowed him up, but self-control was slippery and it was sliding away from him.

"Yeah," Dawson breathed around him. "Come on, give it to me."

Cam watched as his eyes fluttered closed, like Dawson really did want it, and he tumbled headfirst into his orgasm, pulsing against Dawson's tongue.

All orgasms technically felt great, but there was a particular satisfaction in this one. When he collapsed back against the bed, Dawson's hand still pressed into his thigh, it felt like he'd cleared the last bit of cobwebby stress out of his brain.

Any type of way he'd felt about that punt during the game, *gone.*

"Well, that was . . ." Dawson raised himself up and flopped back down on the bed next to Cam. When Cam glanced over at him, he was grinning. The kind of bright smile that Cam could remember seeing so many times on TV in prior years, but had never once seen in person, not since they'd both come to Toronto this season.

"Yeah," Cam agreed. It didn't really matter how Dawson had intended to finish that sentence, 'cause all of the possibilities would be true.

For a moment, he let himself lie there, soaking up the last bit of endorphin rush, not just of his orgasm, but of Dawson lying there next to him, an uncomplicated happiness radiating out of him.

But he couldn't stay. Hookups didn't really sleep over. That was one rule Cam knew like the back of his hand. Funny how it had never felt like an option before, or even like something he'd wanted.

But now he just wanted to not move, to let himself slide into sleep. Wake up next to that same look on Dawson's face.

"Have to say," Dawson finally said, "that wasn't a bad idea at all."

"Not-bad enough to repeat?" Cam asked, even though he already suspected the truth.

Dawson barked out a laugh. "I think you know the answer to that."

Yeah, he did. And it felt damn good.

He should really be going now. They'd established it had been a very mutually satisfying encounter and that they'd be repeating it. There was no reason to stay.

Cam pushed himself upright.

"Where you going?" Dawson asked lazily.

"Back to my place?"

Dawson just chuckled again, a little darkly. Even that was hot. "Why bother?"

Cam almost said, *because you said you didn't want to complicate things, and cuddling together and definitely sleeping together complicates things.*

But Dawson was ten years older than him. He'd been married. Surely he didn't need Cam to explain that to him. If he wanted Cam to stay, then Cam wasn't going to argue.

Not when he didn't want to leave.

"Okay," Cam said.

"Got a spare toothbrush rattling around here, and you can make the walk of shame in the morning," Dawson said sleepily, slinging an arm around Cam's waist, heavy and insistent. "Come on. It's late. Just stay."

It was only a few floors down to Cam's own apartment, but it was cold and empty. Why would he go down there if he didn't have to?

So he settled back onto the bed. "Nice mattress," he said.

Dawson smiled again. "Yeah, isn't it?"

CHAPTER 11

IT WAS THE WEIRDEST walk of shame Cam had ever performed. Probably because it didn't feel like much of one at all.

He woke up when he heard the sound of water turning on, and for a second he couldn't figure out why someone else was in his apartment. But then he opened his eyes and realized that he *wasn't* in his apartment. The walls were just as bare and white as his, though, and it only took a second for him to realize it was Dawson's.

Memories from last night filtered through him, and his breath caught in his throat.

Dawson walked back into the bedroom, shadowed by the night-light in the bathroom. Still naked. No shame on his face.

Though, he was so good-looking—Cam's fingers itched to touch him again—why shouldn't he be comfortable in his own skin?

"Hey, didn't mean to wake you," Dawson said as he slid back between the covers.

He wasn't hungover. Just thirsty, a pale throb in the back of his skull. Easy to dismiss with some water and a very large mug of coffee.

"It's alright," Cam croaked.

Last night, he'd tried to easily bridge the gap between friends and *more*, so Dawson wouldn't feel out of practice about it. But this morning, it was Cam who felt awkward. He'd never woken up in someone else's bed like this before. Never rolled over and wondered if they could pick right back up where they left off.

Dawson's hazel eyes gleamed knowingly as his head hit the pillow. He put a hand on Cam's waist and tugged him closer. "You know," he murmured, "that toothbrush still has your name on it."

Maybe Dawson *hadn't* done this in a while, but he still knew what to say now. Still knew what Cam wanted and didn't know how to ask for.

Nodding and blushing, Cam rolled out of bed. Took care of his business with the toilet. Brushed his teeth. Stared in the mirror for a second. There were a handful of marks on his chest that were new. He pressed a thumb into the bruise and felt his mouth go even drier at the spark of something that crawled under his skin.

When he came back to bed, Dawson was waiting for him and wasted zero time, pulling him underneath his body and it got heated fast. Hands and mouths everywhere, and Cam came with Dawson's teeth in his shoulder, one hand on his cock and the other digging into one of the bruises he'd made on his hip.

"Didn't think I'd like that," Cam said, still breathless as he sat on one of Dawson's barstools, watching as he made them eggs.

"No?" Dawson smirked in a way that was totally not hot at all. *Nope.* "I got a few tricks up my sleeve, still."

They ate their eggs side by side at the kitchen counter while Dawson's knee brushed every few seconds against Cam's.

Cam finished his second mug of coffee and offered to do the dishes, but Dawson just waved him off. "My housekeeper's coming later today. She can do it," he said.

There didn't seem to be any other reasons to stay, but Cam was still hesitating, acutely aware that Dawson was still looking at his mouth.

But before he could suggest going back to bed, his phone rang.

A quick glance at the screen told him he shouldn't ignore it.

"I should probably take this. It's my dad," Cam said, realizing a second after he said it that probably made him look young and a little stupid. God, he could've called his dad back in five minutes—or an hour. But he'd said it, and there was nothing to do but own it.

But there was zero judgment on Dawson's face. He reached out and curled a hand around Cam's shoulder. "Have a good day off and I'll see you tomorrow?" he said, and Cam nodded and that was that.

A moment later his shoes and jacket were back on, and he was in the hallway, picking up his dad's call.

"I texted you," Shane said when he picked up on the last ring.

"Oh. I hadn't been looking at my phone." He hadn't looked at it once this morning. Hadn't even realized it was still in his jeans pocket until it had started ringing.

"Busy night?" his dad asked slyly.

"Uh." Cam genuinely tried to *not* share anything about his sex life with his dad, not because he wouldn't approve—as long as he was safe, Shane hadn't ever cared—but because it was awkward as fuck.

Once in a while, he would gently admonish Cam that someday he *would* want someone for more than just a fun night in bed, and he should at least be open to that possibility. Well, Cam was *not* going to tell his dad that this theoretical person had finally arrived on the scene and that it was his veteran kicker.

"Oh, you don't have to tell me anything," Shane said, chuckling under his breath. "Don't worry about that. Just want to make sure you're doing good after yesterday."

"Ugh, that punt in the second quarter. I know. I should've pinned them right against the line, and I didn't." Cam walked into the elevator, leaning against the back wall for the trip down three floors.

"Kiddo," his dad said, "I wasn't thinking about that at all. Four wins in a row, I figured you'd be celebrating with the team."

"Oh. Yeah. I uh . . .I did. We went out to that bar again."

"We?"

Cam made a face as the elevator doors dinged open. He walked down the hall to his apartment. As expected, it was indeed cold and empty, that sliver of Lake Ontario barely visible out of the window.

He told himself it was fine. He wouldn't give himself away the moment he said Dawson's name.

"Me and a bunch of the guys. Aidan and Levi. Nate. Trevor and Lane. And Dawson too. Of course." Then he'd had to make it awkward by tacking Dawson's name on at the very end and treating it like him being there was special.

He flopped down on the couch, setting the phone on his stomach and turning speakerphone on.

"Dawson, huh?"

Cam groaned in the back of his throat. "Dad."

"Just saying. He's cute, you know? Little older than you—"

"I'm not going to propose marriage to him," Cam interrupted.

"I wouldn't think so. Not yet anyway. He just got divorced, didn't he?"

"Yeah," Cam said. Told himself to fucking shut up. But he didn't. Of course. "Not *that* recently."

His dad just laughed. "So it's like that, huh?"

Cam groaned again. "Daaaad," he whined. "I don't want to talk about it."

"This just a crush on a hot older guy or . . ." He trailed off.

"Or what?"

Finally, his dad sounded even a tiny bit embarrassed. "You really want me to say it? I kinda thought you didn't."

"I don't. I *don't*." But he wanted to talk about it. Last night had been so unexpected, but so good. Cam had hoped that they'd eventually end up in bed together—once Dawson had actually *seen* him, it was like he couldn't stop looking; their chemistry so intense, so *real*—but he hadn't imagined it would happen so soon.

"Kinda sounds like you do," Shane teased gently. "We can talk about it if you want. I know you don't have many friends there yet."

He wasn't wrong. Cam did have other friends, though. Guys he'd played with. Some of his ex–friends with benefits. But even though

Dawson had never really hidden his interest in both sexes, Cam felt like with everything that had happened to him last year, maybe he wouldn't appreciate Cam spreading his private business. Even when it was only to friends who'd *probably* keep their mouths shut.

But he knew his dad would.

Besides, who was his dad gonna tell, even if he was inclined to? Mav, the bartender down at the Wagon Wheel Grill and Bar? His veterinary clients?

"It's . . .we slept together last night," Cam said in a rush.

"He didn't—"

Cam knew what his dad was going to ask before he even got the whole question out. "No," he said firmly. "It wasn't like that at all. We'd both had a few drinks, but I wasn't drunk. And he didn't push me. I . . .*I* probably pushed *him.*"

Shane laughed. "'Course you did."

"And," Cam added, "we had talked about it, a little. Before last night. So he knew I was . . .you know. *Interested.*"

"Kiddo, you've been crushing on that guy forever. I remember how excited you were when he signed with the Thunder this summer."

"That was just a competency kink. He's *so* good." But Cam heard how dreamy his tone had gotten.

It was probably *not* just a competency kink, anymore. Or if it was, it wasn't just because Dawson was so damn good at kicking a football, it was because he was that good of a kisser and so fucking amazing with his hands . . .and his mouth . . .and his dick was just really, really great . . .

"Yeah, we get it. He's real dishy." His dad was laughing now. "I'm happy for you, Cam. You deserve a good guy in your life." There was an unspoken *finally* at the end of that sentence.

Cam had known he should've prefaced this whole thing by explaining that it was casual. A friendly hookup. His dad wouldn't have understood it, but that was fine. He was old and didn't understand the breadth of the gray area between platonic buds and wildly in love.

When Cam didn't immediately respond, trying to formulate exactly the right sentence to explain what he and Daws discussed, his dad groaned.

"No, don't tell me you're gonna do this casual business again."

"It's fine, Dad," Cam argued.

"You know, you *can* like people. You can date people. If you wanted to, of course." Shane tacked that last bit on, belatedly. Cam rolled his eyes, even though he was pleased, deep down, that his dad cared so much about what *he* wanted.

Still, of course, he was trying to fit Cam and Cam's feelings into a normal-sized shape. But then, this morning Cam kept trying to *not* cram his own feelings into that normal-sized shape.

It had been hard, because even though Cam had never dated before, he imagined that might be what it would be like in the mornings.

Slow and sleepy and nice.

Rotating around each other like they were meant to be.

"Yes, Dad, I do know that. But it's not like that. He's . . .you said it yourself. He just got divorced. We're both on a new team. It doesn't have to be serious."

Shane hummed under his breath.

"I just think, might be hard to feel that way about a guy, even a guy's football skill, and then meet him and start uh . . ."

"Dad," Cam said, his face flushing bright red. He was so glad they weren't video chatting right now.

"You know what I mean. Would be hard to *not* feel some kind of way about it. So it's okay if you do. You can tell me. Even if, uh, you can't tell him."

For a split second, Cam did consider telling his dad. Did consider spilling the half-baked feelings that were rumbling around inside of him. But Cam thought it would be worse if he said it all out loud. It might actually make them real.

For now, they were just amorphous floating *maybes*.

"No, it's okay. I'm good."

There was a long, pointed silence.

"Stop it, Dad." Cam huffed with embarrassment. "I swear. It's fine. I know how to do this. And it's good."

"As long as you think it's good," Shane said gently.

Cam rolled his eyes. He'd gotten way more than he'd expected, and from his vantage point, Dawson had acted without even really thinking about it. If Cam had asked for more, asked to stay even longer, he didn't think Dawson would've turned him down. How could it be anything *but* good?

"It's better than good. It's great," Cam confirmed.

"And you're okay about the punt from yesterday's game."

"I think you need to get out more," Cam declared. "Obsessing about my personal life. Probably rewatching every punt a hundred times."

"Stop it," Shane said, laughing. But he didn't deny it, either.

"You're still coming for Thanksgiving, right?"

His dad's voice was soft over the phone. "Couldn't stop me, bud."

Dawson had never, not once, thought what dating Aidan Flynn might be like.

He was beginning to think this was what it was sort of like, but in a super fucked-up, polyamory sort of way. Like maybe what those stupid dating shows felt like when they got down to the last few contestants and the girls kept eyeing each other suspiciously from across the room.

He'd not really thought about it one way or the other when Aidan had suggested they grab sushi tonight.

He hadn't considered whether Aidan would come alone or not. If he had, he might've said that Aidan would bring his boyfriend, Levi.

Not that he'd bring his good friend, once-teammate and now *current*-teammate, Mo Jeffries.

Mo and Dawson shot each other looks across the table like they were both thinking the same thing: *wow, dude, this is so fucking awkward. Aidan's got no matchmaking instincts at all.*

Not that Dawson thought this was a setup or a date.

It wasn't.

Just a weird fucked-up platonic date, because Aidan had decided in his head, where terrible ideas transformed into great ideas, that since Aidan and Mo were friends and Aidan and Dawson were friends, that *Mo and Dawson* should become friends.

While Dawson was neutral to *meh* on that particular idea, but he wasn't against it, either. Mostly, he was against the awkward, stilted first-date small talk that Aidan had whipped out. Like he had a pocket full of notecards filed with conversational openings.

When Dawson saw Levi at practice tomorrow, he was going to ask if he was right.

Dawson interrupted Aidan's in-depth analysis of the AFC North's playoff hopes, dotted with a few dry, impersonal comments comparing his own play to those four quarterbacks. "Dude," he said, "why didn't you bring Levi?"

Aidan shot him a pseudo-hurt look. "Why would I do that? This is a *friends* kind of dinner." He looked over at Mo, who only looked torn between amusement and resignation.

Dawson gave Morris Jeffries an appraising once-over. He didn't seem like a bad guy. It wasn't his fault that Aidan had been in love with him. Or that he hadn't wanted to get all up in Aidan's business. Dawson didn't want to either. Maybe Mo had also seen Aidan puke in a bush once. They'd been playing together long enough it seemed like a possibility.

"I can do things without my boyfriend," Aidan continued, complaining now. "I don't know why you think I can't. Or that I *shouldn't*. We have nice, healthy boundaries, we're so—"

"Trust me, we know what 'nice, healthy boundaries' you have," Dawson retorted.

Aidan rolled his eyes. "For the hundredth time, we were not *making out* in that storage closet. Levi had something in his eye. I was just helping him out."

"Being a real bro," Mo said pointedly.

Maybe Dawson could like this guy more than he'd thought he might.

"A real bro would've gotten on his knees," Dawson said.

Mo choked out a laugh, and Aidan looked torn between outrage and embarrassment.

"Do you ever take anything seriously?" Aidan hissed to Dawson.

Dawson picked up his green tea and wished that Aidan hadn't guilted him into getting this instead of a nice sake. They had a good list here.

"Lots of things," Dawson said. He'd taken Cam seriously last night. Had thought about it a dozen times today: Cam spread out on his bed, gorgeous and glowing, with Dawson's marks all over him.

"You're ridiculous," Aidan said, shaking his head. He looked over at Mo, like *can you believe this guy?*

"I don't know, he's kinda funny," Mo said.

Aidan made a half-grimace, like Mo liking Dawson hadn't been the whole point of this whole freaking exercise.

And if he hadn't been here, out in a dim corner of this sushi restaurant, maybe he'd have found a reason to head down a few floors and see if Cam was up for a repeat already.

He'd seemed into it this morning. Had looked disappointed when his phone had rung, and Dawson had felt the echo of it too, deep down.

"So, Mo, how's it been being back in Toronto?" Dawson said, deciding that if they were going to get through the next hour, he was going to need to make an effort. Otherwise, Aidan would probably whip out his notecards and make every single person at this table miserable, including himself.

"Wait a second," Mo said, straightening. "*How* did you say it?"

He exchanged a knowing look with Aidan.

"What?" Dawson was confused.

"You said it like *Toronto*." Mo said it normal. Exactly like Dawson had. Exactly like Dawson had expected it would be pronounced.

"And?"

Mo and Aidan exchanged another glance. "It's not . . .well, it's *Toronto*," Aidan said, a little apologetically.

"That's what I said," Dawson said.

"No, you pronounced the *t*," Aidan said, chuckling under his breath.

"Do you . . .not?"

"Not if you want to sound like you actually know what the fuck you're talking about," Mo said bluntly.

"Huh. Okay. So . . .*Toronto*?" Dawson slid the *n* right into the *o*, like the *t* didn't exist.

Aidan gave him a supportive nod. "Yeah. Better."

"Better," Mo agreed. "And yeah, it's good to be back. I never wanted to leave."

Aidan pursed his lips together. Dawson remembered when Aidan had lost his mind, acting in a completely uncharacteristic way, and had held out on his *own* contract, threatening not to play until the Thunder had given Mo his own matching contract.

But they hadn't and Mo had ended up going across the country instead, signing for tons of money with the Raiders.

"You shouldn't have had to," Aidan muttered under his breath. Probably still feeling some kind of way that his bid to keep his best friend around hadn't panned out.

"We've talked about this, dude," Mo said. "It was for the best, in the end." His expression turned sly, teasing. "I bet Levi would agree with me."

Aidan straight up blushed. Not something Dawson was used to yet. Maybe he'd never get used to it.

"Oh, that's so damn cute," Mo teased. "That's probably why he didn't bring Levi. He was worried he'd be bright fucking red the whole time."

"No, he didn't bring Levi 'cause he wants us to be friends," Dawson said to Mo.

Aidan flushed even redder, but before he could refute the accusation, Mo said, "Yeah, that was pretty obvious."

"It was not obvious," Aidan argued.

"Dude, you came prepared with icebreakers," Dawson said.

Mo laughed. "You told me he'd known you a long time. He does know you, Flynn."

"Oh, I *know* him," Dawson said.

"Is this going to be a whole thing now," Aidan complained, like again, this hadn't been his whole plan this whole fucking time. Of course, he probably hadn't intended for Mo and Dawson to become friendly by ganging up on *him.*

"Oh yeah," Mo said. "You knew him in college, yeah? At Michigan?"

"Yep," Dawson said. "Met our freshman year. Dorm living, baby."

"Daws," Aidan tried to interrupt again, but that was not happening.

"Oh, I bet you've got some good stories."

"Let me tell you about Halloween, sophomore year," Dawson said, leaning forward.

Mo was already smiling, anticipating how bad it was going to be.

"I can't believe you actually remember anything about that night. You were drunker than I was," Aidan grumbled.

"And yet I was *not* the one who spend half an hour in a bush, puking my guts out," Dawson said.

"Oh, man, you didn't." Mo laughed and smacked him on the shoulder. "Didn't realize you were such a partier back then."

"I wasn't," Aidan said at the same time that Dawson added, "Why do you think he puked for that long? He never partied. Too busy being a super responsible big bro."

"Fair," Mo said.

"Never drank tequila again," Aidan muttered.

"Smart man," Dawson said. "You can't handle it."

"Speaking of tequila," Mo said, turning to Dawson. "Your rookie alright today?"

Dawson froze a little. Then forced himself to relax. Mo had no idea what he and Cam had done last night. He only knew that Cam had joined Trevor and Lane for a round of tequila shots. And then a second round—Dawson had been watching, so he'd seen Mo take one too.

"I'm sure he's fine," Dawson said, like he hadn't been right there to witness every single bit of Cam's morning after. And he *had* been fine. Fine enough to wake up this morning and be totally into another round. Then there'd been that look in his eyes after breakfast, like if his phone hadn't rung, Cam would've been perfectly willing to go right back to bed.

Aidan raised an eyebrow. "You didn't check on him?"

Shit.

He'd played it too casual, and now Aidan was worried he'd left Cam out to dry.

"Of course I did." *Checked on him with my tongue in his mouth.*

"Daws," Aidan warned.

"Will you quit worrying about him like he's the next coming of Riley?" Dawson bitched. "He's a grown man. Perfectly capable of handling his own shit."

Perfectly capable of handling my *shit, too.*

"Unfair," Aidan argued.

And yes, it was a tiny bit unfair that he'd brought Aidan's little brother, Riley, into this. He knew what Aidan was like—how he *had* been, before he'd gotten his head out of his ass—about Riley.

"Hey, he's allowed to make one crack about Riley," Mo said. "You friend-matched us. And totally brainstormed conversational topics with Levi before you showed up tonight."

Aidan huffed. "You guys *should* be friends. And not just so you can gang up on me. I know I'm . . ." He shrugged. Like he didn't have to finish that particular sentence because both Dawson and Morris knew exactly how Aidan could be, better than just about anyone else.

"Ridiculous? Over-committed? Over-involved? The opposite of chill?" Mo smiled, like all of those things actually made him like Aidan better. And Dawson discovered he agreed. Those things were what made Aidan *Aidan*, and as much shit as Dawson gave him, one of the huge benefits of coming here and playing for the Thunder had been reuniting with his old college buddy again.

"Yeah, yeah, I know it." Aidan was smiling though. "Joke's on you, though, 'cause Levi actually likes those things about me."

"Proves he's a good guy who's worth you," Dawson said. He wondered what Mo would say. There'd been a time when Aidan had hoped that Morris might be that guy for him. But then Levi had come along and Aidan had realized he and Mo were much better as just friends.

"Couldn't agree more," Mo said, and his smile was both warm and completely genuine.

Aidan looked visibly relieved by this pronouncement.

And maybe it hadn't just been that Aidan thought he and Mo should be friends, but that he was still feeling out this new iteration of his friendship with Mo.

Dawson didn't think he'd ever been brought along as a buffer before. Probably because everyone on earth would know he'd be fucking terrible at it. But who else was Aidan going to bring? He couldn't bring Levi—that would have been more awkward, not less.

Dawson had been his only choice, but he still felt an unexpected surge of warmth towards his old friend.

"We're all so happy for you," Dawson said, reaching out and patting Aidan on the shoulder. "Finally growing up and falling in love."

"For real," Mo said and his gaze was soft and affectionate. Platonic affection, Dawson was relieved to realize.

They'd be okay. And maybe Aidan was actually right—though he'd never tell *him* that—and he and Mo could be friendly, too.

"You make it sound like I'm like your rookie," Aidan complained. "I'm thirty-three."

"Shhhh, dude, I don't know if I'd say it that loud," Dawson joked.

"God, you're the worst." But Aidan was smiling, looking not-very-secretly pleased at how this had all gone. "But seriously, you *did* make sure our new punter got home safe, in one piece? Made sure he was still alive this morning, right?"

Dawson sighed. Maybe this was inevitable. "Don't be weird about it, okay?"

Aidan's face morphed into an expression that made it crystal clear just how weird he was going to be about it. "You didn't. While he was drunk?" he hissed.

"Oh my God, he was *not* drunk." Dawson was not going to go into the exact ways he'd known that. But suffice it to say, the excellence of Cam's hand-eye coordination had made that clear enough.

"Dude, congrats," Mo said, and he raised his fist for a quick bump.

Aidan glowered. "Don't encourage him. Cameron is young. Naive. Worships the ground Dawson walks on."

"I know. It's pretty great." Dawson said it flippantly, but he meant it seriously, too. Because it wasn't just Cam's hero worship that was a balm on his wounded pride, but his relentless positivity, too. All that sunshine lighting up the dark shadowy corners of his mind.

"Daws," Aidan said, frowning. "I *mean* it. Don't fuck him up, okay?"

"Don't fuck him up or don't fuck him? 'Cause I'm only interested in one of those, and it can't be a freaking mystery which it is."

He'd known Aidan was going to be stupid about this, and so far he'd delivered on every expectation. But Dawson imagined that if he'd found out later—it would've been so much worse. There had to be some bonus for Dawson being at least reasonably upfront about this. He wasn't hiding anything, because there wasn't anything to hide. Nothing to be ashamed of. Cam was a friend and they were just enjoying each other. Having some much-needed fun.

"I wanna know how it went down," Mo said, surprising Dawson.

Here Aidan was, scowling like an angry cat, and Mo was actually encouraging Dawson to talk about it. Maybe he'd dismissed Mo too easily.

"It wasn't exactly a secret he was interested," Dawson said.

"God, your ego," Aidan muttered under his breath.

"Because he *told* me," Dawson continued, shooting Aidan a smug grin. "Anyway, we were walking home, and he was being all sweet and sunshine-y and shit. You know how he is, *everything's gonna work out, Daws!* and well . . .I can only resist so much." Dawson shrugged.

"Unbelievable." Aidan had the nerve to morph from an offended cat to a scandalized grandmother. Dawson was going to send Levi a text to tell him that whatever he'd been doing to unbend Aidan was clearly an ongoing process, and he should put his back into it, still.

"*He* kissed *me*, what was I supposed to do? Turn him down? He was into it. I was into it. Don't tell me I need to draw you a diagram on how that goes," Dawson said.

"I would've said yes, but then there's Levi," Mo said frankly. "And that guy does *not* need a diagram."

Aidan went brick red again. "I'm not going to let you distract me with your comments about Levi, okay? Do I need to talk to him?"

"To Cam? About what?" Dawson knew Aidan would probably be like this. But there was still a whisper of unease that rocked through him. Did Aidan, one of his longest friends, actually think that he was no good for anyone? It was one thing for *him* to worry about it, in the dark solitude of his empty apartment. It was another entirely for a semi-objective third party to suggest it might be true.

"Dude," Mo said, before Aidan could answer. "They're hot for each other. Let them fuck it out. They don't need a freaking intervention."

"Mo," Aidan chided, more gently. Because this was Mo, and he probably always would have a soft spot for the guy. Purely platonic now, but still *soft*.

"Did you stage an intervention when Ri got together with Landry?"

"No, but he wanted to," Dawson said, because he was still smarting from Aidan's comments.

"I did *not*," Aidan protested. "I just wanted him to have someone good for him, and Landry's one of the best guys I know. I was always happy for them."

That uneasy feeling in the base of Dawson's stomach grew.

"Please, *please* do not tell me you're going to suggest Daws here isn't a good guy, 'cause I barely know him but I'm gonna throw down for him, anyway." Mo shot Aidan a steely look, born of long knowledge of Aidan's bullshit.

"No, no, no. Of course not." Aidan said it hurriedly, shooting Dawson an apologetic look that soothed over most—if not all—of the sting. "I didn't mean it like that, Daws. Just . . .I know you're still hurting. And that kind of hero worship, it feels good, right?"

"'Course it does," Dawson agreed. "But that's not all it is. Not anymore."

He'd known that, too, of course. It was why the Bad Idea had morphed into a Less-Bad Idea.

"What do you mean?" Aidan asked, but at least he'd downshifted from *demanding* to *genuine curiosity*.

"We're friends now. And now we're friends who're hooking up." Aidan's face did something complicated and Dawson had to add, "And that's *okay*. We're both good with it. We talked it over."

"Less hot," Mo said.

"Don't encourage him, okay?" Aidan said wryly.

"Just saying. Having a long-drawn-out discussion when you're supposed to be getting naked? Kind of a boner killer."

"Oh, we did it *before* we got naked," Dawson said. "After the security guard caught us making out in the basement of that big shiny gold bank building."

"Oh my God," Aidan muttered.

"It was raining, so we took the PATH. It wasn't like I'm regularly in the habit of making out in public places," Dawson retorted.

"I don't care where you were," Aidan said.

"Reminder: you were making out with *your* boyfriend in that closet," Mo said. "At *work*, nonetheless."

"For the millionth time, he had something in his eye."

"Or in his pants," Dawson crowed.

The waiter arrived then with their sushi. Aidan looked torn between indignation and relief that maybe he might get out of this whole conversation.

They shifted into small talk—talking about their next opponent, the Titans—and how spicy this wasabi was, and how Dawson still had his Iowan white-farm-boy palate. They finished eating, and Mo went to the bathroom after Aidan had grabbed the check.

"Hey," he said, glancing up at Dawson as he finished filling out the credit card slip, "don't freak out, okay?"

"Oh, God," Dawson said, exhaling hard. "What is it now?"

"No, no, it's not bad. Shit." Aidan made a face. "I'm not doing this right. I just want to say I didn't mean to be so judgmental about you and Cam. You've got a good head on your shoulders—"

"Maybe last year," Dawson inserted.

"No," Aidan said, shaking his head. "No, you do *now*. What happened last year had nothing to do with who you are as a person, Daws. Brynn wanting to leave and her dad stealing—that wasn't *you*. That was all them. And what happened after? Anyone would've gone through it. You just had to do it in front of the whole fucking NFL."

Dawson took a deep breath, his throat suddenly tight. "Right."

"I'm just saying, you're a good person. Not *were*. *Are*. And if you're starting something with Cam, even if it's casual, then you know what you're doing."

"Do I?" Dawson questioned.

Aidan shot him a suffering look. "You told me yourself. You guys are friends. You've got chemistry. Who am I to say that it's a bad idea that you hook up? You're smart. Too smart to make a stupid mistake."

"Nobody's too smart to make a stupid mistake when their dick is involved," Dawson observed.

Aidan huffed. "Dude, I'm trying to tell you it's okay. Stop playing devil's advocate here."

Dawson knew it, though he wasn't just doing it for Aidan's sake, but his own. Still, whenever he thought about last night, regret was the last thing he felt.

Instead, all he experienced was an undeniable eagerness to do it again, as soon as possible.

"Okay," Dawson said. Because he was going to do it again, and he *didn't* want to feel guilty about it.

"Good." Aidan gave him a nod and, as they got up from the table, a quick hug. "Don't forget that, okay?"

As Dawson walked back to his building, he couldn't help *but* think about it.

Sure, Dawson had an empty apartment waiting for him. But Cam's apartment was almost certainly empty too. They didn't *have* to be alone, now. They got along great. Dawson thought he could even hang out in companionable silence with Cam. And the sex had been *hot*, with indicators pointing towards it getting even better the more comfortable they became with each other.

Before he could overthink it, he pulled out his phone. **You around?** he sent.

CHAPTER 12

CAM WAS SLUMPED ON his couch, movie playing on the TV, but he wasn't watching it.

He was staring at his phone, trying not to be a creeper as he attempted to justify texting Dawson.

It's been less than twelve hours.

But he looked like he didn't even want you to go.

Normally, Cam wouldn't have overthought this. If he'd wanted to text, he'd have texted. Said something casual and simple. Not *u up?* but something similar, maybe.

Sure, Dawson was a teammate, but he'd hooked up with teammates before. It had *still* never felt as loaded as it did with him.

Maybe it was the way he'd woken up and the first thing he'd seen had been Dawson's face, toothpaste still crusted in the corner of his lips. Hazel eyes bright and delighted that Cam was still here, still in his bed.

That was some permanently brain-altering shit. Or else, it seemed like it was, because here was Cam, obsessing over composing the perfect text that might draw Dawson down to his apartment.

"Fuck it," Cam said, and began to type out, **your apt is probably just as empty as mine. you wanna—**

But before he could finish typing, a text appeared above it. A text from Dawson. **You around?**

Cam legitimately dropped his phone on the couch in surprise and then scrambled to pick it back up again. Had he? He *had*.

Cam sucked in a hard breath. Shit. Shit. *Shit.*

Yeah, he sent back. Then stupidly hit *send* before he could add more. Now he was going to double text, like a doofus. But then, Dawson was old. He might not know how bad double texting was. So he added, **In my apartment.**

Then groaned out loud, because that was even worse. He was going to have to add another one.

Triple texting. Everyone Cam had ever known was going to be embarrassed by him right now.

587, he sent next.

Five minutes later, Cam had barely had time to check his hair in the mirror before there was a knock on the door.

He took a deep breath, trying to calm his racing heart, telling himself that this didn't *mean* anything, only that Dawson was probably horny and lonely—same as him—and went to open it.

Dawson was dressed in a smart wool coat, the shoulders and the crown of his head dusted with droplets of rain, and dark jeans. He looked good enough to eat, and here Cam was in a ratty pair of ancient gray sweatpants and an even more ancient Western T-shirt.

"Hey," Cam said, trying to sound normal about this as he opened the door wider, letting Dawson in.

Dawson walked in and shot Cam a smirk. "Triple texting, dude?"

Cam flushed warm. "Guess you're not *that* old."

Giving him a look, Dawson gave the apartment a vague look around. "Not *that* old," he confirmed, his smirk deepening as he unbuttoned his coat and hung it up, right next to Cam's. Setting his shoes right next to Cam's sneakers. He was wearing a dark blue button-up underneath, the sleeves rolled up to expose a very nice pair of forearms.

No question, there was a part of Cam that wanted to lead him right to the bedroom—their apartments were laid out the same way, so Dawson would know where it was—but before he could, Dawson wandered into the living room.

"What are you watching?" Dawson asked, taking a seat on the couch right where Cam had been sitting.

"Uh, one of the *Fast and Furious* movies. It was on," Cam said. Not that he'd been watching it. He'd been glued to his phone instead, trying to figure out how to get Dawson here.

Well, now Dawson was here. Sitting on *his* couch, looking up expectantly at Cam.

"Never seen them," Dawson said.

"Seriously? *Seriously?*" Cam told himself not to get distracted, but it was hard, because he'd thought, more than once, that Dawson was old—not *gross* kind of old, but clueless kind of old—but this proved it.

"What?" Dawson was grinning, like Cam's incredulity was cute.

"They're more *your* generation," Cam teased as he sat down next to Dawson, "but they're classics. Kind of like someone else I know."

Dawson was still smiling. "Been a little busy the last couple of years."

"*Still*," Cam said.

"And hey, you call me old one more time, I'm gonna have to prove the opposite." Dawson leaned in, and it was so easy to close the gap between them. Like it was the most natural thing in the world.

Dawson's mouth opened under his and they kissed for a long moment before Cam leaned back.

"You know, you kinda kiss like an old person," Cam joked.

Dawson's eyes lit up, and a second later, Cam was being pushed backwards on the couch, Dawson's thigh hot and heavy between his legs, his tongue in Cam's mouth.

He might be shorter but Dawson was heavier, surprisingly muscled for a kicker, and Cam went limp under his weight as Dawson tangled a hand in his hair and twisted his head at precisely the perfect angle to keep kissing.

"Been thinking of this all day," Dawson panted into his mouth. "All fucking day."

Cam's cock kicked in his sweatpants. "Shit. Me too." He'd thought it would be really freaking amazing if he could convince Dawson to come to his place tonight. But Dawson wanting it just as badly as him, wanting it badly enough that he'd been the one to reach out? Cam felt like he was floating on cloud nine.

Dawson pulled back, his dark pupils swallowing up almost all of the hazel. "You're so . . ." He trailed off, hand that wasn't supporting him cupping Cam's cheek.

"So?" Cam prompted, even though he wasn't sure he could hear what Dawson thought of him, without his cock—his heart—his soul—exploding.

But instead of answering, Dawson just groaned under his breath and kissed Cam again, like he couldn't stay away from his lips for longer than a moment.

They made out for a few minutes, the pleasure spiraling through Cam as he imagined all the different ways they might get off together. But one thought kept overriding all the others. Something he wanted so badly he nearly burned with it.

It was tough, but he broke apart, pressing another absent kiss against Dawson's neck. He smelled so good. Like citrus and the spiced cookies that his dad always baked at the holidays.

"Hmm?" Dawson murmured. He was staring at Cam like he'd give him anything he wanted, and so it was easier than he'd expected to voice exactly what he craved.

"Would you uh . . .be interested in um . . ."

Dawson raised an eyebrow. "Yeah?"

"Fuck me," Cam whispered. Not a question, but a statement. A declaration.

Dawson didn't look surprised or disgusted. "Yeah? You want that?"

It wasn't tough to nod his head. "Yeah. *Yeah*. Um, yeah."

"Oh God, yeah." Dawson rubbed a hand over his head. "Baby, you don't gotta even ask." Then he grinned suddenly. "Not that you actually *asked*."

Cam flushed and reached behind him to pull his T-shirt off. The moment it hit the floor, his fingers found the buttons on Dawson's shirt, plucking them open one by one.

"Wait, *here*?" Dawson asked incredulously as Cam tried to reach around to shuck Dawson's shirt off, now that it was finally unbuttoned.

"Why not?" Cam's mouth ended up on Dawson's neck again, sucking a mark into his pulse point. If Daws could leave marks on *him*, then he could return the favor.

"Um, *well*," Dawson muttered.

"Lube's in the drawer in the coffee table," Cam said.

Dawson froze. "*What*?"

Cam squirmed under Dawson's weight, pressing him into the couch. "Do I need to give you directions? A map? I kinda thought you'd want to take point here."

Sitting up, Dawson gazed at him incredulously. "*No*. I don't need directions or a fucking map, and I sure as hell am gonna fuck you. But, you, *you*—"

Cam ordered himself to not be self-conscious or to feel exposed by Dawson's gaze. Or what he was about to make him admit.

"Thought about it, okay? In the shower, this afternoon, and I thought, maybe." Cam shook his head like he was trying to clear it. But his dick was so hard, and he just wanted Dawson to *take* him.

"But *I* texted *you*," Dawson said, in the exact same way Cam had said last night, *I kissed you*.

"Might've been about to do it myself," Cam admitted quietly.

"Shit," Dawson said and stumbled backwards getting up. For a split second, Cam thought he'd pushed too far, too hard, but then he realized Dawson was shucking his jeans off and yanking the drawer in the coffee table open. He made a satisfied noise in the back of his throat and then he leaned over Cam again. That smirk was back in full force, and Cam groaned as Dawson palmed over his hard cock and then tugged his sweatpants down.

"I'm gonna fuck you into this couch," Dawson said in a low, determined voice. "And then I'm gonna fuck you into your mattress, next."

Cam's breath caught in his throat. There was no air in this room, and then there was even less of it when Dawson leaned over, kissed him hard, and then slid his hand between his thighs.

Knew the moment Dawson discovered why he'd been thinking about it in the shower.

"Oh fuck, you didn't . . .you *did*." Dawson groaned into Cam's mouth as he kissed him harder. Two of his slicked-up fingers sliding into him easily.

"Was thinking if I hadn't left this morning," Cam panted. The pleasure was fizzing through him now, bubbles exploding under his skin. Turned out that Dawson's fingers were even better than his own; even better than in the fantasies he'd spun this afternoon.

"Didn't want you to go either," Dawson admitted in a low, wrecked voice.

If Cam was thinking—which he was *not*—he might admit that this was not like any other hookup he'd ever had. It was so intimate, Dawson breathing in his mouth, two fingers buried deep in him, moving perfectly like this wasn't the first time they'd ever done this.

"Come on," Cam begged.

But Dawson didn't move. Well, he did. His fingers were working him so good, and then there was a third one, Cam nearly choking on the feeling as they slid inside.

"Not yet. I'm enjoying myself," Dawson said. He paused. "And you are too. I can tell. God, the way you're taking me. I can't—" He bit off the rest of his sentence, a low groan escaping him.

Cam was usually above begging. He usually didn't *have* to beg.

But Dawson was making him crazy enough that he might do anything. Say anything. Be anything that Dawson asked for.

"Could take you better," Cam muttered, digging his heels into Dawson's back.

"Yeah? Okay. *Yeah.*" Dawson shuffled backwards and twisted his fingers one last time, the pads stroking his spot just right, and Cam's cock twitched against his abs.

"Yes, *please*," Cam said.

Dawson gazed down at him. "No condom?" he asked.

"Don't need it. Bet you don't either," Cam said.

Dawson nodded. "Yeah. No. I've been tested. And you too?"

Pulling him in, Cam murmured against his mouth. "Come on, Daws. I know you want to."

Groaning deeply, Dawson nodded and lined up, pushing in slowly.

Ever since Dawson had arrived in Toronto, this had been a satisfying and reoccurring fantasy. Dawson's cock carving out the perfect place inside him, deep and real and true. But somehow the reality was even better, leaving him panting and weak-limbed, only able to lie there on his couch and take it as Dawson began to fuck into him with slow, even thrusts.

"Shit, baby, you feel so good," Dawson said, head hanging down, hair in his eyes. Cam reached out and tangled his fingers in it, pushing it back so he could see Dawson's face, and that made it even better. Everything was white hot and electric as Dawson found the angle that made him cry out and then pushed and pushed and pushed him.

Cam was aware of how much stupid nonsense he was babbling, but he couldn't stop, it all spilling out of his mouth in a torrent, the pleasure unlocking something inside him.

He gripped Dawson's shoulders and just didn't care. Rode it out.

"Gonna," Dawson panted what could have been a minute or an hour later. Cam felt so good he could float here, almost forever, he thought, Dawson's cock a perfect weight inside him.

He wanted to come, but he didn't *need* to come.

They could just keep going like this, forever.

But then Dawson sped up, thrusting fast and hard, and suddenly that need rose to the surface.

Cam reached for his cock and gave himself a stroke and then another, barely touching himself, because he knew it wasn't going to take much. Sex had been good, but it had never felt like this before. It would be so easy to get addicted to this feeling, and Cam didn't think he was alone. Dawson's face was creased and slack, eyes rolling behind his head as he gave one last thrust and then he shook, coming hard.

He only needed one last touch to follow, cock twitching in his hand as he unloaded onto his own stomach, clenching around Dawson's cock as they both came down from their orgasms.

Cam flopped back onto the couch, panting.

"God," Dawson said and carefully bracing himself on the back of the couch, pulled out. He chuckled under his breath. "We're definitely . . .uh . . .going to make a mess."

Cam felt a throb of satisfaction deep down at the thought they *could*. "Grab my T-shirt. That'll work for the worst of the cleanup."

Leaning down, Dawson did, haphazardly wiping up most of the mess from Cam's stomach and between his legs.

Once that was done, he let the fabric fall back to the floor, and before Cam could suggest that he come back down with him, Dawson was already doing it, cuddling up close, an arm slung casually across Cam's chest.

"Damn, that was so good," Dawson murmured, reaching up a bit so he could press a kiss to one of the marks on Cam's collarbone that he'd made last night. "You have the best ideas."

"Your idea to come over," Cam said, and that was still something he was going to reach for whenever he felt sad or lonely.

"Your idea earlier." Dawson's fingers curled into Cam's skin. Like they wanted to dig in and not let go. Honestly, Cam would let him. Cam was beginning to think he'd let him do anything he wanted.

"Fifty-fifty on the credit," Cam suggested.

"Sixty-forty. Sixty to you, 'cause the fucking was your idea." Dawson snorted, and it was so cute he could barely stand it. He was that particular combination of snarky-sexy-cute that seemed to be the perfect key to Cam's lock. Maybe that was why the sex was so good.

Maybe that was why he was beginning to wonder if he'd ever get enough.

"I'll take it," Cam said.

They were both quiet for a long minute.

Then Dawson spoke up again. "Had dinner with Aidan and Mo tonight."

"How was that?"

Dawson snorted again. "Kind of horrible. Kind of awkward. But it got better. Mo seems like a good guy."

"Yeah?"

"*He's* never seen Aidan puke in a bush," Dawson said. "But despite that, they seem like pretty good friends. Good enough that Mo had no issue helping me gang up on him."

"I will never get used to that," Cam said honestly.

"Yeah, you will. One day you'll walk into the locker room and Aidan Flynn will just be another guy on your team."

For a split second, Cam considered asking if that was how Dawson wanted Cam to see *him*. Just another guy on the team. A guy he hooked up with sometimes. A teammate he worked with on the field. That he could shoot the shit with. But that in a year or two or five, he'd barely remember.

But Cam didn't, because he wasn't sure he'd like the answer.

"But," Dawson added, and Cam could feel him grinning even though he couldn't see it, "you'd better *never* see me as just another guy in the locker room, rook."

Cam let out an unsteady breath. He hadn't asked, but he hadn't *had* to ask. "I don't think we're in any danger of that happening."

"Didn't think so," Dawson said smugly.

Maybe he'd never been in a relationship before, but Cam *had* had a decent number of hookups in his life, and it had never felt like this with any of them. Even the regular friend with benefits he'd had his junior year at Western had been totally different.

Maybe he needed to stop being so worried about freaking Dawson out, no matter what he said, because he seemed right there with Cam—no hesitation and no pulling away.

Cam relaxed into his arms. At least until Dawson said, "I told him about us, by the way."

"What?" Cam flailed, until Dawson wrapped his arms around Cam until he went still.

"Don't freak out," Dawson said. Chuckled. "Guess I should've led with that part. It's cool. Aidan's cool."

Cam craned his head so he could look Dawson in the eye. Shoot him a look because he already knew the truth. Aidan was *Aidan,* but Cam also didn't really think he'd ever been cool a day in his life.

"Okay, fair. Aidan's not usually cool. But he was cool about this. At least after I reassured him that I didn't take advantage of you."

"Seriously?" Cam squawked. "He thought you would? He thought you *could*?"

"Warned me off you and everything. But that was stupid and I told him that."

Cam wished he wasn't so quick to blush, because he was bright fucking red right now. "He *didn't.*"

"Tomorrow you should definitely tell him how shitty that was," Dawson said.

"Ha. *No.* Just . . .oh my God. He was *worried* about me?"

Dawson smacked him on the arm. "Stop it. You're making me jealous."

And that was something Cam was going to have to unpack. Later, though. "I just don't *get* it. I'm fine. I didn't need—why *did* he?"

"Good fucking question. The easiest answer I can give you is that you've met plenty of older brothers in your life, but you've never met an older brother who older brothers like Aidan does. Is he better than he used to be? Sure, yeah, absolutely. But it's like he saw you, saw some of Riley in you, and it was like he couldn't help himself. But he agrees that it was ridiculous."

Cam didn't know what to do with all of that. "He did?"

"Well. Yes. *He* didn't use that exact wording—"

"No? I can't imagine why," Cam teased.

"Shut up, you," Dawson said affectionately, voice gooey and fond. Something else for Cam to unpack on his next sleepless night. "But I pointed out that you know what you're doing, and I *definitely* know what I'm doing—"

"Modest, too." It was impossible not to keep teasing, not when Dawson reacted like that. Like he was offended but also delighted. And every time Cam made Dawson smile like that, it was like someone handed him a gold fucking medal.

"Are you telling this or am I?" Dawson asked archly.

"If you'd get on with it, you are," Cam said.

Dawson laughed and tucked him more firmly into his embrace.

"Anyway, I made sure he knew that this wasn't just because you worshipped the ground I walked on. Being older and amazing, the way I am."

It was impossible for Cam to hold back his cackle. "Oh, sure."

"He was very reassured by this."

"Can I worship for the way you fuck me into the mattress?" Cam wondered.

Dawson's fingers stroked up his arm, all the way up to his shoulder, tracing the tendon of his neck. "Not gonna stop you."

"So he's not gonna like . . .freak out on me?"

"On you? Nah. But, rook, he was always going to freak out on *me*. That's why I told him. I didn't want to hide it—hide *you*—like some dirty secret. This way he knows and he knows the score and it won't be an issue later, if he pulls his head out of Levi's ass and realizes what's going on."

"Am I supposed to be blowing you up for that, too?" Cam wondered.

Dawson made a faux-outraged sound. "I don't know how Aidan ever thought that you had any kind of hero worship going."

"I do," Cam said. Because he *had*. But it was more than that, now. He knew it. He'd known it, even before he kissed Dawson last night. They were friends—more, too, but Cam shied away from identifying exactly what that *more* was. It was fine and plenty enough for now that he knew the *more* existed. And more than enough that they were lying here, like this.

"You're cute," Dawson said drowsily. "You wanna go to bed?"

Cam did. But he also knew he'd be regretting it tomorrow if they did what he'd suggested earlier. Running was already going to be a bit of a challenge.

But if he said he wasn't interested in round two, would Dawson leave? Cam didn't really want Dawson to leave.

"Uh, yeah. Yeah, we can do that." Maybe he could suggest he give Dawson a blowjob to stick around.

But then Dawson was crawling over Cam's body, still naked, and offering him a hand to help him up.

"I know what you said," Dawson said, "but uh, we can just . . .sleep? If you want. Or I could go back—"

"No, don't go," Cam said, and for a second he had a bad moment that he'd said too much, but Dawson's expression softened. "And yeah, I'm good with that. Let's just go to bed."

Dawson smiled. Slung an arm around Cam's shoulders. "Bed it is," he said. "You got a toothbrush for me, rook?"

Nobody would ever know, because he was *not* going to be telling Dawson that he'd popped down to the corner drugstore to pick up a handful of brand-new toothbrushes just in case he worked up the nerve to ask Dawson to come over. Just in case he worked up that nerve and about ten more—Dawson coming over and then Dawson actually *wanting* to stay.

But he shouldn't have worried, because Dawson was the one who'd texted. Dawson who'd invited himself over. Dawson himself suggesting that he wanted to stay.

"Yeah," Cam said. "I got one for you, Daws."

Dawson smiled, unexpectedly soft and sweet, and Cam let go of another bit of the worry he'd been carrying around all day. It *wasn't* just him.

He wasn't alone in this.

CHAPTER 13

"ROOK WAS A LITTLE slow today, but faster than yesterday," Marty said knowingly, tilting his head towards where Cam had just wrapped up his jog around the edge of the field with Joey.

Dawson looked up from where he was stretching. Tried not to flush.

Yesterday, after practice Nate had noticed the marks littering Cam's torso and had made a few joking comments and then Mo had joined in.

Aidan had shot both of them a look, but the damage had been done, and everyone in the room—and then probably everyone in the building—knew that the rookie had been hooking up. Not with Dawson necessarily, but anyone who had been paying any kind of attention probably knew it was him.

And Marty was too observant, and had been doing this for way too long, to not guess the truth.

Dawson had assumed that he might've dodged the inevitable yesterday, but now Marty was giving him the kind of look that spoke volumes about how he hadn't escaped at all.

"Are you gonna lecture me about this like Aidan did?" Dawson wondered.

Marty's eyebrow skidded upwards. "Aidan lectured you?"

"Warned me? Lectured me?" Dawson shrugged. "I'm not gonna fuck the rookie up."

"Never thought you would," Marty said.

"I guess it *was* you who wanted me and Cam to get closer."

"Oh, it's 'cause of what *I* said now?" Marty chuckled. "I told you to hang out with him. That's all." But he didn't look upset or disappointed. He actually looked . . .well, if Dawson was going to call it anything, he would say Marty looked absolutely *not* surprised.

"Yeah, yeah. You probably guessed this was gonna happen." Marty probably had. Cam's crush had been visible from space.

But he wasn't sure how Marty had known that Dawson, when he finally started seeing the rookie, would figure out that once he started noticing him, he wouldn't be able to stop.

"I don't know if I'd go that far. But I thought you two would find some kind of common ground," Marty admitted. "Glad to see you did."

"Yeah, yeah," Dawson said, but he *was* glad. He liked to think that even without Marty's prompting, he'd have noticed Cam eventually, but he was glad it hadn't taken him *that* long. Because it not only felt great to be having regular sex again, but he hadn't even realized how much he'd missed having someone around he really liked. Someone to make laugh. Someone's space to share. Someone to text when his apartment was feeling particularly empty.

"Let's kick some balls," Marty said. "Actually—let's do the ladder."

"Ugh, the ladder." Dawson made a face.

The ladder was a particularly nefarious invention of Marty's where Dawson had to kick three field goals each at graduated intervals, starting at twenty-five yards and moving back five yards every time. Each time he missed, he had to do twenty pushups.

It wasn't so bad from twenty-five yards to the fifty or so. But after? The last time that Dawson had done the ladder, by the time he'd gotten to the sixty-five-yard field goal, his arms had felt like they were gonna fall off.

And *then*, Marty always wanted him to work back the other way.

"The ladder's good for you. You're gonna appreciate it, later. And I'm sure the rookie will too."

"Ugh, I regret you finding out about that."

Marty grinned. "If you've got time to sex up the rookie, you've got time to put in the work on the field, Hall."

"I hate you," Dawson said. But he grabbed a ball and a tee from the bin by the bench and headed out onto the field. They were working on the smaller field today, away from the rest of the team.

Set up his first field goal. Hit those three. One after another after another.

Moved back another five feet. Hit another three, right through the center of the uprights.

Thirty-five yards. Same thing. Forty, and it was still easy.

He misjudged one of the three on the forty-five-yard length but it still barely sneaked inside the left upright.

Fifty, still money.

Marty made some noise about how it was only going to get harder from here, and Dawson already knew that.

Still, he was deep in the zone, totally locked in, and nailed the three fifty-five-yard field goals. Barely heard Marty as he clapped when the third one went in.

Dawson set up for the first sixty-yard attempt. Took a big breath and then another. This was a long field goal, even for him. He'd only made one sixty-yarder in a game. Could make them more easily in practice, especially kicking off a tee, but that didn't mean they were *easy*.

It was a long way, and with the longer distance he had to put a lot more force into the kick, and with that additional force came a stronger chance that his aim wouldn't be as solid.

Dawson eyed the uprights, sixty yards away, and did his mental calculations. Felt pretty good about them, but despite his best efforts, his first attempt went slightly wonky, clanking against the right upright, and flying off, making it his first miss.

Reluctantly, he got down on the ground. The first twenty pushups weren't so bad. But even if his arms weren't aching now, he knew just how much they'd be aching by the time Dawson was done with this hellish exercise.

Thankfully, he made the next two field goals, even at sixty, and then he moved on to sixty-five. He nailed the first, and then missed the next two, and by the time he was done with *those* pushups, he was mentally flogging Marty for ever having been born.

He hadn't even noticed that Cam had wandered over, but after he finished the second set of sixty-yarders (missed one, got two—the second one barely cleared the bottom bar, but even though Marty made noise about it, Dawson decided he could fuck right off), he was startled when he heard Cam's voice behind him.

"Looking good," Cam said.

Dawson flicked his glance behind him and made a face. "If you're here to say anything about my pushup form . . ."

"Oh, I'm not," Cam said. He pulled even with Dawson, like he'd decided it was okay to occupy Dawson's space bubble.

Normally, when he did this, Dawson didn't *want* anybody in his space. God knew he'd complained to Marty enough times at the beginning of the season about Cam approaching him on the sideline.

But somehow, when Dawson hadn't been paying attention, Cam had become the exception to the rule. Maybe not on the *sideline*, but here at practice? It almost felt right to have Cam's attention on him.

"How's it going?" Cam asked.

"Marty's a sadist, that's how it's going," Dawson complained.

"Only caught a few misses." Cam hummed under his breath. "But then, I don't know if the stick is the best way to motivate you."

"What, you wanna be the carrot?" Dawson said it as a joke, but his pulse jumped anyway.

Cam shrugged, but the smile he shot him was full of mischief. "Why not?"

"Daws!" Marty called out. "Stop taking a break. Your arms aren't gonna fall off." He hesitated. "Probably!"

Cam tilted his head in closer. Murmured, "How about for every one you make over fifty yards, I'll give you a blowjob?"

Dawson knew what was coming, but he still choked on air. "I've got *six* more field goals over fifty yards."

But Cam just batted his eyelashes innocently. "Yeah? Well, you'd better get to it."

He wasn't even sure Cam was wrong—a blowjob for a successful field goal might be better motivation than pushups for a miss—but he should have expected how his pulse raced, his mind already drifting to how it might happen. How it might feel. Cam's mouth, tight and hot and wet and so fucking perfect, around him.

Predictably, even though he gave himself a long moment to regain his focus, a few deep breaths to try to even his breathing out, on the first fifty-five-yarder, the ball sailed right past the left upright.

"Damn," Dawson muttered under his breath. He dropped down and counted to twenty as his arms shook through another set of pushups.

When he lifted himself back up, he caught a flash of a knowing smile on Cam's face. But that wasn't what made his whole body heat. It was the subtle five fingers Cam flashed him.

Okay. He was going to focus in. There was no way he was going to give Cam a reason to give him a *four* next. He had this.

He was so locked in, body falling back on the mechanics he'd been drilling into it for the last fifteen years, he barely noticed when he finished fifty-five and went on to fifty.

Cam might've made some kind of approving noise as the first of his fifty-yarders went between the uprights. Marty definitely said something, but Dawson couldn't be fucked to figure out what it was. He was getting this shit *done*.

He'd known, because the way they were with each other made it obvious, that the sex with Cam was going to continue. It was too good to quit, and even if it hadn't been, he wouldn't have *wanted* to stop. But the fact that Cam was making these kinds of promises—

No. He cut that thought off hard and fast. He had one more to get. More than that, of course, because he still had to work his way back down to twenty-five yards, but one more that *counted*. One more that Cam had promised him a reward for.

Dawson lined up, but the focused zone he'd dropped into before was hard to find, and he thought he got close, but still, with his body growing tired from the strain of so many long kicks, it just barely missed.

"Shit." Dawson exhaled sharply. He looked over at Cam, but his grin hadn't dimmed, and sure enough, he flashed him four fingers.

Four wasn't six, but it wasn't anything to sneeze at either, and the thought of it, all that pleasure, got him through the next set of pushups.

Dawson couldn't say the thoughts of Cam going to his knees again—*four more times*, even—completely eliminated the exhausted shake of his arms as he finished the last pushup of the set and stood, but they didn't hurt, either.

"Come on, Hall, finish up strong," Marty called out encouragingly.

It wasn't easy, but Dawson pulled the remainder of his focus tight around him, and even though his whole body was tired, finished the rest of the ladder with no more misses.

He didn't let himself relax, even though anything under thirty-five was a cinch, until the last twenty-five-yarder went through the uprights.

"Good job," Marty said, coming up to him. Dawson fist-bumped him tiredly. "Little uneven in spots, but a good effort."

Dawson made a face. He wasn't about to tell Marty why a certain section had been both easier *and* harder.

"Eh," Dawson said. He could've focused harder. He could've probably made one more than he had. But like Marty said, it was a pretty decent effort and he wasn't going to beat himself up about it.

"You're getting there, kid." Marty patted him on the shoulder. "Good practice. Take a load off, okay?"

Dawson nodded absently. He didn't disagree. Could he be better? Sure, he could always be better. But he was handling this shit better than he had during the summer.

The first time Marty had ever made him do this, the second day of training camp, he'd missed a hell of a lot more, the fatigue and soreness in his arms distracting him from what he was doing with his form.

After, when he'd slumped down on the bench, emptied out with exhaustion and frustration, Marty had put a hand on his knee and explained, matter-of-factly, without an ounce of sympathy, that the ladder trained you to empty the mind of distractions.

Dawson had experienced two simultaneous thoughts: *one*, he was really fucking glad Marty hadn't seemed to feel sorry for him, because that might've been the straw that broke the camel's back, and *two*, that he'd truly believed before that his focus *was* solid. That he was better than any other kicker in the NFL at putting it all aside and doing his job.

But then, he'd realized later, when he'd lain on his couch, ice packs strapped to every limb, that either he'd gotten complacent, or that had never really been true. Because if it had been, then the prior season wouldn't have gone the way it did. If he was right, he'd still be in Baltimore, not alone on a cheap IKEA couch in an empty apartment in Toronto.

Dawson couldn't say that was the turning point, but he looked back and that was the first moment he'd really wanted to fight to get his career back. His *life* back.

After he dragged himself into the locker room and changed, taking his sweet time under the hot water of the shower, there was nothing more he wanted than to go home and collapse back on that same couch. Order takeout. Veg out in front of the TV and hope that he might still be able to raise his arms tomorrow.

Abstractedly, he knew that he and Cam had carpooled this morning, but him coming up to Dawson after he finished dressing was a nudge that not only wasn't it up to him, he *had* plans.

"Come on," he told Cam, "let's go grab some dinner."

"Yeah?" Cam looked eager, like a puppy. "Where at? Are we exploring again?"

He wouldn't have said that his plan for the night was particularly elaborate. A noodle place that Nate had recommended, and then back to one of their places. Maybe some reciprocal blowjobs. Falling into bed. Cam's head resting on his shoulder, his arm around Cam's waist.

But he was *tired*.

Still, he tried to dredge up the enthusiasm he'd had this morning, when he'd formulated the plan over coffee and listening to Cam humming in the shower.

"Yeah, we can do that," Dawson said.

But instead of asking where they were going, Cam just gave him a look. "Come on," he said, "I've got this."

"Got what?" Dawson was confused. He could marshal the last of his brain cells together. Find some unknown well of strength.

But Cam was already wrapping an arm around his forearm and tugging him in the direction of the parking lot as he pulled the keys out of Dawson's hand.

"What are you doing?" Dawson asked again when Cam only shook his head.

"You're dead on your feet," Cam said. "We'll go out some other time."

He slipped into the driver's side like he drove Dawson's car all the time.

"I can drive," Dawson grumbled. "I'm not *that* bad off."

"Sure," Cam said lightly. But he wasn't budging, and so Dawson finally opened the passenger side door and got in.

They were halfway back to their building when Cam turned to him and asked, "What do you want to order for dinner? We'll get it delivered. I know when I get overworked like that, I always want a hot bath. You don't have a bathtub at your place, but I've got one at mine."

That seemed to be the biggest difference between their two places—both nearly the exact same layout, both equally nearly empty—but Dawson had a bigger shower and no tub, and like Cam had said, he'd gotten the tub.

"You don't need to—"

But Cam interrupted him before he could finish the admonition. "If you're gonna say you don't need taking care of, save it, okay?"

"Why?"

Rolling his eyes, Cam said, "It's okay to let someone else handle shit for once—and don't you dare fucking say I can't. I was okay before you came along."

Cam didn't need to specify what he meant when he said *before you came along*. Obviously it wasn't the beginning of camp. Or even the beginning of the season. Back then, Dawson's gaze had slid over Cam like he was just there, like he wasn't anything really worth noting.

But back then, it had been the same with every other guy on the team. Even Aidan, who'd been an old friend.

Different. Not what you're used to. A cruel and unusual punishment, exacted by an unforgiving universe.

Now, Dawson was beginning to understand that this change wasn't all bad. Marty was a good coach. He was learning things. To find his focus when it didn't want to be found. To be more graceful under pressure. To weather any storm. Then there was Cam, who was new and different, but the kind of new and different that Dawson had realized he *wanted*.

"Okay," Dawson finally said. "If you want to, I'm not gonna stop you."

"Oh, you're gonna let me, huh?" Cam teased, glancing over, the look in his eyes soft.

"Seems like I can't stop you," Dawson said. Even though he probably could. Well, *normally*, he might be able to. But probably not tonight.

"What do you want for dinner? Still want noodles? Chinese? Pizza?"

"Pizza?" Dawson's mouth watered. They were both usually pretty vigilant about the meal plan, and pizza was not on the meal plan.

"I think you've earned it today," Cam said. "Aidan told me about this place he likes. Not sure if they deliver downtown . . ." But at the next light, he was on his phone, calling them up.

Dawson barely paid attention to the conversation, except to chime in that he wanted anything but pineapple, thank you very much.

Cam shot him a look that said, *you'll take what I give you and like it*, and that shouldn't have been a turn-on. Not when Dawson was as tired as he was, but it turned out that just about everything Cam wanted to do was a turn-on these days.

God, he'd missed having regular sex. Because that was what it had to be, right? All those extra endorphins he didn't usually have, swimming through his system, making Cam so goddamn irresistible.

Cam hung up the phone and drove them the rest of the way to the building, parking Dawson's car in his numbered spot without being prompted.

It made Dawson wonder, absently, just how long Cam had been paying attention.

"They're gonna make an exception and deliver here," Cam said, checking his phone when they got into the elevator. "Should be here in about thirty. You wanna get in the tub first?"

Cam's voice was so soothing and comforting, it was easy to just nod his head, and then a second later, he thought about what Cam had just said. "Wait, what do you mean they're gonna make an exception?"

"Technically we're out of their delivery zone, but when I dropped Aidan's name, the guy was open to it," Cam said.

"Aidan's name and the promise of a big tip, probably," Dawson said.

Cam flushed. "Maybe."

The elevator dinged open, and as they headed down the hall to Cam's apartment, Dawson nudged him. "You didn't have to do that. We could've gotten anything."

"You had a rough day," Cam said. "Honestly, it's fine. I don't mind."

"Just—"

Cam opened the apartment door and took Dawson's hand, squeezing it firmly. "Stop it," he said. "It's okay. You're tired. Not just physically, but mentally. I know what kind of toll that sort of practice takes on you. I've been there. Just let me handle it, okay?"

The last of Dawson's anxiety drained out of him. It was okay to put himself into Cam's hands, at least for a night.

"Come on," Cam said, tugging him in the direction of his bedroom and its attached bathroom. "I'll get the tub going."

It was a big tub, nice and spacious, long enough and wide enough for two, probably, but Cam didn't seem like he was getting in as he ran the water.

Sure enough, Cam looked over at him expectantly as the tub began to fill. "You gonna strip down?" he asked, his expression *almost* innocent.

"You just wanna get me naked."

"Pretty much always," Cam confirmed with a bashful grin.

It was flattering. Dawson knew he looked good. But he hadn't really cared in so long, his body morphing into a tool for his job more than a way to give and receive pleasure.

Dawson let himself look Cam up and down. He was in gray sweatpants, clinging to his slender thighs, an old T-shirt tight across the chest. He looked good, too. But then, he'd always looked good to Dawson—once he'd learned to pay attention, anyway.

"You getting in with me?"

"Not this time." Cam flashed him a smile that promised that some other time, he wouldn't be saying no.

"Aw," Dawson said, disappointed even though he'd known what Cam was going to say.

Cam just patted him on the cheek. "Come on, baby. Get in. I'll listen for the pizza."

He'd just taken a shower, hot water on his sore, overworked muscles, but floating in the tub felt heavenly.

Tipping his head back, Dawson closed his eyes and just let himself exist.

When he opened them again, the bathroom was dim and he realized Cam must've turned off most of the lights. There was a big fluffy towel sitting on the edge of the tub.

He heard hushed voices and realized a knock on the door must've dragged him out of his hot-water-induced stupor.

Getting out was going to suck, but Dawson braced for it and realized that the towel was still warm—had Cam even put it in the dryer for a few minutes to heat it up?—and that made it less awful when he finally dragged himself out of the cozy cocoon of the tub.

He dried off and threw his sweatpants and T-shirt back on, heading into the living room.

Cam was in the kitchen, and there was a big pizza box on the counter, delicious smells wafting out of it.

"Hey," he said, smiling, "I was just about to go grab you."

"I'm good," Dawson said, and realized he meant it. "Where do you want to eat?"

"Why don't we throw something on the TV?" Cam suggested. "You want to find something while I put these plates together?"

That seemed like the very least Dawson could do. He flipped the TV on and then realized it wasn't as easy as it seemed, because he had no idea what he should put on.

For a split second, his fingers hovered over the remote buttons, but then he realized exactly what he should pick.

A minute later, Cam walked in, carrying two plates filled with salad and heaping with several slices of pizza each.

"Hey, you—" Cam stopped and then glanced over at Dawson, a surprised smile on his face. "You want to watch *Fast and Furious*?"

"You told me I should watch it," Dawson said.

"There's like a billion of them, though," Cam warned. "And they're very stupid."

"The good news is that's about the speed I'm up for tonight—very stupid. Lots of brainless explosions. No thinking required."

It sounded really good, and it turned out it was even better than it sounded. Him tucked under Cam's arm, and then after Cam took the plates back to the kitchen and put the food away, Cam tucked under *his* arm, sleepy and soft.

For the last five nights they've shared a bed for four of them.

If Dawson was thinking about it, he might be worried that it was too much, too fast, but it was hard to be worried, especially when they seemed to be on the same page.

Especially when the movie ended and Cam stretched, yawning, and after getting to his feet, put out a hand for Dawson.

For a second Dawson thought he might lead him to the front door and finally tell him he needed to go home, but there was no hesitation at all in Cam's footsteps as they passed by the front entry and headed instead to Cam's bedroom.

CHAPTER 14

CAM THOUGHT HE AND Dawson were being *fairly* circumspect. Sure, there'd been the day after in the locker room, when Nate had teased him about all the marks Dawson had littered over his skin. Nate hadn't known who'd left them, but by the time they'd left the practice facility at the end of the day, it seemed like most of the guys suspected who it was that Cam had hooked up with.

Still, they weren't flirting or touching or being anywhere close to what Cam would call *obvious*. Not around their teammates. Dawson had told Aidan—and Mo, because he'd been there, at their dinner—but that was only because Aidan had been surprisingly worried about Cam.

Still, Cam thought they'd been pretty chill about what they were doing.

At least he thought that until Nate cornered them after the walk-through, Gatorade bottle in one big hand, and said, "So, when's the wedding date?"

Cam froze, but Dawson froze *worse*.

If Cam looked at their defensive captain and thought, *I wonder if I could kill him with my mind*, he decided that nobody could blame him. He and Dawson weren't *dating*, and on top of that, Dawson had just gotten out of a bad marriage, topped off by an even worse divorce.

"What the fuck," Dawson said pleasantly, after he unfroze.

Nate shrugged unrepentantly and rolled his Gatorade between two big hands. "You two just seem particularly . . .*close* recently."

Dawson had been very firm upfront about defining what this thing was between them, but then had proceeded to act like he'd never said anything at all. Cam was half-expecting to hear Dawson knock on his door later and stay the night in his hotel room bed, because it wasn't like they'd spent almost *any* nights apart since the first one they'd shared. But Cam was *not* interested in calling any of this mixed messaging out, especially not in front of Dawson.

That was a surefire way to freak him out.

And if Dawson freaked out, he would probably stop, and *God*, Cam really didn't want to stop.

Dawson frowned. "I don't know if that's true."

But it *was* true. Cam didn't need Dawson to confirm it, because he was living it.

Obviously if given a choice, he was going to choose both doing it *and* talking about doing it, but he was happy enough to settle for just doing it.

"Come on, you're practically glued together." Nate glanced over at where Aidan and Levi were standing next to each other. They weren't touching, but they didn't have to be for it to be obvious they belonged together. The message Nate was sending was clear enough.

This, Cam decided, had gone far enough. "Not really," he said.

Nate squinted. "I don't mean right now, I mean like you're always fucking together. And then there was Cam's hookup—"

"Dude, be chill," Cam interrupted. "It's cool." He slid a sideways glance at Dawson, who looked torn between looking offended and freaking out.

"Yeah, it's not all that serious," Dawson said, sounding like he meant it.

Sounding like he hadn't spent the last week in Cam's bed. Even when they *weren't* having sex. Cam might've been offended by Dawson's words, but then he knew the truth.

He knew where Dawson was spending his nights. Tucked right up next to Cam, like he couldn't stay away.

"Yeah, it's good," Cam said. *Better than anything I've ever had.*

"So what, you're just fucking?" Nate laughed under his breath, a little bitterly. "Okay, sure."

Dawson surprised Cam then. "You okay, Bishop? Not like you to angst about what everyone else is up to. Don't tell me you're taking lessons from Aidan these days."

"No," Nate said, frowning. "It's . . ."

"I'm *sure* you've heard of a hookup," Dawson said, patting Nate on the arm. "And if you haven't, I'm sure there's someone out there who might be willing to educate you."

"Maybe Ramsey?" Cam asked, pasting an innocent expression on his face.

And yep, there it was. Nate went a dark brick red.

"That guy," he muttered. "Fuck no. I wouldn't touch him if he paid me to. Besides, some of us want someone to be there in the morning."

Dawson barely blinked, and that was the funniest part of all, because he was *always* there in the mornings. Soft and sweet and leaning up against Cam, hands warm from a mug of coffee, pressing a kiss to Cam's neck, like he was saying without words, *thank you for being here, thank you for being you, thank you for everything you do.*

If Cam kept getting that version of Dawson, he was hardly in the position to even want more.

"Sure," Dawson said casually. "That's called being a friend."

Dawson was not stupid, and Cam could fully admit to having a soft spot for the guy a mile wide—a crush and maybe even more, now that Dawson was in his bed and he was in Dawson's—but he could be very stupid sometimes.

Right now was one of those times. But Cam wasn't going to correct him.

"Oh yeah, right. Totally," Cam agreed, shooting Dawson an approving grin.

Nate rolled his eyes. "And you wondered why I asked to begin with," he muttered.

Cam would've known why he asked, but only if Nate was somehow creeping around their building, watching them while they were alone together.

"I'm sure there's a guy out there for you," Dawson said, and Cam elbowed him in the side. First off, Nate wasn't *that* off the mark, and second off, the guy was clearly fucked up about Ramsey, and it wasn't nice to be patronizing about it.

"Be nice," Cam admonished.

"What?" Dawson squawked. "I was being supportive."

"So was I," Nate countered. "Making sure you know that if something was going on, it would be cool."

"Well, thanks," Dawson said. "If something happens, we'll keep that in mind."

His phone rang, and Dawson pulled it from his pocket, frowning at the screen. "It's my lawyer. I gotta take this," he said. Shot Cam a look. "See you later?" he said, in a way that made it crystal clear that the *later* wouldn't be tomorrow, at breakfast, but later tonight, when he came to Cam's room.

Dawson was out of earshot when Nate turned his attention back to Cam and raised an eyebrow. "*If* something was going on?"

Cam knew he'd realized what was up, but it was still hard to explain it. Especially to Nate, who was intimidating at the best of times.

"He's just . . . the divorce and all," Cam stammered.

Nate's expression turned sympathetic. "He's not fucking around with you, is he?"

"Not in the way you think. He's not using me or anything. Or if he is, I'm using him right back—" Cam broke off, deciding he was doing an absolute shit job of explaining any of this. "He says it's just a hookup, but he's treating me like . . .like a . . ." He didn't want to say it, but it was hard not to at least think it. *He's treating me like a boyfriend.*

Cam wondered if he'd need to actually say it for Nate to get it but his expression made it clear that he'd filled in enough of the blanks himself.

"Don't let him get away with that shit," Nate said.

"Why not?" It was fine. It was more than fine. It didn't matter what Dawson wanted to call it. Only that he kept wanting to *do* it.

"Listen, the guy's been through it, sure, but you're a good kid."

Cam made a face.

"No, I mean that in the best possible way," Nate said hurriedly. "A good *guy*. He's clearly fucked up from his whole . . ." He waved his hand around. *Marriage. Divorce. Theft victim. Self-implosion.*

"Yeah," Cam agreed. "Which is why I'm not gonna worry about what he's saying. Only what he's doing."

Nate didn't look convinced. "Yeah, that seems like a bad idea."

But how could it be a bad idea when it felt so damn good?

"Not so far," Cam argued.

Nate just sighed. Patted him on the shoulder. "When—and I'm not saying *if*, but *when*—you need me to kick his ass, you just have to say the word, okay?"

"What? You don't need to ever kick his ass," Cam argued. Yes, maybe Dawson was acting a little clueless right now, but he'd been through a lot. He was allowed to be confused.

"Aidan was right," was all Nate said.

"What about?" Cam asked, even though he was afraid that whatever Aidan had said about him was not exactly flattering. Sure, Aidan had been worried about him, but only because he was apparently convinced that Cam couldn't handle his own shit.

But Cam could. Cam *was*. He was good. So fucking good. How could he be anything else when Dawson was coming to his room later?

Nate didn't answer the question though. Just patted him again. "Just make sure you're safe, rook," was all he said.

Cam watched him go, confused as hell and more than a little offended. He was *twenty-two*. He didn't need to be lectured on how to have safe sex.

Dawson felt a little bad about leaving Cam to Nate's well-meaning but completely incorrect assumptions. But he'd read the plea deal that Simon had sent over and hadn't been thrilled by what it had laid out, in black and white. Barely any punishment at all. There was a part of Dawson that wanted to talk to the prosecutor directly, but he hadn't pulled that lever yet.

Simon, his lawyer, had inferred and then straight up told Dawson that it was better if he was the go-between between Dawson and the prosecutor. But if Dawson was going to seriously consider putting his stamp of approval on this kind of plea deal, then he wanted to talk to the guy in charge.

Maybe Simon would have more information on how he could contact the prosecutor directly. Some advice on how to make that meeting happen. He'd probably have to convince Simon, but at one point, Dawson had been a fairly persuasive guy. Maybe he could dredge those skills up again.

"Hey, Simon," Dawson said.

"Sorry to call the night before a game," Simon said. "Hopefully it's not too late. I didn't check where you were at."

"It's earlier, 'cause we're in Indy," Dawson said. "Besides, not even curfew yet."

"Good. I wanted to check in about the plea deal I sent you last week." Simon said it casually, but there was something—faint and maybe just a figment of Dawson's overly paranoid imagination—off about the way he said it.

"I looked at it," Dawson said. "I'm not sure I'm on board."

There was a part of him that just wanted it to be over. *Let it go, man,* that voice told him insistently, *it's over. The only one who gives a shit still is you.*

But how could he let it go when it felt like the only person who *did* give a shit anymore was him?

"Dawson, we talked about this," Simon chided.

Dawson thought a little resentfully that *Simon* had talked about this. Talked *at* Dawson, in fact, but not really *about* Dawson's concerns.

"Yeah, you did," Dawson said.

"Alex and I are in agreement. You need to put this behind you. The last thing you need right now is to dredge all this crap up again. You're fitting in on the Thunder. You guys are five games in and five wins in. There's no reason to keep wanting to punish Ackerman."

This was so ridiculous that Dawson didn't hold back his eye roll. "Maybe the reason is because nobody else wants to punish him."

"The plea deal punishes him plenty."

"Yeah, restricts him to his seven-thousand-square-foot mansion with its putting green, its sauna, and a freaking in-ground pool. A real punishment."

"House arrest isn't nothing," Simon reminded him, not very gently.

He and Simon had been friends for a long time. Simon had been his first lawyer, when he'd gotten to the NFL. A fellow teammate had recommended him, and he and Simon had hit it off. When Dawson had lived in Baltimore, they'd even gone golfing together.

But now, suddenly, Dawson wondered if Simon *was* on his side.

Why else wouldn't he want Ackerman to pay the same way Dawson did?

"He stole my money, Simon. A lot of fucking money."

"He's starting to repay it. That's part of the terms of the plea."

"Yeah, God knows where he got *that* money," Dawson muttered. He'd seen it filling back in his accounts. But it didn't feel right to him, because in his mind, once a thief, always a thief. Anything Ackerman paid him back might be just as dirty as the money he'd taken from Dawson in the first place.

"Daws, you know why he took your money. It was supposed to be a loan, a stopgap measure, and he'd always intended to put it back."

Yes, that was the official story. The story Ackerman had told Brynn, which was why she was still talking to her father.

But Dawson had never believed it.

"That's bullshit," Dawson said, temper rising in his throat. He paced in his room. Back and forth. He was done playing nice. Simon should know that by now. Should know *him* by now. "He never intended to put it back. He thought he could take it and cover it up and I'd never notice. And if Brynn and I hadn't divorced, he'd never have gotten found out."

"Maybe," Simon said, not sounding convinced. "But regardless if what he said is true or not true, it doesn't matter now."

"It matters to *me*," Dawson argued.

"Yes, that much is clear," Simon huffed.

"I want to talk to the prosecutor about the plea."

"Dawson," Simon warned. "You know why that's not a good idea."

"I'm doing great here. You said it yourself. If I want to talk to them, why shouldn't I?"

"You know why." Simon didn't need to say it.

Dawson swallowed his arguments. He didn't want to fuck himself up again. He *didn't*. But he also didn't want Ackerman to spend the next few years lounging by his pool and enjoying his putting green, sleeping between thousand-thread-count sheets, and never, ever really paying for what he'd done.

"I'll think about it," Dawson said uselessly. Simon wasn't wrong. That was the worst part of this. Maybe he should be prioritizing his own emotional well-being over some potentially misguided desire to punish his ex-father-in-law for his "temporary loan."

"Good," Simon said. "I'll tell the prosecutor's office you need a few more days, but I'm sure that when you're back in Toronto, you'll give the plea another look and it'll look better, yeah?"

Dawson was not convinced of that, at all, but he would at least try. He owed himself that much, didn't he? Simon had said it himself, he was fitting in great in Toronto. Rejuvenating his battered reputation. Why *did* he want to drag it all back out again? He should want to let it go.

"Okay," Dawson said.

He hung up and flopped down on the bed. For a second he lay there and told himself the story Simon had tried to sell, once and then twice and now a third time.

He wanted to believe it was true. That this was the best he was going to get. But there was a feeling, tickling at the back of his throat, in the base of his stomach, that felt the same now as it had when he'd first begun to realize what Ackerman had done.

Like Simon wasn't only on *his* side. Not anymore.

But that would be crazy. That would be Dawson being paranoid again, sure that everyone was out to get him. And everyone wasn't.

It *was* a white-collar crime. Simon had been telling him that from the beginning, but also from the very beginning he'd mentioned more than once how lucky all the victims were that Dawson was included in their ranks because he brought attention and publicity to a case that might not have gone anywhere otherwise.

But Simon's narrative had changed. Now he was eager to get Dawson away from this as fast as possible.

That might be because Dawson *had* struggled so hard last year. It might be a selfless action—Simon hoping that Dawson could redeem himself and resuscitate his career. Or it might be for another reason entirely.

His phone, on the bed next to him, vibrated, and he glanced over.

It was a text from Cam. It only read **684.**

His room number.

Cam hadn't invited him, but the invite was there anyway, in between the lines.

After Cam had gone out of his way to mention that he didn't have a roommate on this trip, he'd intended to head over to Cam's room just before curfew hit, but now he was in kind of a shitty mood and wasn't sure he should.

Of course, if he didn't, he'd just sit and stew. Feel worse, instead of better. Because Cam was always like magic—mellowing Dawson's grumpiness effortlessly, like he wasn't even trying to do it, it just *happened*.

With that thought lingering, Dawson picked himself off the bed. Changed into a pair of loose shorts and an old, comfy T-shirt, brushed his teeth, pocketed his phone and his room key and headed towards room 684.

Cam opened the door with a pleased smile. "Hey," he said. As soon as Dawson stepped in the room, Cam was wrapping an arm around his waist, more touchy-feely than he'd been downstairs. Tugging Dawson against his body until they were pressed together.

"Hey, rook," Dawson murmured back.

Cam's hair was damp from a shower. Dawson reached up and pushed it back, tangling his fingers in the waves.

"How was your call?"

Dawson made a face. "Frustrating." He almost added he didn't want to talk about it. Because he'd thought he didn't. But now that he was here, in front of Cameron, he realized that wasn't true at all. He *did* want to talk about it. He wanted to exorcise all of it, and let Cam take away the sting, one bit at a time, until it was gone.

Maybe he should feel guilty about using Cam that way, but then Cam said, "You wanna talk about it?" in such a hopeful voice, like he *wanted* to do that for Dawson. Like it wasn't too much of a burden for him, at all. Like he was willing to take it on, for however long Dawson needed.

"Ugh, I shouldn't—"

"Yeah, you should." Cam tugged him over in the direction of the bed and they sat down on the edge of it.

It was evidence of how conflicted Dawson was that being on the same bed as Cam only gave him the vaguest pulses of arousal.

"I don't want to just dump on you every time so you'll just make me feel better."

Cam frowned. "Trust me. You don't. We're friends, right? Friends listen, Daws."

It wasn't hard to fold, especially since Dawson had realized he *did* want to talk about it.

"Alright. Well. You know how I told you Ackerman's defense is pushing for a plea?"

Cam nodded.

"Well, my lawyer is too. He wants me to just go along with it. I'm not against it, but . . ."

Cam frowned. "Yeah, you are."

For a second, Dawson didn't say anything. But Cam wasn't wrong. He *was* against it.

"Yeah. You're right. I'm against it. But I don't know if it's just me being . . .petty?"

"*Petty*?" Cam's jaw dropped. "The guy was your father-in-law. Practically your fucking family. You trusted him because of that. Then he stole from you. Wanting him to pay for that isn't being petty; it's totally justifiable. Is that what your lawyer keeps telling you?"

Dawson shrugged. "Not exactly. Simon just keeps pushing for me to go along with the plea deal. And it's a cushy-ass plea deal. Sure, it would mean it's over, and I *do* want it to be over. I do. But fuck, not like this."

"Then tell him no." Cam said it so simply, like it was that simple, even though it wasn't.

"It's not entirely up to me. The prosecutor is only really giving me an opinion because I'm . . .God, this sounds awful, because of who I am." Unease at admitting that spiked through. He'd never bought into the mysticism of celebrity. He was just a regular guy, who was really good at one thing and had worked hard to get better at it, and then because of a combination of luck and circumstance, had gotten rich and famous because of it.

"So?" Cam wondered. "You told me yourself that the case might not have gotten anywhere if you weren't an NFL player, and that part of why you did that was not just for you, but the other victims too. You don't need to be embarrassed to admit it."

Dawson didn't know when he'd gotten so fucking transparent. "I'm not . . .not really."

Shooting him a knowing look, Cam reached over and squeezed his thigh. "So why don't you talk to the prosecutor directly? Can you do that?"

"That's a thought I've had. But whenever I bring it up with Simon, he keeps shutting it down."

Cam didn't say anything, just waited him out. Because yeah, there was more, and somehow Cam had guessed it. Dawson didn't know how; he was only grateful he had.

"It makes me feel like there's something else he's not saying," Dawson continued. "Like he's hiding something. I've worked like hell to not go around being paranoid that everyone's gonna let me down. That everyone's gonna do something shitty. To let go of the belief that I'm an easy mark, ready and willing to be taken advantage of. And this makes me think of that, all over again. But it might just be me. I don't know."

Cam just squeezed his knee again. Tipped his head against Dawson's shoulder. There was something in the way that felt; like Cam didn't believe even though Dawson had admitted to all these doubts and flaws, that he'd struggle to hold on to Cam. Like Cam would trust that he'd hold him up, both literally and figuratively. It made him feel less like a weak, clueless idiot.

Maybe Cam didn't even know what that did, but Dawson was beginning to think that it didn't matter if he realized it, only that he was doing it.

"What if it's not just you?" Cam asked softly. "And even if it is, it's a justifiable fear, Daws. You got let down by someone you trusted. Simon should understand that, and he should be going the extra mile to reassure you, not close down communication."

"Yeah?"

"Yeah, I still think you should reach out to the prosecutor yourself. If you don't set these fears to rest, you *won't* be able to move on."

"You don't think it'd be overstepping?"

"If it is, then it's your right to do that," Cam said firmly.

Dawson let out a breath. "Yeah. Yeah, you're probably right. Of course, I worry this is going to fuck me all over again. I've just gotten my feet under me here. Doing good. Maybe Simon's right that it's just a distraction."

"And you worrying about it isn't a distraction?" Cam raised an eyebrow.

Dawson hadn't really thought of it that way, but that was a good point. "Fair."

"I think if you don't set your mind at ease—make sure this feeling you have is just a feeling, and that's all it is—you're not going to be able to make a decision, and move forward, either way," Cam said.

Dawson sighed. "How did you get so smart, rook?"

Cam's cheeks flushed an appealing pink. And Dawson realized that he'd done it again. Just being here with him, talking it out, had pulled all that awful, peace-shattering poison right out of him. Suddenly, he was aware again that they were on the edge of the bed and Cam was just showered, hair drying rumpled from Dawson's hands earlier.

"Grateful you are," Dawson murmured and leaned in, and he supposed at some point he should stop being so surprised that it was so easy between them. That it felt natural to press their lips together. Not necessarily because he wanted to start something—though if he was being honest, he kinda did—but because it felt right to do it.

Cam opened underneath his mouth, groaning in the back of his throat as Dawson deepened the kiss.

He couldn't help himself, tucking his fingers underneath Cam's T-shirt, pulling it off, enjoying the feel of his bare skin as he went. "God, you feel good," Dawson murmured under his breath. Not sure if he was saying it for Cam or for himself.

It felt even more natural to give Cam one last kiss, their tongues tangling together, and then slide down to the floor, pulling Cam's sweatpants off as he went.

"You don't—"

But instead of letting him finish, Dawson pressed his mouth against Cam's inner thigh. Enjoyed as Cam let out a shaky gasp of approval, his cock twitching.

No, he didn't have to. He *wanted* to. He wanted to give back a little of the peace and pleasure he kept discovering in Cam's arms. In his bed. On his couch.

With that in mind, he leaned in, licking up the length of Cam's cock. Enjoying the way he trembled above him. How his fingers dug into the comforter. The tension in his jaw.

It had been a while since he'd sucked dick—at least the length of his marriage to Brynn, and a year or two before that—but he'd forgotten how good it felt, even for him. How much he loved having his partner's pleasure in his hands. Oral sex in general was something he enjoyed, but Dawson didn't think he'd ever felt this insane about it before, like he wanted more and more, until Cam was filling up his mouth with his come.

Cam's hands dug into his hair, and he groaned above him as Dawson took him deeper. He had to be a little careful. Definitely more careful than he wanted to be. But he didn't want to choke and die, either. Not when it was this good, and his own dick was so aroused that he didn't think it would take more than the pressure of his hand to lose his self-control entirely.

It was a little slow going, needing to remember all his tricks, but he was slowly beginning to pick them up again. And learn more too. That curling his tongue around the head made Cam choke out a moan. All the places he was especially sensitive. The way he shook when Dawson cupped his balls and with a spit-slick thumb, slid behind them, pressing into his hole.

"Fuck, I'm gonna—" Cam broke off as Dawson sucked harder, wanting it all. "God, feels so good, babe."

Dawson shuddered at the pet name. Hadn't thought he'd like it, but he liked everything with Cam.

Barely got his hand on his own cock as Cam began to shake, come spurting down his throat. He was right; it didn't take long.

One or two strokes and the right kind of pressure and he was coming in his shorts.

Panting, he slumped the rest of the way down to the floor. Cam's hands were still tangled in his hair. Gentle now, brushing it away from his forehead.

"Damn," Cam murmured. "That was hot as hell."

Dawson cleared his throat. "Yeah, uh, I was probably a little out of practice."

"Couldn't tell." Cam's smile was so bright it was hard to look at, but Dawson did it anyway, gazing up at him.

He was probably going to regret coming in his shorts in about five seconds, but for right now, Dawson decided he didn't care. It wasn't like he hadn't slept naked with Cam before.

Truthfully, he was pretty sure it was even better that way.

"You feel better now?" Cam asked, looking like he knew the answer to that question.

Dawson sighed. "Yeah. I do, actually. Except for you know . . ." He waved at his crotch. "The whole *making a mess like a teenager* thing."

"Bet you were a cute teenager." Cam's dimple popped, he was smiling so hard.

"Not as cute as I am now," Dawson teased. He took Cam's outstretched hand and flopped down next to him on the bed. He should go get cleaned up, but in a minute. This was too nice to not enjoy, especially when Cam's knee bumped Dawson's and then didn't move away.

"You're magic," Dawson murmured, glancing over at him and the words coming out before he could stop them. He was sure he'd have to explain himself, but Cam didn't ask. His smile just softened, eyes glued to Dawson's face, like he couldn't look away.

As much as he tried to pack up last night's conversation with Simon and put it away until after the game, the thoughts lingered in Dawson's mind.

He turned over what he'd said to Cam and what Cam had suggested he do as he ate breakfast. As he took the bus over to the stadium.

As he got ready for warmups.

"You're quiet," Marty said as he headed onto the field with the rest of the special teams group.

"Focused," Dawson said, even though he wasn't sure that was what it was.

But he didn't want to let the distraction in. Didn't want to vocalize it, because what if he was right, and it fucked him up? He couldn't go through that again. Especially not now when he was beginning to really feel like Toronto was a great place. The winning was nice, no question about that, but the way the team was coming together was the real bonus.

And then there was Cameron.

Dawson had never expected he'd find something so good with the rookie, but it was hard to deny just how much he was enjoying it. Best hookup he'd ever had, hands down.

Marty raised an eyebrow. "Yeah? That's good."

"I'm always focused," Dawson argued.

"Then why are you so quiet about it today?"

Dawson didn't want Marty picking at the scabbed-over wound. He wanted to ignore it, especially until after this game was over. The Thunder had won five straight games to open the season and the sixth was riding on the line, today. Marty should know that and leave him the fuck alone.

Cam mostly had. They'd shared a few murmured thoughts this morning—general chitchat about the game and the city and the choices on the buffet spread—but Cam had seemed to sense that he still had the Ackerman situation on his mind and had mostly left him alone to pack it all up and put it away before the game.

Dawson let out a frustrated noise. "I don't know, I just am, okay?"

Marty shot him a knowing look. Chomping at the omnipresent ball of gum in between his teeth. "Just checking in."

"Well, I'm good."

Marty didn't look convinced, which was additionally annoying. "I'm dialed," Dawson added. "Locked the fuck in."

"What's that phrase that old English guy liked to use? You protesting too much, Hall?"

"*No*," Dawson complained. "And that's fucking Shakespeare, you heathen."

"Yep, that's the guy," Marty said cheerfully.

Dawson rolled his eyes and didn't stomp off, though he was fairly tempted to do it. But if he had, Marty would've figured out he was annoyed. Might've figured out that he wasn't as locked in as he wanted to be.

He went through his warmups and all his progressions. Everything *felt* fine, but there was still a persistently annoying worry in the back of his head that he'd head out to kick a field goal in the middle of a game and everything would hit him at once.

He'd never frozen before. Not once. Not even during the worst of his meltdown last year. But it was always there, hovering as an awful possibility in the back of his mind. Usually easier to ignore, but persistent nevertheless.

Cam wandered over in his direction after the kickoff.

"Hey," he said, but even though that was what he said, Dawson knew what he'd meant. *Are you okay?* was written, plain as day, all over Cam's face.

He grimaced. "I'm good, yeah?"

Cam shot him an unimpressed look. "I didn't ask if you were okay. Obviously you're okay."

Dawson didn't even get a second to reiterate that *of course* he was okay, because Cam continued. "Are you not okay?"

"I'm fine," Dawson ground out. "Just . . . there's nothing *wrong*. I don't know Simon isn't on my side, but . . ."

There'd been a time when any kind of sympathy grated. Felt worse than if everyone just ignored what was happening. But Cam's didn't bother him the same way. Maybe because he knew it went more than skin-deep.

"You don't know, but you're going to find out," Cam said. "And even if it's true? Even if maybe Simon's got an alternate agenda he didn't tell you about? That doesn't change anything about you, or what you're capable of. You're still Dawson Hall. First ballot Hall of Famer. As a *kicker*. Fucking extraordinary. You've got the skill. Nobody ever doubts that. *Just you.*"

Dawson didn't know what to say, but *fucking extraordinary* kept echoing in his head. He managed a nod.

"We don't worry about you, not for a second," Cam said and patted his shoulder. "Remember that, okay?"

It was going to be tough for Dawson to forget it now. Especially when he thought of last season, of the Baltimore players tiptoeing around him like they were afraid to even meet his eyes, because what if he fucking missed another field goal and it was their fault?

But Cam was right; nobody was doing that here. Nobody had shirked away from him when he'd missed that field goal two games ago. They'd just clapped him on the back and said, easy, like it meant nothing, even though it meant everything, that he'd nail the next one.

As the game unfolded, Dawson realized he was actually excited to get out there and prove to the guys—and to himself—that it *was* true. He wanted to remind everyone that he was Dawson Hall, one of the best kickers in the NFL.

But of course, that isn't what happened.

He kicked an extra point. And then another. And then another.

Aidan and the offense were rolling, one touchdown after another. Dawson looked up at the scoreboard as the third quarter wound to a close, realizing the score was forty-two to seven, and there was almost no chance he'd be kicking a field goal in this game.

Six extra points, sure, but those were so routine Dawson barely had to think about them. Especially when that was all he was doing.

"Damn," Cam said as the fourth quarter ticked away, Jaden getting handoff after handoff, the Thunder only trying to eat clock to end this game sooner rather than later.

"Is it crazy that I'm a little disappointed?" Dawson asked under his breath.

"That you didn't get to kick today? You kicked six extra points, Daws."

"Not the same, and you know it. Especially when it's a five-score game."

Cam shrugged. "True." Then he shot Dawson a bright grin. "But you're gonna get them next time."

For a split second, he nearly said, *Hope so*, but then realized that was offering the possibility that he might not some much-needed wiggle room. Not allowing it a foothold in his mind, but enough of a gap that it could find a way in.

But he was done with that.

"Yeah," he agreed instead, "I am."

CHAPTER 15

"You gotta tell me," Cam said, leaning into Dawson's space as they settled in the suite seats above the ice, "was this *your* idea initially, 'cause it's fucking brilliant."

Dawson shot him an amused look. "No. It was all Wes. I think he's having more fun than he should torturing Nate with all his comments about hockey being harder than football."

When Clarissa, one of the PR reps, had come into the locker room with an offer to attend the Leafs game tonight, a handful of hands had gone up, including Dawson's.

Dawson had shot him a look, and it had been easy for Cam to raise his, too. What else would he be doing tonight? He'd only planned on dinner and then some TV on his couch. Maybe convincing Dawson to watch the next *Fast and Furious* movie.

But a hockey game sounded like a good time, and they'd all be in a suite, Clarissa said. Free food and drink.

Hard to turn that down.

Cam had not seen Nate raise his hand, unsurprisingly, but then he'd shown up with the rest of them at the suite, a frown on his face and reluctance in every line of his body.

He and Dawson had taken seats towards the front of the suite, getting ready for puck drop, blue lights flashing across the ice, but he was pretty sure Nate was trying to bury his bulk in the back of the suite, like he could hide from where he was.

There was a big enough group of them that maybe Nate *could* hide, but not for long.

Aidan and Levi were chatting with him, Wes with them, while Jaden, Lane, and Trevor were seated in the row of seats across from where Dawson and Cam had settled in.

Cam couldn't say he followed hockey much, but he knew the basics, and the game was fun—fast-paced and full of energy—and with Dawson a warm line beside him, he was having a great time. Everyone else was enjoying themselves, too, even Nate. At least that seemed to be the case, Nate talking and actually laughing, the handful of times when Cam ended up in the main suite area, to grab him and Dawson drinks or to fill their bowl of popcorn.

But in the first intermission, he and Dawson got up to stretch their legs, and that meant they were milling around the suite when the door opened and Ramsey walked in.

Next to him, Nate stiffened. Cam thought for a second he might duck away, but Dawson was on Nate's other side and he nudged him back into their circle.

"Hey, guys, I heard you were around here tonight," Ramsey said with a wide grin, making the rounds, shaking hands and giving bro hugs.

He was dressed in a suit, slate blue that matched his eyes, with a white shirt open at the collar, a diamond-studded chain peeking out, glinting against his skin. Even though Cam was currently kind of obsessed with Dawson, it was hard not to look at Ramsey and *keep* looking, even if looking was all he was interested in doing. The guy was gorgeous, like a model or a painting in one of those big fancy museums.

Nate's mouth was drawn in a grim, annoyed line when Ramsey finally made it around to him.

"Nathaniel," he said, dipping his head. Nate was the one guy he didn't try to greet with a touch. Just kept his distance.

"Your name isn't even—" Levi said, wide-eyed, glancing from where Ramsey was standing, corner of his mouth quirked up in wry amusement, to Nate, who was practically quivering with tension.

"He knows that," Nate said flatly.

Ramsey gave a little self-deprecating shrug. "It suits you."

"It does not." Nate looked the opposite of amused.

Aidan cleared his throat, clearly aware of how tightly wound the tension was and trying to unwind it. "It was good of you to stop by."

"I was already at the game," Ramsey said. He gestured towards the ice. "That's my team."

"The Leafs?" Cam asked, because he hadn't thought so.

"No, the Sabres," Ramsey said and there was something cold and detached in his voice then. "And I played college hockey with a couple of guys on the Leafs. McCoy and Jones. On the third line."

"Oh, yeah, they scored," Levi said. "That was a pretty sick pass."

Aidan shot him a look.

"What?" Levi exclaimed. "It was! I've been watching hockey more. I know what a good pass looks like."

"It *was* a pretty good pass," Ramsey agreed. Cam had half-expected him to avoid Nate—talking or even looking at the guy—once he'd greeted him, but his gaze shifted right to the guy. "What did you think, Nathaniel?"

"No clue," Nate ground out.

"Oh, that's right," Ramsey said smoothly. "Hockey's too good for you. Or you're too good for hockey? I can't remember which it is."

"You did say you'd get him here, to Scotia Bank," Lane pointed out. Trevor nudged him with an elbow, not very subtly.

"I did. You wanna get out there after the game?" Ramsey asked innocently. Or *his* version of innocently, anyway, because Cam had a feeling that guy didn't have an innocent bone in his body.

"No."

"I don't know, I think you'd be okay out there," Ramsey said.

Nate rolled his eyes. "Don't fucking do that."

"Do what?"

Cam had a feeling things were rapidly going south. He could feel Aidan on his other side, tensing, ready to step in if the situation soured even further.

But Nate only barked out a chuckle. "That look doesn't work on me."

He turned and walked out then.

Cam would've been so upset, but Ramsey didn't even look bothered. Just beamed one of those bright supermodel smiles. "Not sure what he's talking about," he said conspiratorially.

The second period was starting shortly, and Cam grabbed him and Dawson another pair of beers and they settled back in their seats, this time Aidan with them.

"That was weird," Aidan said, leaning forward to tuck his bottle of water into the cup holder in front of him.

"Was it?" Dawson asked.

Aidan made a face. "You were there; you know it was. Don't even try to pretend it wasn't."

"Oh, I was there. I wouldn't say it was weird though. Or even remotely surprising. Nate and Ramsey interacting? It's been pretty much the same since the beginning. Maybe it's even gotten worse. You shouldn't have made him come."

"I didn't," Aidan claimed.

"I don't remember him putting his hand up in the locker room," Cam pointed out. Maybe Daws was right and Aidan wasn't *that* scary. Especially when he was so obviously terrible at reading the room. When he thought what had happened was *weird*.

It was, as Dawson said, not weird. And not particularly surprising.

"I just thought . . ." Aidan ran a hand through his hair and made a frustrated noise. "I want them to get along. Wes is always telling me how isolated Ramsey is. I want to include him."

"He's not your teammate, bud," Dawson said.

It was a little harsh, even for one of Dawson's grumpy moods. And Dawson must have known it, because he sighed and added, "I get that you want to help him. It's admirable. It is. But he and Nate aren't going to get along. Just . . .when you want to invite him, don't invite Nate."

"That's not a solution," Aidan said stubbornly.

Cam wondered if that was how he sounded right before he'd puked into the bush all those years ago. Determined not to be drunk and messy, and yet still knee-deep in a boxwood.

"Looks like a solution to me," Dawson retorted.

"Nate's one of the captains of this team," Aidan countered. "I can't just not include him. Besides, it wasn't even *me* this time. It was Wes."

"I didn't have Wes picking up your worst-big-brother-tendencies on my bingo card," Dawson said.

Cam cackled and Aidan glared. But not hard enough to make Cam regret laughing. Especially not when Dawson shot him a smug grin.

"I'm just saying, Wes is Ramsey's friend, right? So if *he* invited him, it must be fine."

"Bro, it did not look fine," Dawson said.

Aidan sighed heavily. "I know. *I know.* Which is why I said it was weird."

"No, your little arranged playdate between me and Mo was weird. This was . . ." Dawson hummed under his breath and then turned to Cam. "What did you call it the other day?"

"Pulling each other's pigtails?"

Dawson snapped his fingers, nodding intently. "Yeah, that's it," he said. "Maybe they *should* hate-fuck about it."

Aidan groaned under his breath. Apparently that noise was permanently on Levi's radar now, because he appeared then, a crease between his brows. "Everything okay, babe?" he asked Aidan.

Aidan made a face. "If I say they're ganging up on me, will you beat them up for me?"

Cam had never seen Aidan Flynn make puppy dog eyes before. If he wasn't currently witnessing it, he wouldn't have believed it was possible. But it was actually fucking happening.

Dawson had continually told him that one day, he'd see Aidan as a guy—kind of a stupid guy, at that—and not as *Aidan Flynn, Superstar QB of the Toronto Thunder*, and yep, this was it. This was the time. It had finally arrived.

"Bro," Levi said in a wounded voice, "they're like two-thirds of our special teams? Who's gonna kick the extra points when you throw four touchdowns like you did on Sunday?"

"Two-point conversions?" Aidan suggested hopefully.

Levi just laughed, like Aidan was the most delightful person in the whole world. Cam wondered if there would ever be a moment for *him* when Aidan came back down to earth and revealed he too had feet of clay. But Cam realized that was probably never going to happen, because Levi already saw all of him and the magic was, he didn't care.

Just like how Cam saw all of Dawson—his insecurities and his worries and his anxiety—and none of that ever fazed him. He was still just as hot for him, still just as eager to kiss him, the next time they were alone.

"Ugh, you're no help," Aidan complained. "Go back to your gossip fest with Trevor and Lane."

Levi leaned down and whispered something into Aidan's ear. Aidan went bright red, and well, whatever that was, clearly there was going to be no lack of magic in Aidan's condo later tonight.

"Anyway," Dawson drawled, "so you *don't* think they should hate-fuck about it? I'd be pretty damn surprised if you weren't behind that idea." He shot Aidan a pointed look and he went even redder.

"It's not that I *don't*, it's that hate-fucking doesn't solve anything," Aidan said, cheekbones going brick red when he got to the word *fucking*. "How does that help him get folded into our group?"

"Aw," Dawson said. "You see the vision too, then."

Aidan shot him an aggrieved look. "Seriously? If you saw the vision too, then why are you giving me shit about it?"

"Because you're actually the most fun person on earth to give shit to," Cam said and then smacked a hand over his mouth when both Aidan's and Dawson's heads swiveled in his direction.

Dawson looked absolutely delighted, but Aidan's jaw was near the floor.

"I told you," Dawson said, laughing now. "Knew it would happen eventually, rook."

"I don't even want to know," Aidan said, but at least his grumbling seemed good-natured enough.

"The answer is exactly what Cam said," Dawson admitted. "It's too much fun to give you shit."

Aidan sighed heavily. "Trying to remember why I was looking forward to you joining the Thunder."

"To kick your extra points?" Dawson teased.

"I'd make Levi do it," Aidan said.

Dawson slapped a hand across his heart and gasped overdramatically. "Replaced that easy, rook. Can you even believe it?"

"Imagine Levi trying to punt," Cam observed. "I'd pay good money to see that."

"Yeah, what about you, Aidan? Not gonna make an attempt on your own? Just gonna serve your boy up to be humiliated?" Dawson teased.

"Who says he'd be humiliated?" Aidan argued.

Dawson looked over at Cam. "He's so dickmatized he legitimately thinks Levi is good at *everything*. Newsflash, bud, he's not."

"Not sure I agree with that," Aidan said primly. "But, to get back to the *actual* topic, which is not how 'dickmatized' I am or how enjoyable it is to make fun of me, but how we can get Ramsey to be part of the group."

"Aren't we already doing it?" Dawson asked. "Wes made sure he showed up tonight."

"We could do more," Aidan said. "We gotta fix his issues with Nate first. I'm gonna talk to him."

"To Ramsey?"

Aidan shook his head. "Nate. There's clearly something going on, and I think we can deal with it. *Without* the hate-fucking. 'Cause there's no way that's gonna solve anything."

"Seems pretty ballsy, thinking you can fix this," Dawson said, but historically, Cam thought Aidan made a pretty good argument that he could.

"And what, you just wanna leave that guy out to dry?" Aidan gave Dawson a sharp look, and Dawson's expression melted from teasing to understanding in a second.

"I get it," Dawson said.

"I'd think you would," Aidan said, nodding. "Didn't leave *you* out to dry either, Hall. Thought about it. But I didn't."

"What?" Dawson looked shocked. "But Marty—"

Aidan picked up his water and stood. "Who do you think gave him the idea?" he asked.

The game was restarting, but Dawson was staring at Aidan's retreating back like he couldn't quite believe what he'd said.

"What is it?" Cam murmured. Not sure he'd followed what had just happened.

"I thought . . ." Dawson shook his head, like he was trying to clear it. "Marty approached me, after Baltimore released me. Everyone else wanted a tryout, for me to come in and kick with some other guys, but not him. The Thunder were the only team to offer me an outright contract."

"You didn't know it was Aidan." Cam was getting it now.

"We hadn't talked in *years*. I mean, the kind of easy small talk you exchange on the field before games, sure, but nothing more than that. I wouldn't have even said we were still friends."

Cam reached over and squeezed Dawson's knee. "Guess you were."

"Guess we were." Dawson sounded mystified still.

Cam didn't know whether he felt grateful that someone had given a shit about Dawson still—and someone who was in a position to do something about it—or a little envious that it had been Aidan. At least he didn't need to worry about Aidan harboring feelings for Dawson. It was obvious how head over heels he was for Levi.

"I think . . .I think Aidan's one of those dudes where if you're one of his guys once, you're one of his guys forever," Cam suggested.

"Yeah." Dawson looked like he was just now realizing this.

"You think he can fix this thing between Ramsey and Nate?"

Dawson shrugged. "If anyone can do it . . ."

A second later Elliott Jones sniped in a beauty of a shot and they were all on their feet, yelling about it. "Shit!" Cam exclaimed as the suite celebrated the goal. "That was *sick*."

"Sure was," Dawson agreed, and they exchanged a smile.

"It's no football game," Dawson said as he let them into his apartment a few hours later, "but that was a great way to spend an evening."

"Yeah, for sure," Cam agreed. "I've not really watched hockey much before."

"Everyone told me this was a hockey town, and I can see that now," Dawson said, toeing off his shoes and hanging up his jacket. Cam followed suit and then trailed after him into the kitchen.

"We're six and oh and I think everyone's getting behind us now," Cam argued. He'd heard that too, though—that Toronto only cared about hockey, about how their Leafs hadn't won a Stanley Cup in sixty-some-odd years.

But there'd definitely been a big cheer from the crowd between the second and third period when they'd shown the team in their suite on the jumbotron.

"Careful, rook," Dawson joked, "you're gonna jinx us."

"Never," Cam said stoutly.

"Yeah," Dawson said and leaned in, pinning Cam against the counter. "I think you're gonna have to undo that, rook. You got any ideas?" His voice was teasing and lit Cam up inside.

When it came to Dawson, Cam *always* had ideas.

Cam wound his arms around Dawson's neck, pulling him in closer. Kissing him with everything he was feeling but hadn't said yet. "Yeah. Take me to bed."

He thought he'd been clear enough, but when they reached the bedroom, Dawson pressing him down to the bed, Dawson still hesitated.

"You're sure?" he murmured against Cam's lips. "Tomorrow—"

"You'll be gentle," Cam said.

"Oh yeah?" Dawson tugged Cam's sweatshirt off, and then his fingers went to the button of Cam's jeans. Tugged them down.

"But not too gentle."

"Wouldn't dream of it. I know how you like it." And he did, by now. So well that it always took Cam a little aback whenever he realized Dawson didn't seem to realize what they were doing. How they were so much more than just friends and fuck buddies. Everyone else saw it. But not Dawson.

Maybe he just wasn't ready yet. When Cam thought of how Dawson had genuinely believed that nobody had wanted him any longer, it was hard to be surprised.

He just needed more time. More patience. And Cam could give him both of those things, freely. Especially when it was as easy as it was tonight, Dawson's mouth hot and sweet on his, his touch leaving trails of aching fire through him.

Pushing Cam farther back on the bed, Dawson teased his cock with his tongue as he slicked up his fingers and slid one in, careful and gentle.

Cam had always thought it would be easier if Dawson's affection was obvious, but tonight, it felt bigger than Cam could hold, the warmth in his eyes and the clear tenderness in his touch.

"Harder," Cam begged, spreading his legs wider. Needing more. Needing Dawson to push him, to push all these feelings away, even for a moment.

"God, you're so hot like this," Dawson murmured, sounding blown apart. He slid another finger alongside the first, but then he leaned in, pressing a soft kiss to the crease of Cam's hip. Cam couldn't squirm away from it. He could only lie there and feel it, the perfect juxtaposition of Dawson's insistent fingering, fast and a little rough, and the soft, thoughtful look on his face.

Pleasure spiked through Cam as he teased a third finger around his rim, rubbing against that spot deep inside. He groaned deep, limbs shaking as Dawson took him apart.

"Come on," Cam begged. "I'm ready—I want it. Want *you*." Dawson needed to do it before Cam lost his brain-to-mouth filter and along with getting fucked into the mattress Cam confessed all the half-realizations and feelings he was still pretending he wasn't having.

"Want you too. So fucking much." Dawson pulled off his shirt. Shoved his jeans down. And a second later was crowding against Cam, skin to skin. "Make me crazy."

Cam made *him* crazy? Cam almost laughed then, a little hysterically. Dawson didn't even know how he was turning him inside out. Making him want things he'd never given a second thought to before.

He looked at Aidan and Levi, with their clear sense of possession between them, and *craved* more. Not from just anyone, but from Dawson. Thought about how Dawson had grabbed his hand during a particularly fraught moment in the third period and held on long past it.

It would've been so much easier—but maybe not better—if all he'd wanted from Dawson was *this*. Him pushing in, cock hard and slick as it moved inside him, lighting him up from the inside out.

His hips settled against Cam's hips, Dawson groaning with it, and Cam turned away, burying his face in his elbow. His face *and* all the embarrassing noises that he couldn't help making.

Dawson gave him a sharp smack on the thigh. "None of that. Let me hear you. Tell me how good this dick makes you feel."

Cam squeezed his eyes shut and then opened them again. Wondered if Daws even knew how he looked right now. "Amazing," he admitted breathlessly.

"Gonna make you feel even better," Dawson said, beginning to thrust in earnest, his fingers wrapped around Cam's knee, that same tender-rough contrast turning Cam inside out.

Cam couldn't even tell him to stop, because it felt too good, too right. He was lost to it. Dawson tucked his body under his, attuning every nerve Cam possessed into his frequency.

A drop of sweat fell from Dawson's hairline to Cam's chest, sliding down his pec, and he nearly cried with it as Dawson found a new angle that had him seeing stars.

"Yeah?" Dawson's voice was breathless. "Like that?"

"I'm gonna—" Cam trembled. He hadn't thought sex could be like this—an otherworldly, magical experience. His whole body felt like it was glowing with it, and a second later, he was shaking apart, come shooting all the way up his chest.

Dawson's eyes screwed shut and he followed.

That, Cam thought, even as the lassitude of all those endorphins surged through him, was better.

Because if Cam looked at him in the eye right now, he wasn't sure even Dawson could pretend that this wasn't what this was.

He'd pretended, over and over, and right now, he couldn't manage it. Only a few days earlier, he'd been full of disbelief when Nate had offered to kick Dawson's ass for hurting him.

Hadn't believed things could ever come to that.

But his heart felt raw tonight. Had seen, a little too well, what it could be like.

If a stranger had looked at Aidan and Levi, and then at Dawson and Cam, he wasn't sure they'd be able to tell the difference. Dawson's clear affection in his gaze, in the way his eyes sparkled when Cam teased Aidan. The possession in his touch. How Cam wanted to give it right back, a constant loop of feedback.

He'd never been in love before, and Cam had always thought it would feel incredible, like flying without a parachute, but now he just felt vaguely sick to his stomach as Dawson groaned, sitting up to grab them something to clean up with.

"You're quiet tonight," he said, after he wiped both of them down and nestled back down in bed, Cam in his arms like that was exactly where he belonged.

You're going to be fine. You'll be fine in the morning. You'll be used to it by then.

Cam still wanted to believe those reminders. Thought they could still theoretically be true.

"Just thinking," Cam said.

Maybe he ached a little, but he still wouldn't trade it. Still had no interest in walking downstairs to his cold, empty apartment. It was just so much *better* up here, in Dawson's. And not because there was anything special about Dawson's place over Cam's. They were still the same. Same basic layout. But wherever Dawson was, that was where Cam needed to be.

"Wanna share?"

Cam risked a glance over. Dawson's hazel eyes were soft and satisfied. Pleased, even. His arm tightened around Cam, fingertips stroking his biceps.

He didn't want to lie. He didn't even want to lie by omission. But he couldn't tell Dawson what he was thinking. *This isn't a hookup. It's maybe* never *been a hookup. Not for me, and I'm pretty sure not for you either.*

Instead, he changed the subject.

"What do you think *is* going on between Ramsey and Nate?"

"I think you nailed it," Dawson said drowsily. "They're pulling each other's pigtails."

"But why?" Cam questioned. "Why not just . . .give in? If they both want it?"

Dawson chuckled lowly. "You've never been burned, have you?"

"What, like romantically?" Cam asked, and Dawson nodded.

"No. Not like . . .not like you mean, I think. I've never been in a real relationship before." *Not like this one.* "Nothing to get burned by."

"Never?" Dawson sounded surprised.

"Yeah. Like hookups. Friends with benefits. That's it."

"Those can go south," Dawson observed. Like that wasn't what he was currently pretending they were doing. The fact that he could bring it up so casually, like it could never go south between them said it all. But clearly, he *had* gotten burned. Cam didn't need any details of his marriage and his divorce to know that. Dawson's hesitation to call a spade a spade made it obvious.

"Well, yeah, sure. But not for me," Cam said. He didn't add, *only if there are feelings involved,* because he wasn't about to invoke the *F* word tonight, of all nights. Not when his heart already felt so raw.

"Lucky," Dawson said wryly. "But yeah, that's my guess. They've got some baggage. One of them, or both of them. Or something else between them. And that always complicates things."

"Baggage does?"

"Well, yeah. But it's really what the baggage produces. *Fear*." Dawson chuckled humorlessly. Like maybe he understood this far too well.

"So they're both afraid, and so instead of doing anything about it, they just . . .avoid it? But they don't want to ignore each other either, so they just what, poke and prod?"

"Yeah, sort of."

Cam snorted. "That sounds childish."

"Yeah, well. Not all of us can be old souls at twenty-two," Dawson said and stretched his back out. But he still didn't let go of Cam. "You're kind of a wonder, you know?"

"I am?"

"Yeah. So honest and like . . .uncomplicated. Easy."

Cam made a face, and Dawson laughed. "I mean it as a compliment. It's a good thing. It makes this . . .it makes this so good."

He had to wonder that if he told Dawson everything he was thinking and feeling tonight, if he would still be singing the same tune. He didn't feel honest or uncomplicated or easy. He wasn't pushing any of that onto Daws, not yet, so of course he still believed those things were true.

Maybe that wasn't right, but he understood too, what Dawson had said about fear. It made it hard to be honest.

Because what if he pushed and he ended up pushing Dawson right out of his bed? He had it so good right now. Had everything he wanted, except the words. And maybe those mattered, but would risking everything to get them be worth it? Cam wasn't sure.

"It *is* good," Cam said hesitantly. "I didn't think it could be so good."

Dawson turned back, curling into him. Amusement on his face. "But you've done this before."

Cam did not roll his eyes but he wanted to. "Yeah, but not like this," he said. "Not with you."

It shouldn't have, but somehow it made it easier that Dawson was dumb and clueless. Truly so stupid to not be able to read between the lines. "Oh, and I make all the difference, huh?" He sounded smug.

For a split second, Cam almost told him that he should be the opposite. Embarrassed, actually, for not picking up on what he wasn't saying. But then, Dawson's certainty that he made it good—that they made it good together—soothed, too.

"Yeah," Cam agreed.

Maybe Dawson wasn't saying it. Maybe Dawson couldn't verbalize it, even to himself, but there was no question in Cam's mind.

He *was* feeling it, too. Just the same as Cam was.

CHAPTER 16

"You've worked your way through all four of those recs already?" Aidan looked at him in surprise, setting down his chicken wrap. "Seriously?"

"We've been going out a few times a week," Dawson said, trying not to sound defensive. He'd wanted to ask Aidan quickly, before Cam showed up in the cafeteria. "Ordered in a few times."

"Okay. I didn't realize you were so serious about it," Aidan said.

"Not *serious*," Dawson said, definitely defensive this time and not sure he could help it. There was just something unsettling about the word *serious* that he didn't want to look at too closely.

Aidan shot him a look. Dawson had known the guy for so long, but it had been awhile since they'd spent so much time together, and he was beginning to recognize some of his tics again. And that look? It never boded well.

"I meant, not that you were serious about the rec list," Aidan said with exaggerated patience. "I meant, you're clearly serious about the rookie."

"What?" Dawson squawked. He was right—or wrong, actually, because this was even worse than he'd imagined. "I told you we're friends. Hanging out. And sure, yeah, hooking up."

"Daws, you held hands with him for the whole third period of the Leafs game."

"That was . . .that didn't mean anything."

"No?" Aidan's eyebrow skidded up.

"I was nervous about the game. We wanted the Leafs to win, and that *was* a stressful third period. Only a one-goal game."

"I've never known you to give two shits about hockey or the Leafs," Aidan countered. "You *or* him. What was the score on their game Friday night? Who are they playing tonight?"

Dawson had no fucking clue. "It's different when you're there, in the arena," he claimed, even though he knew that was shit. Why *had* he reached over and taken Cam's hand? Because he just wanted to, that was why. Because Cam had been clenching it around his leg, worry etched over his face, and it had seemed like a comfort to both of them, when things had gotten nerve-wracking in the third.

"Didn't see you reaching for *my* hand," Aidan said.

"That's 'cause Levi would have chopped it off." Dawson could hear the fear in his voice. Not because Levi was absolutely possessive as shit, but because he'd just been *doing*, not *thinking*. Not about any of it.

But now he was recalling all the nights he and Cam had spent in each other's beds—pretty much every night; not *only* when they had sex, but plenty of other times, too—all the breakfasts and dinners and carpooling. They'd been basically inseparable. Dawson was six movies into their *Fast and Furious* binge, and maybe deeper into something else.

But *no*, they'd agreed it was just hooking up. If that had changed, surely Cam would've said something. If he didn't like what they were doing, he *would've* said something. Dawson believed that, no question. Instead, he was going around looking cute as fuck, all the goddamn time, huge smile on his face, his sweet, sure positivity transforming Dawson's life.

"What about the fact that you stayed in his room when we were in Indy," Aidan said.

"Oh, that's just . . .you know. Hooking up," Dawson said. "Sex. I shouldn't have to explain that to you anymore."

Aidan shot him a pitying look. "Do you remember when Levi and I started dating?"

"You mean, when you were hooking up and were sure that was all it was? But you were actually head over heels in love with each other?" Dawson couldn't help but feel a little smug as he leaned back in his chair. See? He knew what the fuck he was talking about. He could still get one over on Aidan.

But Aidan's expression morphed from pity to . . .*worse*? Nope, that was not supposed to be happening. "Oh, bud," he said.

"What?" Dawson demanded.

"Pot, meet kettle."

"What, *no*," Dawson said. He wasn't in love with Cam. If he was, he'd . . .well, he couldn't be. That was all it was. Whenever he thought about the last time he was in love and how that had ended—in betrayal and ugly words and even uglier metaphorical wounds, and then the capper to the whole nightmare, the logistics of the divorce—he felt sick to his stomach. He wasn't doing that again. Not ever.

What he and Cam had was great. No strings. No worries. No fights. Everything was *golden*.

"You're going on all these dates. You're staying over in each other's places—"

Dawson opened his mouth to argue about that even though he knew it would be a lie.

But Aidan just kept going. "I know you are, so don't even bother trying to tell me otherwise. You both keep slipping up. You spend a night apart since that first night? Have you?"

Dawson wasn't counting. That was the *whole point*, fuck you very much.

"No idea," Dawson said shortly.

"It's not a bad thing. It's a good thing. You're happy. Way happier than you were when you showed up here this summer and it was like you had a little thundercloud hovering over you everywhere you went."

"You're one to talk," Dawson grumbled.

Aidan leaned forward. "Exactly. *Exactly*. I've been there. I was fucking right there, with you, at one point, so I can see it. Way more clearly than you, anyway."

"What does it matter what it is if we're both enjoying it?" In the back of his mind, Dawson knew why it mattered, but if he believed it, then it would mean that it would have to end, because he couldn't go there—not yet and maybe not *ever*—and he was definitely *not* ready to have it end.

"That's a question between you and Cameron," Aidan said sympathetically.

"I came to you for restaurant recs, not a dissection of my personal life." Dawson was annoyed.

"We're all seeing it."

"So what, you're doing to us what you said you'd do for Nate and Ramsey? We don't need any help. We're not stupid; we're *fine*."

"I think that's probably up for debate," Aidan said, and Dawson growled under his breath.

"Just saying," Aidan said, grinning. "Kind of stupid."

"Are you gonna send me more restaurant recs or am I gonna have to go ask someone else?"

Aidan picked up his phone. Typed a few things. Dawson felt his own phone vibrate in his pocket. "There you go, I'd say be safe with them, but . . ."

"But what, now lecturing me and the rook about safe sex is too much?" Dawson snorted. "It's ironic, that's what it is."

But the way Aidan looked at him, like he could see right into Dawson's mind and knew everything Dawson was not thinking about, was galling.

"Ugh, you're the worst," Dawson complained as he pulled his phone out. Checked the list. And yep, despite his general obnoxiousness as a friend, he could count on Aidan for the best spots to visit in the city.

"You're welcome," Aidan said, and he actually had the nerve to laugh about it.

Cam chose that moment to come over to the table, sandwich in one hand and two bottles of Gatorade in the other. He set one of them—Dawson's favorite flavor, blue—in front of him and settled down next to Dawson, hand on his knee as he unwrapped his sandwich with the other.

Aidan just raised an eyebrow pointedly. "Daws was just grabbing some more dinner recommendations for you two," he said.

Dawson was afraid for a split second that Aidan might say more. Might divulge everything he'd just been lecturing Dawson about, therefore not just opening Dawson's third eye, but Cam's as well. But Aidan didn't say anything, *thank God*. He'd known he didn't want anything to change, but even imagining the possibility of it made him squirm in his seat.

"How do you feel about Lebanese?" Dawson said.

"Oh!" Cam exclaimed between bites of sandwich. "I don't know. Not yet anyway. But I'm excited to find out."

"Good," Dawson said smugly. "We'll go there tonight."

Cam smiled at him, slow and intimate and the warmth that bloomed in Dawson's stomach made it surprisingly easy to push away everything Aidan had just been saying. What did he know anyway? This was a guy who'd never really dated anyone—who'd barely even hooked up with anyone—until he was in his thirties. He was clueless. Dawson and Cam were fine. *Better* than fine.

Turned out that Cam was a huge fan of Lebanese.

He devoured the first set of kabobs the waiter brought and it hadn't even been a question for Dawson to order more as he tangled his feet under the table with Cam's.

"This is fucking delicious," Cam said, shoveling another bite of saffron rice and chicken into his mouth.

"Good," Dawson said.

Cam glanced up at him. "You're not really eating."

"I am," Dawson said, but he wasn't really. He was too busy thinking. Too busy watching Cam when he didn't think he was being observed.

Tilting his head, Cam examined his face, an intent expression that shouldn't have made Dawson nervous, but did, anyway.

"You wanna talk about it?"

"Talk about what?"

Cam set down his fork, which really said a lot. "Come on, Daws," he entreated. "You've been distracted all dinner. The food's good and I like to think the company's up to par—"

"It is," Dawson reassured him immediately. He wasn't thinking about what Aidan had said earlier. Well, he was deliberately *not* thinking about it. But he'd gone out of his way to do something else, right before they left the practice facility, and it was making him additionally nervy. He'd considered putting it off after the conversation with Aidan, but he'd put it off long enough, and he couldn't do it anymore.

It hadn't been hard to find the name of the prosecutor on the paperwork. Or very hard to dial up the office and let his name do all the talking.

The person he'd talked to had reassured him that he'd hear from the prosecutor.

Now all he had to do was wait.

Which . . .turned out that was the hard part.

"Then what's up?" Cam asked, crease appearing between his brows. And that wasn't allowed. Dawson would confess to just about anything just to take that look off Cam's face.

"You know how you told me I needed to find out for myself what was really going on with the Ackerman case?"

Cam nodded.

"Well, I'm doing it. I contacted the prosecutor's office directly and well—" Dawson cleared his throat. "I'm hoping that they'll get back to me. Let me know what the real situation is."

"That's great, Daws," Cam said, eyes full of sincerity.

"I hope it is. I'm sure when Simon finds out he's gonna be pissed. Hurt, too, that I didn't trust him." Dawson was sure that he was just being paranoid, and that when push came to shove, Simon was probably going to be justifiably annoyed that he hadn't just trusted him. Why shouldn't Dawson trust him? He hadn't ever done a thing to earn anything else.

"Simon should understand exactly why you need this," Cam said. "If he was a friend, he'd get it."

Dawson *had* tried to trust blindly, but he wasn't any good at that anymore, unable to shake the feeling at the back of his head. He knew if he didn't do something to make sure he knew the whole situation, even if he made his peace with the plea deal, he'd not be able to entirely move on.

Start fresh.

And if he ever *did* want to examine anything that he was deliberately not thinking about—if he ever hoped of making Cameron something more to him than just a friend and a hookup—then he needed to put all of this to rest so he could finally heal.

"I hope so," Dawson said. "And I really hope it's just *me*. That it's nothing."

"We'll see," Cam said, then leaned forward across the table. Eyes intent on Dawson's. "I'm there for you, no matter what. Whichever way it turns out."

Dawson smiled, nodding, and realized as he picked up his fork that he'd never questioned whether *that* was true.

Maybe other people bred mistrust in him, but not Cameron. Never Cam. It was so easy to take his open and easy nature and believe in it, wholeheartedly.

"This is . . .uh . . ." Dawson pushed rice around his plate, picking up little bits of extra garlic sauce. "This is good for you, yeah?"

"Lebanese? I thought that was obvious." Cam laughed. "We had to order more food, Daws."

"Not the Lebanese, though don't tell Aidan that, because he's already bordering on insufferable. I mean . . .uh . . .what we're doing. You and I."

Cam looked up at him, surprise written all over his face. "Did you think it wasn't good?"

"No, no, I did. I *do*. I love it. I—" Dawson bit off the rest of whatever embarrassingly rhapsodic thing he was about to say. "I'm good. I just want to make sure you're good, too. I know we said hookups, and we are, but we're . . .uh . . .spending a lot of time together."

"If I didn't like it, I'd tell you," Cam said.

"Right. Right. I knew that. I did. I just wanted to make sure." Dawson wished now that he'd never brought it up. Of course Cam would've told him if he'd crossed a line, even inadvertently.

"Being here in Toronto, on the Thunder, was good before, but now that we're hanging out all the time? It's so much better. I feel . . ." Cam trailed off before he could finish his sentence, but whatever look he was wearing on his face? Dawson felt the echo of it in his own chest.

At the very least, they were on the same page.

"Yeah, same," Dawson said, and it wasn't hard at all to smile at Cameron then. It came so easy and natural.

"Good, 'cause I love learning about this stuff. Like new food and new cultures. Even if it freaked me out at first."

"You didn't want to look stupid," Dawson said. He got it. He'd been there, too. Maybe it had been a long time ago and he'd had a little more experience with a big city, but it wasn't all that much different.

"Not in front of anybody, sure, but definitely not in front of you." Cam nudged Dawson's foot. "Might've had a little bit of a crush on you."

"Had?" Dawson teased.

Cam flushed. "You know exactly how it is," he claimed.

"Yeah, I do," Dawson said, and it was hard not to sound smug about that. Not when he had Cam in his bed now, the day after that, and the day after that, and hopefully well . . .for a really freaking long time.

Dawson packed *that* thought away before it did any damage.

Well. Any *more* damage.

"I was thinking we could watch another movie tonight, if you wanted," Cam said.

"You mean put the movie on and make out the whole time?" Dawson asked archly. That's what they'd done with numbers three through five, which they'd then had to rewatch later, making an attempt to keep to their ends of the couch.

"Don't tempt me with a good time, Daws," Cam said earnestly.

Nobody could blame him for making sure they were on the same page, because it *was* so good. Cam fit into him—and Dawson was beginning to realize, *he* fit into *Cam*—better than he'd ever imagined.

Cam smiled at him, wide and beautiful, his brown eyes brimming with affection, and Dawson felt a pulse of gratitude so intense, so satisfying, he nearly opened his mouth and said, *Don't ever leave me. Don't ever let this thing between us die. Don't ever go away and leave my life in shambles.* But more damning than anything, *Don't ever hook up with anyone else. Not like Brynn.*

Dawson shoved all that crap away or down—it didn't matter where it went as long as it wasn't in front of his mind—and went back to eating his food, which was, as Cam declared, really fucking delicious.

Cam had cleaned his plate and Dawson was close when he felt a buzz in his pocket. Pulled out his phone and knew, from the Baltimore area code, who it was. The prosecutor was calling him.

"Who is it?" Cam asked. "Is it the prosecutor?"

Dawson nodded, and Cam reached over, squeezing his arm. "I'll grab the check. You go take that call."

"Alright," Dawson said, rising to his feet and grabbing his jacket.

It was cold, but not raining at least, so he flipped his collar up and answered the phone.

"Hi, this is Dawson Hall."

"Oh, good, Mr. Hall. I'm glad I caught you." The woman's voice was light and musical. Not the hard-nosed, very male lawyer that he'd expected. Maybe this was the assistant? He'd only seen N. Kaminski listed in the paperwork.

"Of course," Dawson said.

"I'm Natalia Kaminski, the lead prosecutor in the Ackerman case."

"Oh." *Oh.* He felt very stupid now, unpleasantly reminded of all the times Brynn had told him, rolling her eyes, about how he didn't even realize how privileged he was. He shouldn't have assumed that N. Kaminski was a man.

"I'm very glad you contacted me," she said, forging ahead like he hadn't sounded surprised that she was who was handling the case. "Your lawyer has been . . .well, we'll say, very stringent about gatekeeping your time and attention. I get it. You have a job that requires it, but it's been somewhat frustrating from this side."

Dawson unstuck his voice. "What? You wanted to talk to me and Simon wouldn't let you?"

She sighed. "Yes. Simon's been very eager for us to give attention to this plea deal Ackerman's lawyers suggested, but . . ." She trailed off and Dawson thought he might throw up all the Lebanese food he'd just eaten, right here on this sidewalk.

Simon had said, over and over again, how it was the prosecutor's office who wanted the plea to go through. Not *him.*

"But?" he managed to ask.

"I want justice for you, of course, but there's a whole host of families he stole from. I want justice for *them,* too," she said. "And as terrible as it might sound, you being involved means press and attention and makes people give a shit."

"That's what I want too. I want him to pay. To not spent the next few years in his cushy-ass mansion." Dawson could hear the desperate edge to his voice. The panic rising inside him.

Simon had lied. He'd *lied*. After he knew everything Dawson had been through. How paranoid he'd gotten. How terrified he was to trust anyone. But he'd done it anyway.

"Good. We're on the same page, then."

"In the future, contact me directly," Dawson said. He was sure Simon would have an excuse. A reason why he'd twisted this whole situation. But it didn't matter. There was no earthly explanation he could ever stomach that could justify Simon's betrayal.

"Of course." There was the barest whisper of sympathy in her voice, but she was a professional. She wasn't going to ask. Didn't need to ask, probably. "Give me your email. I'll include you directly on all the correspondence in the future."

"And whatever you need," Dawson said, after he spelled it out for her. "I don't know what Simon told you about my willingness to testify, but I'm ready to do it."

"I'm still hoping it doesn't come to that, but I appreciate it, and the other victims will too," Natalia said wryly.

"That's the idea," Dawson said. It was easier to focus on that, on what he could do, than on the horrible feeling spreading through him, poison running through his veins.

Was it just Simon? Or was his agent in on it too? Had Simon and Alex conspired together to keep Dawson in the dark? The bottom of his stomach dropped out, *again*.

"If you need anything else, don't hesitate to reach out."

"I won't," Dawson said and meant it. He was going to have to involve himself personally. There was the obvious shittiness of how the betrayal felt. But then there was the additional wrinkle that he was going to have to journey back to that mental place where he'd lost himself last year. *Alone*. Without Simon and without Alex.

"Excellent. Have a good night." Natalia hung up.

"Daws?"

Dawson looked up and Cam was standing there, obvious worry on his face. It only hit him that maybe he wouldn't be alone this time.

He'd have Cam. Marty. Even Aidan, mostly because if he caught even a hint of what was going on, he'd butt in until Dawson confessed everything.

There'd been teammates and coaches in Baltimore, of course, but there it had always felt different. Like he only earned their approval as long as he was perfect. As soon as he'd stopped being perfect, their support hadn't exactly *ended*, but it had faded away over time, until it *had* felt like he was alone.

"You okay?" Cameron asked, coming over to him and putting a hand on his shoulder.

Dawson let out a short, unsteady breath. There was the truth and then there was what he might've said, to anybody else.

He'd thought it would be a lot tougher decision, but in the end, it wasn't at all.

"No," he said.

Cam's face creased with worry. "You were right," he guessed.

"Yeah. Yeah, it seems that way. I need to call Simon. And God, *Alex*."

"Alex?" Cam's arm looped all the way around Dawson's shoulders now, pulling him in close.

"My agent." Dawson's throat clogged. Alex had been with him from the very beginning. How could he have conspired with Simon against him? He'd *known* how devastating the blows of last season had been.

"Shit." Cam gestured down the sidewalk. "You wanna deal with them on the walk home or when we get home or . . ."

"I'm going to call Simon first."

"Alright. Whatever you need." Cam's hand slipped down his shoulder and then grasped Dawson's, gripping it tightly and not letting go as they started to walk back towards their building.

He didn't have to repeat again that he was there for Dawson, no matter what the fallout, because Dawson *felt* it. Solid and unshakeable.

Of course he'd felt that way about Brynn too, at one point. But by the time things had come to a head last year, things between them had already disintegrated into ash. Burned up *and* burned out.

Dawson stared at his phone. He was really tempted to call Alex first. He'd known Alex longer. But the way the reality was taking shape in his mind, he had a feeling whose idea this had been. Before this, he'd have trusted Alex with his life. Simon he'd trusted too, but *less.*

There'd always been a worry in the back of his mind that Simon was a little too smooth, a little too easy. He'd told himself it was just the natural distrust of lawyers, but now he looked at that and wondered if deep down, he'd already known the truth.

So he called Simon first.

Simon picked up on the third ring, the sound echoing like he was in the car. "Hey, Daws, what's up?" he asked.

There was nothing to do but rip the Band-Aid off. Dawson had spent enough time shying away from the truth; too much time already worrying that he was right.

"I just got off the phone with Natalia Kaminski," Dawson said bluntly.

"I told you—"

"I know what you fucking told me," Dawson retorted, suddenly full of blinding rage. "I know all the lies you told me."

"They weren't *lies*," Simon said entreatingly. "We were worried about you! You nearly flushed your career down the drain in Baltimore. The last thing you needed was for you to get dragged into all this bullshit again. It's what I kept telling Kaminski, but she wouldn't accept it."

"*We?*" Dawson asked in a low voice. He'd assumed that it had to be Alex, too.

Simon sighed. Admitted reluctantly, "Alex and I. It was my idea, but he went along with it. He was so worried you'd never get over what happened last season, and I told him the best thing was for you to just move on."

"That what you wanted too?" Dawson asked bitterly.

Cam squeezed his hand again. Dawson squeezed back.

Simon must be seeing the writing on the wall, because he actually admitted it. "For the gravy train to keep chugging along? Fuck yes. You know how many clients I got because I had *Dawson Hall* on my list?"

There it was. The bald truth he'd never wanted to see, right out there in the open.

It felt awful; he wanted to fall to his knees and vomit the poison out of his system until it was all gone. But he also knew, different from last year, that it would eventually be okay again. One day he'd wake up and it would be better. Just, *God*, he didn't want to give any of this up. He hoped that it would be better before he could finish what he'd started last season.

Because Simon wasn't wrong. He'd nearly flushed his career away over this.

"You're fired," Dawson said.

"You can't—"

"I can and I am," Dawson interrupted in a hard voice.

"Well, don't be stupid about Alex," Simon said ruefully. "He didn't like it. No killer instinct, that one."

"You mean he actually gave a shit about me?" Dawson asked.

Simon just made a disgruntled noise and Dawson was done. He hung up.

Cam didn't say anything for a whole block as Dawson tried to stop shaking.

He didn't know if it was better or worse that the terrible thing he'd suspected, the worst-case scenario he'd told himself a thousand times was only a product of paranoia, was true.

It would've made him trust his instincts more, except that he'd trusted Simon in the first place. Trusted Alex, too, even though he didn't want to think it was the same. But maybe it was.

"You gonna call your agent?" Cam finally ventured, softly, when they were halfway down the next block.

Maybe it was needy to squeeze Cam's hand again, but he did it anyway. "I should. I *want* to. But I'm so fucking pissed. And hurt. And what if he . . ." Dawson swallowed hard. "What if he knows that and takes advantage of that? What if he weasels his way back in with an apology that I listen to because I don't want him to be as shitty as Simon was?"

Cam hummed under his breath. "I think you're not gonna know one way or the other until you listen to him say it."

"How are you so smart?" Dawson asked wryly. That was better than asking, *how did I get so goddamn lucky?*

"Not sure, but just happy it's helping," Cam said, shooting him a bashful smile.

Dawson nudged him with his hip. "Don't be modest, now."

Cam beamed up at him. "Wouldn't dream of it."

"I think . . .Simon was one thing, but I wanna see Alex's face when he says it. When he tries to worm his way back. When he gives me whatever excuse he's going to cook up." Dawson sighed. "I'm sure that the first thing Simon did was call him up."

"Might help you figure it out," Cam agreed.

Sure enough, it was less than five minutes later—they hadn't even made it back to the building yet—when Dawson's phone began to ring.

Dawson met Cam's eyes and nodded.

"Hey, Alex," he said when he picked up. It was easier to keep his voice steady with Cam's hand clasped in his. Maybe he should've been able to handle it either way, but was it so terrible to take the help when he needed it? Dawson wasn't sure.

"Oh, God, Daws. I'm so sorry." Alex sounded truly, horribly repentant. "I wanted to tell you the truth. I *did*."

As Dawson expected, he did want to believe him. "Then why didn't you?"

"I . . .you were so fucked up last year, Daws. So fucked up. And I know it was the divorce and everything else, too, and once things started disintegrating in Baltimore, it was like you couldn't stop it. But this was going to be your fresh start. I wanted to give that to you."

Dawson hummed under his breath. It was, nearly word for word, what he'd expected his agent to say. "I've got to focus on this game in two days," he said, "but you should come to Toronto for it. We'll talk after."

"Okay. Yeah. I can do that." Alex sounded relieved, like he hadn't just invited him-slash-insisted he come to Toronto at the end of October.

"Yeah, you can. After everything, you'd fucking better."

"I know. It was fucked. The whole situation was fucked, Daws."

Dawson didn't need Alex to tell him that. He'd lived it. He knew exactly how fucked it had been. And how fucked it was that after knowing everything, Alex had still gone along with Simon's plan—if that was what had happened.

Dawson still wasn't sure if he believed it.

"Trust me, I know," Dawson said.

"Yeah. Yeah, you would. Shit. Well, I'll be there. Gonna come to the game, and we'll go out after, alright? Nice dinner, just the two of us."

Dawson nearly said, *make that three, 'cause I want my emotional support rookie to come too,* but he didn't. Because they *weren't* dating, and only someone who was invested in that kind of relationship would be willing to sit through a dinner like this. Because it was going to suck. Dawson was going to have to play hardball. Listen to Alex whine and worry and generally vomit up any and every kind of apology in the hope that Dawson might listen.

"Alright," Dawson said.

"See you in a few days, Daws," Alex said.

Dawson nearly hung up then, but Alex continued in a halting voice, "I really appreciate you being willing to listen. I know you don't have to. I know you already fired Simon."

"I did," Dawson confirmed.

"You didn't have to give me a chance to explain," Alex said quietly.

Dawson didn't want to go into it; why he'd trusted Alex, but something about Simon had always made him feel uneasy. Probably because he was still worried he'd make the wrong call again.

"Yeah, I did," Dawson said.

"Well, I'm glad you did," Alex said. "See you on Sunday."

They were approaching the apartment building now. Cam tapped his keycard against the side door's sensor and they took the elevator up to Cam's floor in silence.

They'd taken off their coats and shoes before Cam turned to Dawson. "You still wanna watch a movie or . . .?"

Dawson took it as a good sign that Cam had already figured out that he didn't want to be alone. He hadn't even asked if he should press Dawson's floor when they were in the elevator. He'd just taken them to his own apartment, no hesitation at all.

That felt new, like something unfamiliar but good, *solid* even, shifting into place between them.

What *did* he want to do? Did he want to half-watch stupid car chases and explosions and way too much masculine posturing, all while he could barely drag his mouth off Cam's mouth for long enough to know what the fuck was even supposed to be happening?

Dawson turned to Cam and smiled. "Yeah, actually, I do. It seems like it might be a good distraction."

He didn't know how much any of this was going to fuck him up.

Specifically how these new betrayals would impact him. How committing to helping Natalia Kaminski might affect his focus and his game play for the rest of the season. It was all a risk. He should be freaking out; he kind of was, a little.

But it was hard to freak out too much when he was pressed up against Cam on Cam's crappy couch, his weight warm and solid and real against his body.

CHAPTER 17

THE BILLS COMING TO Toronto was always going to be a challenge.

Not only were they a good team—a *great* team, really, if Dawson was being bluntly honest about it—but Buffalo was so close to Toronto the stadium was typically split more evenly between the fans of the two teams.

They also came in with a chip on their shoulder, wanting to destroy the Thunder's win streak.

Dawson got it; if the shoe was on the other foot, he'd be heading into Buffalo determined to disrupt *their* win streak.

But the truth was, even though Dawson was new to this rivalry, it *was* a rivalry. The two teams had a history going back years and years, which could be credited to how they'd both been on hot streaks during the last decade plus.

So this game being a hard-fought battle was not a surprise. They'd traded opening drive touchdowns, then both defenses had settled down and they'd traded field goals. Cam and the Bills' punter got work then, the game turning into a chess match of field position.

But right before the end of the half, Trevor caught a beauty of a deep pass from Aidan, and the sideline erupted cheers only for them to sink into groans, Trevor losing the ball when he tried to make another move and get the team a yard closer to the end zone.

When he came back to the bench, anger and frustration evident on his face, Lane reached out for him, but Trevor just batted his hand away, heading to the opposite end of the sideline, muttering under his breath.

"Well, shit," Cam said, as they jogged into the tunnel. Instead of the Thunder scoring a touchdown before the half, the Bills had taken Trevor's fumble and driven down to the thirty-six-yard line and then kicked a killer fifty-one field goal.

Aidan was typically pretty quiet at halftime but Dawson couldn't remember the last time they were even behind at the end of the second quarter.

Today, he actually said a few words about how they were fighting and they needed to keep fighting.

The thought that had been rattling around Dawson's brain since the game had started and that he'd tried so hard to ignore was now pressing in, inexorably: *it's going to come down to you. It's going to come down to you and you're not going to be ready.*

He *was* ready though. He knew how to kick a fifty-plus-yard field goal. He'd done it so many times before. Won a Super Bowl. Won championships. Had faced down the worst pressure a kicker could imagine and come out on top.

He had the mechanics and the skill and he *wanted* to believe he had the focus to get it done.

But the ghost of last season was haunting the corners of his mind still, no matter how he tried to push the memories out, tried to keep his mind squarely aimed on the challenge of today's game.

At the end of the third, after the Bills had made it 20–10 with a long touchdown drive that had made Aidan scowl, Marty made his way over to check on where Dawson was practicing kicking into his net, keeping his leg warm in case he was needed.

With the way the game was going, he was already convinced that he'd be needed.

Marty coming over didn't do anything to dissuade him.

"You hangin' in there?" Marty asked.

"Yeah," Dawson said, leaning over to grab the ball and set it back on the tee. "I'll be ready."

"Nobody thinks you won't," Marty said.

"We gotta get another TD first, before it's even an issue," Dawson pointed out wryly.

Marty waved in the direction of Aidan and the offensive guys, huddling up. "You don't think they've got this?" He didn't need to ask how many late-game drives and game-winning drives Aidan had led, because it was a lot.

Today was no exception. Dawson watched as Aidan shouldered the team on his back and for the first ten minutes of the fourth quarter drove them down the field and pulled them within three points. Mo caught the touchdown in the corner, and the stadium erupted, every fan, whether they were wearing Bills or Thunder blue, sensing an exciting end to the game.

Now the defense just had to get the ball back without giving up any more points, and then Aidan—and Dawson—would have to do the rest.

After Dawson returned to the sideline after kicking the extra point and kicking off, right through the end zone so the Bills returner wouldn't have a chance to touch it, Nate and the defense huddled up and Aidan was already back on the bench, tablet in his hands.

Everyone was prepared to do what it took to win this game. Including Dawson. He went over to his net and began to gather his focus.

There was less than five minutes of regulation time left. The Bills would want to run the clock down with every play. If they got a handful of first downs, it would probably be enough to run the rest of the clock out, even if the Thunder used their timeouts.

There'd been a time when Dawson's gaze would be glued to the field, watching and waiting to see if he'd get a chance to tie the game and send them to overtime.

But he'd learned his focus was tighter if he ignored what everyone else was doing and, instead, kept his attention solely on his task: kicking.

Dawson leaned over and stretched out, carefully, counting to ten and then twenty before moving on to the next position. Then he grabbed one of his balls and set it on the tee, kicking it, over and over until it felt like the feeling of his foot hitting it was echoing through every molecule of his body.

He glanced up once, when the crowd erupted, and saw that Josh Allen had rushed for a first down. That was one. They'd need at least another two if they didn't want Aidan and the Thunder offense to get another crack at it.

And nobody on the Bills *would*. Aidan was worshipped for a reason. He was *that* good. The Thunder had won six in a row, and nobody else was as committed to keeping that streak going more than Aidan Flynn.

On the next play, Nate got a sack. Then on the next, they tackled the Bills' running back behind the line of scrimmage. It was a long third down.

When Dawson looked up, the Bills' punting team was heading onto the field.

Okay, they were hoping to pin the Thunder's offense on one end of the field, with very little time left on the clock—less than a minute—and no timeouts.

Tough, but not impossible.

Now, Dawson couldn't help but glance over at the field between every kick into his net. Aidan rolling to the right, Levi blocking for him like his life depended on it, Lane detaching from his defender and heading towards the sideline.

Aidan hit him for a twenty-yard gain, and suddenly, everything began to feel very real.

Dawson glanced over at Marty. Marty was already looking in his direction. He gave him a nod.

There was another fifteen-yard gain, and then another ten-yard pass.

And suddenly the offense was in the soft part of the field, right at the edge of Dawson's range, but still pretty far to throw a Hail Mary.

They could go that direction, and try to win the game. That was riskier. Less chance of it happening. Or Dawson could go over to Marty, to Coach Robertson, and tell him that he could kick it. It was fifty-nine yards. One yard more than his personal best.

Could do it and *wanted to do it* merged in Dawson's mind. He didn't know where one ended and the other began. But regardless, he found himself walking over to their head coach and meeting Robertson's eyes.

"I can do it," he said.

Robertson gave him a brief glance. "Yeah?"

"Let's go for the tie. Go to OT," Marty added, joining them.

Nodding, Robertson put a hand on Dawson's shoulder. "Go for it," he said.

There wasn't time to do another practice kick. The clock had stopped, because Aidan's last pass to Mo, he'd just managed to get out of bounds before he was tackled.

But they didn't have very long. They needed to get on the field. Get set up.

Marty waved Cam over, and they jogged to where the ball was sitting.

"You ready?" Cam asked, and Dawson nodded.

He didn't need to tell Cam that his hold needed to be perfect. That he was going to need every bit of time he had to get as much drive on the ball as possible. Fifty-nine yards was really fucking far. He could do it. He'd done it in practice so many times. Before games so many times.

But never *in* a game.

Dawson took one deep breath, then let it out. And another.

The clock restarted, only to count down to zero right after Joey snapped the ball.

Cam's hold was flawless, fucking textbook. Dawson even felt like his kick was strong, steady, even.

He nailed the ball, and it soared through the air, the whole stadium holding its breath as it just barely edged to one side of the upright.

The wrong side of the upright.

The hope in Dawson's chest deflated, like a balloon popping.

He'd missed. He'd *missed*.

He could have sent them to overtime. Maybe even given them the game. The seventh win in a row, but he hadn't gotten it done.

He hadn't been good enough. The moment had come, and like so many times last season, he'd fucking whiffed it.

Dawson stared at the end zone, at the crowd beginning to shuffle towards the exit.

He wasn't the hero. In fact he was the opposite. He was the guy who'd fucking blown it.

"It was so freaking close," Cam said, murmuring in his ear as he slung an arm around Dawson's shoulders, beginning to tug him to the sideline.

Like he knew Dawson would stand there and stare at the uprights forever, hoping the outcome would magically change.

Aidan was standing on the sideline, face slack with exhaustion, but eyes still bright blue. He was holding his helmet in one hand but he didn't hesitate to swap it to the other hand and put it around the other side from Cam.

"Hey, Daws," Aidan said.

But even though there was zero judgment in Aidan's voice, it was hard to even look at him. Because what if he saw it when he looked closer.

"Sorry," he mumbled.

"No. Don't do that shit," Aidan said staunchly. "Listen, we could've won that game so many times. And even if you made that—how many yards was it, even? Longer than your personal best, right?—we'd just be going to OT. No guarantees there."

Aidan was being nice, but Aidan also didn't know what he'd had to face just a few days before this game. What he'd discovered about Simon. What he was going to have to talk about with Alex tonight.

Maybe if he'd just let it go, maybe if he'd just accepted the plea deal, he would have nailed that fifty-nine-yard kick.

"No, but—" Dawson tried to argue, but before he could, Aidan interrupted him.

"No *buts*," Aidan said firmly.

"It was fifty-nine," Cam said softly next to them. "And yeah, a yard longer than his personal best."

"Not your fault," Aidan said, nodding over at Cam. "Listen to the rookie."

"He didn't say it wasn't my fault," Dawson muttered as they walked through the tunnel, down the corridor towards the locker room.

All the people who were watching them—the various staff that always were hanging around, they'd see that Dawson was upset. They'd see Cam on one side and Aidan on the other. Like he was fragile, and he wasn't. Not anymore. He was so tired of being a problem to fix. So fucking tired of trying to fix *himself*.

"Yeah, he didn't need to, because I heard what he wasn't saying, and so would you, if you were thinking clearly," Aidan said bluntly.

It wasn't that Aidan's tough love wasn't welcome or convincing, it was humiliating that it was needed at all. Even as he craved the comfort of it and desperately wanted to believe in the truth of it, he still didn't want to touch it.

"You shouldn't be doing this," Dawson said. "You should be, I don't know, licking your own goddamn wounds. Not mine."

Aidan laughed. "Dude, we're six and one. I'm not going to cry about it. It was bound to happen. And honestly? We were *in* that game. It was that close. I get you ten yards closer, give me another ten seconds on the clock? And that game's going to overtime."

"You think it would've?"

Aidan scoffed. "Dude, you saw the kick. It *barely* missed. Ten yards closer? You're money. I'd bet on you every single fucking time."

Aidan did sound very sure. His certainty was reassuring. But then, he didn't have the whole story.

They entered the locker room. It was quiet, but not deathly silent the way it could get sometimes after a bad loss. This was a frustrating loss, but Aidan was right about a lot of things: they *had* been in it, right until the very end.

Dawson just wasn't sure Aidan was right about *everything*. How could he be, when he didn't have all the information?

He turned to Cam. "I'm good," he told him. "I gotta—I'm gonna talk to Aidan for a minute."

Cam nodded, heading towards his locker to start stripping off his equipment.

"What is it?" Aidan asked under his breath. "You *are* okay, right?"

"I'm . . .well, I guess I'm okay." He'd told Cam the other night, when he'd found out about Simon, that he wasn't. He'd had a few days to come to grips with the knowledge. He'd be hearing Alex out later tonight.

"Some shit happened that might have divided my focus, kind of like happened last season," Dawson admitted.

"What shit?" Aidan didn't sound accusatory. Only calm and curious.

"I talked to the prosecutor on my ex-father-in-law's case, and it turns out that even though my lawyer kept insisting everyone wanted my stamp of approval on the plea deal, they didn't want that at all. They wanted the opposite."

"So your lawyer lied to you," Aidan said, pursing his lips together. "Seriously?"

"Lawyer *and* agent," Dawson said.

"Shit. Daws." Aidan put a hand on his shoulder and pulled him in for a quick hug. "Why didn't you tell me?"

Here it came. Aidan was going to say, *why didn't you tell me? Why didn't I know that before we sent you out there to kick the field goal that would've possibly won us the game? I should've just gone with the Hail Mary. Better chance, if your head wasn't in the game.*

"I don't know," Dawson said, shrugging awkwardly. But he knew. It was because he'd wanted so badly to believe he could do all of this anyway. That his focus and his skill were back on the same page and they were within his grasp again. That he could call on them when he needed them again, like he always had before.

"You had Cam, I get that. But, Daws, I'd have *still* wanted to know."

Dawson tried not to feel bitter about Aidan's words, but that didn't work very well.

"Sure, I get it," Dawson said sarcastically, beginning to pull out of Aidan's grasp.

"Wait, no," Aidan said, confusion creasing his face. And then it was even worse when the comprehension dawned. "I didn't mean it like that. *I meant*, I would've wanted to be there for you *as a friend*. I would've still sent you out there to make that kick. You didn't miss because you were distracted from what happened with Ackerman's case this week. You missed 'cause it was a really fucking long field goal, and frankly, it was *this* close to going in. What happened with your lawyer and your agent? I don't think it had anything to do with what went down today."

Dawson wanted to believe it so badly. But it was hard, when last year was right there, hovering in the back of his mind, as irrefutable evidence.

"I know you want to think that's true," Dawson started to say, but then Aidan smacked him, actually pretty hard, on his shoulder pad.

"No," Aidan countered, "I *do* think that's true. But I think the person you really need to convince is yourself."

He patted Dawson again, more softly this time, and turned to go.

"Hey," Dawson said, reaching out and catching his arm. "What do you mean by, *You had Cam*?"

Aidan rolled his eyes. "You cannot be this dense."

"I'm not *dense*," Dawson argued.

"You actually fucking are. He's the first person you told, wasn't he?"

"Well, we were out to dinner, so yeah," Dawson said.

Aidan shot him a long-suffering look. "My point exactly."

"Friends and hookups go out to dinner."

"Not *all* the time," Aidan said. "Listen, if you wanna lie to yourself, knock yourself out. But the moment it fucks up the rookie, I'm gonna be on your ass."

"What, this isn't you on my ass *now*?" Dawson asked sullenly.

"Oh, buddy, this isn't even close," Aidan said, patting him. "You wanna go out to Vault with us? I think Levi's getting a group together. Thought I might talk to Nate, too, if I can get him alone."

"Nah. I'm actually meeting up with my agent."

Aidan raised an eyebrow.

"I already fired Simon. The lawyer. But Alex?" Dawson sighed. "We've been together my whole career. I don't think this was his idea. Not that I'm really in a place to trust anything either of them say, but their stories were at least consistent about that."

"So you're gonna see him in person and judge," Aidan said, always astute.

"Basically, yeah," Dawson said.

"Well, good luck. If you want a drink after—you're always welcome."

"Sure. Yeah. You gonna take the rookie with you?"

Aidan shot him a look. "Oh, now you're worried about him?"

"I never said I wasn't," Dawson argued, even though he knew it would only give Aidan more ammunition.

"Yeah, yeah, we'll watch out for your boy," Aidan said, nodding, a glimmer of a smile on his face as he turned to walk towards his locker.

He finished up, shower and a few questions for the media, before he pulled Cam aside, right before he was ready to head out and meet Alex.

"Hey," he said, leaning against the wall of the corridor, "you going to Vault with the guys tonight?"

"Yeah, I was going to talk to my dad first and change. Then head out."

Dawson felt a pulse of worry. Was Cam going to try to be a hero again? Try to prove that he could walk alone in the city when he didn't *need* to do that? He wouldn't be there to talk Cameron down if he had another panic attack.

Aidan probably could. Lane or Trevor or Mo. But Dawson selfishly didn't want them to. Well, he didn't want Cam to have a panic attack *at all*.

Which was the whole point of this conversation.

"Take a cab, okay? Or don't walk alone. Let those guys pick you up."

Cam smiled at him. "You worried about me, Daws?"

It wasn't hard to be honest. "Yeah. I am. Last time—"

"Last time was different. I was . . .I was cocky. *Stupid*. Thought I could just get over it," Cam admitted wryly.

There were still a handful of people in the corridor, but Dawson decided he didn't give a shit. He reached out and cupped Cam's cheek, and Cam, to Dawson's delight, leaned into the touch. "If it was only that easy," Dawson said.

"I do feel better. Like . . .a more healthy level of fear, if that makes sense?" Cam confessed. "Like, I went out last week to the farmers' market. And that was fine. But you've helped. Helped me see the city as something not to fear, but as something cool and exciting, too."

That hadn't been Dawson's only purpose in taking Cam out, but it was a nice side benefit. He was thrilled it was working.

"I'm glad to hear it," Dawson said.

Cam tucked himself into Dawson's side, and Dawson couldn't help it—he put an arm around his waist, tugging him in closer. "It's probably smart to be cautious," Cam said.

"It is," Dawson agreed. "I don't ever want anything bad to happen to you, *ever*."

Cam gazed up at him, dimples on full display. "That's pretty sweet, Hall."

"It's how I feel," Dawson said, shrugging like it was no big deal. But he knew it was. It was that feeling that he kept pushing back down, like if he pretended it didn't exist, then it didn't.

But that didn't stop him from *feeling* it.

"Good." Cam brushed a quick kiss across his cheek. "I'll be safe, I promise. Even text you when I get there."

"And text me when you leave."

"You'll probably be home by then," Cam said, confusion crossing his face.

"Yeah, you can tell me when you're coming home to me." Dawson realized a second after he said it what that sounded like, but then decided *fuck it*, he'd already said it, hadn't he? And he *meant* it.

Cam's smile grew. "Sounds perfect."

CHAPTER 18

From the moment he met Alex in the hall on the suite level until they reached the restaurant and headed to their table, tucked in the back, Dawson made sure all that came up was the regular small talk.

He asked about Alex's wife and his two daughters. Dutifully laughed at a fun little anecdote about how Marisa, his four-year-old, had somehow gotten into his wife's makeup and had smeared it all over the brand-new cream-colored dining room carpet they'd just had custom made.

They'd briefly touched on the game, Alex making soothing noises about the miss, and reminding Dawson about how that kick had been technically out of his range. "And you almost made it, man," he said, patting him on the back as they sat in the back of the Uber.

But finally they made it to the restaurant and settled down at their table, Dawson picking up the wine list more because it felt good to have something in his hands when Alex leaned in and earnestly said, "I'm so glad I came this weekend."

"Are you though?"

"It was a good game. You guys lost, but it was close; anyone's game, really. Six and one is still fucking amazing, Daws."

"Yeah," Dawson agreed. Didn't mention that seven wins in a row would've been even better. They both knew that, and the thing was, Alex wasn't even really wrong about the argument he'd made. It *had* been close, a hard-fought rivalry game that could've been anyone's, right there at the end. If Aidan had had ten more seconds, they could've done one more pass, and then Dawson *would've* made that kick.

Sent them to overtime, and then all bets were off.

"To be honest, I thought you'd be more upset about it," Alex said, leaning back in his chair, studying Dawson's face carefully.

"That's because you've been obsessing about how last season went," Dawson countered. Aware also of how stupid that sounded, because it wasn't like he *hadn't* been obsessing over how last season went.

"Dawson, we've *all* been, that's why we did what we did. We were worried about you. Well, *I* was worried about you."

"Yeah," Dawson said bitterly, "Simon was just worried about his bottom line."

"About that—it wasn't about that for me."

Dawson tapped the wine list. "Are we talking about it now?"

"I thought that was why I came. So we could talk about it. Hash it out."

"Maybe I brought you to Toronto to fire you in person," Dawson countered. He was still mad. Though the anger had mostly faded, leaving behind a deep and pervasive hurt.

Alex just shrugged. Looking more resigned than upset by that statement. "Maybe, but I don't think so."

The waiter arrived then. Dawson had yet to open the stupid wine list, even though he was holding it, so he asked for a recommendation, and after a quick back and forth, they took his suggestion for a cab that would pair well with steak.

"First, before anything else, I want to say I appreciate you *not* firing me the way you did Simon," Alex said, sounding like he'd rehearsed that particular opening. "You could've."

"Yeah, I could've," Dawson agreed. But he'd known Alex a long time, and unlike Simon, Alex had never given him an uneasy feeling in the back of his mind.

"But you didn't. You gave me a chance to explain myself. So I will. I didn't *like* what Simon suggested, but, Daws, we've known each other a long time, and I've never seen you like you were last year."

"Last year was shit," Dawson agreed.

"No, it was, but it was worse than that. You were—I don't think you even realized how bad you were. Brynn told me that one day she came over to pick something up from your apartment and you were just sitting there in the dark, on the couch, staring at nothing. We were *worried* about you. I wasn't sure you'd be able to face a tryout situation."

Dawson couldn't recall that exact memory, but he didn't think it would probably help to admit he'd done it so many times they all blurred together. How often he'd hidden in his empty, awful apartment, in the dark, and wished everything and everyone would just go away.

"But then," Alex continued, "this job fell into your lap. Marty wanted you and nobody else when the Thunder kicker retired. I was so happy and so fucking relieved. And it was like you woke up for the first time in months. You moved here and started over, but the prosecutor kept wanting to drag you right back to that place. That was the last thing you needed."

Alex sounded genuinely torn up about it.

"It wasn't right to keep it from me. You should've let me make the choice."

"You'd have told me it was your responsibility to do what you could for the case. For all those other people who'd had their money stolen, too."

"And I'd have been right," Dawson countered.

"Yeah, but we were still using your name to get it done. Just not using *you*."

"It was still my call," Dawson reminded his agent in a hard voice. Not wanting to let himself fold to the obvious distress and concern in Alex's voice. That wasn't a lie. He'd been genuinely, really worried about

Dawson, and looking back, seeing it described from Alex's point of view, maybe he should've been.

"Yeah, it was," Alex admitted. "And I'm so fucking sorry that I went along with it. I didn't realize until it was too late that Simon gave a shit for the wrong reasons. By then, how was I supposed to fix it? I just thought if it got settled, then it would be over. You'd move on, because you were doing so much better. Happy, for the first time in a year, at least. I didn't even realize how long it had been or how bad it had gotten, until I saw you today."

Dawson didn't know what to say. He'd known he'd been coming out of it. Known that he'd felt *so* much better, these last months.

But hearing Alex say it that way? He couldn't help but think of what Aidan had said earlier. *You cannot be this dense.*

Because it was Toronto and the Thunder, yes, and it was the support he'd gotten from his teammates, for sure, and the success he'd had here to start the season, but it was more than that too. It was rediscovering his friendship with Aidan. Getting to know some of the other guys like Lane and Trevor and Nate. Being forced to befriend Mo against his will, but discovering he really liked the guy. Finally having Marty as a coach.

But it was more than even that.

It was Cam.

The rookie had wormed his way in and spread his sunshine around, lighting up all his shadows.

Dawson sighed. "I get it. You were only trying to do the best thing for me. He wasn't." He didn't say Simon's name. "But you were."

"I wish I'd seen through it earlier. But yeah, he was definitely a clout-chaser. Only gave a shit about you because you brought in more business. Didn't want you to fall apart because he worried about what it would mean for *him*."

It was easier than Dawson had expected to reply back and *mean* it. "But you were only worried about me."

Alex looked incredibly relieved. "Oh God, yeah. I was. I hoped you'd see that. I . . .I know I fucked up—"

"You can't do that shit again. Not ever again," Dawson stressed.

"I won't. I *wouldn't*. I know it was a mistake," Alex agreed.

Dawson had a feeling he would struggle for some time with who to trust and who not to trust—after Ackerman and then Simon, that wasn't much of a surprise—but he'd always trusted Alex. It wasn't so much building that trust back from scratch but polishing the scratches and pounding the dents out of what already existed between them.

The waiter arrived then, with their wine, and after pouring their drinks and taking orders for an appetizer he also recommended, disappeared again.

"To new beginnings," Alex said, lifting his wineglass.

Dawson picked up his own and tapped it against the lip of Alex's. "New beginnings," he echoed.

"So, what's happening with the case, now?" Alex asked after they'd discussed what they were going to order.

"I told the prosecutor that I'd be happy to do whatever she needed," Dawson admitted. "It *did* freak me out, and then today happened—"

Alex shot him a knowing look and interrupted, bluntly, "You can't think that has anything to do with this."

"Last year—"

But Alex didn't let him say it. "No," he said, as confidently as both Aidan and Cam had been. "That was a whole different thing. That was running out of time—and yeah, could Flynn have thrown a Hail Mary, sure? He could've. But it was chancy, either way. Either throwing to the end zone for the win or having you go out there, at the edge of your range, and try to take it to overtime. Neither was really a *good* choice, but they took the better chance. And you being a stronger chance than Flynn throwing a Hail Mary? I'd think about *that*."

Dawson did. Sat with it for a second. "I can see it," he agreed. "Still . . .I still get worried about it all going down the tubes, again."

"I think anyone would be," Alex empathized.

"I'm going out of my way to make sure that it won't," Dawson added.

"Yeah, you are," Alex said, leaning forward. "You've been *money* since you got here. This changes nothing."

"Okay," Dawson said, and to his surprise, he believed that was true now more than he had five minutes ago.

They ordered, enjoying the appetizer that arrived at the table. It was hard not to, since it was hot cheese, baked and laced with hot honey and thyme.

"So what else is new?" Alex said, after he finished going over some promotional opportunities. All of that probably could've been an email, but it was good—unexpectedly good, actually—to sit here with him and talk about them in person.

And of course, Dawson had *needed* to see his face when he told his side of the story. They'd never have been able to build that trust back if he hadn't.

"Well," Dawson said, hesitating. "I guess I'm . . .made a new friend?" He rubbed his hand on the back of his neck.

"A new friend *friend*?" Alex sounded surprised, but pleased. "And here I remember you declaring that you were never dating again, after Brynn."

"We're not dating. Um. Not officially. Not like that." But the more Dawson was looking at it, they kinda *were*. Just without saying the words.

"Like what, then?" Alex set his elbows on the table, looking fascinated.

Dawson was regretting bringing this up. The thought of officially dating, of being *serious*, still made him feel a little sick to his stomach. The thought of feeling something that could go sour, twisting uncomfortably, deep down.

Never mind how painful it would be if Aidan was *right* about something.

But being afraid of it didn't mean he wasn't already feeling it.

"Like, right now, it's just . . ." Dawson trailed off. *Sleeping together every night. Hanging out every day after practice. He's the first person I want to call when something goes south, but I don't even have to pick up my phone because he's already right there.*

When he thought it, it was hard *not* to see that Aidan might be right. *You cannot be this dense.*

It was humiliating, but maybe he *could* be that dense.

"It's just what?" Alex prompted. "I've never known you to be cagey about someone you're interested in before. When you first went out with Brynn, after like three or four dates, you announced to me that you were going to marry her." Alex made a face. "Come to think of it, maybe that's a good reason to be cagey about it."

Dawson had forgotten about that too. Or maybe *forgotten* wasn't the best term. Pushed it entirely from his head like he could actually pretend he'd never felt that sure, that happy, was probably more accurate.

"So, you're feeling a little burned," Alex continued. "But you like this . . .person?"

"It's a guy," Dawson said. "But that shouldn't be a surprise."

"I knew you were into both. If you're worried it's going to be a problem, it won't."

"I wasn't. I was more worried about . . ." Dawson waved around his head, rolling his eyes. "My whole bullshit."

"Fair," Alex agreed. "So, who is he? You gonna tell me about him?"

Dawson probably should tell him exactly who it was, but he still hesitated. Pushed the last bit of melted cheese onto a cracker and shoved it in his mouth.

"Oh, you don't want to tell me," Alex said, both comprehension and a wide grin breaking across his face. "I bet it's good. Whoever it is, it's gonna make me want to tear my hair out, isn't it?"

"Uh," Dawson hesitated. More because Alex was looking increasingly delighted.

"God, please tell me it's not Flynn."

"What?" Dawson yelped. He had *not* expected Alex to say that, especially because Alex had especially shitty gaydar, and publicly, Aidan was straight as an arrow.

"Just saying. I remember back in your senior year of college, when we first started talking about me repping you, you followed him around like a puppy."

"Aidan's a *friend*."

"So?"

"And," Dawson added, muttering, "if you'd ever seen him puke in a bush, it would absolutely destroy any attraction you felt—if you'd ever felt any."

"I'll have to take your word for that," Alex said. "So, it's a teammate, then?"

Dawson rolled his eyes. "You're not as smart as you think you are."

"Yeah, I am. So who is it? Bishop? He's out of the closet and hot. That's your type, right?"

"I don't have a *type*," Dawson argued.

"Hot," Alex retorted fondly. "That's your type."

"Fine, maybe." But Cam was so much more than just a hot guy. Had been more than a hot guy from almost the very beginning.

Alex huffed out a frustrated sigh. "You're not gonna tell me, are you? You said it was just a hookup, though. Do you *want* it to be serious?"

"I . . ." Dawson trailed off. He wanted to keep doing what they were doing for a long-ass time, that was for sure. He didn't think he'd ever get tired of it. But whenever he thought of putting it into words, of standing in front of Cam, asking him to choose *him* and all his stupid fucking baggage, he felt sick. When he thought of Cam saying yes, he felt sick. Thrilled for sure, but nauseous, too.

"Just because you and Brynn fell apart doesn't mean you can't start over with someone new," Alex said, like it was just that easy.

Just a decision Dawson made. One minute he was on his own, isolated maybe, but in no danger of getting screwed over again, and the next he was half of a couple and *anything* could happen.

Like fear was no big deal.

Dawson swallowed it down.

"It's . . .it's not that," Dawson lied.

Alex didn't look convinced. "I think it's exactly that. Come on, Daws. Who is it? Bishop? Not Jeffries—he's too new to the team."

"And straight," Dawson added.

Alex sighed.

"Okay, fine, *fine*. It's not . . .it's not serious. It's something, but it's not serious." At least saying that made the fear recede in the back of his throat, finally. "It's Cam. Cameron Greene."

Alex looked boggled. "The punter? The *rookie punter*?"

"What? He's hot. He's sweet. He's—"

"He's so young, though," Alex said, having the nerve to sound judgmental about it. "I was sure you'd say it was Bishop."

"Well, it's not. It's Greene."

"Huh. What does he think about this?"

"We're on the same page," Dawson said. "It's cool. It's good."

"Okay," Alex said nodding. "Well, I can see why you'd like him."

Dawson could think of a thousand ways he liked Cam, but he wasn't sure he wanted to hear why Alex thought he liked Cam.

"He's hot, yeah," Alex continued, "and he's sweet, like you say. Worships you, if I remember. You got a hard-on for some hero worship, Daws?"

Dawson frowned. "It's not like that."

"No?"

The fear was mostly gone now, and it was easier to just let his mouth run, everything he'd wanted to say about Cam unstuck. "Yeah, he's hot and he's sweet and he thinks I'm a great kicker. But he laughs and he smiles, like he's so full of brightness he just has to share it. Listens to me.

Takes care of me. Best guy to hang out with, to grab dinner with or just sit on the couch and watch a movie with. And the sex—" Dawson stopped abruptly, suddenly far too aware of what his word vomit sounded like.

"The sex, huh?" Alex teased, leaning forward. "That good?"

"Better," Dawson said smugly.

Alex shot him an unimpressed look, which was confusing until he added, "Kind of sounds to *me* like you're crazy about him. Definitely like you're dating him."

Dawson opened his mouth and then snapped it shut again.

"You even listen to yourself, Daws?" Alex asked gently.

"Trying not to, to be honest," Dawson admitted under his breath. If he listened to himself, he might not be able to keep pretending, and what would he do *then*? "I want to, I want to listen to me and I want *him* to listen to me, too. But I can't do that until I've resolved some of this. I'm . . .I'm not sure how ready I am to commit to someone again. Even if I *want* to."

How could he? When he was still slogging through the worst of the fear? When he was still wondering if he was paranoid at even the possibility of another person betraying him?

There were some days, when Cam looked at him, and the trust and affection in his gaze blew Dawson away. But then there were other times—not whole days, not anything more than single moments, usually—when the fear threatened to swallow Dawson whole. Where he imagined falling for Cam, deeply and completely, and it all went wrong after.

"I think the fact that you're worried about this," Alex said gently, "tells me—and should tell *you*—more about how ready you are. You want to be a good partner. That's *being* a good partner."

That was all Dawson wanted. To be good, and have Cam be good for him, back. Why did it have to be so goddamn complicated? A part of Dawson wanted to just say, *it's so good and easy and simple now,* but he knew they couldn't keep doing this without talking about it. Not forever.

Alex cleared his throat. "But *hey*, you got this. When you're finally ready to introduce us? To make it official? Gonna be a good day."

"Because you know all my embarrassing stories," Dawson muttered, still, pretending his insides didn't warm to the idea of Alex meeting Cam. Not as the rookie punter of the Thunder, but as Dawson's *boyfriend*.

"Sure, we'll call it that," Alex said, his eyes twinkling.

Chapter 19

"Are you for real, rook?" Aidan looked over at Cam like he was losing it, and Cam didn't feel like he was. Okay—maybe he was, a *little* bit. He was beginning to be more comfortable with Aidan and more confident when it came to the starting quarterback. But it had still been a tiny bit terrifying to walk over to him in the locker room, as he finished getting changed after practice, and ask the question.

If he hadn't had a whole plan in his mind, he might have chickened out.

If the plan hadn't been for Dawson, Cam totally would've chickened out.

"Well, yeah, I'm for real." Cam squirmed, shifting his weight from one foot to the other.

"Dawson *just* asked me for more recs, and now here you are, asking too. You gonna take someone out that isn't Daws, rook?"

"No," Cam squawked. Why would he? Dawson was the only guy he wanted.

Aidan spread his hands. "Then why don't you ask him for the list I already gave him?"

Embarrassment crawled up Cam's spine. When he'd envisioned having this conversation, he'd thought Aidan would shoot him at best, *one*, and at worst, *two*, knowing looks, and then rattle off the name of some perfect date-night restaurant and that would be the end of it.

But instead, Aidan was staring at him like that and asking questions that were obviously designed so Cam would confess his entire plan. He'd told himself it wasn't awkward half a dozen times, but he hadn't managed to be convincing enough, yet.

"It's . . .it's a surprise," Cam admitted in a low voice.

Aidan's eyebrows rose. "A *surprise* date. Huh. Well, that's adorable."

"Bro," Levi said, from Aidan's other side, "put him out of his misery. Can't you see how he's squirming?"

"You're no fun," Aidan said, elbowing Levi.

Levi just cackled. "I'm the *most* fun."

For a second, Aidan got lost staring into his boyfriend's eyes, and then Levi murmured something under his breath to him, and his attention suddenly snapped back to Cam.

"You wanna take Daws out, yeah?"

Cam nodded, because if he didn't, he was going to launch into a big long explanation, which *would* be embarrassing, along with half a dozen caveats. He'd already had to endure Nate's warning; he didn't want Aidan to add his two cents, too.

Aidan had already done his share, when he'd apparently warned Dawson before anything had ever happened between them.

"That's cute," Levi declared.

"Levi," Aidan warned, but he was grinning over at his boyfriend.

"What? It *is* cute."

"He's just been practicing so hard," Cam said. He hadn't even needed Dawson to tell him that he was buckling down and focusing on football this week. Cam had been working hard too, but nobody had been working as hard as Dawson. He'd done the ladder twice, and he might have even done it a third time, but Marty had stopped him, telling Daws they didn't need him to wear him and his leg out.

Any time Dawson had when he wasn't at practice, he was looking for another lawyer with Alex's help and then also having several long conversations with the prosecutor as they worked together on the official response to the deal Ackerman's lawyer had sent over.

"Yeah, he's been real dedicated this week," Aidan agreed.

They'd managed to snatch a few moments together. Shared meals over the kitchen counter as Dawson scrolled through emails from Alex about the different lawyers he'd talked to. One night he'd sweet-talked Dawson into another bath and joined him.

And they had, without fail, no matter how busy Dawson was, spent every night in the same bed. Sometimes it was Cam's, sometimes it was Dawson's, but it genuinely felt, at least to Cam, that it didn't matter whose it was, as long as they were in it together.

"You should absolutely reward all that dedication with a hot date," Levi said slyly.

"That's the plan," Cam said, trying not to flush bright red.

"So, where should he take Daws?" Levi said, looking over at Aidan, who just shrugged.

"Oh come on, you're always taking me to cute places," Levi teased. "What about that cute bistro down by the water? In the Distillery District? That place was adorable. Super romantic." He turned to Cam. "I'll text you the address. Order a nice bottle of wine. There's candlelight. And you can walk around the little stores after, and there's even these outdoor firepits. Order some hot chocolate. Cuddle up with him." Levi's expression turned smug.

"I don't know why you're even asking me," Aidan said, flashing his boyfriend a smile. "Levi's got you all covered."

"Next time, I'll just ask him where you've taken him recently," Cam said dryly.

"Ahhhh, the rookie's got jokes!" Levi crowed. "I fucking love it."

"Especially when they're at my expense," Aidan said.

"Exactly." Levi leaned in and pressed a brief kiss to Aidan's temple. "Finish getting dressed, I'm starved."

Aidan looked over at Cam, who was still standing there. "You good now, rook?"

"Yeah," Cam said, noticing that Levi had already texted the address.

"If they don't want to give you a table on short notice," Aidan said, smirking, "just drop my name again, okay?"

"I—" Cam hesitated.

"No, seriously," Aidan said, clapping Cam on the shoulder. "Daws deserves a good night out. He's been going through it, and you know what? You're a good guy, to let him."

Cam wondered now if this was the talk. The one he'd been hoping to avoid from Aidan.

"Yeah," he agreed. "It's not hard to be patient." It was sometimes, but only because there was so much that he wanted and often it felt like Dawson wanted it too, just as much, and yet he was the only one stopping them from having it.

Cam *got* it, but that didn't mean it was easy.

Aidan smiled, a slow bloom across his face. "You're good for him," was all he said, though. No lecture, no warning, no threats whatsoever.

That made it so easy to smile back. "Trying anyway," Cam said.

"Doing better than that," Aidan said. "I know him, so I know how stubborn and infuriating he can be. Plus, I know how heavy his baggage can be." He stood and patted Cam on the shoulder. "He's gonna come around."

And Cam was pretty sure too but it felt good to hear Aidan say that.

"Thanks," Cam said, smiling back.

Before he showered and changed, he called the restaurant. He didn't want to drop Aidan's name—though it turned out that he didn't need to. Turned out the person who answered the phone was a big Thunder fan, big enough that they actually knew who Cam was, which didn't happen all that often, and he was able to fit them in last minute with a prime time and promised that the table would be one of their best.

By the time he did shower, fingers slipping a little nervously on the buttons of his shirt, Dawson showed up, looking tired but pleased.

"You finally done?" Cam asked him as Dawson stripped out of his sweaty practice jersey.

"Yeah, think so."

"Good, 'cause we've got an hour for you to get ready and to get to the restaurant," Cam said.

"Restaurant?" Dawson blinked at him, surprised. "That why you asked me what I had planned for tonight?"

Dawson had told him that he was looking forward to heating up something from their meal service—which they apparently shared, now—and a pair of lazy handjobs.

But Cam had figured they could do a little better than that. Dawson *deserved* more than that. He was always going out of his way to plan things for them to do. Dawson wouldn't have called them dates, but they *were* dates, in every single way that mattered. And someday, when Dawson wasn't so caught up in his own baggage, he'd see that, and until that point, Cam *was* willing to be patient, just like he'd told Aidan.

"Yeah," Cam said, smiling. "You good with that? Or are you too tired?"

Dawson grinned, his smile unexpectedly bright. "To hang out with you? Nah. Never."

"Good," Cam said. He'd been pretty sure, but he'd known there was always a chance he'd be calling the restaurant back and moving their reservation to next week, when things in Dawson's life were a little less crazy.

"I'm gonna go—" Dawson waved towards the showers. "Good thing I brought decent clothes today and not just sweatpants."

But Cam had been thinking ahead, even this morning. "Remember when I told you I liked your ass in those jeans?"

Dawson smirked. "Oh, so *that's* what that was. You've got layers to you, rook."

"I like to think so. *You* like to think so." It was so easy to smirk right back. Dawson made it easy, everything between them feeling so right and so *simple*. Which was why, more than anything, Cam knew that they would make it through this. That on the other side, it was going to be him and Dawson.

"Yeah, I do," Dawson said. "Don't go anywhere, okay?"

Cam knew what Dawson meant. *Stick around so we can head out to dinner together.* Which . . .obviously. But as Dawson disappeared into the showers, Cam thought that maybe Dawson meant something more, too. Meant, also, *Stick around because I think we could be pretty fucking amazing together.*

Well, he didn't have to ask Cam twice.

Cam wasn't going anywhere.

If Cam was putting a mental list together of everything that Aidan Flynn was good at, he was going to have to add *planning dates* to the list.

Because if Aidan had taken Levi here, then he'd hit the ball right out of the park.

The food was delicious, the atmosphere soft and sweet and undeniably romantic, the wine the waitress had recommended perfect. Maybe it wasn't entirely Cam—even if he'd been smart enough to ask for a recommendation—but he was going to take the victory lap.

Especially when Dawson's face was soft in the candlelight, lips red from the wine, his fond gaze never leaving Cam's face as he finished up filling out the check.

"That was . . ." Dawson sighed happily.

They'd had a whole dinner, at least two whole hours, without talking about lawyers or Ackerman. They *had* talked about football, but not the Thunder. Instead, they'd ended up sharing stories from their past, of all the teams they'd been on. Funny anecdotes and rough moments, and everything in between.

He and Dawson had been on a lot of *date*-like dates, but this had all those beat by a factor of ten.

It was so good, and Dawson so clearly comfortable with all of it, his hand reaching for Cam's across the table and squeezing it and their feet nudging together, that Cam was tempted more than once to just *say* it. To put it out there, between them. *This was a date. Did you have a good time? Because I had a good time. We should do this again. Should also get takeout and watch stupid movies with big explosions and car chases and make out on the couch. And everything in between, too.*

But before Cam could work up the nerve, Dawson leaned back in his chair and said it, like it was nothing. But Cam had learned so many of Dawson's tells by now, and he could see the tenseness in the line of his neck, the flash of uncertainty in his hazel eyes as he said, "We should do more dates like this."

He was so surprised he almost said, "*Was* this a date?"

But of course it was. He'd meant it to be, even if neither of them called it exactly what it was.

Instead he kept it simple. "Yeah," he agreed, meeting Dawson's gaze without an ounce of shame that he'd done this and *meant* it.

Dawson laughed ruefully. "I've been really stupid, haven't I?"

"No," Cam argued immediately, shaking his head. "You were . . .well . . ." He wanted to say Dawson had been fucked up, because that had been evident to everyone—Cam more than anyone. But there was still a tiny part of him that didn't want to bring it up, to call it what it so obviously was, because once the words were out there, they couldn't be taken back.

"I was fucked up. You can say it." Dawson's voice was wry. "And we've been doing this for a while. I can see it now. Weird that a few candles made me realize it."

"The candles?" Cam asked stupidly.

Dawson laughed. He was still easy, the last of his anxiousness fading away completely. "I was sitting here, thinking, he's so pretty in candlelight. Wondered, then, when the last time I had dinner over candlelight was, and it struck me, it was with Brynn. Before things got shitty between us. That's what this is, isn't it?"

There were two paths Cam could take. He could play it safe, and say, *yeah, sure it is but it's okay, I don't mind either way.* Or he could do what he really wanted, deep in his heart, in the place where he knew he was in love with Dawson, and he could say instead, *yeah, I know, and it's been okay, but I want things to be different now. Because they're different for me.*

It was too early for Cam to admit his feelings, but he could take the second road without confessing everything.

"Yeah," Cam said. "And it's been okay. But I want things to be different now. They're different for me, now, than they were when we started this." He didn't know if that was entirely, strictly true, because the emotion inside of him didn't *feel* new, but this was good enough for now.

"For me too, and I'm sorry it took me a long time." Dawson sighed and reached for Cam's hand, squeezing it, but this time he didn't let it go. "I want to keep doing this, and I don't want to share you with anyone else."

"Ditto," Cam agreed. Then decided what the hell, he'd lay his heart *mostly* bare. "There hasn't been anyone else. Not for me."

Dawson grinned. "How could there be, when I was taking up all your time, rook?"

"And I was giving it to you," Cam retorted fondly.

"Yeah, you were," Dawson said. He stretched and stood, and this time he reached for Cam's hand again. "Come on, let's go walk around, work off some of this dinner and the wine."

They wandered around the Distillery district for awhile. Grabbed hot chocolate from one of the vendors as they walked around under the white stringed lights hanging between the old-fashioned brick buildings that had all been repurposed from warehouses and factories into shops and restaurants.

Dawson's hand was warm in his, and he didn't seem to hesitate even when a few people recognized them—two of them even asking for autographs and selfies.

"I guess we're just . . .doing this?" Cam asked when the last guy had wandered away after his photo with both of them.

"I'm okay with it, if you are," Dawson said, glancing over at him. "I really am sorry I was so . . .so stupid, I guess. I was worried I wouldn't be good for you. I still worry about that—"

"You shouldn't," Cam insisted seriously. But he'd had a feeling it was something like that.

"I kind of should," Dawson retorted dryly. "I fucked up my last relationship. I wasn't really present. Yeah, she cheated on me, but when I think of how it was, before that happened, it wasn't anything to write home about." He glanced away, like the pain was resurfacing again and he didn't want Cam to see it, but Cam wanted to see every bit of it, every bit of Dawson that he could get. He reached over and, gently holding his chin, tugged Dawson's gaze back to him.

"Neither of us is perfect," Cam reminded him. "I've never been in a relationship before. I might be terrible at it, too. But I think as long as we both want to be good for each other, that's what really matters."

Dawson nodded. "And I trust you—I couldn't do this if I didn't—but every time I think of how my marriage imploded, and that happening again . . ."

"I wouldn't ever do that to you," Cam promised.

"Well, of course you don't think you would. But I can be difficult. Bitchy."

Cam tossed his empty hot chocolate cup and turned to look at Dawson. "You think you being a little grumpy is gonna turn me off? Scare me off? Make me leave you?"

"No, but I . . .I can't go through that again. I've been terrified of opening myself up to it again but then Alex said something the other night. The fact that I want so badly to do right by you, that means something."

"I think so," Cam said. He leaned in and brushed a kiss over Dawson's mouth. His lips were chilly and perfect. "It's plenty good enough for me."

"Nothing's too good for you," Dawson said softly, and Cam knew then, without a shadow of doubt, they were on the same page. Dawson loved him too, but he was still dealing with the remnants of fear and doubt. Cameron had been patient up til this point, and with everything he wanted so close to being in his grasp, he wasn't about to give up now.

"Why don't we go home and you prove it to me?" Cam leaned in and kissed him again, deeper this time. He was allowed. They'd just taken two fan pictures while they were clearly out together, holding hands, and neither of those guys had seemed like they gave a shit.

"I like the sound of that," Dawson agreed.

Dawson had really believed that when the moment came—*the* moment—he'd let the fear or the doubt hold him back.

But in the end, it had been *so* easy. He'd looked at one option, and seen Cam slipping away from him, and the other option meant, just like Alex said, making good choices for himself and for *Cam*, and it hadn't taken any real effort to admit what he'd known, deep down, was true for some time.

He had feelings.

They were dating.

Cam was the guy for him.

He'd meant it—he'd taken one look at Cam in the candlelight and realized he wanted to see him like this all the time, smile bright and eyes shining, happy because *Dawson* had made him this happy—and there hadn't even been a question in his mind.

"God, want you all the time," Dawson said, crowding Cam into the back of the elevator, kissing him fiercely, their hips aligning. "Want to get you so good, rook."

Cam groaned into his mouth, tilting his head so he could kiss Dawson even deeper.

The elevator doors dinged open, and they staggered onto Cam's floor, Dawson's hands tucked into the back pockets of Cam's jeans, cupping him possessively.

"Yeah?" Cam asked breathlessly. "What do you want?"

Dawson just laughed, still a little shocked—in the best possible way—that he could have this. That he could take it with both hands and hold it and *keep* it.

"You," he murmured, leaning into Cam's back, mouthing at his neck as he tried to get his keycard swiped.

He finally got the door open, something Dawson was absolutely going to make fun of him for, maybe between rounds one and two, and they stumbled into the dark entryway.

It was funny, because Dawson had been tired before, worn down between the season and this week's hard practices and all the bullshit with untangling his legal responsibilities with Simon. Alex had been a big help, additionally proving just how loyal he was to Dawson, but it had still been a lot.

But now he didn't feel tired at all, excitement and arousal buzzing under his skin. It had been too long since he'd gotten his mouth on Cam. Too long since he'd had the energy to do more than perfunctorily get each other off, in long lazy showers or in the mornings before they had to drive into the practice facility.

He wanted to spread Cam out and get him naked and take his time. Kiss him everywhere. Make him squirm. Make him *beg*.

But to do that, he needed to get Cam to the bedroom first, and Cam kept laughing and twisting out of his grasp.

"Goddamn it, *stay*, and just *let me*," Dawson begged, sounding a shade of desperate himself.

"You gonna make me?" Cam teased, looking down at him with a look that sent Dawson to his knees. Metaphorically, right now, and possibly literally in a minute.

"God yes," Dawson said emphatically.

He'd just pinned Cam to the first flat surface he could find—the little wall between the entry and the kitchen—tucking a thigh between Cam's legs, swallowing his groan when he rubbed their dicks together, when a light went on.

For a single bewildered second he'd thought Cam had reached over and turned it on.

But then he was looking over, right into the eyes of a stranger.

No. Not a stranger. A guy who could be exactly how Cam would look in twenty-plus years.

"Shit!" Cam exclaimed and scrambled out from underneath Dawson's grip. "Dad!"

That was the boner killer of the century right there.

Dawson would be disappointed by that fact, but the truth was, meeting Cam's dad was definitely going to be better if he *didn't* have a boner.

"Oh my God," Cam continued as the man stared at where Dawson still had an arm wrapped around his son's waist, "I can't believe you're here. You didn't tell me you were coming in early!"

"I thought it would be uh . . ." The guy made a wry face and rubbed the back of his neck. "A nice surprise. So, surprise?"

"Dad," Cam said a little hesitantly, and then he was detaching himself from Dawson and throwing himself into the older man's arms for a tight hug.

"Can't believe you're here," Dawson overheard Cam murmur into his shoulder. But even though Cam's dad's gaze flicked to Cam once, and then twice, he returned to staring at Dawson each and every time.

Well, *fuck.*

They'd just agreed they were dating. That they were together. Dawson felt—well, he actually felt pretty fucking good about that. But it was one thing to feel good about it, with Cam's dad a shadowy amorphous figure still in the back wilds of Montana, and another entirely to face him, *now,* in Toronto. With half a boner, still.

Cam's dad turned to him, and Dawson trying not to panic, panicked a little. He could *not* face his brand-new boyfriend's father, whose name he suddenly couldn't remember, with even a *little* bit of a boner. He thought about Aidan puking into the bush. Thought about the gulp of rancid milk he'd taken once in college. Thought about the moment he'd gotten a call from his forensic accountant last year.

And *yep,* that last one was the boner killer of the fucking century.

"You must be Dawson Hall," Cam's dad said, extending his hand.

Dawson shook it, trying to not shake anywhere else. Cam's dad had the same warm, friendly brown eyes as Cam, but they were narrowed a bit as he took Dawson in.

Dawson didn't blame him. Dawson came with baggage, *capital B,* and he was also older. He'd been lectured enough by Aidan and co to know how it might look, and he wasn't sure what Cam had said to him.

"Shane Greene," he said. And *thank God,* Dawson didn't need to ask him what his name was. Armed with his boyfriend's dad's name *and* no boner, he was going to ace this shit.

"Great to meet you," Dawson said, nodding. Trying to remember what he'd said and done with Ackerman, when he'd first met Brynn. But as soon as that thought crossed his mind, he froze. This wasn't going to be the same. It *wasn't.*

It was getting easier to recognize the sudden onset of fear and combat it. But it still *happened.* Dawson still didn't fucking like it.

"Heard a lot about you," Shane said casually, but the way he was eyeing Dawson was *not* casual.

"Dad," Cam protested hotly, a flush rising on his cheeks.

Shane turned to his son with a mischievous grin. "Oh, but I *have*."

And Dawson wasn't totally relaxed about it, but he could breathe now, at least. It didn't *seem* like Shane Greene had come to Toronto to interfere or, God forbid, intervene.

"Oh yeah? I wanna know everything he said," Dawson said, trying to be casual too.

Cam rolled his eyes and elbowed Dawson gently in the ribs. "Come on, don't encourage him."

Dawson flashed a conspiratorial smile to Shane and was pleased to see a shadow of the same look appear on Shane's face.

"Next time," Dawson said. "It's late. I should get going back to my own place." He was proud of pretending that he and Cam hadn't been making out against the wall like they were on their way to the bedroom. His voice barely wavered at all, even though the thought of going back to his own lonely apartment felt like hell.

There'd been a time, last year, when he hadn't been so good at doing hard things, but he must be getting better at it, because it didn't feel great, but it wasn't the end of the world, either.

"Really?" Cam's pout did make it a little harder. And *God*, he did want to stay here. Did want to go to Cam's bed the same way he had been every night since they'd started dating—and the irony of him finally seeing the light on that, tonight, when he couldn't actually do it anymore, wasn't lost on him.

"Yeah." Cam drifted closer to him, a hand on his hip as Shane inclined his head and moved deeper into the living room, clearly trying to give them a little privacy.

"He's not going to be weird about it," Cam protested in a low voice. "And he'll stay out here. The couch is a pullout."

"Cam," Dawson murmured.

"I'm just saying. I don't want you to go."

"Trust me, I don't want to go either, but I also don't want to start this thing with you the wrong way, especially with your dad here. I know you've missed him." Cam had said it more than once, and Dawson remembered the wistful look in his eyes as he had.

"Yeah," Cam agreed. "He really wasn't supposed to be here for a few weeks. I thought we'd have time . . .to you know, *talk* about it."

"Cam, it's fine. It's really fine," Dawson reassured.

Cam tucked his head closer, into Dawson's shoulder. Dawson pressed a kiss to the side of his head. "Really?"

"Am I disappointed? Yeah. A little bit. But it's also okay. I get it."

"At least . . .give me a goodnight kiss." Cam pulled back, his chin tipped down.

"I thought I had already done that," Dawson teased.

Cam leaned in closer, licking his lips.

And Dawson was only a man, he could only fight his inevitable desire so long, even with Shane Greene only half a room away.

Still, he kept the kiss relatively PG-13. Slid a hand down to Cam's hip and kept him anchored with at least an inch between them. Couldn't risk getting hard again, especially when it had been so difficult to fix that situation earlier. But of course, he hadn't anticipated that even a little bit of Cam's clever tongue would make him want to use it everywhere.

He should've, based on prior experience, but Cam did something to his brain. Blew out all of his good intentions and any possible normal thought processes. Made him irrational. Desperate. Wild.

Dawson broke off the kiss, breathing hard.

Cam's brown eyes blinked down at him. Soft and hot on his face. "I'm gonna miss you tonight," he admitted quietly.

It was impossible not to bare his heart—or at least part of it—when Cam was looking at him that way, his own feelings written clearly across his face. "Ditto," Dawson agreed. "But it's not gonna be forever."

He didn't want to ask how long Shane was going to be staying, but he didn't have to.

"Long enough," Cam grumbled good-naturedly.

"We'll find time, and after us being around for awhile, maybe it won't be weird for me to stay," Dawson said optimistically.

Cam reached up, cupping his cheek. "Gonna hold you to that."

"You'd better." Dawson had meant it to sound joking, but it came out earnest and heartfelt.

Cam smiled and took a step away from him.

Dawson nearly reached for him again, but he held back. Shaking his head a bit to clear it. The problem was he wanted to keep swimming in the ocean of Cam and never surface for air. Even though he knew he needed to.

"Hey, it was nice to meet you," Dawson called out, waving towards Cam's dad in the living room.

At least Shane seemed amused, not upset. "Yeah, you too. Don't be a stranger." He chuckled. "Not that I thought you would."

Dawson pressed one last kiss to Cam's cheek and headed out the door before he dragged out this goodbye any further.

Before he decided that he wasn't saying goodbye at all.

Still, at least there was a silver lining. Cam's dad clearly knew who he was, maybe even what they were to each other, and he hadn't seemed like he disliked Dawson.

That was something. Dawson could work with that.

Maybe with time, he wouldn't feel that fear slithering around in the base of his stomach when he thought about making nice with another romantic partner's father.

Surely, that had to get better.

Especially when it was obvious, just from getting to know Cam, that Shane Greene was nothing like how Richard Ackerman had been.

CHAPTER 20

Cam was impressed.

His dad waited until the next morning, even until he was done with his breakfast and nearly done with his coffee, before he turned to him with a wry smile and said, "So you and Dawson Hall, huh?"

"Daaaaad," Cam whined. He'd known it was coming. Had lain awake last night, alone in his bed for what felt like the first time in months, and not only missed Dawson, but wondered what his dad was going to say about it.

He couldn't pretend with Shane; he never could.

"Just saying, you two looked . . .uh . . .pretty cozy there."

Cam wanted to sink through the floor. "*Dad*."

"I'm just saying. I'd have let you two go, but I thought if I did, I might see more than I bargained for."

Turning towards the sink, Cam could feel how red hot the skin of his neck was, exposed by the loose collar of his T-shirt—though if he was being totally transparent, he was pretty sure this was actually *Dawson's* T-shirt.

"You don't want to talk about it?" Shane asked.

"About me and Dawson nearly having sex in front of you? No. Really, I don't. I don't know what gave it away."

His dad just laughed. "No, I'm not even *that* enlightened. I mean, do you want to talk about how you're in love with him?"

Cam didn't really want to talk about that either. Not that it was bad. It was not bad. The furthest thing from bad. But he'd barely gotten a chance to do a mental fist pump that he and Daws were finally on the same page, relationship-wise, never mind actually *celebrate* that Dawson knew it too.

Rinsing off the plates in the sink, he took a long moment to compose himself before he finally turned to face his father.

He'd been hearing since he was a kid how his dad had a kind face. And it was kind now. The basic level of kindness, sure, but also more, like he'd gone out of his way to keep every bit of judgment out of it.

"Last time we talked about him, you were still determined to keep it casual," Shane pointed out, leaning forward, his elbows propped on the counter. It was still a little unbelievable to Cam that his dad was here at all, in Toronto and in his apartment.

There was the truth and then there was the carefully constructed fabric of unspoken semi-truths and fictions he and Dawson *had* been operating under. Though they *had* cut through them last night. Come clean with each other. Or *mostly* clean, anyway.

Cam *hadn't* told Dawson he was in love with him, even though he was pretty sure he was. Even more sure now, because his dad had taken one look at them together and had known. Not just wondered, but *known.*

"Not anymore, though, I think . . ." Cam swallowed his concerns, and bared his heart. "I think it was never really very casual between us."

It was what his dad had been claiming for a month, but to give him credit, Shane didn't immediately say, *I told you so.*

"Yeah? You guys talk about it finally?"

"We're starting to, yeah. Last night, we went out and it was a real date. I meant it as a date and Dawson thought it was a date, too. So we're . . .um . . .dating."

Shane smiled, full of genuine happiness. "That's great. You're happy about it?"

"Fucking thrilled," Cam said, then shot his dad a look. "Would've been a little happier if you hadn't showed up right in the middle of the *we're boyfriends, now* celebration."

"Sorry," Shane said, wincing. "I really thought the surprise would be good. And you've been a little distant—"

Cam opened his mouth to argue. He hadn't been *distant*. Okay. Maybe he had been, a little bit. Sticking to texts, instead of calling. But he'd been busy, and if he was being totally honest, preoccupied with Dawson.

"You don't have to argue about it," Shane said gently but sternly. "It's okay if you were. I know it's okay. I should be . . ." He trailed off. Looking, to Cam's shock, a little guilty about it. "I should be okay with it. You're a grown-up. Making your own life. I should let go, easier."

"Should you?" Cam wondered. He couldn't imagine a world in which they weren't close, even if they weren't in the same geographic location. Maybe that was because for so long, it had just been the two of them, and also because his dad had *never* held him too close. Just close enough, as far as Cam was concerned.

He'd always wanted Cam to fly.

"I should," Shane said wryly, looking guilty, still. "But I don't want to."

"Well, I don't want you to. I know I've been busy, and not calling, the way I should." Cam felt guilt surge through him. Sure, his dad had his whole life back in Montana, but now that Cam really thought about it, it was probably somewhat empty without him in it.

"I'm not here because you didn't call as much," his dad admitted. "I'm just . . . I don't know, I just felt like I needed to see you. I know we said in a few weeks, for Thanksgiving, and through the holidays, but . . ."

The words Shane wasn't saying were easy enough to hear.

"You know you're always welcome, Dad," Cam said softly. "I know the couch isn't very comfortable, but I'm happy for you to stay."

"Even if I put a crimp into your relationship?"

"You aren't," Cam insisted. Even though he kind of had, already.

Still, he wanted to believe what Dawson had said, which was that in time, with Dawson and his dad becoming more comfortable together and Dawson and Cam growing more used to their relationship, it wouldn't be weird anymore for Dawson to stay over.

Or for Cam to go with him to his apartment.

"Kinda am," Shane said dryly. "Sorry about that."

Cam decided he didn't like it when his dad looked guilty. It was even worse when he sounded guilty. Like he was gate-crashing on Cam's life, when he wasn't, not at all.

How could he be when Cam was so genuinely happy he was here? When he'd missed him, too?

So he changed the subject. "What are you doing about the business while you're gone?"

"You know it gets slow in the winter," Shane said. "And there's another vet in town, now, so it's not just me. I'm . . ." He cleared his throat. "I'm not as needed as I was before."

"Silver didn't edge you out, did she?" Silver was the other vet in town—she was much younger than Shane, at least two decades younger, and had been a few years ahead of Cam in high school, but they'd known each other. The town was small enough it was impossible not to.

"No, nah, nothing like that," Shane argued, but there was an edge of melancholy to his voice that Cam didn't know how to ask about. He'd never heard his dad sound like that, before.

"What did she do?" Cam asked. It was easier to focus on Silver than it was on Shane, who despite his silvering hair, had never seemed particularly old and definitely never defeated. But there was something now, and Cam didn't like it.

"Nothing. Really." Shane laughed, but he didn't sound very amused. "It's fine. Silver's great. And her being around in town means I can fuck off and come to Toronto and visit you."

"Alright, if you say so," Cam said. But he didn't really believe all that was true. There was something going on with his dad, and he was going to get to the bottom of it. "I *am* really glad you could get away. Come to Toronto. It's a really cool city."

"What happened to you being apprehensive about it?" his dad teased gently.

Cam flushed. "Well, Daws and I have been doing some exploring. Since, you know, he's new to Toronto, too. And that's been really cool."

"Seeing it through the eyes of love, huh?"

"Shhh, you can't say that shit, he's going to freak out again, and I don't want—"

Shane's gaze sharpened and he interrupted. "Dawson is going to freak out if he finds out you're in love with him? You mean, he doesn't know?"

"Well, not *yet*," Cam soothed. "Of course not yet. We just got together, officially. It's . . .it's a little fast for big love confessions."

"Not when he's in love with you, too."

"Dad, you don't know that's true," Cam argued, even though he was pretty sure Daws *was*. There was a way he looked at him, like they were the only two people on the planet, and Cam had always imagined that was how someone in love might gaze at him.

"I saw him. I saw you. Definitely saw enough," Shane teased.

"That's just—" Cam broke off. He didn't want to say it was just sex, because even he knew that it wasn't. They hadn't been apart for a single night in weeks, and they weren't fucking every night. A *lot* of nights, sure, but not every night. And yet Dawson had never wanted to leave his bed, or wanted Cam to leave his.

"Cam, son, you can believe whatever you want, but you two are serious about each other."

"I want us to be," Cam agreed in a soft voice.

"You'll get there."

Cam had been believing that was true since the very beginning and nothing had ever made him sway from that belief. Maybe that was what made it easier to be patient, now.

"Anyway," Cam said, "you'll get to see how cool Toronto is, now. And you'll have to come in, meet the guys."

"I'd like that," Shane said.

"I bet you I could even get you into the facility. You could come work out. Watch some practices," Cam said.

Shane raised an eyebrow. "You'd want that?"

"Dad, you've never been weird about me being a football player. I can't imagine you're going to start now."

"You really wouldn't mind?"

"Dad, what are you even going to do while you're here?"

"Play tourist? Catch up on my reading? Become a lump on your couch?" Shane chuckled self-consciously.

On the counter in front of him, his phone buzzed. It was a text from Dawson. **Still up for carpooling this morning?**

It wasn't everything Cam wanted, but he'd take it anyway.

"Well, enjoy that stuff today," Cam said. "I'll talk to Coach Robertson today and Marty—I'm sure they won't mind."

"I don't want to be a bother. Or an imposition." His dad was looking awkward again. "I should've told you I was coming. Should've not come until we'd planned."

That was just bullshit, and Cam wasn't going to pretend otherwise. Slipping around the counter, he pulled his dad into a tight hug. "No," he told him firmly. "I'm glad you're here. I'm glad you came. I missed you too."

"You were just close at Western. I knew this would be an adjustment . . ."

Cam got it. It had been hard for him, too. "We're gonna figure it out," he promised. "But now I gotta get to practice."

"You driving in with Dawson?" his dad asked pointedly, grinning.

"Yeah," Cam said. "But I'll be home for dinner. We'll go out. There's a lot of good places around here. And if you don't wanna go out, we can always order in."

"Yeah, apparently you've gotten good at that," Shane teased, reaching out to ruffle his hair. "And you know Dawson is welcome, too, if he wants to join."

He'd assumed that, but he wasn't sure he'd ask. Dawson had seemed chill enough but Cam didn't want to force the issue so soon, even if he already knew he'd miss him tonight.

Things with Dawson were *so* new, and still a little unsteady, and then there was the specter of Richard Ackerman hovering. The last father of a partner that Dawson had had, it had gone just about as badly as it could go.

"We'll see," Cam said noncommittally.

"Alright." His dad reached out, squeezing his shoulder. "Have a good practice, kid."

Dawson was already waiting in the car when Cam arrived in the parking garage. When Cam slipped into the passenger seat, Dawson leaned over and gave him a nice long kiss. Nice enough and long enough that Cam was disappointed when Dawson pulled away, shooting him an apologetic grimace.

"Wish we could keep doing that, but traffic's bad today. We gotta get going."

Cam sighed. "I missed you last night."

"Yeah," Dawson agreed as he pulled out of the garage. "But it's okay. Your dad's cool. You should spend time with him, while he's here."

Dawson said it so casually. *Your dad's cool.* Cam wanted to believe it, but there was still that voice in the back of his head that kept reminding him that he'd *just* gotten this. He wasn't going to force his father on Dawson, not when he clearly had so much baggage about fathers-in-law. *Understandable* baggage about fathers-in-law, frankly.

"I was thinking tonight I'd take him to that Ethiopian place we walked to last week."

"He ever have Ethiopian?"

Cam shrugged. "I hadn't either though, and it was fucking delicious."

He didn't offer for Dawson to join them, and Dawson seemed okay with that, and they downshifted into small talk about practice and the upcoming game Monday against the Jets.

"I'm excited, it's my first Monday Night Football game," Cam said.

"Now we know why your dad showed up. He wanted in on the Monday Night Football hype," Dawson teased.

"I can't blame him for that," Cam confessed.

"Just remember, rook, it's just another game. Primetime, sure, but you're built for that. How many great punts did you make during Western's game against Wisconsin? That was the highest-pressure situation you'd been in, and you killed it. And Monday night? You're gonna do it again."

Dawson's glance over was warm and supportive. Cam wanted to hoard it all, bask in the knowledge that he had such a great boyfriend and such a great teammate. Someone who really wanted him to succeed not just because he was also wearing a Thunder uniform, but because he cared about *him,* about Cam.

When they made it to the practice facility and headed into the first meeting that seemed to be the overall tone of the coaching staff. Sure, it was a Monday night game, but it was just another game. Another chance to get a W. To wipe away the sting of their first loss, last week.

Cam only had a quick moment after the first all-hands-on-deck meeting to grab Coach Robertson, asking him about his dad. Coach gave him a look. "He normal about shit?" he asked, and Cam didn't have to ask what shit he was referring to. Some guys' dads would show up and act weird. Try to coach still. Interfere. Prove that they somehow knew best. Cam had been around too many quintessential sports dads to know exactly what Coach was talking about.

"The most normal," Cam said.

"He's cool," Dawson said, chiming in. Even though he'd only met him for fifteen minutes the night before.

"Sure thing, tell Marty to get him some credentials," Coach said, nodding.

But as they headed to the locker room to change before practice, Cam was still stuck on what Dawson had said.

"You've barely met him and you vouched for him," Cam pointed out as he pulled on his practice jersey.

"It's not about meeting him," Dawson explained as he bent into a deep stretch. "It's about knowing *you*. You're refreshingly not fucked up about your dad."

"Neither are you," Cam said. He didn't say anything about Ackerman, because this wasn't about him, but he lingered in the back of Cam's mind anyway.

"Takes one to know one, rook," Dawson said with a grin.

Marty worked them hard at practice, but forced Dawson to call it quits early. "You're gonna fuck up your leg, and then both Robertson and the rook here are gonna have my head," Marty said, unexpectedly serious.

Dawson made a face but let it go without arguing.

He was quiet on the drive back to their building.

Cam toyed with a fraying edge on the hem of his sweatshirt. Wondering if he should say the thing that was lying between them, unsaid. That his dad wasn't like Ackerman. That Dawson would never have to worry about that happening with Shane. Cam knew he didn't have to say it out loud for it to be true, but he also knew that the most dangerous aspect of fear was that it wasn't based in logical reality.

His dad wasn't a money manager. He wasn't ever going to even have an opportunity to steal from Dawson. But he didn't have to, not for him to freak Dawson out.

"You still thinking about the Ethiopian place?" Dawson asked as he pulled into the parking garage.

"Yeah. I am. I think he'll like it. Toronto's such a cool melting pot. I want him to experience some of that while he's here," Cam said.

He had to wonder if Daws was asking because he was angling for an invite, but then the moment passed, and Cam was no longer sure.

"Yeah, he should," Dawson agreed. He parked, and when he got out of the car, pulled both their bags from the back. Set them on the ground and pulled Cam into him. First into a brief but passionate kiss, which melted into a warm, supportive hug. "Gonna miss you tonight," he murmured into Cam's ear. "Missed you last night, too."

He'd already said that, but Cam didn't want to assume he was talking about the hanging-out part of the evening. Maybe he was just talking about the way they curled up in bed together to fall asleep. Or about the activities they did *before* they fell asleep. Cam missed those too, even though it would only have been a few nights without them.

If he was being really honest with himself, he missed *everything*.

He was just used to having it all, Dawson in every way he desired him. The last thing he wanted was to push too hard and lose it. Patience wasn't easy, but he'd already been patient. He could be patient a little while longer.

It still sucked to split up when they got up to Cam's floor. Dawson brushed a last kiss across Cam's upturned mouth before he got off the elevator. "Have fun tonight," he said.

"I'm trying not to rush him, but this kinda sucks, if I'm being really honest," Dawson complained to Aidan as he tugged his pads on. Aidan was already dressed, lounging against the side of Dawson's locker.

Cam had already gotten dressed and exited the locker room, because the social media team wanted to take some pics with him and his dad, here to watch him play his first Monday Night Football game. Otherwise, Dawson might not have said anything.

But it was going on five nights now, and he was tired of Cam brushing him off. He'd thought when they'd finally gotten together, for real, there wouldn't be any more bumps in the road. But as cool as Shane seemed, he was proving to be a major roadblock.

"You're sure he's okay with you being a guy?" Aidan wondered.

"Cam's *gay*. And from anything he's ever said about his dad, he's like the most supportive." Dawson sighed, pretty sure it wasn't *him* that was the issue, but it was hard to say, because Cam hadn't once invited him to hang out with him and his dad.

He'd seen Shane a few times in passing, around the practice facility. Once Shane had gotten the green light to spend time there, Cam had even stopped carpooling in with Dawson.

He'd tried to explain it away, to excuse it, because of course Cam would want time one-on-one with his dad. But it didn't matter how subtly Dawson hinted that he wouldn't mind getting to know his dad better, nothing had happened.

"Then what's the deal? I thought you guys fixed this," Aidan said absently, seemingly way less worried about this particular drama than Dawson was.

"I just . . .it's weird, isn't it? He was all-in before. Patient and supportive and shit. And then Shane gets here and it's like he's pulling away." He'd already said it sucked, but he was *so* tempted to add that again.

Aidan shot him a look. "Have you talked to him about it?"

"Of course not," Dawson blustered. He tugged on a beanie and grabbed his helmet. "How would I even ask? *Hey, Cam, does your dad think I have cooties?* I don't fucking think so."

"You are actually the worst communicator on the planet."

"Says the second-worst communicator on the planet," Dawson complained.

"Exactly. I'm qualified to say just how shitty you are. Just fucking *ask* him, Daws. You're in love with the guy, how hard is it possibly to say to his face, *I'd like to get to know your dad while he's here.* You want to be serious about the rookie? This is your way to do it. Not fucking him every night."

Dawson made an outraged noise. "I—that's ridiculous, coming from you."

"Is it though?" Aidan asked smugly. "I'm just saying, I knew *my* boyfriend's parents forever. Long before we started dating. I got this in the bag. You're still trying to figure out where the bag even *is*."

"I hate you," Dawson complained.

Aidan patted him on the shoulder. "The truth hurts, bud."

Dawson made a face. He knew he was going to have to say something, but right now, he needed to put this problem from his mind and find his focus. Sure, this was a different issue than what had potentially distracted him last week, when he'd missed that long kick, but he wasn't willing to take a chance, either.

However he was going to deal with this situation would have to happen after the game was over.

Maybe the crap with Ackerman was difficult, with no easy fixes to be found, but he had to believe that he and Cam could figure out how to coexist, in a relationship, with Shane around.

But Dawson shouldn't have worried about tonight's game.

The offense, which had been stymied last week by the Bills' suffocating defense, didn't have issues at all with the Jets.

"Thank God they traded Sauce away," Mo mentioned during halftime. He was up to a season high 125 yards receiving, with two touchdowns already, with nobody on the Jets able to cover him, once they'd traded away their best corner in Sauce Gardner.

Dawson had kicked three extra points and a single thirty-four-yard field goal, which the Thunder had only settled for because Acker had had a holding penalty and they'd run out of chances to get the first down.

Robertson had felt good going into half with a twenty-four-to-three lead, and nobody could really blame him.

But of course that meant that Dawson had barely had any reason to push himself. He was partly annoyed, partly relieved.

"I've only punted once," Cam said to him as they sat in front of their lockers.

"A killer punt though, rook," Dawson pointed out with a smile. "And hey, are you actually *bitching* about that?"

"No, just . . .I'd rather *do* something," Cam said. "And it's not like I didn't hear you complaining to Marty about three extra points and one . . .what was it? One *measly* thirty-four-yard field goal?"

"Practically an extra point," Dawson said.

"Exactly," Cam said, chuckling under his breath.

"I just want a chance to prove I can do it," Dawson said, leaning in so only Cam could hear him. "I wanna prove to everyone I'm not that guy who missed last week."

"You mean the guy who missed a *fifty-nine*-yard field goal? That was right on the edge of his range? Yeah. Okay." Cam's knee nudged his. "Stop being such an overachiever, Daws. Nobody thinks you need to prove anything."

But maybe it wasn't about proving something to everyone, and more about proving it to *himself.*

He didn't want to need that reassurance, but there was a deep-down part of him that was screaming for it.

That kept reminding him that when he'd let the team down last season, it had cost him the rest of what he'd had. And this season, somehow, he had even more to lose.

But the second half didn't deliver on the opportunities Dawson was hoping for. He kicked another extra point, when Aidan hit Lane on a sweet buttonhook route, and he took it fifty yards to the end zone.

After that, the Thunder offense, up thirty-one to three, took a relatively conservative approach.

It meant that Dawson spent the rest of the game riding the bench, watching as Jaden, the Thunder's running back, took chunks out of the tired Jets' defense, and Cam kicked several more deep punts. Pinning the Jets' offense inside the ten, twice. More than earning *his* money.

It was a solid win, a complete team victory—offense, defense, and special teams combining to prove, in a primetime game, just how dangerous the Thunder was going to be this year.

Dawson was not surprised when Aidan announced in the midst of the raucous celebration in the locker room that everyone was coming out to Vault tonight, to revel in the team's first half of the season success.

He *was* surprised when Cam shuffled over to him, outside the locker room, and unlike what he'd expected Cam to say—that he was skipping to spend the time with his dad—that apparently Aidan was insisting that not only Cam show up but that he bring Shane, too.

"He's our good luck charm, apparently," Cam said with a shrug. But he was smiling at Daws, like he was pleased he didn't have a reason to bail. "I even reminded him that he only showed up after the last game, and he pointed out that we lost that game. Our only loss of the season."

It was a little silly—typical Aidan superstition—but Dawson wasn't going to argue with it, because he *wanted* Cam to come tonight. He'd missed him with an ache he hadn't imagined could be possible. Even better that Aidan had figured out a way to make sure Cam brought his dad, too.

Maybe Dawson could figure out a way to talk to him. Try to bridge this weird distance that had fallen between him and Cam. Make sure Cam knew that Dawson thought Shane was cool.

"I'm not gonna argue with it. Unless *you* want to argue with Aidan," Dawson said wryly.

"No way," Cam said.

"You *were* fucking awesome tonight, rook," Dawson said, slinging an arm around him and squeezing Cam against his body. He could see Shane making his way down the tunnel, and maybe a few days ago, he'd have removed his arm. Not forced Shane to witness their PDA.

But Dawson had missed him so much he wasn't willing to do it. Not anymore.

"Thanks." Cam tilted his head down towards Dawson's and, to Dawson's delight, leaned in a little closer, even though Shane had now joined them.

Cam only detached briefly, to give his dad a hug, and then he went right back to Dawson as he said, "Hey, Dad, you up for going out?"

"Sure," he said. "You coming too, Dawson?"

"Planning on it," Dawson said casually, even though a catastrophe would have to dislodge him from Cam's side, after what felt like *days* apart.

"Good." And the little nod of approval Shane gave him then told him that if someone was trying to keep them apart, it wasn't him.

Which left only one person, and Dawson was determined to get to the bottom of why Cam would be pulling that crap.

CHAPTER 21

From everything that Cam had told him, his dad had lived his entire life in a small town in Montana, too. But he was only enthused and comfortable the moment they walked into Vault.

None of the apprehension Cam had displayed in the dirty alley was present, and Shane melted into the crowd around the bar, exchanging small talk and ordering a drink like this was the kind of shit he did all the time.

"Yeah," Cam said, even though Dawson hadn't actually said any of this out loud, "he's always like this. Comfortable around people. Always been a little in awe—and a little jealous—of it."

Dawson chuckled. "You're good with people, rook."

But Cam only laughed and shook his head. "Not like him."

"Well, how about this—just be good with me, okay?" Dawson tilted his head up and pressed a quick kiss to Cam's temple.

Cam beamed. "Yeah. I can do that."

"Good."

Ramsey appeared then, doling out his usual smiles and charm, sprinkling them wherever he went, and next to them, Nate tensed. Didn't frown, but looked clearly uncomfortable as Ramsey wound his way closer and closer, like he was skating in circles, narrowing down his final destination.

Dawson wondered if Aidan had talked to him yet. It was unclear if he hadn't gotten around to it, or it just hadn't been nearly as effective as Aidan was hoping for.

Sure enough, Dawson had just grabbed his and Cam's drinks from the bartender when Ramsey reached his final destination.

Unsurprisingly, it was right next to Nate.

"Bishop," Ramsey said, inclining his head. He was in a slate-blue sweater tonight, his chain just visible, glittering against his throat.

Nate only rolled his eyes. "Playing nice, huh?"

"I thought that's what I *always* do," Ramsey retorted mildly, seemingly not bothered by Nate's adversarial attitude.

Dawson exchanged a knowing glance with Cam.

"Yeah, wonder if you can actually fucking stand any of us," Nate grumbled.

"Oh, but you're my *favorite*, Nathaniel," Ramsey teased.

Nate made a face, and Dawson decided that he'd heard enough. Whatever Aidan said, it had *not* been effective. Maybe it was time to throw his own hat into the ring. He nudged Cam, giving him a subtle look over at where Duke and Jack were hanging out. Cam nodded back, message clearly received.

"Hey, Nate, I was gonna ask you something," Dawson said, sliding in between where Nate was leaning against the bar and where Ramsey stood. "You got a minute?"

The thundercloud on Nate's face lifted a bit. Like he'd just wanted an excuse to leave Ramsey alone. But then, as Dawson led Nate over to one of the high-top tables, he caught Nate glancing backwards.

Right at Ramsey.

Before Dawson could try to parse the expression on Nate's face—was it longing or frustration or annoyance or possibly a semi-toxic combination of all three?—it was wiped clean.

"So, what's up?" Nate asked, leaning his elbows against the table.

Oh shit. Dawson had told him he was going to ask him something. Which meant he needed to ask him something.

Dawson scrambled. "Uh, you might've heard I had to fire my lawyer."

"Yeah, I did hear. That sucks, man. Sucks that people keep taking advantage of you." Nate's tone was genuinely sincere. He wasn't a man of many words but the words he did say always seemed heartfelt. Which was why it always seemed odd that Nate seemed so adamantly against Ramsey, even from the beginning, when he'd had no real reason to dislike the guy.

Dawson shrugged. Wondered how he could subtly segue from him firing his lawyer to the subject of Ramsey. Maybe if he just kept going, it would come to him.

Should've just left this to Aidan. He's way better at this shit.

Aidan *was*, but Dawson was discovering how good it was to be part of a team again, to be *really* part of a team, and he didn't want to just take a back seat anymore and leave all the hard shit to his old friend.

"Thanks," Dawson said. "I was wondering if you had any recommendations. Knew anyone who was really good at handling contract stuff. And wouldn't be against seeing me through the rest of this trial with Ackerman."

"Yeah, my guy's great. I'll text you his number."

"That's awesome." *See, Hall? Two birds, one stone.*

"No prob." Nate glanced back at where Ramsey was standing, now chatting easily with Wes and Mo. Dawson knew what that look felt like. Wanting to go over there, even though he knew he shouldn't.

It was what gave him the push to finally say something. "You seem like a real helpful guy," Dawson said.

Nate looked over at him. "I do?" he asked, smile tilting up the corner of his mouth.

"Well, yeah. I've been through it, sure, but it sounds like that guy's been through it too." He waved over at where Ramsey had just made everyone in his relative vicinity laugh.

"Not you too," Nate said.

"Listen, I don't know what your issue is—"

"Yeah, you don't," Nate retorted. "And you're not gonna. Did Aidan suggest that you talk to me? I can handle my own shit."

Dawson did not mention that it didn't seem like that was true, at least when it came to Ramsey. Nate had a good six inches and fifty pounds of pure muscle on him. He wasn't *stupid*.

Optimistic, maybe, but not stupid.

"Of course you can," Dawson soothed. "And no, of course Aidan didn't put me up to anything. *Would* Aidan do that?"

Nate chuckled darkly. "No. He'd never want someone to pull something off where he failed."

"Exactly," Dawson said. "We're just both saying similar things, because it's so obvious."

"What's so obvious?"

Damn. Dawson had really hoped that he wouldn't have to go into more detail than that. That Nate would be self-aware enough to understand exactly what Dawson wasn't explicitly saying.

"That you want to go talk to him," Dawson offered.

Nate frowned. "I absolutely fucking don't. That guy is a menace. Always showing up and throwing his weight around, like anybody gives a shit about some washed-up hockey player who can't get on the ice."

Dawson opened his mouth to suggest that assessment was both too harsh and also a little too vehement in its denial, but Nate shot him a dark look and stomped off.

Well, shit. Now he probably wasn't going to get Nate's lawyer's info, either.

So much for two birds, one stone.

He tipped his drink back against his lips, finishing the rest of it. Wondered if he should head back to the bar, get another. Find where Cam was and maybe persuade him to go make out in an empty bathroom.

But before he could, his phone vibrated in his pocket. He checked it, and once he saw Natalia Kaminski's name, he picked up immediately.

"Hi, Dawson. Sorry to call so late," she said apologetically. "Do you have a moment?"

"It's alright. Let me just see if I can find a quiet spot," Dawson said. He set his empty glass down on the table and headed off to check out the different rooms that spun out from the main bar. He hit pay dirt in the gaming room, which was still empty. In an hour, it would be full in here, with the guys playing pool and darts, but for right now, they were all still congregating at the bar.

"Okay, I'm good now," Dawson said, leaning his hip against the back of one of the long leather couches.

"I told you we were talking to Ackerman's lawyers. They didn't like that we rejected their last plea," she said.

"No, they wouldn't like that. He wouldn't either." Dawson assumed if he hadn't blocked Ackerman's number forever ago, he'd have called up Dawson and demanded to know why he was being so difficult. And Brynn might have interceded on her father's behalf, but he'd told her months ago that he wasn't willing to listen.

"No," Natalia agreed dryly. "But after finding out what we didn't like with the original plea deal, they came back with another option."

"Yeah?" Dawson wasn't expecting it to be much better than the last one, but he supposed they had to earn their money—*his* money, probably—somehow.

"I'll send it over," she said, "but the gist of it is that he's willing to do time."

"Not just house arrest?"

"Not just house arrest."

Dawson was surprised.

"I was surprised too," Natalia said when he was stunned into silence. "But I think they're worried."

"Sounds like you've got them exactly where you want them," Dawson said.

"Yes and no." Natalia sighed. "I'm willing to consider it. I wanted to get your temperature on it first, though."

"How much jail time?"

"Less than a year. At a low-security prison. It might be what he gets with a lenient judge. But it would mean he would have to file a guilty plea, Dawson. And it would mean we could start moving forward with a restitution plan for you and the other victims."

Dawson didn't know what to say. "What do you think?" he asked, because he *wasn't* sure.

"I think it's honestly a good compromise, and it frees up resources to go after more criminals," Natalia said. "And it frees *you* up."

"Me?"

"I know what kind of burden this is on you, with your career. You've given a lot of time and attention already, and with your job and your stature, that's not easy. I know that. This would allow you to put it behind you, forever."

There was no way that didn't look appealing. It *did*. Natalia was right, as she usually was.

She was right about everything, except one thing.

"I don't care if it's easier or not. I don't want *my* ease to be part of this," Dawson argued. "I don't care what this means for me, as long as justice happens. I've got a good—a *great*—support system, here. My agent's working on the lawyer angle."

"He's been great," Natalia inserted.

"And to be honest, it doesn't feel like I *haven't* put it behind me."

Dawson froze.

Hearing what he'd just said. Realizing he meant it. He *had* put it behind him. The legal issues were just that—wrapping it up in a pretty bow, sure, and making sure Ackerman paid for his crimes was appealing, additionally—but *he was over it.*

He'd gotten past it.

And maybe it wasn't just Cam, but it was a *lot* Cam.

His love and support had been there when he'd needed it most, and now all Dawson wanted to do was tell him . . .well, *shit.* To tell him he loved him, too. That he was the most important person in Dawson's life, and that he couldn't see that ever changing.

"If that's the way you feel about it, then I'm considering proceeding," Natalia said cautiously.

"You should," Dawson said. "I'm sorry, though, I . . .there's something I have to do." *Something I have to say.*

Aidan was right; he'd been incredibly stupid and even more incredibly dense.

This feeling, buoyant and certain, wasn't new. He'd been in love with Cam for *weeks*, and he hadn't told him. That wasn't okay, and what was even more *not* okay? That he'd been trying to be better. To do better. To do *right* by Cam.

How could he do that if Cam didn't know how he felt?

"No worries," she said, chuckling under her breath. "I'm just glad I caught you. I'll send the plea deal over, and you can let me know if you change your mind."

"I'm not going to change my mind." *About this. Or about Cam. Ever.*

"Alright, then. I'll keep you updated."

Dawson had just hung up, ducking out of the game room when a person he hadn't expected to see intercepted him. And before he could find Cam.

But he couldn't look frustrated, because this was Cam's dad, carrying two drinks, making it obvious that his destination had always been Dawson. He couldn't look impatient or frustrated.

Dawson tried not to tense and failed.

"Hey," Shane said, setting the whiskey in front of Dawson. "Saw you were empty."

"Thanks," Dawson said.

Shane waved in the direction Nate had stomped off, earlier. "He didn't seem very happy."

"He wasn't," Dawson said wryly. "Hopefully he gets over it."

"He'll get over it. You guys are a team," Shane said.

"Yeah," Dawson agreed.

Though he really, really hoped that he didn't have to ask Aidan to intervene if Nate *didn't* get over it. He'd be extra annoying about it. Chide Dawson for doing the kind of work that Aidan was better suited to, and the worst part was that Aidan probably wouldn't be wrong.

Then Shane adjusted his stance, leaning in a bit more, lowered his voice, and said, "Kind of like you and Cam."

It shouldn't have taken Dawson so long to realize, but it hit him like a physical blow that Shane had come over here to give him the freaking shovel talk.

Like five minutes too late. Five minutes after he'd already realized his feelings.

"Yeah?" Dawson said warily.

Maybe he deserved one. He didn't know how much Cam had told his dad about what they'd been doing—or what Dawson hadn't been saying.

But he'd fixed it, hadn't he? He'd gotten over his fear. It wasn't an easy thing, and some moments he *did* worry, but he meant what he'd said to Natalia.

He'd moved on. He was ready to start this new chapter of his life, with Cam next to him.

And Cam seemed to want to do the same. Unless, of course, Dawson was counting how he seemed to want to keep Dawson and Shane apart.

Maybe that was why he'd been dreading this. Shane threatening to dismember Dawson if he hurt Cam. Well, that was ridiculous, because if that ever happened, he'd have to get in line. Aidan had already declared he would, and Levi would no doubt be right behind him, like he always was, and then there was Dawson himself.

"Just wanted you to know you're always welcome with us. I didn't know if I'd like you, Hall, but it's hard not to, when you make Cam so happy."

Dawson wasn't sure he was keeping up. "Wait . . .what?"

Shane frowned. "I don't want to end up being your third wheel, but—"

"It's not me that's making that decision," Dawson pointed out softly. "I'd be there every single day, if he let me. If he wanted me there."

Dawson didn't say who *he* was, but he thought it was pretty dang obvious.

"What? Seriously?" Shane looked shocked. "Cam is—why would he—that doesn't even make sense—"

But it was beginning to make sense to Dawson.

He'd gotten a glimmer of an idea, and now that he had, the thought kept growing in his mind. Making more and more sense the longer it sprouted.

Of course, explaining it to Shane was going to mean coming clean about a lot of things, but that was probably something he should do anyway.

"I think he's worried about putting us together because of my experience with my ex-father-in-law. But not just that, but how freaked out I've been about starting something serious and real with him. He doesn't want to rock the boat, now that I've finally gotten my head out of my ass," Dawson admitted. *And now it's so out of my ass.*

"*Have* you gotten your head out of your ass?"

"Well, yeah," Dawson said, and he had, more than he could say to Shane. "I told him I want to be together, like for real, for serious, everything. But then you showed up and he seemed to panic. I get it now. He was worried your presence would remind me of things I want to forget."

"Your ex-father-in-law," Shane said steadily.

"He did some bad stuff. Stole money from me and others. But I know you're not him. I never thought you'd be him."

"You're divorced, too?" Shane said it so casually, but there was an intent look in his eyes. And maybe this was more of a shovel talk than Dawson had thought it was.

Dawson nodded. He could make excuses. Mention how Brynn had cheated on him. But the cheating had been only a symptom of what had gone wrong between them.

"Lot of tough breaks," Shane pointed out.

That was not a lie. Dawson had been struggling since they'd started falling over, like dominoes, but there was no question things were looking up. Looking bright.

"Yeah, it's been tough," Dawson said. "I won't lie about that. But I'm solid. I won't . . .um . . .force all of my baggage onto Cam. I'd never want that. He deserves better."

Shane hummed under his breath. Swirled his glass of whiskey. "Now you won't, but you were doing it before?"

"Not anymore," Dawson repeated firmly. He'd never been more sure of anything in his life. He *loved* Cam, he was pretty sure Cam loved him back, and they weren't going to fuck this up. Dawson would go to any length to make sure of that.

"Not sure how much Cam's told you, but my wife died young. Cancer took her when Cam was only eight." Shane sighed heavily. "It was an absolute shit time. For what felt like forever after that, I kept thinking, the rest of the sky's falling. The worst shit was always around the corner. I had to learn—had to *teach myself*—that wasn't fucking true."

"I'm still learning how to do that, too," Dawson admitted.

"It's all about hope," Shane said wryly. "Finding it and keeping it. Even if it's hard. Especially if it's hard."

Shane patted him on the back. "Think about it," he said. "And talk to Cam. Make sure he knows how you feel." He picked up his drink and wandered back over in the direction of the bar.

Ironically, maybe if Dawson hadn't realized how he felt, this might've been the realization, but Shane had literally come in five minutes too late.

He *had* deliberately let himself drift along this path without considering what the path looked like.

But he couldn't drift anymore, not just because of what he'd realized, like a lightning strike during his conversation with Natalia, but because Shane's words reminded him so much of what Cam had said to him, in the PATH, right before they'd kissed for the first time.

Sometimes, Cam had said, *we just have to stay the course. Have hope that things will turn around. Even if it seems like they won't.*

He'd listened back then. Holding on to the grains of hope he'd managed to hoard away had convinced him it was a good idea to get involved with Cam. To let his light shine into the dark corners of his life. And the more he'd let Cam in, the more he'd realized that everything *could* be good again. He could find happiness and satisfaction and a soul-deep connection with someone again.

It wasn't just Cam tugging Dawson back into the sunlight.

It was this team, rallying around him. Aidan being the friend he hadn't even realized he was missing. Marty being the kind of steadfast and zero-shits-given coach he'd always needed and never had. Alex, who'd gone above and beyond after the Simon disaster to be the kind of agent he needed most right now. Even Natalia Kaminski, who was determined to fight against Ackerman's lawyers and make him pay the price for his theft.

But even when it wasn't *just* Cam, Cam was undeniably an enormous part of it. He'd brought light and joy and love back to Dawson's life.

It hit him like a ton of freaking bricks, *again.*

Love.

There was no question, Dawson thought as he tested the way that word felt inside his head, but also, mostly, inside his heart. He'd told himself he wouldn't fall hard or fast again, but even though it was hard, none of it felt too fast. Instead, it felt just right.

It was easy to hope, or *easier*, anyway, when he loved someone the way he loved Cam, and now that he knew, Dawson wasn't going to waste a second more of his time pretending otherwise.

Now that he'd realized that this warm, intoxicating feeling he kept putting his hands up to and basking in was *love*, he wanted to tell Cam about it as soon as possible. He wasn't sure how much longer he could keep the words in. And he was *not* going to just blurt them out in front of all the guys.

When he reached where Cam was over by the bar, his group of Duke and Jack merging at some point with Mo, Ramsey, and Wes, it felt so good and so right to just put his arm around him and tug him in. To let that calm certainty and happiness that he knew was love, now, wash over him.

"Hey," Cam said, tilting his head down. "How was Nate?"

"Not good," Dawson said.

Cam made a face. "Well, you tried."

"Yeah. Hey . . .so . . ." They'd been here for a bit at least, but Dawson still felt a little guilty tugging him away from the party, especially when it was a party he'd earned. Well, they'd *all* earned it, but definitely Cam.

"Yeah? You wanna get out of here?"

"For sure."

Cam deserved so much better than that. Maybe not the full romantic treatment tonight, but he could say the words—hopefully words Cam wanted to hear—and give him a really good orgasm.

"Good." Cam smiled at him deeply enough his dimples popped. "I just gotta find—"

"Hey, kid, you looking for me?" Shane appeared then.

"Oh good, Dad, I *was* actually." But then Cam hesitated again, like he was rebooting.

Shane drew him—well, *both* of them, actually—away from the crowded bar. "Kid," he said seriously to Cam. "You gotta stop worrying about everyone so much."

Cam looked surprised. That he'd been called out? That Shane had realized?

"Dawson, back me up here," Shane said, glancing over at him.

"Yeah, seriously. I'm not going to freak out if we hang out with your dad," Dawson promised. "He even seems pretty cool."

Cam flushed bright red. "I didn't . . .I wouldn't . . ."

Shane ruffled his hair but it was Dawson who spoke up. "Yeah, you did. And it's cute. Sweet. Real thoughtful, actually. But unnecessary."

"Yeah, I wanna get to know your guy, kiddo," Shane said, and it was Dawson's turn to flush. But not with embarrassment, with pleasure.

"You're really—it's not a problem?" Cam gazed down at Dawson.

"Not a problem. But . . .maybe not tonight?" Dawson suggested.

"Yeah, you guys go to Dawson's place. I'll hang out here a bit longer, then head back to your apartment, if that's alright?"

"Perfect," Dawson said, reaching down and tangling his fingers with Cam's, squeezing them. "You good, babe?"

Cam gave him a grateful look. "Yeah. Yeah. I'm really good."

"Good." Dawson nodded and glanced over at Shane. "I'll see you around, yeah? Have a good night."

Unexpectedly, Shane grinned and tugged him into a quick hug. "Yeah. For sure."

They said the rest of their goodbyes. Dawson felt a little bad that he didn't see Nate anywhere. He'd been hoping to spot him at some point so he could try to smooth things over, but he was nowhere to be found.

Oh, well. He'd text him tomorrow. Make sure they were cool. Maybe even apologize for pushing him too hard, though in Dawson's humble opinion, he *hadn't*.

When they finally got outside, Cam said, "Do you wanna walk home or should we grab a cab?"

It wasn't ridiculously cold tonight, and they both had jackets, so Dawson said, "Let's walk. We should probably talk about what happened with your dad."

Cam groaned, but he didn't argue, so there was that, at least.

"I meant what I said in there," Dawson said when they were outside. "You don't need to protect me from him. He doesn't freak me out."

"I . . .yeah, I *was* worried. Things were so new, and I didn't want to . . ." Cam trailed off and took a deep breath. "I just didn't want to push too hard."

"It's not pushing if I want to get to know him, and he wants to get to know me," Dawson said gently. "Also, let's be honest. How new were things, really? We were dating for months."

Cam's eyes went big and round and he stopped right there on the middle of the sidewalk. But before he could say anything, Dawson continued. "I know we talked about it a little on our last date, before your dad showed up, but I want to make it clear. We're together. I want to do right by you. I don't want to impose on your time with your dad, but the last thing I want is for you to think you need to protect me from him. I don't need to be."

"Yeah?" Cam tipped his head down. His eyes were soft. Full of an emotion that Dawson thought he could identify. *Hoped* he had identified correctly. "You like me, huh?"

Here it was, the opening Dawson had been waiting for. Had been *hoping* for.

"Little more than like, rook," Dawson murmured, pulling him close against him.

Cam's mouth notched open. "Yeah? I . . .yeah, me too."

Leaning in, Dawson brushed his mouth across Cam's. "You want me to say it?"

"Been waiting," Cam admitted.

"I love you," Dawson said.

Cam grinned. Kissed him back. But not nearly as long as Dawson was hoping for. Too soon, he was breaking it off. Still smiling like Dawson was the best gift he'd ever received. "I love you, too," he said. "So much? I didn't even know—"

"I didn't either," Dawson teased.

"Didn't think I could be happier than when I actually got drafted. Or when I found out you were signing here, with the Thunder, but . . ." Cam shrugged, his whole face lit up with love and joy.

"Turns out things get even better."

"You wanna show me how good?" Cam suggested.

And it was so easy to lean in and kiss him again. Longer, this time. Deeper. When he finally lifted his head, they were both breathless, and Dawson didn't hesitate this time. "Come on," he said, "let's go home."

Every inch of Cam's skin felt like it was humming and alive with desire and with love. He crawled up Dawson's body, pressing him down into the mattress, drunk not on booze but on the way Daws was looking up at him, like he was the most gorgeous thing he'd ever seen.

The walk home and travel up to Dawson's floor had felt endless—far too long until they got to touch each other the way they were both dying to, but now that they'd gotten here and they'd both gotten naked, he didn't want to rush. Cam wanted to take his time.

He'd only ever get to have *first time, in love and together forever* sex once. It was always so good with Dawson, and had been from the very first time, but Cam was ambitious and he wasn't willing to settle for just very good.

"God, I want you," Cam murmured, leaning in and brushing his mouth against Dawson's, who just groaned beneath him. "Want you so bad."

"Think I want you more," Dawson echoed breathlessly. "You're so—"

He gasped as Cam ground down on his cock, hard and leaking underneath him. Cam wanted to sink down on it. Grind endlessly until neither of them could take it anymore. Until they fell right off the edge together. As close as two people had ever been.

"You like that?"

"I fucking love that," Dawson said. His head was tilted back on the pillow, pleasure already creasing his face. "Fucking love *you*."

If Cam had thought Dawson taking his time to express his feelings meant that he wasn't going to be willing to express them very often, it turned out he was very, very wrong. Dawson had already told him half a dozen times on their way to their apartment building, and once he'd gotten naked, Cam had already heard it twice.

Every single utterance made him grin and the last two had made him giggle.

"Wish we could *just* . . ." Cam trailed off. He ground down again. Already imagining how Dawson's cock would feel deep inside him. But Dawson was big enough and he still had to walk tomorrow. Well, maybe not *tomorrow*, but in two days, and he'd already taken enough flack for Dawson fucking him so good he could barely jog properly.

"I got you," Dawson murmured, leaning over and snagging the lube from the drawer next to the bed. "Come on, baby. Let me touch you."

Cam didn't need Dawson to ask twice. He shuffled closer, lifting his body in invitation. Groaning as Dawson cupped his ass and then slid a finger between his cheeks.

"Like that?" Dawson murmured.

"More," Cam begged. Pleasure was fizzing along his spine and he was already so hard his cock ached.

Dawson must have had the same thoughts as Cam though, because he didn't rush. Fingered Cam open slowly and deliberately, waiting until he was begging for the next finger before he finally gave it to him.

"I'm so ready," Cam pleaded. "Want you *now*."

"Patience," Dawson countered, but his voice was rough and his other hand was clamped hard around Cam's hip, fingers digging into his flesh. Probably leaving bruises.

God, Cam *hoped* he was leaving bruises. He wanted to look in the mirror tomorrow and trace the evidence of this night, of Dawson's love, imprinted on his body.

"I know you want me."

"Baby, I'm *dying* for you," Dawson ground out. He sank three fingers in and twisted them, making Cam groan hard.

"You can baby me all you want tomorrow. But tonight? Tonight, I *need* you."

Dawson dug his teeth into his bottom lip and then dragged Cam down, kissing him hard and insistent, his tongue fucking into his mouth as his fingers fucked into his body.

When he finally let him up, Cam let out a happy, relieved sigh as Dawson slipped his fingers out and slicked up his cock.

"Come on, rook," Dawson whispered.

Cam didn't need any more encouragement. He circled his fingers around the base of Dawson's dick and then took it in one long, breathless slide.

It felt so fucking good. But it wasn't just the ecstasy lighting him up, but the awe and relief and utter joy in Dawson's expression as he gazed at him.

Bracing a hand on Dawson's chest, Cam wiggled even deeper and they both groaned in tandem. Dawson's hands clamped around his hips again, and he didn't begin to thrust but instead just grind deeper still.

Cam gasped.

"Feels good, huh?"

"Feels amazing." Cam squeezed his eyes shut, because for a second, it was almost too much to take—Dawson looking at him like that, like he wasn't just a person but he was a miracle, like he was Dawson's everything—but then he opened them again, because how could he miss it, either?

Maybe it would feel like this again. Maybe it would feel even better.

Maybe in a year or five years or ten, they'd still be in love. They'd still be wild for each other. But Cam thought they both understood now that this feeling couldn't be taken for granted.

He was going to grab and hold on to every moment with every bit of strength and determination he had. Even if that scared Dawson away. Even that was too much for him.

But the way Dawson groaned his name—and what he'd told Cam in Vault tonight—told him that he'd worried about that too much.

He *could* have this. Could have *him*.

"I'm so lucky," Cam panted as he rose and sank down. Swiveled his hips.

Dawson was full of breathless, incredulous laughter. "Are you kidding? I'm the lucky one. The luckiest. I never thought—but now here you are, and God, you are perfect."

Cam wasn't perfect. Not by a long shot, but on one point he could agree as he fucked down onto Dawson's cock harder, feeling his orgasm growing closer and closer. From the red flush on Dawson's cheeks and the way his hips kept stuttering it seemed that Dawson was, too.

But even if Cam wasn't perfect, there was *one* way Dawson was right.

"No, but I'm perfect for you," Cam murmured, leaning in and kissing him. Dawson's hips thrust harder and faster, and a second later, Cam was coming hard, burying his face into his neck.

He felt rather than saw Dawson's orgasm, loving the way he shuddered beneath him.

It made total sense to just stay collapsed onto Dawson's body. Especially with the way Dawson kept stroking his back and murmuring words about how wonderful and gorgeous and flawless he was. How good he felt. How Dawson never wanted to let him go.

Cam pressed a kiss to his neck. Nuzzling in closer. "Well," he said right back, "I'm not letting you go first."

"Okay, rook," Dawson said, his chuckle a rumble that Cam felt throughout his whole chest.

CHAPTER 22

November

Nobody had ever asked Dawson, but he thought it made absolutely no fucking sense to have the only Canadian team in the NFL play on Thanksgiving.

American Thanksgiving.

Yet, that was exactly what the Thunder were doing. Flying to Dallas, to play the Cowboys in their annual Thanksgiving game.

"It's stupid, yeah," Marty agreed, as Dawson did his final stretches before kickoff, "but it's pretty cool that we'll get a long break after this."

Dawson couldn't deny that. In the three weeks since Shane had shown up in Toronto and he and Cam solidified their relationship, they'd been working on finding a happy medium between Cam spending time with his dad, Dawson *and* Cam spending time with Shane, and Dawson and Cam having enough time to indulge in the alone time they both desperately craved.

Playing earlier in the week, on a Thursday, meant that they'd have a nice leisurely ten days before their next game, and two extra days off next week.

"We're looking forward to it," Dawson admitted.

He'd already told Cam they were spending one of those days doing absolutely nothing but lazing around in bed—and if absolutely necessary—on the couch.

Maybe figuring out what this thing between them looked like had been a little bit of a challenge, especially with Shane around and the additional time demands of the football season. But despite all the possible pitfalls and the fact that Cam had never had a relationship before and Dawson's last one had ended catastrophically, he wouldn't trade it for an easier road. Dawson was sure he'd been happier, at some point in his life, but if he had been, he couldn't think of when that was.

"Good conditions," Marty pointed out, glancing around.

"Marty, it's a fucking dome," Dawson said dryly.

"Yeah. You wanted to push your distance, a good time to try something, maybe. Just throwing that out there."

In the weeks since missing the fifty-nine-yard field goal against the Bills that would have sent them to overtime, he'd been working hard on upping his personal best distance. Trying to get more comfortable and more consistent in the upper range of the 50s. It was hard, but Dawson was also determined that he wouldn't fail to deliver. Not again.

It was a work in progress, but Dawson felt reasonably certain he could kick anything under sixty yards in a game, but in the last three weeks, he'd barely been tested.

Kicked plenty of extra points. Even some field goals. But nothing over fifty yards.

Dawson was still afraid he might miss—and what missing might mean for this team and for his career—but he wasn't letting fear dictate his life anymore.

He'd won the guy, and now he was going to own this new professional opportunity too.

"Tell Aidan to be less spectacular," Dawson said, trying not to sound whiny and only mostly succeeding. Special teams guys around the league would roll their eyes if they could hear him complaining. Teams with great offenses who didn't need their kickers to bail them out or their punters to play a field position battle were the best kind of teams to play for.

But Dawson still craved a chance to try a long field goal again. To have it be the difference between losing and winning. To put that fear to bed, one last time, with the kind of decisive act that made it really fucking hard to rise again.

"Sure," Marty said wryly. "You wanna tell him or are you gonna let me do it?"

Dawson just chuckled and picked up his helmet to head out onto the field for the kickoff.

Cam intercepted him before he left the sideline. "Kick some ass, baby," he murmured to him, the touch of his hand lingering on Dawson's shoulder.

It felt like he'd spent the first two or so months of the season terrified of distractions on game day, and how they might negatively impact him and his performance, but Dawson was discovering that some distractions actually weren't distractions at all. Cam was the best and brightest of those.

"Love you," Dawson murmured back. He reached out, squeezing Cam's waist.

"Love you more." He swatted him on the ass, grinning. "Now, get out there."

Dawson jogged out onto the middle of the field for the opening kickoff.

From the beginning of the game, it was obvious that even though the Thunder had five more wins on the season than the Cowboys, they'd shown up today determined to show out for their holiday crowd.

They pushed defensively, causing Jaden to fumble the ball, setting the Cowboys up with a short field and their first touchdown.

Then one of the corners—who was notorious throughout the league for his interceptions and who Aidan had spent the last week sweating over—picked off one of Aidan's passes, even though it had been a hard-fought ball with Mo.

And just like that, the Thunder were down fourteen to zero, barely into the second quarter.

Dawson watched from his usual spot on the sideline as Aidan prowled back and forth in front of the bench, extorting not just the offensive line to do better, but all the position guys, too. Lane and Trevor. Mo. Jaden.

On the next drive, the Thunder drove farther down the field, Aidan actually using his legs to run for one of the first downs, something he rarely did anymore.

They made it to the fifteen-yard line. Second and three.

"I'm not worried."

Dawson glanced over to see that Cam had drifted near.

"Do I look worried?" Dawson asked.

"A little, yeah. I thought Aidan's eyes were going to pop out of his head when that guy wrestled that pass away from Mo."

Aidan's expression *had* been a little funny, and it would have been even funnier if the Cowboys hadn't scored on the very next play.

Dawson shrugged. "They're gonna get some points on the board."

"Short-ish field goal for you," Cam pointed out. He knew how much Dawson yearned to prove himself. And how that proof wasn't for anyone else but him.

"They're gonna get a touchdown," Dawson said confidently.

Aidan must have agreed, because the next play he handed the ball off to Jaden, who made a beautiful cut and then another, spinning right into the end zone.

"See?" Dawson said, after he and Cam finished high-fiving about it. "Told you."

"He gave the ball to Jaden because of that fumble, yeah?" Cam asked.

"Something like that," Dawson said. Jaden had gotten his redemption. Mo had caught two important passes on that drive, getting his.

But now Dawson wanted his own.

And it wasn't kicking extra points or thirty-five-yard field goals.

Still, nobody was complaining when after that disastrous first quarter, the Thunder went into the locker room at the half tied fourteen all.

During most games the tone on the sideline in the second half had been relaxed. Jovial. In several of the games they'd played this year, they'd been leading by enough points that Wes and some of the other backups had been in by the end of the game.

But not today.

The Thunder traded field goals with the Cowboys, Dawson heading out and not kicking the longer field goal he'd wanted to try, but instead a forty-yarder. Not a gimmie, by any means, but not the fifty-plus he still wanted.

The third quarter ticked to a close, the score still tied. Cam was even getting more work than normal, the Thunder punting on several drives. But he was steady and excellent, both times pinning the Cowboys against the ten-yard line.

Every time Cam came back to the sideline after a great punt, Dawson left his space bubble, giving him a high five and a few words of encouragement. He was tense, but focused, a feeling that seemed to extend to everyone on the sideline.

It was an unspoken assumption that whoever made the worst—or last—mistake would be the team to lose this game, and all fifty-two members of the Thunder were united and determined it wouldn't be on them.

Midway through the fourth quarter, Aidan led the Thunder offense on a tough, gritty drive. Jaden routinely making five-yard runs out of plays that shouldn't have gained him more than a yard or two, at best. Aidan made a handful of great throws, and Mo made at least one spectacular diving catch that was bound to end up on at least a few highlight reels.

It wasn't the normal kind of offensive fireworks the Toronto Thunder displayed but Coach Robertson was always talking about how teams who wanted to take it all, at the end of the season, had to win all different kinds of games.

This was definitely different from their usual, but maybe that was okay.

Aidan ended up taking the ball himself, running it in the last few yards, to get the touchdown, and that felt representative of the whole game. It was probably really good that he was going to get a good break after this. Probably good for *all* of them, Dawson realized, his own neck stiff and tense with the anxiety, no matter how he tried to loosen it.

Up seven, the game headed into the last five minutes.

It was up to the Thunder defense to preserve the lead, but the Cowboys seemed determined to not let the Thunder come into their stadium and come from behind and win the game.

They might not have had as many wins, but they still had offensive weapons, and they used them.

Dawson watched with disbelief as they converted a third and twenty-four, after a Nate sack and another tackle for loss.

There were forty-five seconds left in the game when the Cowboys tied it up.

Aidan didn't usually approach him during games.

But Dawson wasn't surprised to see him coming over, sweat beaded on his forehead, his hair matted with it, helmet in his hand, blue eyes tired but blazing with determination.

"Hey," Aidan said.

"Forty-five seconds, that's plenty of time," Dawson said before Aidan could ask.

He was already steeling himself for what would be his task. But before he could do his part, Aidan had to do *his*: get the Thunder close enough for Dawson to make the kick.

"How much do you need?" Aidan asked.

Dawson almost told him he knew his max. Aidan knew his stats, same as he knew everyone's on the team, inside and out.

But that wasn't what Aidan was asking.

"Get me within sixty, and I can do it," Dawson said.

Aidan raised an eyebrow.

"It's a dome," Dawson added. "And I've been working hard."

Aidan didn't argue. Didn't question. Just patted him on the shoulder and said, "You got it, bud."

And just like Dawson trusted Aidan to deliver when the game was on the line, like he'd done so many times before in his long and storied career, Aidan was trusting that Dawson was going to do the same.

Dawson realized it didn't matter that he'd missed the last fifty-nine-yard attempt he'd tried. Dawson had looked Aidan in the eye and told him he could do it, so Aidan believed him.

He'd known, of course, that the team trusted him. That *Aidan* trusted him. Dawson had always had a feeling that the person he was really trying to prove he was back to was actually himself.

But it had never been driven home as much as it was in this moment.

Dawson glanced over to where Cam was standing. He was apart, too. Palms flat against his thigh pads, expression wiped of emotion, as Aidan took the field to get Dawson the yards he needed so he could try the field goal.

Like he'd sensed him looking, Cam glanced over, too. Smiled wide, and it hit Dawson hard and real fast, like Cam had a line straight to Dawson's heart.

Maybe he did.

It was not easy. The Cowboys were sensing blood in the water. They probably wanted to go to overtime.

But Aidan was not going down without a fight. He hit Mo on a gorgeous slant pattern. After the catch, Mo, not the biggest guy in the universe, made an extraordinary effort and shucked one defender off and then sent another sprawling with an epic stiff-arm, taking the ball twenty-five yards down the field.

Thirty to go.

Aidan's next pass went to Trevor, Lane giving him just the block he needed to spring him free. Lane got the next, hovering on the sideline, so that he could make sure the clock stopped right after his catch. Five seconds left.

There it was. That was all they had time for. Marty looked over at Dawson and nodded, approval and certainty in his eyes. Dawson took one last practice kick into the net, and headed out to do what he'd been wanting for weeks.

Cam met him on the middle of the field. He didn't touch him, but he didn't need to. The look in his eyes was enough.

Aidan had gotten him just enough yards.

Dawson did the calculation in his head and realized it wasn't sixty yards, but fifty-nine.

For a split second, that threw him. *You tried this before and you didn't pull it off.*

Yeah, he had. He'd been married before, too. Been part of a team. Neither of those had worked out but that didn't mean you didn't keep trying. That you gave up hope or gave up on yourself.

Especially not when Dawson believed that he *could* do it.

Cam lined up.

With one second left on the clock, Joey snapped the ball. Cam caught it and flawlessly positioned it for Dawson's foot.

He was the only factor of this play left. The *most* important factor.

Dawson's foot hit the ball and it felt good. It would have the distance, if he hadn't sacrificed his aim for the strength needed to boot it fifty-nine yards.

He held his breath as the ball sailed through the air and only let it out as it split the uprights. The referees called it good and a second later he was suffocated by a crowd of excited, happy Thunder players.

Dawson was pretty sure that was Cam's arm around him, Cam's face buried in the crook of his neck. His voice telling Dawson, "I love you so fucking much, you absolute beast."

It wasn't that hard to believe it, not anymore.
And it was even easier to hope for it.

EPILOGUE

Five months later

Dawson's phone rang just when they rounded the corner out of the elevator with the couch.

"Shit," Dawson exclaimed, three-quarters of his figure hidden by the end of the couch.

"We should have paid for movers," Cam said, for at least the tenth time.

"No, just . . ." Dawson swore again. "Let me get this balanced against the wall so I can answer. Natalia said she'd be calling today."

"Or we could have used any of our friends. Our football-playing friends," Cam teased, hearing the strain in his voice as he held up his side of the couch, watching as Dawson tried to juggle it and then press it with one hand to the wall of their apartment building.

Dawson shot him a look, full of heat, that promised retribution later. The sexy kind of retribution, no less.

Cam hoped that they'd both be up for the sexy kind of retribution. They were only a few pieces of furniture into this move, and already he was wishing he'd put his foot down and hired movers anyway.

So what if he and Dawson were just combining their apartments essentially as they moved into a bigger place? So what if it wasn't even *all* the furniture, because his dad had decided to stick around, more long-term? He'd taken over Cam's lease, and even though Shane kept arguing he didn't need much, Cam hadn't wanted to leave him with nothing.

They *still* should have hired movers. Or taken Nate or Wes up on their offers to help move them. Cam was pretty sure Trevor and Lane had stuck around Toronto too, and weren't flying home to Arizona for another week, at least.

The point was, they could've had help. Instead Cam was now holding up three-quarters of this couch as Dawson pulled his phone out of his pocket and shoved it between his cheek and shoulder.

"Hey? Oh, yeah, good to hear from you."

It was Dawson's *I'm a grown-up* voice, which meant that it probably *was* Natalia. Cam felt marginally less annoyed then.

His dad had mentioned this morning, as they'd chowed down on donuts and coffee he'd brought over, that moving tested every relationship. Cam had argued they didn't need testing. He and Dawson were so solid.

But Dawson's determination to not hire movers was possibly going to be the first real test. Not the Thunder's season. Not the case against Richard Ackerman. Not even when Cam's dad had shown up right when he and Dawson were still in the middle of figuring their relationship out.

Nope, it was going to be this couch.

Cam groaned under his breath, wishing he'd gone a little less hard at the gym yesterday.

Dawson kept nodding, adding a comment or two on the phone, but Cam couldn't hope to decipher what was going on, not until Dawson got off the call and explained what he'd heard from Natalia.

Progress was being made in moving forward on going to trial. In a few weeks, Dawson had told him that he'd need to head to Baltimore for another round of interviews. It was looking likely that he'd need to take the stand.

Finally, he hung up, right when Cam thought he might lose his grip on the couch.

"So," Dawson started to say, the smile evident in his voice, even though Cam couldn't see his whole face.

"Tell me while we move this stupid couch," Cam grumbled. "My arms are gonna fall off."

"Aw, baby, are you tired already?" Dawson joked.

"Fuck yes."

"It was all good news," Dawson said, changing the subject, shouldering more of the weight. "Ackerman's lawyer came back with another deal. Even better this time. Natalia thinks they're really panicking about the possibility of going to trial."

"The possibility of going to trial *and* the possibility of you taking the stand like a goddamn avenging angel," Cam added. "He's gonna plea out and plead guilty and go to jail for a long-ass time."

"That's the hope. Natalia feels like there's a very good chance we can make him pay without having to call our bluff," Dawson said. He chuckled tiredly. "I'm so fucking relieved."

"Me too," Cam agreed. They'd talked more than once about how committed Dawson was to seeing this through, but if he didn't have to while getting the outcome they all wanted? That would be even better.

They'd finally made it down the hallway, and to the open doorway that they'd propped open on their new, bigger apartment.

This one had a shower *and* a tub, as well as a second bedroom, because both of them hoped that the next time Dawson's parents came to visit from Iowa, they wouldn't need to stay in a hotel. They could stay with *them*.

Cam had met them briefly at the end of the season, but he was looking forward to getting to know them better. The five of them, including his dad, merging into a new familial unit.

There'd been a time when he'd been secretly terrified that *Dawson* might be terrified about this, but so much of what he'd been through and how he'd emerged from it on the other side had proven once and for all that Dawson wasn't about to let a little residual fear scare him away.

Not when it came to what he really wanted. And Cam really believed, without a single doubt, that what Dawson wanted was Cam and *them*.

They finally maneuvered the couch into the empty living room and set it down.

Dawson let out a gust of a sigh and flopped down on the comfortable surface.

"What are you doing?" Cam asked, even as he fell down next to him. "We have like . . .a whole bunch more shit to move."

"I know," Dawson said, shrugging. He turned and pressed his head into Cam's shoulder. "I think I screwed up. We should have hired movers."

Cam could only laugh. "Oh yeah?"

"For sure, rook."

"Can you still call me that?" Cam wondered softly. "I'm not a rookie anymore."

"Baby, you're *always* gonna be my rookie." Dawson tilted his head up and pressed a kiss to Cam's mouth. It felt as good as the first time. Maybe even better. Who had Cam been kidding? There was always going to be energy—and time—for sexy retribution.

"Oh God, we should have knocked."

"Dude, I *told* you to."

The voices surprised Cam and he pulled away from Dawson, craning his head towards the apartment's entrance.

He supposed he shouldn't have been surprised to see Nate and Wes walking in, Lane and Trevor trailing behind them.

"You guys need some help?" Wes asked innocently.

"They managed the couch and then collapsed on it," Nate said seriously. "I think the answer is *yes*."

"How'd you know?" Dawson asked.

"Shane sent us," Trevor said. "He said you two were trying to be stupid and heroic, and you didn't need to do that."

Cam laughed. "Yeah, he'd say that."

"And he'd be right," Dawson said wryly, pulling himself upright and then holding his hand out so he could help Cam up too.

He took it and pulled himself off the couch with a half-hearted groan. "I'm so glad you guys are here," he admitted.

"Me too," Dawson said.

Cam elbowed him in the side.

"What?" Dawson retorted. "I *am*."

"You didn't want to hire movers."

"Well, these aren't movers, they're our friends." Daws shot him a lopsided look. It was adorable, and Cam's heart squeezed. He loved him so much. Even when he was being too literal and a little bit grumpy. Probably even more when he was being too literal and a little bit grumpy.

How could Cam resist? He was so fucking cute when he was bitching—and then there was the benefit of Cam enjoying brightening his mood after.

"Shane said he was almost done packing some of Dawson's kitchen stuff. Should we head there first?" Wes asked.

Dawson exchanged looks with Cam. "God bless your dad," he said.

Cam couldn't help his smile. It was more than that, though. He knew he was beaming at Dawson. He'd expressed enjoyment and appreciation that Shane was around. He'd said more than once how much he just plain liked Cam's dad, which Cam got, because he was pretty freaking awesome. But he'd still never believed that Dawson would be standing here saying those words.

"Yeah," Cam agreed, brimming with happiness.

"Ew," Nate said as he glanced between them. "Maybe we did just interrupt something."

"Hey," Wes retorted mildly, "it's not like you aren't plenty gross sometimes."

The corner of Nate's mouth quirked up. "Fair."

"Yeah, yeah," Dawson said. "The kitchen at my place. That sounds like a good place to start."

They all trooped out and Dawson turned to Cam. "I'm so fucking glad your dad texted them," he said.

"Yep," Cam agreed. "Now say, *Cameron was right.*"

Dawson just laughed. "Not gonna happen," he claimed, even though they both knew better.

"How about you just say . . .you're happy they showed up?"

"I did?" Dawson countered.

"*And,*" Cam added with emphasis, "that you're not alone anymore."

Dawson pulled Cam into him. Pressing a kiss to his temple. "Well, I already knew that," he teased. "Never gonna be alone again."

-

Don't miss *Hell or High Water*, Ramsey and Nate's much anticipated love story, coming in spring 2026. Read a free preview here!

-

To read more about Ramsey's history at Portland U, check out the Portland Evergreens hockey series.

INTERESTED IN READING MORE OF
BETH'S BOOKS?

CHECK OUT A FULL LIST OF TILES
BY SCANNING THE QR CODE
OR VISITING HER WEBSITE

WWW.BETHBOLDEN.COM/BOOKLIST

WANT TO FOLLOW BETH?

MAKE SURE YOU NEVER
MISS A RELEASE?

SCAN THE QR CODE BELOW
OR VISIT HER WEBSITE
FOR A SOCIAL MEDIA LIST,
NEWSLETTER SIGNUP,
AND SO MUCH MORE!

WWW.BETHBOLDEN.COM/ABOUT

* 9 7 8 1 9 6 4 6 9 1 5 2 7 *